B E T H

The
Crocodile
Fury

Published by Arrow Books in...

...

...

Published in Great Britain by The Women's Press Ltd, 1996
A member of the Namara Group
34 Great Sutton Street, London EC1V 0DX

First published in Australia by Angus & Robertson, 1992

British Library Cataloguing-in-Publication Data
A catalogue record for this book is available from the British Library

ISBN 0 7043 4466 1

Printed and bound in Great Britain by
BPC Paperbacks Ltd

*For Choo Kwei Heong,
my other grandmother*

ACKNOWLEDGMENTS

As well as oral stories I have referred extensively to the following: Frena Bloomfield, *The Book of Chinese Beliefs*, Arrow Books, London, 1983; Wolfram Eberhard, *A Dictionary of Chinese Symbols*, Routledge, London, 1986; Haji Mohtar bin H. Md. Dom, *The Bomoh and the Hantu*, Federal Publications, Kuala Lumpur, 1979, *Malay Superstitions and Beliefs*, Federal Publications, Kuala Lumpur, 1979, *Traditions and Taboos*, Federal Publications, Kuala Lumpur, 1979; J. N. McHugh, *Hantu Hantu*, Donald Moore, Singapore, 1955; Martin Palmer (ed.), *T'ung Shu*, Vinpress, Kuala Lumpur, 1990. The pig ghost was adapted from 'Sung Ting-po Catches a Ghost' in Yang Hsien-yi and Gladys Yang (translators), *Ghost Stories of Old China*, Asiapac, Singapore, 1986; and the bandit initiation from an account of a secret society ritual in the *Penang Gazette*, 2 August 1867.

Many thanks to Drusilla Modjeska, my editor, for her editorial advice, encouragement and patience; to George Papaellinas, Barbara Brooks, Margo Daly, Matthew Noble, Alexandra Pitsis, Marlene Jones, Mick Dark and Sita Subramony for assistance and support both literary and otherwise; to Yong Tze Tein for confirming the ghost; to Paul Gillen for bearing with the bully and me with humour, edits and insight; to my family for incalculables; and to Arnie Goldman who first said so.

This book was written with the assistance of an Ethnic Affairs Commission Fellowship, and a Project Grant from the Literature Board of the Australia Council, the Federal Government's arts funding and advisory body. Final revision was greatly assisted by a Fellowship at Varuna, the Writers' Retreat and Centre managed by the Eleanor Dark Foundation. I am deeply grateful to all.

An extract from *The Crocodile Fury* appeared in *Previews II*, Sydney Writers' Festival, 1992.

CONTENTS

*This is a story
my grandmother tells*

ONE

SHE GIVES ME
AN AMULET

Grandmother's voice rings in my ears: *Always spit three times to avoid bad luck. Never look behind you when walking alone at night, even if someone taps you on the shoulder. There are three candles around a person's head, one at the back and one on each side. Never turn your head sideways suddenly, it'll snuff out a candle and ghosts rush in to get you.*

I've spent most of my life in a convent. That's the place to begin. The convent is on a hill on the edge of the city, next to a jungle reserve which swallows and spits out trucks full of soldiers every day. In the jungle is a tribe of monkeys headed by a one-armed bandit which leads forays into the staffroom to steal food. Although the teachers are used to this, they run screaming whenever monkeys swing in the doors. Seeing their example, girls run screaming too, at every opportunity. Convent girls are known as the Screaming Nuns.

The hill with the convent and the jungle is where rich people and poor people send their girls. Here young girls are brought in who are too noisy or boisterous or too bossy or unladylike or too disobedient or worldly, or merely too hard to look at, or feed. This is the convent's reputation. Here, hard-to-look-at girls are kept in special dormitories and fed, and taught to do sewing and weaving. Here noisy boisterous bossy young girls are turned into young ladies who are honest, obedient and humble. They are taught to read and write, to figure numbers and cross their knees when sitting, to play netball and poach perfect eggs, and also to bob when they see the nuns and the priest, and to know Jesus to love Jesus and to serve him in this world and the next. The convent on the hill is the oldest and the best in the whole city. Its halls are wide, its ceilings held up by shiny pillars around which two disobedient girls can swing. Its floors are tiled in places with imported tiles, its doors carved from the heavy woods of ancient jungle trees. Its walls are thick enough to contain the shouts of the most boisterous girl, its dormitories with their sparse beds and wire-screened windows and bare floorboards echoing with deliberate nuns' footsteps at bedtime, are formidable enough, yet homely enough to quieten the giggles of even the naughtiest, the sobs of even the most homesick girl.

Over the years the convent has grown in spurts. A new dormitory is added when the nuns have raised enough money, and a proper laundry, a much-needed wing for the orphans abandoned at the door. Over the years the convent has eaten at the edges of the jungle, growing like an odd-shaped beast with mixed foundations and roof-shapes, and the paint on some parts peeling, on others almost new. Sometimes the convent swallowed parts of the jungle whole. In the playing fields great jungle trees spread their roots, over which naughty convent girls clamber at playtime. In the evenings gusty jungle winds shed jungle nuts and seeds onto the lawns and flowerbeds, which grow into sturdy jungle seedlings naughty convent girls have to weed out with their bare hands at lunchtime, if they are caught being bad. Jungle vines and creepers wind their way inch by stealthy inch over the wire fence, under the drainpipes, through the cracks in the brickwork to leave stubborn brown stains when ripped away. Convent girls drape the ripped-away creepers around their necks and shoulders, they perch twisted crown-creepers on their heads and dance in wild sneaky circles when the nuns aren't looking.

'Girls! Behave like young ladies, girls!' the nuns cry, clapping their hands in horror, looking.

From the time I was a small child I have always known I would go there.

'That is your school,' Grandmother said, stopping to point, making my mother lift me so I could see. My mother heaved me onto her shoulders, sweat beads glistening her neck. I wound my arms around her. 'That's where your mother went,' Grandmother said, 'and where you will go.'

From the bottom of the hill we could see the ridged roof of the convent over the dark shapes of the jungle trees. Sometimes a jungle wind scurried the treetops in waves. The roof hunched solid amidst this movement the way Grandmother made me hunch my muscles, legs and arms and shoulders taut as I copied the flexes and stretches of her morning exercises, the curve of her lungs expanding, the rhythm of her tiger breath. As we watched, the roof, solid, rocked and crested on the wave of the trees. I clapped my hands, telling Grandmother what I could see.

'Good,' Grandmother said.

Before I ever saw the convent I knew the shape of its buildings and the grain of its wooden floor under bare feet. The swing of its heavy doors. I knew the smells that crept in from the jungle in the evenings and the early mornings, and the way moonlight slashed through the shuttered windows where my grandmother once stood. I knew the slide of the cleaning cloth from her daytime fingers, and the way she stood, instead of working, with her face pressed to the glass.

'Are you listening?' Grandmother demanded.

I knew the way the corridors twisted, and the weird-shaped rooms one came upon at sudden corners, and the way, if one was sharp-eyed and canny, one could sometimes see a hidden door. But where these doors and rooms and twisting corridors led to, I did not know.

'That's why you will go there,' Grandmother said. 'To see.'

That's the place to begin. The convent on the hill where I spend most of my days and some of my nights was famous long before I was sent there. Once, before the nuns took over, it was only one building, a shambles, a mansion abandoned for years by everyone except the jungle. The mansion had been ransacked long ago. It was filled with rubbish and decaying furniture, its fine marble floors were heaved and prised apart by jungle roots as thick as a young girl's thigh. Its windows were hung with jungle creepers allowing only a feeble light. Once it was the headquarters of bandits. Then, the headquarters of soldiers, where informers sidled for their monthly pay-outs, and the screams of bandits, communists and other enemies of the city echoed through the halls. Once, long before that, a rich man lived there, in the mansion that later became the convent library, the ghosthouse, and when he lived there it was filled with exotic treasures. The gardens were filled with exotic plants and trees brought back from the rich man's travels: the Rose of India, the juniper, the rain tree, the great hog plum. The rich man was a collector of the exotic. He came from far away. Every year he set out searching for something new. He planted a garden as far as the eye could see. When he stood in sunlight the natives were moved to silence, even the ones who served him, who saw him day after day. In sunlight the rich man looked as if he was dipped in gold. When he turned suddenly, golden sparks rippled the sunlit air.

The rich man cut back the jungle and built the mansion from stones carved from a foreign country, and glass blown and tinted by foreign craftsmen, and mixes of sand, mosaic and masonry made up of secret foreign formulas. Only the dark beams and floorboards, the bones of the great building, were taken from the deepest jungle. Only the natives who built it left traces of a local presence in the rich man's mansion:

their drops of sweat mixed in with the foundations, their blood and crushed limbs marking the beams that held the ceilings up. Their stray hairs and skin scuffs cemented forever between the bricks. The rich man built a funicular railway to the top of the hill, an ornate toy with open-air cars carved and gilded with creatures from foreign mythologies: mermaids and men, a Gorgon, Winged Gods and Sirens, the Faerie Queen. Its sidings were trimmed with silver, its leather seats stained the colour of the sea. At the top of the hill he built a pavilion cityfolk called either The Boil or The Pearl, depending on who was listening. From the hilltop the rich man could see the whole countryside, the curve and swirl of the jungle, the city seething. On the horizon a faint hairline: the sea. The rich man's mansion perched on the hill like a shimmering palace the likes of which neither the hill nor the jungle, nor the city growing steadily around them, had ever seen; an incomplete palace, for the rich man was never satisfied. When he was home, builders and carpenters forever plagued the place, working in remote corners, adding Grecian columns, an attic garden, constructing curved staircases to rooms he later decided he did not want. The rich man walked the length of his mansion followed by foreign henchmen clutching at plans and papers, cursing silently behind his back. He lined the mansion with hangings intricately woven in foreign climates, still smelling of the lands from which they came. He hung the windows with deep velvet curtains that swallowed the light in shades of ruby, emerald, midnight blue. The rich man surrounded himself with the furnishings of a tasteful and gentlemanly life; nothing pleased him more than to lie on one of his luxurious couches, holding an invaluable object, a latest acquisition, in the palm of his hand. A jewelled miniature, an ancient vessel in perfect proportion. The rich man turned the object this way and that, he ran his fingers over its curves and sharp edges. He gazed out his windows at the jungle-edged sky.

Long before the convent became a convent it was famous for the parties the rich man threw. The rich man's parties were the talk of the city. Poor cityfolk gathered at the gates to listen to the blare and tinkle of the foreign music, to sniff at the cakes and sweetmeats, the strange perfumes. They jostled one another to glimpse the endless surge of rich foreigners, of planters, government officials, merchants, pale-faced adventurers, wives and daughters dressed in every shade of the rainbow streaming through the doors. Soldiers hired for the evening herded curious cityfolk back into line, they smashed bottles of home-brewed alcohol, waved their hired truncheons at any sign of over-excitement, of curiosity turning to spite. The rich man's parties lasted all night, all-night music blared from his mansion, all-night dancing and shrieks of laughter greeted each dawn. The rich man crooned with the dancebands he hired, he bobbed and swayed with the dancers hired to bob and sway till they dropped. He filled fountains with champagne enough to spill from a thousand glasses, to be lifted in salute at midnight to where his lover stood. The rich man's lover was young and beautiful. No one knew where she came from. The lover was brought by the rich man into his house in secret, kept in his quarters both day and night for weeks with no one allowed to see her. Then, one day, she was led out, leaning on the rich man's arm, swaying slightly. A shimmering white gown enveloped the lover's body, billowing as she walked. Her fingers curled on the rich man's sleeve. Her eyes seemed now bright, now milky. Over her scented oils and powders hung always a salty tang of the sea. The lover stood at the top of the stairs at the rich man's parties, her head tilting to one side, with the light and laughter rushing towards her. People peered upwards. My grandmother stared from the shadowy curve of the stairway, standing tiptoe, arching her neck. Grandmother wore her best servants' clothes, her face powdered, kitchen grease carefully wiped from her hands. She clenched her hands, staring upwards. In the glittering lights the lover's skin was white china, her hair like a sheet of night. Her face as smooth as stone under water. The rich man bought the lover tight silken dresses with slits up the sides, which she never wore. He begged her wear her hair loose, swinging past the backs of her knees. The lover stood for hours on the upper balcony with the music and laughter floating towards her and she raised her glass, and smiled in the direction of the sea.

That's the place to begin. The hill with the convent and the jungle is called Mat Salleh Hill. It is a hill of many old sayings, the site of stories going back to a time when no city skyscrapers mushroomed towards it, no suburbs crept out in every direction, no city smog threaded its jungle trees. No convent of brick and marble sat halfway up its slope. The hill with the convent and the jungle is the city's oldest landmark: long ago fisherfolk from the outlying islands knew the city, even before it became a city, by the peak of its hill. The hill's peak is curiously twisted, humped with green-fringed boulders in the shape of a woman turned away from the harbour, in the act of turning back. Simple fisherfolk still guide their narrow-bottomed boats laden with gifts and offerings through the treacherous island channels mazed southeast of the city to appease the gods and spirits of the hill. Jungle spirits live there in profusion, so the stories say, and hill spirits who look like monkeys, or very small men. There too rest the spirits of the dead awaiting reincarnation, and the gods of thunder and lightning, of fire and fruitfulness, of earthquake and the seven hundred winds. Once every city child knew this, and bowed their heads when facing that way. From certain angles, squinting past certain buildings, the woman turning can clearly be seen.

'Where?' demands the bully.

'There!' I point, seeing the woman through buildings and around corners, crowning curved bridges, looming over straggly city trees. A woman turning is one of the things my grandmother has taught me to see.

'Good,' Grandmother says.

The hill with the convent and the jungle is visible from the many outlying islands, from far out at sea. Sometimes playful sea spirits weave its image in foam and seaspray, they strengthen it with seaswells, twine sea mists around it to perfection so sailors and traders from faraway places are fooled into seeing land. So potent are the spells of the playful sea spirits that before the sailors and traders know it they have landed, they have dusted their clothes and stamped their sea-weary feet and are walking the waters as carelessly as if on land. Before they know it they find themselves flailing. Insubstantial shapes swirl around them with the heads of beautiful women and the bodies of seadragons, they are caressed by fishfaces armed with human limbs, by human shapes with scaly ridges down their backs. The playful sea spirits snatch at their clothes, tease rings from their fingers, knives with handles of ivory or silver from their belts. Before they know it the sailors and traders find themselves sucked to the watery depths.

This sea east of the city with the hill for its landmark has been notorious from days of old. It is famous for its unruly sea snakes and dragons, its typhoons and seasqualls that defy weatherworkers, its pranks of wind and water: a sudden drop of the barometer, sea monsters slashing great gashes in rudders and anchors, sea spirits rising to snatch live humans to the seabed, to be imprisoned in overturned pots. Cityfolk laugh behind their hands when they hear of the survivors' wild tellings, a favourite old saying upholds local wisdom that only the foolish by playful sea spirits are fooled. Careful fisherfolk with their gifts and offerings and humble attitudes are never caught out. In these parts it's well-known that the land and sea spirits, and those of wind and jungle, and the ones living in rocks and trees have no love of humans beyond a tolerance easily turning to spite. All manner of spirits have to be watched for trickery, even the most passive and friendly, the ones favouring woks and zebra crossings, have to be flattered and appeased. Local cityfolk know, though nowadays my grand-mother says more and more are forgetting, that though the spirits who share the city, the jungle and the sea with humans may have once been human, or vice versa, their memories, like human memories, are short. Unlike humans they feel no pity, no remorse. It is useless to remonstrate or sulk for drowned comrades or ships sunken, useless to shake your fists. Even helpful spirits may inadvertently do harm. Their ghostly natures are fixed by one overwhelming desire, be it food or a substitute, or vengeance for those who are wronged, or tricked. The overwhelming desire of hill spirits is to possess people's origins: the place they come from, the shape of their faces, their true names. Hill spirits are famous thieves. They are the most mischievous of the spirits, and will cause havoc whenever they can. They have only one arm and are black and hairy. Hill spirits keep human origins in a pouch in their cheeks. When they call a person's true name, that person will have to go. That person will become the hill spirit's slave. Once every city child knew this and covered their faces when stared at, and shut tight their lips when strangers asked their names.

When my grandmother was a girl, nobody in the rich man's mansion wanted to sleep with her. Grandmother slept so deeply her breath was a rumble that heaved out of her body, that slithered along the bedclothes to slip into the other servants' dreams. The other bonded servants woke in fright, feeling Grandmother's breath in their dreams. They used their feet to push her away. They dug her stomach with their toes and pinched her arms, but nothing would wake her. Even from the farthest corner of the kitchen she could still be heard. Grandmother slept with her arms and legs splayed, she slept like a watermill. Some nights she churned. Some nights she kicked and punched in her sleep, panting as though undergoing great feats. Other nights she rose to walk the kitchen in wavering circles, trampling everyone underfoot. Some nights the other servants woke to see what looked like a cloud of fireflies winking around her head. One servant or another woke to sit bolt upright at midnight, staring at Grandmother in irritation, in fright. Grandmother's face at midnight was not her petulant daytime face, her stubborn headstrong face that she turned to the other servants when they were cruel, when they forced on her the chores nobody wanted to do. Her night-time body was no relation to the daytime one she disobeyed the senior servants with, disappearing for hours on end, reappearing to slop through her work without a word of apology or explanation. At night Grandmother was otherworldly. She walked with her sleeping breath rattling the kitchen windows, her voice a hoarse whisper coming from lips that did not move.

The other servants ganged up against her. 'What? What did I do?' Grandmother shouted as they ringed their beds with lucky talismans and reflected eight-sided mirrors in her eyes to confuse her. They slept clutching their newly blessed crosses, their wooden beads. They tied Grandmother to her pallet, yet woke at midnight to find her arms and legs unbound, her body stumbling this way and that. Her hair flying, though there was no wind. When the other servants could stand the nightly interruptions no longer, they carried Grandmother slumped between them down the steep and gloomy stairway to the basement, to the room without windows. When they found her work unsatisfactory they dragged her there, and when she was naughty, or a precious lamp was broken and no one owned up, or when Grandmother was deliberately stubborn, when she flew into a temper, and refused the work they set her, and answered back. 'Who? Who are you going to tell?' the other servants cried, slamming the door behind her with the slam of a door not soon to be opened. 'You'll stay there till you're sorry, beast!'

My grandmother hated this room, the punishment room. The room was nicknamed Grandmother's because no other culprit was sent there as often as she. In the mornings when she woke to the dark walls around her and her limbs stiff from lying twisted and the door latched from outside, Grandmother blinked and rubbed at the dark with her fingers. Grandmother shouted and beat her fists. The punishment room was in the lowest part of the house, the furthest corner of the basement. Its walls were two feet thick, its door barely shuddering though her fists swelled up red. The floor was bare and dusty, the dry earthy air rattled in her throat. Grandmother crouched with her cheek to the door, rocking, slapping her palms against the wood. Some days she beat and shouted for hours before anyone remembered.

My grandmother believes in ghosts. She believes in gods and spirits and demons. She is old now, so sometimes she mixes them up. When she was younger she had an extra eye. 'Where? Where, Grandmother?' I ask and ask, but she can never be sure. Sometimes she points to her forehead, sometimes her left cheek. My grandmother's extra eye suddenly opened when she was hit on the head with a frying-pan ladle. Fat from the pan spat in the arc of the ladle to splash her forehead, her left cheek. The ladle shattered on impact and the lump on my grandmother's head was a boiled egg, a shiny knob. Grandmother's eyesight blurred. She was in between ages at that time, almost fourteen years at the count of the calendar, no longer a child, not yet a young woman, at the in-between time given to general bouts of dizziness and reeling, but Grandmother was strong. She was the youngest bonded servant at the rich man's mansion, the most inferior, and used to pots and pans and ladles landing on her arms and legs and head without warning, yet she fell faint and lifeless from that blow as though cut with one stroke.

'You've killed her!' the kitchen workers cried.

'Huh!' the Number Two Kitchen Maid grunted, grasping the shattered frying-pan ladle. 'The beast! This beast is so tough, even if I beat her twice as hard, she won't die. Aiya, beast! Get up! You think today's a holiday, or what?'

Slowly Grandmother pushed herself upright. Above her head dark shadows were swirling. Grandmother blinked. The world was filled with a sudden churning, a surging of ribbons of darkness and light that sucked the colour from the floor, the walls, the woodstove, the kitchen, the world through the window, everything. The opening of her extra eye surprised her so that she felt no pain. She stared at the grainy faces of the kitchen servants crowded around her like black-and-white altar pictures of ancestors long dead. Grandmother leapt to her feet, shrieking. She raced from that ancestor-filled kitchen in one leaping shriek. The knock on the head with the frying-pan ladle that opened her extra eye also drained my grandmother's world of colour. At first the colourless world terrified her. Later she learnt the advantages of seeing in black-and-white.

My grandmother knows about ghosts. She is great at giving advice. When Grandmother advises she sits in her special chair just outside the doorway. Knowing clients steer her to her chair when she's absentminded; in her special chair Grandmother's advice always works. She sits shaking her wrinkled feet in their clogs, she cups the shape of the ghostly advice in her hands. I pause my notetaking to watch her fabulous handshapes until she shouts 'Be serious!' to give me a fright. Grandmother examines my notes. She can't make out the scribbles but she likes the lines to be straight. Someday she will write a book, she says, from these notes. That is why I must write neatly, I must press my pen to mark the paper firmly so the words will never fade. Someday Grandmother will write a proper book, with pages edged in gold and covers of shiny red leather. She will dictate and I will write.

Ghosts live in dark dank places like deep in the jungle, or a basement, or school and public toilets. Never go into the jungle or the basement, or a school or public toilet alone, always check if the lights are working. Always make sure you carry a torch. Never cut yourself in the jungle by accident, never leave blood droplets on a basement floor. If jungle or basement ghosts are lurking, this will rush them out with bulging eyes and tongues wildly lapping. Never leave used sanitary pads lying around. If a toilet ghost devours one, the unlucky person will die soon after.

When Grandmother was younger she used to be a famous ghostchaser. In her heyday her door was always crowded with prospective clients: red-eyed men and women, haggard from the disturbances of ghosts. In those days Grandmother was paid with day-long feasts that swelled her belly, with live goats and chickens, even nuggets of gold. Nowadays her front teeth are gapped and pitted with the gold that had to be dug out when times got tough: when Grandmother lost so much face her ghostchasing reputation was spoiled, and later, when her extra eye closed, and the clients who were once so fawning and eager crossed themselves and slammed their doors. Nowadays my grandmother still gets a client or two, but no spectacular jobs. Customers step in cautiously where once they shoved and jostled. They merely ask for a passport for the dead, stamped with Grandmother's tiger seal for safe travelling through the underworld, or a ghost wedding for their lonely dead, or a question-and-answer session to see how their ancestors are. Nowadays my grandmother's clients are local people, who have seen her in her heyday and know the power of her charms even if they don't immediately work. In the middle of our front room is a blackened incinerator that in the old days used to swallow up offerings, sending them off to hell with a great whoosh.

'Whoosh!' Grandmother shows me, puffing her breath so my hair flies back.

The convent on the hill next to the jungle is where I met the bully. That's the place to begin. When the bully and I first met I went to stand beside her, as my grandmother told me. The bully stood with her legs stretching her skirt, her head turning to stare. Her shadow was black and solid in the morning sunlight, mine a dark whiplash cleaving onto hers. The bully jumped at the touch of our shadows. Suddenly she smiled.

The bully in school is a girl twice my size. She is wide and sullen with arms meaty and hands that curl into fists. The bully lives in the convent. When the day girls go home she stands at the gate to watch. The nuns found the bully on the doorstep, wrapped in newspaper and a scrap of red cloth. Her sign is the bullock; her strength, the earth, on which the bullock stands firmly. When the moon is full the bully creeps into the jungle to rub thick clots of earth onto her skin. The bully is wild, covered with marks from where the nuns beat her. When the Old Priest died he left her his camera. He said it would tame her, seeing life frozen a moment at a time. He left her his knife, once owned by a famous bandit, an eversharp knife, good for cutting fine edges on photographic paper. The bully and I are crazy about photography. The bully likes taking pictures and developing them, and I like watching.

'The best place in school,' the bully says, 'is the darkroom.'

Everyone knows the bully is mad. If someone says: *I dare you to spend the night in the toilet in the library all by yourself*, she will do it. If someone says: *I dare you to make that girl take off her underpants and dance on the table, and not tell*, she will do it too. Everyone is afraid of her. The bully wears her hair short and draws charcoal pictures in the toilets and picks at her nose, especially when teachers are watching. She says the nuns are going to kill her. To bury her in the jungle and rub out her name so no one will know. The bully takes pictures for evidence. She has pictures of all the nuns: nuns eating, nuns sleeping, nuns perched on the loo. Pale nun shapes pacing the corridors at night. The bully goes to confession every week. She cries when there is thunder and lightning and says the Our Father in one breath. She is going to heaven whatever the cost, but the nuns say: *No chance!* Unless the bully mends her ways. The nuns say the bully is bad. While she sleeps the devil will come to get her. The bully wants to see the devil. At night she curls her fingers around her camera in anticipation. She sleeps with her eyes open to be sure.

Before my grandmother lets my mother take me to school every morning, she insists on doing my hair. Grandmother's old hands hold the comb in a trembling clasp, her knob-boned fingers pull at my roots. I stand hopping from one foot to the other while she scrapes at my skull. She divides my hair untidily, rubs knots between her thumb and forefinger to give my hair bulk.

'Ow! Grandmother!' only makes her pull harder.

'This knot is so you will keep your eyes and ears open,'

she mutters. 'This one so your head won't turn. This, so you won't forget your old grandmother. This so you'll find your way home.'

When Grandmother has finished, my long braid pokes out this way and that with knots. Grandmother stands waving at the door, her lips curling with satisfaction. The braid she has knotted is so tight it pulls my eyes up at the corners, it gives me slanty vision so I walk crooked. All the way to the convent my mother pulls me straight. When we reach the convent she pulls me into the laundry where she works. Slowly, patiently, she loosens Grandmother's knots until my scalp itches from the blood rushing back. She rubs my temples until the glittering black behind my eyelids goes away. Until I can see. My mother knots my hair ribbons in place. She pats my cheek. 'Before you go home,' she says, 'come here first, and I will put them back.'

Before my mother became a Christian she was convinced that her luck was bad. My mother's badluck hung on black hooks from her shoulders, like wings. As she walked it brushed the earth behind her. My mother picked up this badluck when she was just a child and did not know the techniques of badluck evasion. That morning she stood at the scene of a murder the night before, watching the blood spots on the path slowly browning. The spots bunched like flowers on the path that led through the field from my mother's house to the river. My mother dropped her bundle of washing. In the distance she could hear the echoing shouts of her brothers and sisters at play. She could see the churn of the river where it met the sea. On each side of the clustered spots was a handprint, one faint, the other heavy, holding the spots together. My mother bent to inspect the handprints more closely. She touched the tip of an outspread finger with her own. Although she did not know it then, this was when the badluck hooked itself onto her back.

'Was it heavy?' the bully asks, flexing her own broad shoulders on which, if anything dared to hook itself, she would immediately know.

'Can't you see how she is bent over?' Grandmother cries. 'She thinks she's passed her badluck on to Jesus, but see how she's bent!'

My mother carried the badluck home when she finally ran to tell about the murder. The body twisted into the undergrowth reached out its arms to make her run faster. The moment she entered the house, everything changed. The shadow of the badluck coloured the whole front room. My mother tripped on the doorstep which was raised to prevent demons from entering. Her outstretched arms broke her fall. Her palms slid to a stop along the knotted wood, leaving skin, picking up splinters. Her palms made two marks on either side of her head, one faint, the other heavy. From that day everything began to go wrong. Rising with eyes brimful and palms scraped ragged, my mother felt the unfamiliar weight of the badluck on her shoulders. As she grew it spread itself more evenly. It bent her knees, making her shuffle, and drooped her head, and hung like lead in her hands so that even the things she touched with the lightest touch spilled, and cracked, and shattered. The badluck slipped into my mother's blood. It weighed down the corners of her mouth.

Slowly her reputation spread. When the people of her village saw her coming they spat three times and turned the other way. They sprinkled salt into her footprints and covered the faces of babies when she passed. No one looked her in the eye. My mother's family, already burdened with too many debts and children and worries, decided to send her to the city with the Auntie who came to recruit servant girls. My mother sat in the back of the taxi listening to the creak of the wheels over the ruts and potholes, under the weight of her luck which tipped the taxi sideways. Other village girls slipped against her, grumbling. Her tears splashed dark spots onto her new red dress. When my mother had been beaten for spoiling the rice or holding back the rain or bringing sickness to the family, she had felt the badluck quiver on her shoulders. She had felt it rise in her throat in lumps of varying sizes. Even years later, after she became a Christian and no longer believed in this luck, in unguarded moments she sometimes felt its roundness, its black smoothness, at the base of her throat. But try as she might to spit it out, my mother never could.

The city with the convent on the hill next to the jungle is a city of many old sayings. There is a saying, as the old saying goes, for every day of the week. The sayings flash through the city as quick as a monkey's hand, in a week a new saying might be on everyone's lips, from the road sweepers clutching their bristle brooms to the city officials riding around in air-conditioned cars. The city gobbles up sayings like candy, like soldiers gobble evil bandits, like bandits gobble innocent city boys and girls. Some are forgotten in the time it takes a hen's droppings to cool, others appear and disappear like a coconut approaching the seaside, others stick around like a new mother-in-law. At the convent the nuns teach us even newer sayings by rote. Every morning convent girl voices rise singsong in the convent air. *A stitch in time saves nine. As red as cherries, as white as snow. Take care of the pennies and the pounds will take care of themselves. One bad apple spoils the whole barrel.* When I take the sayings home to Grandmother she swirls them around with her tongue. She pokes them into one cheek, then the other, then spits them out.

'What?' Grandmother shouts, pretending she hasn't heard rightly. 'What's that? What *snow*? What *pound*? What *apple*?'

The new sayings go into one of Grandmother's ears then out the other, but the old sayings stick like mud. Grandmother rattles them off by heart, looking at us sideways. The older the saying the better. The nuns are as clever as crabs teaching crab babies to walk straight but when the elephants fight, the mousedeer will die in the middle, and the bodies after the battle will be as cold as a sea spirit's embrace. Grandmother rattles off one saying after another, without repetition, all in one breath. The bully, my mother and I stand counting them off on our fingers. There is only one saying we know we will hear twice. Of all the sayings in this city of jungles and glowering clouds, my grandmother's favourite is about a creature who can't be controlled. When Grandmother speaks of this creature she always slows her breath. She becomes pensive, her eyes cloud over, her hands lie still. Sometimes she is so awed she has nothing to say. The creature is called the land crocodile. *Beware the land crocodile.*

Imagine this beast, this human-shaped terroriser of innocent girls, as running from tree to tree. Usually he wears nothing but a loincloth and carries a knife. He lives on the edges of the jungle so he gets the best of both worlds. When things get too hot he fades into the safety of the trees and when the urge takes him, out he creeps to jump at victims—young girls usually, but old women too, if he's desperate. He holds them down and pokes them with his knife to make them scream. The crocodile's body is hot but his knife is as cold as ice. When he's on a rampage his whole body swells, he lets out a sound that is low and throbbing, that fills young girls' and old women's heads with the hum of a thousand insects, the shudder of earthquakes, the toppling of great jungle trees, so they fall over faint and panting. When the crocodile is on a rampage he gives off a red glow. When a young girl is deflowered or a man seduces someone else's wife, or your daughter is stolen, your faithful assistant led astray, you can be sure it's with the help of the land crocodile. A girl unlucky enough to be touched by the crocodile will forever be branded with wild ideas, with tempestuous fevers. She'll never listen to her elders, she'll never do what she's told. Such a girl will become a lifetime victim of passions so itchy she'll never be able to sit still.

Grandmother is terrific at descriptions but that is as far as she will go. It's bad luck the convent is next to the jungle, she says. Bad luck for some: the ignorant, the arrogant, the unprepared. Land crocodile. No wonder the nuns make everyone pray all the time, such a danger lurking at the door. My grandmother gives me an amulet to wear whenever I go to school. When the amulet is frayed from running and jumping, when it's torn from being caught on a button or ripped from my neck by the bully in play, Grandmother will light her incense and special candles. Grandmother will dig into her box of special charm papers, she'll polish her scratched reading glasses and dip her brush into her special mix of red ink and fresh chicken blood. Grandmother will grip firmly. She'll frown in concentration, steel her breath to make me another, just as strong. Every year my grandmother gives me a new amulet, with increased protection power. Every year there is increased danger.

'Just before the end of your second life cycle,' she promises. 'Just before you turn fourteen I will give you my strongest amulet, my most powerful charm.' Grandmother lifts a corner of her shirt to show me her strongest amulet. She carefully fingers one side of her belly, then the other, then twists to see where it has gone. I cup the amulet in my palm when she finds it, press my cheek to its warmth.

'Why then, Grandmother? Why not now?'

'Because then you will need it,' Grandmother says.

My grandmother sends me to the convent on the hill next to the jungle in spite of danger because Grandmother has a plan. A plan for getting back face, for killing two frogs with one stone, two ghosts with one ghostchasing spell. Two enemies with one fiery stroke. Every day she awaits my return. She sits in the doorway with her eyes fixed to the front gate until I come home. When I stay at the convent for the night she sleeps with her eyes slit open from worry. The amulet swings from my neck or around my wrist or in my pocket as light as air. My walk to the convent is as light as air, as crooked as a crab baby's, it's a scuttle here and there to look in through shop windows, to crouch at a pedlar's mat strewn with trinkets. To ease the tastiest sweetmeat, hot and steaming, from under a streethawker's nose. My grandmother sits chewing her lip, her temper crusty. Her old bones are like iron, immovable, her body like the anchor of a ship tug-tugging against it, while my walk to the convent is a walk on waves. My chin lifted for whistling. Grandmother makes me wear the amulet whenever I go to the convent, to that crocodile-infested area, because it's there she has her plan.

'What did they teach you?' she asks when I return. 'What did you learn?' She feels for my charm to check it's not broken, she shivers and shakes with relief. She gets out her notebook and pen; sits worrying, grumbling, stumbling her finger after my penstrokes as I race along lightly, swiftly. I arch my arms as if eating her paper. I grin at her frown. My pen swoops in hunger.

My grandmother gives me an amulet to wear whenever I go to school because it's there I'll reach the end of my second life cycle. It's there I'll see for myself. I'll learn the true meaning of the crocodile.

TWO

THE BEST
PLACE IN
SCHOOL

That's the place to begin. The hill with the convent and the jungle is called Mat Salleh Hill. Rival schools call it Mad Sailor Hill. Once, so long ago no one remembers exactly when, a storm swept in from the east so suddenly it took everyone by surprise. In those days the city had yet to become a city. Simple fisherfolk lived in huddled shacks along the coastline. They lived on seafood and scavenging, they wore rough cloths woven with their own hands and lived in woven houses, and strung themselves with necklets made from shells and twigs and leaves. They ate fish skewered on bamboo splinters, fruit plucked fresh from the jungle trees. The storm sent the people scurrying inland. It gobbled up their shacks as well as their mangrove swamps and lagoons, it blew the coast so ragged no one but the oldest people recognised it. The storm was like the oldest storm in the oldest people's memory. It raged for as long as the oldest storm, gobbling and spitting day in and day out while the people huddled in caves and makeshift shelters. They laid out offerings to appease the sea spirits, they cowered at the sight of the storm spitting and gobbling, devouring what belonged to the land, throwing up junk and treasure from the belly of the sea.

The storm stopped as suddenly as it began. The people left their shelters to find the coast littered with the storm's leavings: the bloating remains of sea creatures, scraps of rope and sail, the dangling bones of ships, and crates and boxes, whole or smashed, wedged amongst the mangrove roots. As the oldest people did after the oldest storm, the people stood watching the morning glint on the storm's leavings. The new and cockled splinters of the boats and ships tossed high on the back of the storm, now dashed to shore, would make new shacks, the boxes and crates would contain all sorts of things for which the people had no names. The people shaded their eyes, staring down the length of the coast. As the oldest people did after the oldest storm, they saw amongst the wreckage and dead sea creatures the bodies of men of different shades and sizes, pale men and dark men lapped by the water, side by side. They saw a group of pale men, some flopped in an untidy huddle, others stumbling awkwardly about. The people approached this group cautiously. The oldest people remembered other groups which had proved unfriendly. When they were near enough they called out to signal their approach. 'What news? What a big storm, ah? Are you well?'

A scurry of excitement ran through the group as they neared. One of the pale men leapt to his feet. 'Run!' he screeched. 'It's the cannibals!'

'Will you be staying long?' the people asked the pale men, politely avoiding the wild gaze and the screeches of the first pale man, who brandished a branch of driftwood, then plunged up the beach and into the jungle.

'Boy! Come back!' the other men shouted in their own language. 'Follow him, men!'

Some of the pale bedraggled men plunged into the jungle after the first pale man. Some of the people trailed after.

'Don't let the jungle sounds fool you,' they called. 'He's going this way!'

The pale bedraggled men and the people pushed further and further into the jungle. The land tilted upwards, their bodies bent forwards with the climb. But though they craned their heads and ran tiptoe, they could not see the first pale man. They neither glimpsed the jungle mists stirring nor the jerk and sway of the jungle plants as he passed. The only evidence of the first pale man's existence was the cries that leapt back to pierce them, the screeches interweaving with a myriad other jungle sounds so that they were surrounded by a web of screeching, cackling and cawing, as well as the sounds of the other pale men, the brush of their bodies through the bushes, the snapping of twigs and branches underfoot. The people slipped through the jungle like water. It seemed to them the pale bedraggled men blundered recklessly, trailing behind them a path of tattered jungle plants and scarred treetrunks for anyone to see. When the climb curved upwards sharply the people refused to go any further. They refused to climb the hill where the jungle spirits and hill spirits swirled thickly, where the local deities lived. 'Come back!' they called. 'We cannot go there, we have no offerings! We'll make them angry!'

Soon the pale bedraggled men also turned back. They followed the people back through the loose folds of the outer jungle to the beach where the other people and pale men were already sharing food and water, shifting through the wave-shaped combs of sea junk and treasure for anything that could be used. The other people and pale men were talking to each other with broken bits of each other's language, and wide-armed gestures, hand signals, bodily leaps. Already the other people and the pale men were exchanging smiles, and sounds to name each other; they were weaving the beginnings of stories with their eyes and hands and lips.

'Where do you come from?' the people asked.

'How long will you be staying?'

'Your brother has the sea fever, ah?'

'What is your brother called?'

As the oldest people did after the oldest storm, the people helped the group of pale men to build their own shelters, they shared their food and clothing with them, watched them gather strength enough to set off down the coast to where bigger settlements of people lived. They watched them hail a passing fisherboat, or take to sea in a boat of their own building. The people gathered on the beach to wave them farewell. Neither the pale men nor the people, though they went many times to look, ever found the first pale man, though at night they sometimes heard a shrieking singsong, a wild crooning on a jungle wind.

'He lives with the spirits,' the people joked with one another. 'He's so pale they think he's one of them!'

'What is your brother called?' they asked. 'Perhaps the gods won't mind if we name his new home for him.'

'Oh, that one!' the pale men answered in their own language. 'He's a mad sailor. Mad Sailor! That's what he's called.'

'Safe journey!' the people waved.

'Don't worry,' the pale men called over their shoulders. 'We'll come back safe!'

So the people rolled the first pale man's name in their mouths, and from that day until this, the hill has been known as Mat Salleh Hill.

That's the place to begin. The convent on the hill next to the jungle is where rich people and poor people send their girls. Here all kinds of girls get to mix together, they rub shoulders at morning assembly, bump into each other as they march from class to class. They call to each other across the playing fields, go about in groups of favourite twos and threes. Before I went to the convent nobody offered to go with the bully. The bully stood amidst the calling, marching, shoulder-rubbing convent girls with her mouth scornful, her eyes following them here and there, her feet almost setting out in that direction. Her ancient box camera was slung for company around her neck.

The bully in school is a girl older than the oldest girl in class. She is tall and sturdy, with knuckles shiny and bones too big for her face. Her body stretches her uniform, her breasts make two lumps on her chest. No one knows exactly how old the bully is. Every year she looks the same. Other girls get taller or wider, or slimmer or shapelier with each passing year, but the bully always looks the same. She grew until she was fourteen, my grandmother says, the end of her second life cycle. Then the bully stopped.

'Why, Grandmother?' I ask. 'Why?' But Grandmother can never be sure. She frowns at the bully across the room. Finally she shrugs: 'Didn't know which way to grow.'

'One day you will be the same age,' Grandmother tells me. 'Then you will be older.'

When I was allowed into the convent the bully had been in the same class for years. Other girls came and went but the bully always stayed. The bully always stayed the same: no bigger than the biggest girl in class, no older-looking than the oldest-looking girl. The bully is allowed to attend only certain lessons: catechism, needlework, history, morals, craft. The bully rushes to these lessons from her various chores. She comes from the kitchens smelling of onions and steaming ricepots, of the boarders' lunch of curried stew. She comes from the toilets smelling of disinfectant, from the storerooms trailing cobwebs to mark her exercise book.

'How many times must I tell you to wash first!' the teachers cry, chasing her out.

When the class breaks for recess it is the bully's job to clean the blackboard and tidy the chairs. Everyone can tell when the bully cleans the blackboard. She covers it from end to end with the sweep of her arm, with mountainous streaks. When the class goes for sport it is the bully's job to carry the equipment. It is the bully's and my job because we are charity students, but the bully pushes me away. The bully spits onto her palms and rubs them briskly. 'You hold the door,' she says.

Balls and bats, hockey sticks, nets and racquets, all sling

bouncing from the bully's back. The bully has muscles on her arms that pop in and out. She balances hoops and markers against her belly. She walks hunched and sullen, scowls at the teachers and knocks tables and chairs crooked as she goes past. No matter how the nuns try to teach her she never does anything with good grace. The bully is lazy, slovenly. She has to be nagged and scolded constantly before she will do the chores the nuns set her to earn her keep.

The only place no one can nag or scold the bully is the darkroom. In the darkroom the bully is king.

'Do a somersault,' the bully says. 'Stand on your head.'

The bully watches as I tumble over and over. There is space for three somersaults from wall to wall. I stand waving my legs in the air.

'What next?' I cry. 'What next?'

When the bully can think of nothing I flop to my feet beside her. I snail-walk the way she walks, carrying equipment, bending over with arms stuck out like bats and balls. I make the sullen face of the bully, cheeks blown out, lower lip drooping. I grunt the bully's sour grunt. Passing, I make as if to tweak her ear.

'Shh!' the bully says.

In the darkroom the bully is always listening. Hearing clipped footsteps, the rustle of starched skirts, the low murmur of the nuns. The darkroom is the bully's secret, buried in the furthest corner of the library basement, where nowadays nobody thinks to go. Its walls are windowless, its door half-hidden by stacks of costumes and old school-play props. The nuns have locked the darkroom, bolted it for good, but the bully has a key. In the darkroom the bully shows me her equipment, hoarded over the years. The box the Old Priest packed up for her before he died swings its cover open. It is filled with ancient photographic materials, the bully's camera, the special scrapbook she is beginning, her dog-eared book of rules. An album pasted with yellowing photos on pages shiny with age. The bully and I pore over these photos. She points to them with her knife. Beneath some are captions of time, event and place, in the Old Priest's tiny copperplate hand. *Digging the well. Uncovering the flagstones in the courtyard. Sister setting up the scriptures class.* As I read the captions the bully peers into the photos. Her eyes are cat's eyes, hardly blinking. She examines each photo an inch at a time. Black-and-white faces stare back at her, either pensive or grinning, or twisted with concentration. The bully looks at their mouths one day, at their eyes the next. One by one she passes them to me. Bodies lean this way and that, and there are accidents: blurry feet and gravel, black photos crossed with hairlines of light. The scaly close-up of a hand. Although the bully looks at the photos over and over, every time she looks she thinks there's more to see. She bends her oldest photo to the flickering lamp.

'Something moved,' the bully says.

In the darkroom the bully becomes laconic. The bully's cowhide, which she wears outside the darkroom, becomes like pulp. Here she licks at the thin welts from the cook's bamboo cane that she doesn't even notice outside the darkroom, here she gingerly flexes her scabbed ankles. She blows on her bruises to unfreeze the blood. Here the bully and I are completely free. We sit laughing and giggling for no particular reason. We try on costumes dug sneezing from their stacks outside the darkroom, do somersaults until the bully tires and stops me with a friendly slap. We lie panting on the floor. Sometimes the darkroom floor is so cool it feels like water. In between chores and classes the bully and I fall asleep on a floor that smells stale and briny, rich with the smells of our sweat, and older richer smells, which make us toss and turn in sleep, in dreams of our heads under water, our bodies drifting on the cold hard bed of the sea.

When I first got to the convent I followed the bully around, as Grandmother told me. Weeks later the bully led me to the narrow stairway tucked into a seldom-used corner of the library, behind a shelf of dusty books. She opened the door with the sign *Strictly No Entry!* so I could pass. I peered into the library basement as she swung her torch beam past cardboard cutout jungles and a shiny slivered moon to the black of the darkroom door. The stairway plunged steep and gloomy. The old wood swallowed our footsteps as down we went.

'The *best* place in school,' the bully pointed, nudging me forwards, arcing her arm towards the darkroom in a generous sweep.

My grandmother knows about ghosts. She is an expert on ghostly sightings, on the habits and hungers of spirits and demons, on ghostly vengeance or favour reaching to spook humans from the other side. Grandmother has creaked down many a steep and gloomy stairway, she has peered under beds and cupboards, swung her lantern into corners where any ghostly favour or vengeance might be lurking, ready to spring. She has gripped her never-fail matches and ghostburning candles, stabbed her special ghostslashing knife at shadows daring to come too close. The path towards the fulfilment of a ghostly favour or vengeance, Grandmother says, is more convoluted than that of humans, having to travel an indirect route. But sooner or later, by ways and means human or animal, discerning or otherwise, the message gets across. Such is the nature of unfinished business: never resting until it's paid back. Only powerful wisewomen are known to turn the path of unfinished business somewhere else. Even powerful wise-women are sometimes caught out. When Grandmother was no longer young, such a message wound its indirect way towards her, through the passing of the wet and dry seasons of her living, despite the habitual twists and turns she made in hope of confusing just such a message. It paused when it finally saw her, dropped like a stone from the sky, like a frying-pan ladle, to flatten Grandmother where she stood. The message dropped on her like a curse gone wrong. It struck suddenly, with great precision, to close my grandmother's extra eye.

'How did it do it, Grandmother? How?' I ask and ask, but she can never be sure. Sometimes she assumes the posture of fast movers, of lightning and electricity, other times she merely shrugs. The ghostly message leapt from the jungle to attract her attention, it hit the butt of a bandit rifle against her head in the exact spot of the long ago frying-pan ladle that first opened her eye. Grandmother staggered under the blow. In the instant before falling she saw before her not the old bandit, toothlessly grinning, but a woman dressed in shimmering white. The most beautiful woman my grandmother had ever seen. The woman smiled at Grandmother, her smile dispassionate, one hand held out as if in greeting. Grandmother's eyes widened. She jumped with recognition. The rifle butt shattered on impact and the lump on her head was a boiled egg, a shiny knob. Grandmother's eyesight blurred. She staggered to her knees and immediately pressed her head to the ground. She held out her meagre belongings: her bowl of coins, her lucky talismans, her red handkerchief. The bundle of scraps she'd wrangled from the porkseller only that morning. Grandmother bowed and bowed until the pattern from the road was printed on her forehead. The bandits stood in a circle around her, not knowing they were messengers, laughing.

'Too old to fight,' they cried. 'Too ugly to screw! Too tough to eat!'

They pushed the blunt edges of their knives into the folds of her belly, knocked their homemade truncheons against her shoulders and neck. Grandmother heard through the roar in her ears a scuffle break out amongst them. The sound of bodies pushing against bodies, a voice crying, 'Aiya, who's this? Comrades! Do we bully old women? Let her be!' The circle of faces jumped and dipped, dark faces, pale faces, old ones, young ones, ones she seemed vaguely to know. One with a cracked and flaking skin, with eyes black and glittering. Grandmother folded her body inwards, bowing and bowing. The closing of her eye surprised her so that she felt no pain. The arrival of the ghostly message, so unexpected, filled her with regret at her lack of expectation. For the first time in years she saw colours dancing and whirling around her. Later

Grandmother collapsed, expecting her head to be lopped off with a rusty bandit sword, but the men had already gone.

Before her extra eye closed, my grandmother was the most famous ghostchaser in the whole city. Not once did she imagine she would one day sit shaking her legs in the doorway, waiting for customers to come. For years Grandmother's business went so well she was thoroughly worked off her feet. Grandmother was so busy she even had to buy herself an assistant. In those days she was no longer young, her back was bent, her hair streaked with grey. So Grandmother went out to look for my mother. Grandmother had noticed my mother, who worked at the local brothel, whom the brothel keeper screamed at from morning till night. My mother was a young girl in those days, but already she walked with her shoulders stooped and her head permanently lowered. Her feet shuffled even when she wasn't lugging groceries or emptying slop-buckets, or moving furniture upstairs and downstairs according to the brothel keeper's latest whim. My mother walked as though carrying a great weight. She neither ducked nor flinched from the blows aimed at her, though once she cried out 'Auntie!' and Grandmother heard from the other end of the street. My mother's eyes drooped at the corners where heavy tears trembled.

'Take her!' the brothel keeper exclaimed when Grandmother asked. 'Look at that face! I'm sorry I promised her parents I'd look after her, she's brought me nothing but badluck. I took her from the village, I gave her good clothes and food, but is she grateful? Does she try to be nice? All she does is mope around the place, turning customers off! If you take her she'll only bring you badluck. Aiya, old friend, you so eager for badluck, or what? Take her next time.'

Grandmother felt my mother's liver, which was stiff to the touch, meaning she could withstand great shocks. She studied her brow, which was low and hairy, meaning she was timid but would not die of fright. She examined her tongue, large and rounded, meaning she wouldn't talk back. 'I'll take her,' Grandmother said.

My mother's large hands were good for carrying ghostchasing equipment: a bucket, some rags, some gunpowder and lamp-oil, a bag of spells and seals, a cloth soaked in menstrual blood. A live chicken, beak tied with string, temple prayer beads, a cross. Since every ghost was different, Grandmother never knew what she would need. Some ghosts were no more than bits of leftover anger or envy, some had human characteristics, fear of closed spaces or water, others thought they were gods or saints or fairies, others didn't even know they were dead.

Grandmother watched the slope of my mother's back under the weight of the tools. When they went ghostchasing my mother would have to carry everything so Grandmother's hands and thoughts could be free. Grandmother carried only her special ghostslashing knife, to be used when things got extra tough. Its handle was charred and misshapen, as though it had been through many battles, its salt-crusted blade was a menacing sight. The magic knife sent all kinds of ghosts and demons screeching in terror. Its burnt smell warned what their fate would be. Even Grandmother did not like to see the knife, she kept it for emergencies, she handled it with great care. She looked at my mother's hands, which were square-fingered but nimble, which cut and folded paper quickly, neatly. She examined her eye whites, poked her in the ribs. 'Eat more,' Grandmother said. 'Eat slowly. Do eye exercises. Drink this.' Even though she was no longer young they went out on jobs every day. Sometimes, after a flood or famine, or a bandit raid on government offices, an accidental soldier massacre in the squatter areas, or if a single ghost was particularly strong and stubborn, they didn't come home for weeks.

Once Grandmother and my mother were called to the convent by the caretaker whose hut was next to the ghosthouse. The caretaker was a timid, shuffling man, not old but not quite young, grey-haired from tragedy and already stooping. The caretaker's wife had recently died, suddenly, like a tap on the shoulder, some said of disappointment, others of grief. The caretaker walked the convent with his eyes swelled up from sorrow, his chores performed automatically, his awe of the Old Priest and the nuns who spoke to him kindly but sternly growing into an awe of life. The caretaker peered over his shoulder every now and then, suddenly, to see if life was sneaking up for another tap. In those days the convent ghosthouse was already famous throughout the city. Convent days were famous for their occasional bangings, cacklings and screechings, convent nights for books flying from their shelves in neat order, troops of see-through soldiers patrolling the halls. Bandit shadows slumped in unlikely corners, pointing to wounds that bled no more. Convent afternoons spied an occasional sad woman in shimmering white, pausing for an instant at the top of the stairs. When convent girls ran screaming the nuns cried 'Nonsense!' and set them Hail Marys for overactive imaginations, litter duty for playing tricks. Even the caretaker and his wife learnt to live with the ghosthouse happenings, although after their son was born she became superstitious. She stood staring at the library for long moments before coming to bed. 'Badluck place,' she muttered, snapping the windows shut, pasting protection charms over the door. 'Aiya, how to clear them out?'

After the caretaker's wife died the activity for which the ghosthouse was famous became even more pronounced. The bangings, cacklings and screechings banged, cackled and screeched more often and loudly, the beautiful woman at the stairway was joined by other shapes and shadows, the soldiers by swirlings in the courtyard, pale ghostlights under the stairs. The caretaker and his son awoke each midnight to shiver in bed. They crept to their window, the boy clinging to his father with his eyes squeezed tight. Tears streamed down the caretaker's cheeks.

'Aiya, Wife!' he swung the window wide open. 'What are you doing? Can't you go yet? Why make so much noise?'

The figure in the ghosthouse window turned for a moment to stare. She wore the same determined look she wore in life, her see-through hands placed on her hips at the same determined angle she placed them, in life, just before embarking on any unpleasant but necessary chore. The caretaker's wife stared for a moment, then turned. She hunched her shoulders and split like shards of light into a dozen directions. The caretaker watched, horrified, as not one wife but a dozen raced and flitted all over the ghosthouse, poking into this corner where a huddle of shadows fled squeaking, jabbing behind those doors where fluid shapes became sharp and brittle, poking and jabbing and shooing all manner of heads and entrails, ink-black blobs and eyeless humps from their hiding places in a frenzy of ghostly housekeeping.

In the morning some parts of the library looked as if great battles had happened, others as if they had been hastily tidied, books and magazines strewn about, then put back wrong. All the furniture would be rearranged. Every morning the nuns ordered the caretaker to move everything back. Groups of naughty convent girls on punishment duty huddled together peering over their shoulders, sorting the magazines and books. The caretaker and his son lugged at the furniture all day, bumping into each other, jumping at every sound. Their necks were heavy with an assortment of colourful charms. When they finished the nuns crept into the ghosthouse to pray. The Old Priest sprinkled holy water and hung crosses over the doors, watched in horror as the holy water sizzled on the cool marble floor. The nuns sent pleas for a first rate exorcist from their home country, but no exorcist came. The Old Priest tried different masses, blessings and fastings; he emerged with his cassock crooked and the ends of his hair singed. The ghost-house would be quiet for some nights, then it would start again. Ghostly dancers spilled into the courtyard, a man covered in teethmarks raised his glass in salute. The shimmering woman at the top of the stairs turned to smile at the caretaker's wife and her frenzied cleaning.

'Wife!' the caretaker cried, burning furtive offerings at the ghosthouse window every night. 'Aiya, Wife, you're dead! Do you hear me? No need to clean any more. Your husband's sending you food and journey money. Aiya, Wife, please go!'

But the caretaker's wife took no notice. More bangs and crashes filled the night-time ghosthouse, more unearthly voices shrieked their protest, then wept as though the world was coming to an end. The caretaker and his son grew black rings around their eyes from the strain.

When the caretaker came to see my grandmother, she cracked her knuckles in anticipation. She flexed her arms and sucked at her teeth. 'Auntie,' the caretaker began, 'the nuns don't know I came. I can't stand it, I'll pay Auntie myself, but I haven't much money . . .' The caretaker twisted his sweatcloth out of shape while Grandmother airily waved her hand.

'Aiya, business is good,' Grandmother said. 'This time I've got interest. Got charity. Don't worry. This time I do for free.'

My grandmother hadn't been to the ghosthouse for years, not since the nuns took over. Some months earlier she'd foreseen her return and had waited patiently. Grandmother shouted at her young assistant, who scuttled about preparing everything. They waited. The caretaker asked Grandmother to choose an auspicious ghostchasing time. The nuns were so fierce he begged her to scan her almanac for a time when everyone was sleeping—in the dead of night.

When my mother was a young woman she met a young man as she was turning a corner. Rain dripped over the edge of the convent corner to splatter their faces and hair. My mother heard a sharp intake of breath. She and the young man bumped shoulders, accidentally, for an instant their shoulderbones locked. Through their thin shirts their skins slid grazing against each other. My mother's gaze lifted from its usual sweep of the ground to the young man's face. Both she and the young man took a half-step backwards. Their eyes were exactly level, their bumped shoulders and arms curved for balance curving at the same angle, aching at the same spot.

The young man and my mother held their heads the same way, slightly lowered; they held their bodies alike, gingerly, like bodies guarding secrets too fragile for the world. For an instant my mother and the young man stood rooted like a mirror image of each other, like accomplices. Then her gaze reverted to its old angle, her mouth mumbled excuses, her body slipped around the corner and the young man, away.

This, the young man said, *was their first meeting*.

This, my mother says, *was not*.

When my mother was a young woman there was an instant between the time she was a girl and the time it seemed to everyone she became a middle-aged woman, worn, the features of her face caved in. In that instant my mother was a young woman, no more, no less. Her head and shoulders ceased their habitual stoop forwards. In that instant the badluck lifted from her shoulders with the merest shrug. Her face took on its natural expression, the expression that was hers before the badluck knocked it off course. Her eyes widened slightly. Her gaze abandoned its usual scuttle to linger on shapes and colours unseen before, on smoke curls from the woodstove, cobwebs caught in sunlight. Her chin sank for long moments onto the palm of her hand. In that instant, which seemed to my mother to last both an eyeblink and forever, she stood poised on a hinge: turning a corner. My mother stood there, perfectly balanced. She could swing either way, but she stood there, an eyeblink or forever, perfectly still. In that instant everything stopped. Gone was my mother's badluck past, disappeared her badluck future. My mother felt young, and light. When the instant passed, an eyeblink or forever later, everything, my mother, my grandmother, the ground, the air, the world, was irrevocably changed.

Although she dared not look, my mother heard the young man pause on the corner. She heard him turn a half-circle towards her. So deliberately, so quickly it seemed to her of their own volition, her feet stumbled their way over the uneven stones of the passage, her hands pushed open the heavy door. Her body slipped into the warmth of the familiar. My mother leaned for a moment against the shut door, breathing the moist air of the everyday place, the workplace, where the sinks and tubs and piles of washing etched their comforting hard edges and the only ghosts rising to meet her were damp and fleeting ones, puffed out then disappeared with each hiss of laundry steam. My mother drew a hand across her brow. She tidied her already tidy clothes, tucked imaginary loose strands of hair behind her ears. She walked her slow measured walk past the piles of clothes that needed sorting, past those that needed extra scrubbing and soaking, and the ones needing only a quick final rinse: to the centre of the room. In the centre my mother felt solid.

Although she did not hear him my mother knew the young man entered. She knew the young man leaned against the door as she had, breathing as she had, but unlike her he walked a faltering walk to the centre of the room. The young man stood directly behind my mother the way some ghosts like to do. Some ghosts will wait for a turning, to show those foolish enough to turn their frightful ghostly face. The young man smelt clean and earthy. He smelt like smooth jungle rain. My mother stood solid, not turning her head. Some ghosts were sneaky. They knew about body temperature and the tingling places on the back of the neck, and delicate smells. The young man dropped his rainsoaked jacket and the bundle slung over one arm. He reached his arms around my mother, gathered his body to hers. His hands seemed too scarred and wiry to be ghostly, his skin too rough for enchantment; his body too brittle to make havoc out of mischief, human ache out of ghostly spite. The young man rested his head on my mother's shoulder, nestled his breath in the curve of her neck. It was then that the badluck shifted, suddenly, swiftly. The badluck crouched tiptoe, ready to spring. My mother leaned into the young man in surprise.

Imagine this hill as it must have been all those years ago. Surely the jungle was still here then, they say it is an old jungle, that is why it must be preserved. How could an exotic garden spread its way over the jungle-covered hillside as far as the eye could see? The rich man must have hired an army of gardeners who slashed and burned and uprooted, even now-adays the old convent caretaker sweats pure salt leading naughty convent girls on garden duty in a losing battle to keep the jungle back. The convent garden seems to shrink with every year. Five paces over the straggly wire fence and the jungle trees stand tall and sturdy, as if they have been standing forever. The jungle canopy hangs with a weight of leaves and branches laced and relaced to allow only an underwater light. The jungle light sinks sluggish from chinks in the canopy to the leaf carpet as it has forever, as if forever is the time jungle sunlight takes to sink to hand height, to spill a drop like water on my palm. Perhaps the rich man really grew jungle trees. Instead of fountains and pavilions and shrubs from faraway places, planted with gusto then allowed to run wild. Instead of a track slashed in a straight line to the top of the hill, eating everything in its path. Perhaps the rich man parted and carved and cemented gently, unscathingly. For all that's left of him in this jungle, he may as well have let the jungle be.

But how will the bully and I know? Every time we walk in the jungle it seems to have changed. Traces of the rich man and his lover shift their shapes like jungle mist. The stories we unearth are like the ruined fountains and garden statues we stumble over, showing only their broken pieces, their missing bits. The bully and I only know what we're told, what we see. Deep in the jungle we discover stones laid in strange patterns, whether bandit stones signalling long forgotten messages or soldier stones laid for a soldier game, the bully and I don't know. We push our toes to disrupt any neat pattern, kick jungle earth and leaves onto any other human sign. The bully considers the jungle her own. She makes her own marks: moss carefully scraped in intricate patterns, rocks overturned to show their moist underbellies where insects scurry from the light. Chalk arrows in every colour and direction to confuse anyone else on a jungle walk. Anyone else on the lookout for jungle treasure like the bully and me.

In the jungle I follow her closely, as Grandmother has told me. Grandmother's special leaf and root collection bag is tied round my waist to steady me, her never-fail matches and ghostburning candles knock reassuringly against my side. I shiver and shudder as I follow the bully. I stare around me in terror at what my grandmother has told, as Grandmother shivers and shudders at the thought of me in the jungle. But still she says I must go: that is part of. her plan. The bully is a jungle expert. Even new girls know this, even hardcore girls who say they know everything come asking the bully for jungle advice. Which woods are smoothest for carving love hearts to be distributed on Saint Valentine's Day, which leaves will sprout between book pages, which fruit sends a tingle like electricity along convent girls' tongues. The bully knows the many paths of this jungle and the places where people can rest. She has walked it so often she knows where to look. *There is a grave in its centre*, Grandmother says.

Walking along the jungle paths the bully and I keep a lookout for the place where the many tracks meet. We keep a lookout for the crocodile. We follow the path of the troupe of monkeys, spy the one-armed leader in trunk and branch shapes, hear its cry like human teasing in the canopy overhead. The bully and I race after the monkeys, we bend breathless with our hands on knees. We see the marks made by the soldiers' boots. Soldiers play at being soldiers in this jungle reserve. Some play good guys, others play bandits and communists, and they chase each other along the tracks. They chase monkeys and young girls too, that is what Grandmother says. My grandmother feels sorry for the bully. She says there is a shadow following her.

The lessons in school that the bully likes best are history and storytelling. These are the lessons she tries hardest to follow. But no matter how the nuns scold and explain the bully can't tell the difference between the two. She mixes up her exercise books, draws gnomes and fairies in historical battles, makes kings and queens from faraway countries ride in bullockcarts to the guillotine. The nuns throw up their hands, they mark the bully's painstaking pictures with a large red cross. During history lessons the bully is forever sticking up her hand, which the nuns pretend not to see. The bully is forever saying 'Please, Sister . . .' when they ask does everybody understand. The bully sits at the back of the class, not lulled like other convent girls by the nuns' lilting accents, not scribbling whatever they say as fast as she can. The bully sits chewing her lip. 'Please, Sister,' she blurts.

The bully can't imagine the faraway battles and treaties, or the kings and queens in their strange garb and hairstyles, she can't memorise dates for peanuts, can't see what faraway places and people have to do with her. How they and she fit. Of her two favourite lessons she likes storytelling best. The nuns are more lenient at storytelling. They don't shout at the bully: 'Because that's what happened, my girl!' Sometimes they even let her take part. For storytelling convent girls go to the front of the class to tell a story they know. Stories of local saints and heroes are allowed, tales of loyal servants who stay with their masters while others turn traitor, and those of soldiers bravely battling enemies to keep the city safe. Convent girls have to tell their stories from memory, without any prompting, without hidden notes. The ones who tell the best story, with the best action and without stumbling get an A for expression. They get gold stars to paste next to their names.

'Who can tell the story of . . .' the nuns ask, and the bully bounces up and down. The bully rattles her desk at the back of the class and sticks up her arm. She grunts and strains so the nuns will see her, but no matter how she tries the bully is seldom chosen. 'Be quiet,' the nuns say. 'Not you.'

Everyone knows how the bully tells stories. The bully rushes to the front of the class, then turns, then stands gaping. She is so excited she doesn't know where to begin. She mixes the story up, starts in the middle, then goes to the beginning, then diverts, starts again, forgets how to end. The words rush from the bully's mouth in spurts that tangle the story with her breathing. Convent girls laugh behind their hands and shout encouragement and questions and comments to confuse her. They stamp their feet, watching how the story and the bully twist and turn. The bully tries her hardest to tell her stories the way the nuns say, but she never gets them right. The words vein her cheeks with red, they block her eyes and ears so the nuns have to hit a ruler against a desk to make her stop.

'You've had your chance,' the nuns exclaim, sometimes laughing, sometimes angry. 'Go back to your seat!'

The nuns say the bully's way is not the way to tell a story. Convent girls must learn to do it properly. A story starts at the beginning, with a description of the people and the place of the story. David was the shepherd of Judea who wrote psalms and became king. Mat Salleh was one of the first pioneers to open up the jungle; he founded this city, braved the wild beasts and savages, and finally succumbed to a jungle fever that shrivelled his brain. Convent girls must stand erect and stick to the facts. No one is interested in whether David clipped his own toenails, the nuns say, which makes convent girls fall about laughing. People want to know how he became king. They're not interested in what the evil bandit King Crocodile ate in the jungle, or his evil desires, they want to know how and where the brave soldiers captured him. How they ensured ordinary cityfolk's safety by ending his evil reign. No one is interested in the way the thread tied to the bully's finger to remind her to sweep the corridors suddenly brings back a crucial part of the story that she has forgotten to tell. Convent girls must speak plainly and clearly until they get to the end. They must remember that the last word is not the true end. Every story has a meaning which can be applied to the lives of convent girls. Only when they see this meaning does the story end.

'What did you see today?' the nuns ask.

Convent girls must store these endings in their exercise books to read over when they are free. That is the way they will learn wisdom. When convent girls only want to waste time chattering, or running and jumping and playing the fool, they must think of the hardworking squirrel who lives on his stored nuts in winter while the playful squirrel dies of hunger. In times of adversity they must flick through their books to follow the tough little train struggling up the hill, like the long ago train forging its way to the top of this very hill, never straying from its track. *I can I will I can I will I can I will*, puffing and panting all the way. And on the way down, *What a relief I could I did I could I did.* Unlike the bully, who stammers and strays and questions and confuses her story, convent girls must remember to always keep on track. They must remember that these are only stories. That real life is full of inconsiderations, but here everything fits.

Grandmother says: *Never fit your body into the natural curves and hollows of the earth or rocks or trees, for these are the resting places of spirits, who won't appreciate being sat on, or coming back to find you there. Never play hide-and-seek at dusk. If you hide in dark corners at dusk, you will never come out again. You'll die and turn into a mouldy corpse and only be discovered a hundred years later. Never disturb someone who is sleeping for the spirit leaves the body when it sleeps. This is called dreaming. The dream is the wandering of the spirit in search of adventure or to finish business the awake body has forgotten, or failed to do. One way to get back at an enemy is to wait until she is soundly asleep. Powder the enemy's face a ghostly white, draw coloured patterns on her cheeks. Put shoeblack over her eyebrows and toothpaste above her lip. When the wandering spirit wanders back, it won't recognise its body. It will get a great shock and flee. Your enemy will sleep forever.*

My grandmother knows about enemies. She knows about bullies too. She says all things must be endured. The one who endures will win. Grandmother shows me the steps to be used in the pursuit of endurance and victory. These are the roots of life. One step after another, each like walking a path. *First: learning to see. Second: controlling the breath. Third: reçog-*

nising the enemy. Fourth: learning their ways. Fifth: writing the rules. Sixth. Seventh. Grandmother makes me write these down. Whenever she thinks of a new step she pushes her notebook towards me. She shows me how to make the sign *Avert!* which will stop a demon in its tracks. She swishes her cane when I miss a step, pretends not to hear when I say I need a camera, I need a new notebook, a map of the ghosthouse, a single track through the jungle on which to walk. I need a compass, and something for blisters and thirst. I need a magic knife.

[faint show-through text from reverse page]

◄ **THREE** ►

RECOGNISING THE ENEMY

On the day my grandmother's extra eye closed, she stirred on the roadside with a head so light she thought a rusty bandit sword must have separated it from her body. 'Wah, so light,' Grandmother marvelled. 'No wonder ghosts can fly.' Grandmother lay by the roadside waiting to see what would happen, whether anyone would arrive to guide her passage to the underworld, whether the world, now that she'd reached the other side, had changed. The closing of her eye, although then she did not know it was closing, spread bands of sparkling colour around her. Only faint traces of the black-and-white world she was used to remained. Grandmother waited patiently. Gradually she noticed the slight movements of her body, the twitch of her toes and ankles, and her elbows bending, her fingers feeling for her severed head. Her hands reaching for her porkscraps, her talismans and coins. The slight movements of her body prickled Grandmother with a myriad scraping aches.

'Wah, so much pain, no wonder they come back crying,' she mused before her fingers noticed that her neck was unsevered, her belongings lying unpilfered by her side. Grandmother sat up, slowly, painfully. She gathered her scattered porkscraps, her broken bowl of coins, the talismans now streaked with dust from the road. She stumbled home in a daze and lay in bed with a temperature of a hundred and six degrees. She lay tossing from side to side, soaked in sweat and spittle and piss. My mother turned her gently and wiped her. 'Not so many! Not so many!' Grandmother cried, seeing shadows surging round her bed, hissing and leaping like flame. For an instant the old bandit leered out of the mass, brandishing his bandit rifle to make Grandmother jump. The beautiful woman stood immaculate in her shimmering white gown, her hand held out, her smile like a promise. The bug-eyed shadows of Grandmother's ghosthouse girlhood stretched out their hands. Then the individual shapes faded, the shadows around her bed merged and swelled. Their black-and-white shapes were cut through with colour, their voices shrilled and whispered, begging Grandmother to deliver a final message, a last farewell. My mother scribbled the messages Grandmother translated. The shadows thinned with her fever. The colours she had not seen since girlhood leaked slowly but surely back into her sight.

'Stand still!' Grandmother told my mother. 'Face west, face the jungle-covered hill. Bow three times. Bow once! Bow twice! Bow three times! Say farewell to your Mother and Father, your Third Uncle, your First Sister, your Second and Fourth and Fifth Brothers. Now they are going up the mountain, they are climbing the hill. They are joining the spirits on the hill!'

'Farewell Mother, Father, Uncle. Farewell Sister, farewell Brothers. Farewell,' said my mother, tears streaming down her cheeks. She had not seen her family since the brothel keeper came to her long ago village to take her away.

When my grandmother's extra eye first opened, the swirling dark and light bands of its opening, the icy clarity of its vision filled her with dread. The eye fitted shapes to the familiar chorus of disembodied whispers that had accompanied her since birth. The colourless map it fixed over everything terrified her. Years later, when she realised that the swirling colours caused by the swing of the bandit rifle were no passing eye ailment but the closing of her extra eye, that too filled her with terror.

The story of the ghosthouse is a story to strike terror into the heart of any young girl. Faint echoes of the story linger about the convent, even away from the library, even through the fumes of disinfectant, weedkiller and holy water the nuns spray around the old buildings, into the old gardens where convent girls sometimes get hysterical and jungle weeds grow wild and strong. Even through the disapproving stares and clipped cries of 'Nonsense!' of the nuns. The echoes of the story whistle their way along the corridors, weaving in and out of the classrooms, through keyholes, around teachers, over the pages of open textbooks to zoom like hornets into this or that girl's ears. If convent girls listen too closely it will drive them silly. It will drive them bad. This is what the nuns say.

The bully and I have a photo of the story of the ghosthouse. This is how we know it is true. The photo of the story of the ghosthouse is part of the bully's secret collection. In the darkroom we examine it hard, and often, and long. We trace our fingers along its tattered edges, touch the tips of our tongues to its blistered surface to see if it has a taste. The bully's photo is fire-damaged, on its blackened back are four grey fingermarks where it was snatched from the flames. The photo is filled with shadows, only by looking long and hard can we see.

'What do we see?' the bully whispers. In her excitement she adds new creases to the photo, she crushes the corner I hold. The bully digs her fingers into my arm until my starched uniform crackles. I look at the photo sideways, which Grandmother says is a good way to see.

'A face,' I say. 'We see a woman's face. A most beautiful woman.'

'What else? What else do we see?'

'Another face. A man's.'

The bully smooths out the photo. The others in her collection slip and slither onto her lap. The bully's shoulder pushes against my shoulder, her cheek touches mine as we crane to see. The faces in her oldest photo are so close together that when we look carelessly we see only one face.

The story of the ghosthouse is a story convent girls long to hear. Convent girls lean their ears against the library walls at lunchtime, they listen around corners and pillars when anyone is talking, nuns or teachers, the old cook and sweeper, the laundry maid and ancient caretaker stopping for a chat. Convent girls crowd together in the dormitory in a tent of blankets after lights-out, shushing each other with their elbows, tilting their heads sideways, straining to hear.

'I heard music,' convent girls whisper.

'I heard footsteps, but no one was there when I turned.'

'I heard fire, I smelt burning.'

Convent girls huddle together in the warm dark of the blankets, leaning their bodies against each other with arms and legs crisscrossing and heads pressed close. Their whispers thread the warm dark air. Sometimes they twirl a torch so the blanket cracks give off a pale swirling light. Sometimes a cool night wind slips under the blankets to tickle their spines. On nights like these, when they're quiet and lucky and the lookout sees no sign of the night sister doing her rounds, convent girls may spend long minutes listening for the story of the ghosthouse, twisting their bodies this way and that to snag each passing whisper, giggling and shivering with fear. They may gawk for long moments at the shapes the whispers mesh into, the wraith-shapes growing out of the dark. They may look up, startled, to glimpse a recognisable form in the corner of their eyes. A beckoning figure behind the door of the furthest toilet, a sad woman at the top of the library stairs. A tilted profile, a hand reaching to rest at the base of a slender neck. They may see the rich man's lover with bare shoulders and hair swinging past the backs of her knees. Under the tent of blankets convent girls may shudder deliriously.

The glimpse of the lover at the top of the stairs is a glimpse of the lover in moonlight, an alabaster lover frozen for a moment like the arch-backed statues frozen tiptoe on the stairway rail. This is how the blanketed whispers say they have seen her. The lover doesn't stand half-leaning over the railing with arms slung around the statues guarding the top of the stairs. She doesn't stand like convent girls do, though in the mass and surge of girls you could almost miss her, she's no bigger than a girl. The lover doesn't stand swinging her ankles, calling down the stairs for girls who are slow. In moonlight she stands frozen with her back to the stairway and it seems to the whispers that everything is frozen with her. Even the calls of the convent girls, their swinging ankles and scampering footsteps hang frozen. The lover has just climbed the stairs. She stands as if she has been standing forever, the stairs just climbed, one hand curled over the banister rail. The lover stands in moonlight even in the middle of the day. In moonlight she stands whitened, even her black hair whitened. She stands draped in a plain white gown that fountains round her feet. The whispers have never seen the lover's feet. Her step is as light as breathing, her touch like a kiss of air.

Then the lover sighs, and it seems she has been sighing forever. The lover's sigh is a ripple that slides from her lungs, that droops her lower lip as it leaves her body, as it slips down the folds of her gown to sag its tortuous weight down each and every stair. Sighing, the lover moves from the top of the stairs towards the open doors of the balcony. Her hair swings lightly, her carelessly worn gown slips from her shoulders. Moonlight glimmers the lover's pale skin. Her gown trails in the pattern she weaves between the tables and glass cabinets holding precious objects, the gilded stands and pedestals on which carved figures lie. The lover pauses to consider one object, then another. Her fingers trace their various skins: the cold Venetian cupids poised with golden arrows, the African tiger still warm in its ivory leap. The Ming vase five centuries old. From the walls the empty eyes of the masks and paintings from far-off places watch her weaving walk through the maze of artefacts that tower over her, that fit into the palm of her hand. The path she walks to the balcony doors is a collection of the exotic. As she passes, statues reach their finely wrought arms to pull at a sleeve, to snatch a handful of gown, a clutch of hair. Every now and then the lover pauses to listen. At the doors she suddenly stops. Her head jerks sideways. The whispers stop also. The lover slowly begins to turn her head. At the window her head slowly begins turning. That is when the whispers either stand rooted to the spot, or bolt shrieking. Rooted to the spot, or shrieking, the whispers never agree on what they see. Some say they see the saddest and most beautiful face, the face of the Virgin, the face of a queen. Others see a burned hag's face, fire-licked to leather, with its lips stretched wide as it leaps from the moonlight with a deafening howl. Others say they see in moonlight only the billowing hair and skin like the underbelly of a fish: there is no face.

The terror of the ghosthouse is a terror worth risking the wrath of the nuns. It's a terror like the one that courses through convent girls' bodies as they lean against the wire fence looking at the road winding to the lights of the city, watching the trucks of soldiers rumbling past. It's a terror like the soldiers waving and winking broadly and convent girls raising their hands aflutter, winking broadly back. It's like the one that chases after them when they run helter-skelter through remote parts of the convent, down seldom-used corridors, up dusty stairways to lean out a topmost window, jostling each other as they scream: 'Murder! Murder! Murder!' Shrieking with laughter as the terror snaps at their heels and they race back down. In the blanketed dark, the terror changes from something that snaps to something that licks at the backs of convent girls' necks. The terror licks with long slow licks, and drips down their skins like warm coconut sugar. Like an icicle drop. It widens their eyes in surprise and horror, it makes stalwart girls who cannot see the whispers, try as they may, groan and grumble and tear at their hair. Only the bully shuts tight her sleepless eyes, twitching her own uninvited blanket around her, turning her scornful bully's back onto the giggling, hump-blanketed terror of the girls.

The story of the ghosthouse filtered through the years: the nuns will not tell it so someone else must. My grandmother was a girl when this story happened. She worked in the kitchen of the house that is now the ghosthouse, the library. She ran errands, carried water, washed the floors. Grandmother did a skip and a spin whenever the rich man passed her. The rich man stopped to watch. Grandmother spun in fairy circles, her usually flat feet no longer hitting the earth in hollow slaps, but flashing in and out and up and down, lighter than air. When Grandmother finished, the rich man patted her head. Grandmother came running at his whistle. When he whistled, she dropped everything, she made faces at the sullen faces of the other servants as she ran. She stood waiting long past her bedtime as the rich man's house filled with couples who glittered, who tinkled their voices, and smelt light and airy, like fruit Grandmother had never eaten, flowers she had never smelled. Grandmother stood waiting for the rich man's signal with her mouth watering, her eyes like bits of rounded glass. She wore her best clothes, her arms and legs wiped clean of kitchen grease, her face patted with cooling powders to an unnatural white. When the rich man signalled, Grandmother leapt to the centre of the room. She jumped and spun till the rich man signalled her to stop. Her face ran in sweat streaks, her skin glinted brown through the powdery mask. The rich man ordered the danceband to play faster and faster. His guests crowded around my grandmother, their cheers and claps rising louder and louder, their voices jabbing like the rhythmic jabs of her arms and knees. When the rich man finally signalled, Grandmother crumpled, she bent over double, heaving her breath. The claps were a thundering roar over the roar in her head.

'Bravo!' the couples cheered.

'What a clever little girl!' they called. 'What an ugly child! What a darling! Where did you find her?'

'None of ours could do any better!'

The rich man fondly tweaked Grandmother's ear. He waved her back to the kitchen where she went on wobbly legs. He made the other servants be nice. He bought Grandmother holiday suits that turned them sour with envy, fairy dresses for a fairy dancer in pale pinks and lemons, and her favourite red. A pyjama suit so red only its buttons were brighter. When Grandmother first came to the ghosthouse she was given brand-new servants' clothes. She was sent to the rich man's bookroom, his business room, into which businessmen, soldiers and city officials disappeared and reappeared clutching sheafs of papers. An impassive houseboy stood to attention soundlessly opening and shutting the door. Grandmother stared at the books lined from floor to ceiling as she entered, she breathed their layered smells. That was her first sight of the rich man, the one she never forgot, lines of books behind him, a shaft of afternoon sunlight grazing the top of his head. The smells Grandmother had never before encountered, musk and paper, leather and wood, leaked into her nostrils to spoil every other smell. Grandmother breathed deeply. The rich man beckoned her forwards, he tapped her shoulder to still the wondering turn of her head. Grandmother's shoulders were ridged through the cloth. Lifting her shirt the rich man discovered her back crisscrossed with scars. He turned her around, his mouth wry, his eyebrows lifting. The rich man looked to Grandmother like the gods on family altars, both terrible and kind, whose lifted eyebrows could start thunderstorms, raise meek waters to floods.

'Are you a bad girl?' he asked, flicking her chin. 'What have you done?'

The rich man bought Grandmother toys and allowed her to wander about his house wherever she liked. He liked the shape of her face. He liked to run his hand over the ridges on her back. The rich man's hands were smooth. He liked the way she ran her fingers over his palms, trying to find a line. Her serious brow and piercing stare amused him. He allowed her to touch his antique treasures, his precious statues and carvings, and his clockwork toys that marched in solemn circles, and the mechanical clocks that spilled music and whirling figures in place of ordinary chimes. The rich man let Grandmother's curious hands follow the path of his miniature railway, meandering under bridges into tunnels, around jungles and seasides, over hills and towns spread over half a room. While Grandmother wandered, touching this or that, the rich man lounged in an armchair, watching.

'Break anything and you are gone!' he called out suddenly, cheerfully, making her jump. His eyes were deep and serious when Grandmother looked. 'Break something and I'll throw you to the beasts in the jungle. Come here! Won't you do your dance?'

The rich man gave Grandmother complete freedom, as long as she performed her chores satisfactorily, and gave the other servants no more than her fair share of cause for grumbling. As long as she was never sulky or stubborn in his presence, as the other servants complained, and broke nothing, and replaced everything exactly where it was found. As long as she was deathly quiet when the rich man wanted a quiet like death, or chirpy, prattling in her singsong voice if that was what he asked. In some moods the rich man became sentimental.

'Do you love me?' he asked, cupping her face with his hand.

'Yes!' Grandmother cried, the expected answer.

'Are you mine?'

'Yes.'

'Remember it. Body and soul!' The rich man laughed, bored, slipping her from his knee.

As Grandmother wandered here and there, looking, marvelling, the rich man lounged in his chair, listening for a breaking sound. He wrote curt replies to overseas letters, kept account of his business in ledgers larger than both her spread-out hands. Every now and then he tilted his head to show he was listening. Grandmother had complete freedom in his house as long as she was like a shadow when shadows were his desire, or laughing when that was, or dancing, or bursting into her child's loud monotonous song. Sometimes her singing was all the rich man could bear, even though it sent the other servants scampering with hands pressed to their ears. Sometimes Grandmother's singing was all that was needed to break a particularly sombre mood. The rich man sat deep in his armchair long after she had finished, the hand on his glass so pale, his chest so still that Grandmother was filled with terror, thinking her song had killed him dead. Then the rich man would suddenly smile. The rich man's smile streaked into my grandmother. Grandmother had complete freedom in his house as long as she broke nothing, and did exactly as he desired, even better if she guessed his desire before he knew it: his bedroom slippers when he was tired, a journal from the homecountry that he'd misplaced, a drink mixed to perfection in his favourite glass.

When my grandmother was a young girl she knew what complete freedom was—she had it. Complete freedom was belonging, body and soul, and my grandmother had it. As long as she broke nothing in the rich man's house and was polite and cheerful and reasonably clean, and he never saw her when his lady guests were visiting, unless they asked and she was called. When the rich man's lady guests were visiting Grandmother wandered from the kitchen to the doorway of his quarters. She stood listening to the coiled laughter springing from those shut-off rooms, and the clipped conversation, and the silences that stretched for much too long. She stood unmoving, her forehead split with frowns, until one of the other servants, or even the rich man's personal manservant, came to hiss her away. Scowling, Grandmother went. When the rich man sent for her she broke nothing, and was clean and cheerful. These were the rich man's rules. To Grandmother they were easy.

'Body and soul!' he cried, ruffling her hair. 'Listen to the jungle beasts!'

The rules unbroken, the rich man in one of his sudden boisterous moods, Grandmother would be seized by strong arms that threw her into the air and swung her in a playful circle, a squealing arc. Grandmother would be cuddled in the crook of an arm so firm she thought she was sitting on stone. Her arms allowed to wind themselves around a sweet-smelling neck, her cheeks planted with kisses that left a delicate sting. The floors of the rich man's house were polished in those days; wherever anyone walked their feet left marks. The other servants polished and polished but some marks never went away. Grandmother's footprints were flanked by other lighter feet, hop marks, slide marks, the skid marks of sudden leaping. When the rich man was at home, the other servants cursed, and polished, their work never done. When he was away they pulled at Grandmother's ears. They beat her till her legs were striped with welts. 'It's not me!' Grandmother screamed, ducking, but the house was filled with evidence: the trailing smudges of small feet walking.

When my mother was a young woman she met another young woman walking in the street. This was before my mother became a Christian. The other young woman was the most beautiful woman my mother had ever seen. She stopped to smile at my mother when they met. Her smile was blinding, her eyes pinpoints of light. This meeting happened at the time my mother walked the streets of the city every day, looking into every face for a sign. At this time, not yet a Christian, she looked at everyone suspiciously. Old women, young children, men whose stares slipped from her face to graze the anxious curves of her body. At this time my mother's gaze was a wild thing, red-eyed, bold. She met everyone face to face. She stopped short in the middle of the street, staring, sending cars and motorcycles screeching and skidding. People shouted curses, leaned out of windows showing their fists. My mother walked on—seeing, unseeing. This was the time she stopped looking like a young woman. This was the time my mother's instant passed.

Not yet a Christian, she walked every day, starting early, rubbing the sleep from her eyes. Ignoring the growls of her belly, the aches of her swelling feet. Every day my mother walked searching for her disappeared husband. She pushed against the other bodies hurrying along the sidewalks, raced after familiar shapes slipping around corners. Catching up, she stopped short an inch from the person's face. She stared hard. How hard it was to sift through the features of a person's face, which features were they, the ears, the eyebrows, the nose, the lips parted, the eyes slightly widening. Which were the signals separating danger from safety, the possible enemy from the possible friend? Which would be able to tell her where somewhere safe was? In those days my mother could put nothing together, her hands shivered uncontrollably. Her words came out so broken people blinked their incomprehension, they gave up and turned away. The city my mother walked in was a city of splinters, of disconnections, the sidewalks searing her feet against the creak of a hawker's barrow, against a slice of the smog-hazy sky. The faces she stared into were fractured into features never amounting to a whole. To my mother these eyes were friendly, but not these lips. This chin stuck out belligerently, this was familiar, but not this line of yellowed teeth. My mother stopped to stare; wrung her hands despairingly.

'Where are you going?' Grandmother shouted each morning. 'Useless! Come back!'

But my mother stumbled from the house without turning, without hearing Grandmother's calls that brought the neighbours hurrying to their gates. My mother dragged her feet one after the other away from the house, from the unmade breakfast, the unmended convent linen, the charms unprepared, and Grandmother shouting, Grandmother slapping her palms against the door in anger, and the neighbours adding their voices to call her back. Already my mother felt tired, so early in the morning, but still she rose with her mouth purposefully set. Every morning she left my grandmother's house without turning, placing one foot resolutely after the other as though setting out on a great journey. As though walking a dream.

Grandmother says: *This is how the story first started. First of all was the number One, which is the number of completion and loneliness. When the Big One first moved, its breath produced the male principle yang and when it rested it produced the female principle yin. The energy that gives life to these two principles is chi or the breath of nature. People who understand and can control the breath have the power to influence nature. Among the most powerful breath controllers are mediums and spirit speakers, who are usually women. A medium finds out early in life what her role is. Looking at the hand of a medium you will see the life line cut short. In exchange for a longer life, a medium makes a deal with the spirits, she agrees to become their voices and eyes. If a medium tries to stop speaking for the spirits they will torment her until she drops dead. Mediums who speak for good spirits extend their lives by doing good deeds. Others are not so lucky. A medium who is controlled by an evil or mischievous spirit is a frightening sight. One famous medium was taken over by a runaway monkey spirit for seven months. During this time she chattered unintelligibly. She ran around the temple terrorising devotees, breaking altar candles and climbing the temple pillars when the monks gave chase. The monkey spirit is the most mischievous of all the animals. Children born under the sign of the monkey have the characteristics of the monkey spirit and must be controlled relentlessly, otherwise they will cause havoc.*

My grandmother is the enemy of havoc. She is the keeper of an ancient knowledge, the enemy of newcomers and people who disregard rules. Unlike the nuns Grandmother says there is no one track that everyone must follow. Everything moves in a pattern of dips and rises, goodluck curves, treacherous folds. Everything has a place. Good or bad, wherever the pattern takes you, there you will go. How you cope depends on your wits, on how good you can see. No one leaps from the pattern to be saved. Grandmother is the enemy of strangers who enter households and change everything according to their whim. Who turn favour to neglect and make havoc where everything was once nice. She is the enemy of unfinished business that doesn't go her way. In fact my grandmother has so many enemies the bully and I can't count them on our fingers, we even run out of toes. Grandmother makes enemies left, right and centre. The neighbours opposite who have turned Christian, who stand in the street with their golden-edged books and leaflets driving customers away. The debt collector who didn't show respect. The young rival ghostchaser around the corner charging people half-price. Walking down the street Grandmother stops on every corner, her gaze roving like a challenge. Her voice grates ready for a fight. The bully and I walk faster. We make enemy chalk marks on the window sill that run over the edge. But my grandmother's oldest enemy is the one who takes up her time. Only her oldest enemy keeps her sitting in her special chair by the doorway late into the night, plotting and planning a way to make the old enemy pay: a way to win. My grandmother was born under the sign of the tiger. In life she is as fierce as her sign. She's as determined as a tiger to win. No man or woman who has looked into Grandmother's tiger eyes would dare to cross her. The tiger is the guardian at the gates of hell, known as the King of the Mountains, and even its shape, carved into stone, can scare demons. When Grandmother shows her tiger face even the fiercest demon would run shrieking.

'Show me, Grandmother. Show me!' I plead.

When Grandmother shows me, my eyes widen till the irises are ringed with white. My mouth falls open and I screech in terror so loudly the bully screeches too. The bully follows my mother home from the convent thinking she will have a relaxing time, but here her hair stands up in fright. Grandmother and the bully leap from their chairs. 'What's the matter?' my mother comes running as I hop from foot to foot. Neighbours peer over the fences, a radio is abruptly switched off. My shrieks snake out not in all directions but towards

Grandmother. White-faced, she signs *Avert!* and I can hold the shriek no longer. I skip nimbly away, my mouth snapping shut. I make my cheeks into pouches to hold back my laughter but it breaks out in bursts, like bullets.

'You bad girl! You monkey!' Grandmother cries, hobbling, swishing her cane. 'Teasing your old grandmother! Wah, I thought you really turned. Wait till I catch you, beast!'

My mother rushes after Grandmother, scolding, grasping Grandmother's arm in case she falls. Grandmother's clothes flap around her, filled with sudden gusts of wind. Only the bully sits back in her chair, chewing her lower lip. The bully sits oblivious, rocking gently, flexing her tongue in surprise.

The enemy of convent girls is everything outside the convent. This is what the nuns say. The biggest danger to girls is their inability to tell the difference between the enemy and friends. This must be the biggest part of their training. Good convent boarders from good sheltered backgrounds think that everyone is their friend. The teachers and nuns have to line them up in rows and take them outside to experience the enemy first-hand. These trips are called school excursions. Convent girls go on school excursions to rubber estates and rural villages where the enemy wraps itself in the clothes of ignorance, backwardness and poverty. Stomachs that bloat under flapping shirts. The girls go to museums where the enemy is the past, filled with superstitious ancestors who walk naked and pray to the devil disguised as rocks and trees. They go for nature walks along the jungle tracks where the enemy are groups of boys from other schools, wild monkeys, soldiers who tramp or stand around in twos and threes, winking and calling, and whistling their sour breaths.

There are different ways of dealing with the enemy but the best method for convent girls to follow is avoidance. The convent girl's greatest weapon is fear. If convent girls practise avoidance and listen to their fears, they will lead tranquil, productive lives. Everything will be in order. Chances are they'll never do anything wrong. If they are good and do as they're told no enemy can hurt them. Divine providence will be their protection. A convent girl's best defence is to keep her eyes lowered, her mouth shut, her ears open. To never go out at night, and walk everywhere in groups, and emulate her elders, and follow their advice.

'Will we always be able to do this, Sister?'

'Yes, easily! By always thinking what Jesus would do, by putting your palms together, by following—'

When convent girls go outside the convent they huddle together for protection against the enemy. The nuns show us maps of where the enemy lurks in its greatest numbers, charts of what behaviour is likely to attract it. All enemies come from the devil, who has many guises, each requiring a different response. In the villages convent girls are told to hand out Bibles and tins of sweetened milk, to line the streets in cheering rows when new factories are opened. In the city they must walk looking neither right nor left, and make the sign of the cross when they pass the temples and hovels where the devil reigns. They must never cheapen their lips with red or their eyes with bands of black or silver, or wear skirts that lift in the wind to show their knees. Whether in the jungle or the city, they must stick to the paths that are marked, the roads they are familiar with, the places their elders allow them to go. When an enemy approaches they must crowd together, sometimes lifting their fists in a show of defence, sometimes giggling and pointing. Sometimes both. They must poise their legs, ready to run. Groups of giggling cackling convent girls with fists raised and legs poised to run are a sure deterrent for certain types of enemies.

The enemy of the bully is an amorphous creature that the bully can't quite see. This enemy changes its shape daily. Some days it is a mist that hangs around the bully, twining itself in and out of her clothing, bristling the hairs on her neck. Some days it's a dull thudding in her ears. Others, a piercing as sharp as bone. The bully never knows when or where the enemy will hit. If she suddenly twists to slap at the back of her neck it's because the cold fingers of the enemy have tapped her there. If she jumps from her seat in the middle of a lesson, you can be sure it's the enemy's touch that has made her leap.

'Outside!' the nuns shout, and the bully has to pick up her book and pencil and stand outside the classroom where passing girls and teachers can stop to shame her.

The nuns say the bully's enemy is her temper, which is ridged like the dried backbone of a fish and just as brittle. A single word can make the bully's temper snap. When the bully was a child she ran screaming down the corridors when she didn't get her way. She tore out her hair in bunches and beat back at the nuns when they smacked. She kicked and punched when they tried to put their arms around her, when the night sister swooped for a cuddle she ran shrieking away. The nuns say the bully's enemy is her stubbornness. The way nowadays she shows her anger by slamming things onto tables, by sliding muttered curses out the sides of her mouth. The bully's enemy is her instability—her bad stock. Her mother who was a washerwoman, a wild girl, a virago. Her father whom nobody knew.

'That's your father, your father!' convent girls chant behind the bully's back when they see the rubbish collectors with their hoarse cries and arms blackened to the elbows.

'That's your mother!' they point to the women with bloated bellies squatting outside the sundry shops, digging for scraps of onions and chillies from the discarded piles.

The bully turns, raising her fist, baring her teeth. The convent girls flee.

In the darkroom the bully and I sit cross-legged, knee touching knee. The darkroom harbours no enemies of the bully's, its stale briny air, unlike the air outside, carries no hidden barbs. Here the bully can twist and jump without fear of scolding, she can tell as many stories as she likes without being stopped. She neither has to raise her fist nor bare her teeth. In the darkroom the bully and I touch foreheads, we sit with our eyes squeezed shut, our lips pressed together, imagining we will never part our lips or open our eyes. The bully and I sit on the cushioned mats she has sneaked into the darkroom, imagining the dark is a place we can hear, we can see. An in-between place, like babies in limbo, like the spirits of the dead my grandmother says are waiting for reincarnation at the top of the hill. In the darkroom the bully and I stuff cotton into our ears. We trail our fingers over each other's faces, cup each other's shoulders and elbows in our hands. No one is allowed to talk, to peep. The bully and I imagine we are underwater creatures, morsels curled in a shell. The first to flutter an eyelid or let past their lips the tiniest sound, a murmur, a sigh, even too hurried a breath, will lose. Behind my eyelids the dark grows to enormous proportions, in my ears the silence of cotton is a pounding like drums. The minutes swell and stretch until I lose sense of everything except their stretch and swell. The bully and I become alternately large then small, large then small: enormous, then the head of a pin. We become infinite. Then nothing. Infinite, then nothing, so that it seems my eyelids must flicker, my lips part not on the tiniest but the largest of sounds. It seems I must fail the test the bully has invented to see if I come up to scratch. In the infinite dark, the nothing dark, only our fingertips, our hands, our knees touching knees, hold me silent. Hold me still.

The bully's face is set so sullen even the dark can't change it. Touching her face I shrink, I grow to size. The bully's face is earth into which I dig my fingers. Her skin is treebark, her elbows scabby, her neck unwashed. Her bully's face taut like a mask. Only her chest and stomach feel soft through the shirt, only her fingers in the dark are unlike her usual bully's fingering: uncertain. The bully traces a clumsy spiral from my shoulder past my armpit to my side, the path of ticklers and torturers, to see if that flutters my eyes. She pokes a sudden sharp finger into the space between my shirt and waistband to see if that prompts a hurried breath. But Grandmother has taught me to breathe. The bully stops on a patch of rough skin just above my knee fold, on the inside of one thigh. She fingers the raised and regular pattern, scaly, smooth when she rubs one way, snagging when she pulls her hand back.

'What's that?' the bully asks, breaking the game.

'Nothing,' I quickly pull down my skirt. I pull the cotton from my ears, slide away from the bully to light our darkroom lamp. 'You lose,' I say. 'That was easy! What will you give me?'

'What was that?' the bully demands. But in the light my skin where the skirt is lifted is smooth.

'What will you give me?' I repeat, sticking out my chin, taunting.

But the bully is used to losing. The bully is frowning at her finger where she felt the rough skin. 'Anything you like,' she says. 'What do you like? Photo? Rulebook? Borrow camera? Anything!'

'Promise.'

'Anything you like,' the bully nods.

'Tell you later,' I say, which makes her shake her fist because she doesn't like to be kept waiting. The bully doesn't like suspense. She wants to know everything *now*. She comes towards me with lips pursed and fingers working like the fingers of torturers and ticklers to make me giggle even before she reaches me, as if already the bully is torturing and tickling, already I'm in the corner and she's blocking the way. 'Stop!' I splutter, even though she hasn't started yet. I skip across the room.

'Tell me now!' the bully threatens.

When things get too much for the bully, she sneaks away to see my mother in the convent laundry. My mother has worked in the laundry for years, since long before I was born. Its walls are covered with her pictures of saints and prayer scrolls, its shelves with the plastic flowers she made herself. Its air is filled with the warm soapy smell the bully and I think of as hers. The bully stands on the doorstep, breathing deeply. Unlike the nuns, teachers and girls my mother is always pleased to see the bully. When the bully arrives she stops to stand with hands on her hips. 'How big you are growing!' she exclaims, although the bully hasn't grown for years. My mother sticks out her hand to show the height of the bully when she first saw her all those years ago, lounging around the chapel door. 'Aiya, have you eaten yet?' she asks, plucking a treat from her pocket for the bully, a slice of sugared melon or a fizzy sweet.

When the bully arrives at the laundry it is a surprise to see the bully's face, even the bully would be surprised to see her face cracked open with smiles. 'Auntie,' she replies politely. 'Thank you, Auntie.'

Unlike the nuns my mother says the bully's enemy is not her quick-snapping temper but her lack of memory.

In the laundry the bully stands watching the flames hissing under the ancient tubs. She watches my mother measuring detergent, slipping the piles of dirty sheets and pillowcases into the water, stirring the foul-smelling brew. When the bully tires of watching we turn to stand at the window, leaning our foreheads against the steamy glass. Outside, the troupe of monkeys slide down branches, flexing their tails. They hang upside-down, drop with dull thuds one after another to snatch at the pile of leavings my mother has put out. Fruit veined with bruises, vegetable peelings, nutshells and scraps of meat, all are nimbly scraped at, sucked and swallowed. Inedible parts fly in all directions. The one-armed monkey crouches at the top of the pile, deftly picking the choicest bits. Its fangs gleam huge and yellow at any other monkey daring to come too close. The bully opens the window to lean kissing noises at the one-armed monkey, she stretches her hand invitingly, snaps her fingers, but the monkey pretends not to see. Its old grey eyes echo the dart of its hand. Only now and then does it lift its head to stare directly at our window, to make snarling monkey faces back at me.

'Good monkeys!' my mother calls from the doorway. 'Food for you, good monkeys! No need to steal!' My mother smiles as she returns to stir her washing with a wooden paddle. 'Sheet soup,' she tells the bully and me. Steam lifts the damp hairs on her forehead, surging around her like the enemy mist that comes to plague the bully. I make faint marks on a workbench with a rag leaking blue. I make the bully's profile, her heavy jaw, the jut of her chin.

The bully's enemy unfurls in this moist atmosphere around my mother. Its hold unclenches amidst the crackle of firewood, the wet slurp of the sheets: in the companionable echo of my mother's silent bends and turns, her rolled-up sleeves, her clogs that clack on the damp cement. The bully watches my mother greedily. My mother says the bully is greedy for memory.

'Why?' the bully asks. 'What happened? When did that happen?'

'Wait,' my mother says, wiping her brow. 'Grandmother will tell.'

When the bully cannot wait she kicks her foot against the wall because now the wall is her enemy. She picks flecks of paint off the windowsill with her nail. She waits for my mother to tell. About when my mother was a young woman and a young man's magic knife accidentally touched its handle to her belly to make an ashen mark which sank into her belly and sat there aching, and seven weeks later started to grow. About how my mother gently stroked this ache. The bully waits for my mother to tell about the time my mother, my grandmother and I went to pay homage to the sea, and how when they weren't looking, I rose from the makeshift altar, my hair suddenly unfastened, my dress flapping, suddenly shimmering white. I stood for a moment, turning, then ran like a demon spirit into the sea where I almost drowned. Grandmother's hobbles could not hope to catch me, her desperate screams made everyone look. The bully waits for the part where my mother squeezed saltwater from my hair as she cradled me, as Grandmother tweaked my ears to bring me back. Unlike any of the other stories she hears, the bully remembers my mother's careless sketches exactly. When convent girls taunt her she repeats the feel of my mother's gentle stroking and the scrape of salty hair on her head. When they accuse her of lying she shouts the warmth and firmness of the cradling arms. 'I remember!' the bully shouts, her face growing redder and redder. The bully pushes girls over when their taunts become too loud, their cries for 'Proof! Proof! Proof!' When they scream for the teachers, she breaks into a run. She kicks and kicks at the wall.

In the laundry my mother works on oblivious to the bully. Sometimes she will tell, but usually she won't. The bully is always hopeful. Sometimes the bully strikes it lucky, and my mother will absently begin. Spinning expertly on her clogs, arm muscles gleaming as she lifts the sheets to the wringer, she'll give the bully the gift of her stories. Then, midway, she will suddenly stop. She will grow pale, although the bully doesn't notice, and stand with lips drained and features frozen as though seeing an unbearable sight. The bully doesn't notice but I have seen my mother wear this look many times. I've seen her wear it when her hands are idle, when she's resting for a moment, or when there's a sudden loud crash or bang, or the rumble of passing trucks or soldiers' footsteps, or when Grandmother sometimes jokingly, sometimes serious, orders my mother to stand still. 'Bow three times,' Grandmother tells my mother. 'Bow once! Bow twice! Bow three times! Say farewell to your husband. He is running into the jungle, the city. He is running away.'

'Farewell, husband,' says my mother, who has not seen my father since the soldiers plunged after him into the jungle. Grandmother, sometimes joking, sometimes serious, will hobble towards my mother to shake away her trance. 'Aiya, just joking!' Grandmother cries. 'Useless, can't you take a joke!'

My mother has worn her pale frozen look many times, but only when she can't help it, when she thinks she's alone in her room or the laundry or the kitchen, where no one can see. It is my mother's look of terror, forbidden by my grandmother, worn when my mother is faced not with fierce apparitions, chairs flinging themselves towards her, severed fists rising from gravesides, not when she's faced with my grandmother's ghostchasing adversaries, but with an enemy of her own. When my mother's enemy comes face to face she stands petrified, the careful balance of her daily life, of prayers and calloused knees, washtubs and sheets, of soup-making and caring for an old woman and children, each in their proper order, with their proper attention, is thrown into disarray. My mother stands petrified, waiting for the enemy to go. If she neither moves nor thinks the enemy will slowly fade. Unlike the bully's, her enemy is not an amorphous creature but one she can see quite clearly. My mother's enemy is solid, it's a thing that beckons, a hard reflecting thing, like glass. Her enemy is slit down the middle like the split of an axe: before and after she became a Christian. It comes only when summoned, when my mother gives in to our plaguing and starts her stories. When she forgets and looks into her memory. Then the enemy shimmers around the corner, or behind her, waiting for my mother to turn. I can only see my mother's enemy by squinting, by sneak-wearing Grandmother's special sunglasses to cut out the glare.

I run to wrap my arms around her, to unfreeze her, to call her back. She reaches for one of her statue saints. The warm moist plaster reminds her where she is.

'What happened next?' the bully persists.

'Wait,' my mother recovers, her body relaxing as she turns to smile at the sullen face of the bully, to pat the bully's sour head.

'Wait,' she encourages, because now, no matter how the bully begs, my mother won't continue. She won't tell no matter how the bully asks. No matter how the bully wishes it my mother isn't the keeper or the teller of my family's memory.

'Ask Grandmother,' my mother says.

The bully and I watch the monkeys dart back up the hill into the jungle, first the one-armed monkey, then another, then two, then the whole bunch. Their fur streaks silver through the canopy.

FOUR

MY FLESH
IN LAYERS

The upper balcony of the library is the place. The place to find things.

'Lie down,' the bully says. 'Lie down and pull your skirt up. Like that. Higher.'

In a corner of the balcony are the footprints, two tiny feet marks, side by side. To an undiscerning eye they look like patches of moss or watermarks, but Grandmother has taught me to see. What was the lover thinking of as she stood at the railing, did she lean her weight against it, did she shift from side to side? How the breezes must have played with her hair, that heavy hair. From where I am lying I can hear the music. I can see the dancing in the courtyard, the rich man raising his glass. The couples swirling round and round. I can taste the waiting on her lips, in the salty lick of tongue on lips.

I rise from where I am lying to stand squarely on the footprints. I put one foot down, then the other. I smile. The lover's footprints curl around my feet like well-worn shoes. The bully tugs at her camera strap impatiently. She frowns in concentration, squinting from one eye.

The story of the ghosthouse filters through the convent years. It echoes down the hallways after the footsteps of the nuns, along the rows of girls lined up for morning assembly. Convent girls stretch from side to side, they stick their heads out of line, lift their hands to cup their ears. Sometimes the wind from the jungle carries faint cries.

The rich man came to this city before it became a city. He cut a path beyond the seaside squatter town and camps, beyond the traders and townsmen with their shops and newly built houses which seethed and swelled now this way, now that. The rich man cut a path inland through the jungle to its highest point, where legend had it the bones of a foreign sailor were scattered, a place known as Mad Sailor Hill. The rich man dismissed the tales telling of this badluck place and purchased the whole hill with its jungle from the city officials, dirt cheap. From this highest point he imagined he could see everything. He stood on the highest point for hours, seeing everything. He built his house in the shadow of this point, where the midday sun hardly burned. From his newly built house he could see shapes peering from the cut-back edges of the jungle. His servants whispered, pointing to these shapes; the shapes, stopping, made their skins prickle, their knees weaken, the day's meat smell rancid, the day's rice go cloudy with mould. The jungle shapes huddled the servants together in the night-time kitchen, some burning joss sticks, others winding their arms and necks with strings of protection charms. But though the rich man shouted and beckoned, though he rushed out with foreign sweetmeats as an offering and his gun for caution, he saw nothing but the shapes in the corners of his eyes.

'Bandits,' the servants whispered. 'This place famous hide-out, Master.'

'Jungle spirits, Master,' they said behind their hands so the spirits wouldn't see they were tale-telling. 'We make trouble, mess up their house, they come make trouble, mess up ours.'

The rich man made the servants burn their joss sticks outside and rostered the men to watch at night. He let them plant a ring of thorny pineapples around the property, which they said the spirits couldn't cross. Sometimes the rich man himself kept watch, but he saw fewer and fewer shapes. In time there were no shapes at all, only more paths following his path from the sea, more processions of planters, traders, miners and missionaries with their odd-shaped baggage trains borne by the natives. He saw more houses built. The rich man himself came and went. He would be home for months, then absent the rest of the year.

When the rich man was home the house on the hill echoed with the wild and frequent parties some cityfolk said brought it infamy, others fame. The expatriate merchants came, the heads of foreign trading companies, and government officials as well as the rich local businessmen and playboys, and the native aristocracy. Everyone who was anyone scrambled for an invitation, even the expatriates, even though locals and natives alike were cordially shown in. That was the rich man's novelty. At his parties one rubbed shoulders with everyone. The rules of colonial society were suspended and those unappreciative of the suspension stayed away. As for the rest, if they did not come for the lavish servings of food and drink, or the sudden exotic entertainments, jugglers and acrobats one week, a dancing bear another, they came for the music and dancing, the atmosphere that crackled from the moment they entered, so that their eyes acquired a sparkle, their hands fluttered to neckties and neck flounces, their mouths widened to an all-embracing grin. If rich cityfolk did not come for that they came to grasp hands in firm handholds and press powdered cheeks together, to huddle in clusters according to colour and rank and name. If not for that then merely to rate the rich man's fine gardens and interiors, to listen to outrageous whispers about him in the shadowy corners of the courtyard, and examine his taste in hangings and paintings, in antique collection and imported champagne.

Some nights the rich man stood apart from his own parties, he stood like a plantation manager, a mining headman, a master of some kind or other, who has presented the workers with an unexpected holiday, with ingenious amusements, decadent freedoms of mind and body to drive them wild. The rich man stood apart, indulgent, his smile promising no repercussions tomorrow, for the excesses of tonight. Tomorrow the workers would not be whipped, though the gossips might be busy and the city matrons purse their lips. The rich man stood nodding to this or that acquaintance, bored. Some nights he threw himself into the thick of the celebration, he pressed his body to any wild dancer, leapt onto the bandstand to slump against the grand piano, and croon. Slumping against the grand piano, crooning, his drunken slur was just melancholy enough and sweet enough to wring from even the drunkest planter a moment's silence, from the most jaded planter's mistress a hand clasped to a wistful breast. Crooning, the rich man observed the length of the room with narrowed eyes. Under the polished chandeliers his head was a blaze of gold, his wineglass a cut of light.

When the rich man was home, the deep velvet curtains of the house that later became the ghosthouse were always pulled back. The windows were thrown open. The house on the hill pulsed against the jungle like a beacon. When the rich man went away it echoed emptily. Its windows were shuttered against the moist jungle air, its curtains drawn against the bleaching light. Its corridors rang out not with the quick click clack of a houseful of revellers but the footsteps of a single child. When the rich man was away, his servants were not the white-clad shadows weaving their way through the parties laden with offerings of food and drink, charming every guest with their hurried efforts to secure every comfort, their deferential bows and limpid looks. When the rich man was away he would hardly recognise his men and women. He would stare at the wholly unshadowlike lot of them, dissolved from their white crispness into so many lumps of brown and yellow, shiny with perspiration, sallow with endless eating and drinking. If he ever saw them, his voice would cut through them like a knife, would jolt them from their lolling stupor on the woven mats in the courtyard, from their chattering of high-pitched voices like jungle apes. But the rich man never saw.

Each time he returned he found his house spic and span, his servants lined in neat order to greet him. Each return he found the city changed; he found it closer to becoming the city. Now it would have lanes in place of the jungle tracks, now streets straddled by shophouses. Increasing numbers of different-coloured peoples were striding along; different-coloured voices snaked the city air. From his house the rich man glimpsed not the shapes that slipped and blended into the jungle's edges, but the lamps from other houses. He snapped his eyeglass shut. He built a fence around his hill, fixed a stake to its foot with a sign bearing his name, which the servants frequently cleaned and replaced, and replaced and cleaned. He hired soldiers to patrol his boundaries, to keep both bandits and jungle spirits out. Then the rich man went back to his travels, to the sea.

When my grandmother was a young child she walked the streets of this city fearlessly. When she was a young child the city was where she lived. Grandmother awoke each morning with bustling city sounds in her ears, dusty city sunlight in her eyes. She pushed against her brothers and sisters to lean out the creaky wooden slats of their upstairs window, watching the city street. When Grandmother was a young child the city was not yet a city but to her it seemed enormous, its rooftops seemed to stretch forever, only the ragged jungle around it signalled its end. In the city's centre a child could imagine that no jungle surrounded her, no wild animals were waiting to gobble her up if she did anything wrong. My grandmother and her brothers and sisters almost fell out the window, shouting and waving their good mornings, calling to the bullock cart drivers, the egg and noodle pedlars, the market women with goods piled high on their heads. Some mornings they woke to shrill screechings and the sounds of running, they rushed to the window to see the bodies of bandit sympathisers and tax evaders slashed where they stood. Those were the days of the Knife Wars in the city, long preceding the Paper Wars, long heralding the Wars Underground, in which my father disappeared.

When Grandmother was a child she lived in different parts of the city, but she never forgot the bustling quarter where she and her family first stayed. Later, when she left to be bonded as a servant in the rich man's mansion, still she awoke to hear the city's distant bustling, to smell its smells faintly and imagine its sunlight on her skin. Grandmother stood at the window of the rich man's mansion, imagining the city followed her. She crept to the upstairs balcony to watch its sprawl. In those days the city almost reached the hill next to the jungle on which my grandmother lived. Grandmother turned her back to the jungle, she shivered at its sight. To her the jungle was a dark throbbing heart. Everything that was frightening poured out from this heart: animal shrieks to send her running, smells to wrinkle her nose, jungle fogs that snaked along the paths from the jungle's centre to curl under rocks and over fallen treetrunks onto the tarmac roads that steamed in the cool of night.

When Grandmother first came to the rich man's mansion she lay each night with her eyes open, her small body stretched taut. Each night she crept from her bed to walk the roads that led to the backstreets and nightmarkets of the city, and the lanes where people never slept. The shapes lurking in shadowy archways, the men grouped in drunken circles on the pavement, laughing and shouting, talking-story, gambling, did not scare her. She passed ragged gangs of street urchins and secret society members without a second glance, barely noticed the bandits swaggering around in what they thought was a good disguise. At the places where the street hawkers huddled their carts, people stopped to ruffle Grandmother's hair. Women placed a scented finger under her chin and blew into her face to make her laugh. They slipped sweets into her pyjama pockets and offered her bowls of steaming melon soup. When

Grandmother smiled they let her pass. My grandmother wandered the city with wide eyes, drifting past beggars, pedlars, couples who made one shadow as they walked. She spent her nights in the city, walking, looking for the shophouse with the particular window from which children hung, laughing and pointing, overlooking the street. Grandmother looked and looked. Every night she walked searching. The abandoned shapes of sleeping servants became a grumbling rise and fall of city streets, of bridges hooking sluggish city streams into place. Later my grandmother learnt to lean from different windows. When she left the rich man's mansion she learnt to sleep with her eyes still and her limbs spread carelessly, the sleep of the exhausted.

Nowadays convent girls have long learnt to lean from different windows. They've long learnt to sleep with their eyes closed tight, no matter the bumps and shuffles that shudder the convent night. Convent girls stick special hand signals out special windows, one wave meaning *All's Clear*, two waves and a fist, *Danger! Here come the Nuns!* Convent girls walk sedately, hand-signalling behind the nuns' backs, they announce dormitory meetings, *Get the blankets ready!* Their young girls' bodies tremble with what they have seen and what they have to tell. Nowadays they go to the library in pairs. They count their footsteps and half-shut their eyes, but still there are things to be seen. Flittings across the gamesroom and peerings from under the stairs. The black frock coat of a priest poking through a mark on the chapel wall, the bloated body of a water-tortured woman, the glowing entrails of a bandit belly slit from side to side. Once convent girls saw the shape of a man who stared at them hungrily. The man was covered with teethmarks and his mouth was stretched with calling. His mouth hung open, a cavernous pit spitting fire and ashes, his eyes squirted tears that sizzled his skin. He flung his arms wide open. 'Hungry ghost! Hungry ghost!' the girls ran screaming and their ears were boxed and ice cubes shoved into their collars before they saw sense. Once a girl who was studying alone in the library wouldn't stop screaming. The nuns had to block her mouth with a rag and order the prefects to hold her, one prefect for each wrist and ankle. The girl struggled and kicked so hard her skirt flew up to her shoulders. A growing red patch stained her pants where the cloth had slipped and the prefects dropped her, running to wash their hands. Only the bully dared go into the library alone. Only the bully and I, with her knife and my amulet, dare go.

'Watch me,' the bully commands, puffing out her chest. 'Are you ready? Here I go.'

The bully goes into the basement of the ghosthouse where the fiercest spirits are said to live. Where cardboard castles with bent turrets and windows of glass paper leap from the dark at crazy angles in the swing of the bully's light. Where wigs of yellow wool are heaped untidily amongst golliwog costumes and Christmas tinsel and Mary's blue veil. The bully descends into the gloom. The old wood swallows her footsteps as down she goes. She grips her bandit's knife with its charred handle as though it's a sword. The props and costumes of long forgotten concerts rustle as the bully strides past.

'We're going to close the door,' convent girls call, pressed one against another, their lit-up faces in the doorway as pale as moons.

'Where are you, ghost?' the bully cries, stabbing at the dark with her torchlight. 'There's no ghost in here! Only a coward ghost!'

'You'll be mad in the morning,' the girls call in quavering voices. 'Your face will be blue with terror. You lips will hang slackened and your hair stop growing, and your eyes roll inwards to look at your brain.'

Before they can close the door the bully's torch beam arches across two dangling feet above her head. The bully's light dips wildly. Her gasp echoes the stifled cries of the girls. The feet above her head swing gently, long splayed feet with curving toenails and dirt-encrusted heels.

'Aah!' the sound, half-scream, half-sigh, rushes out of the

bully, who snaps her mouth shut because it's her reputation to neither scream nor sigh.

'Run! Run!' the girls cry, ready to run.

'Spit on it! Spit!' they aim arches of spit from the doorway, which fall short.

But the bully's own mouth is dry. Slowly the bully swings her torch beam upwards. The light slides over the folds of a grimy white gown, over rust-coloured patches, the matted ends of long black hair. The bully stands rooted to the spot. Her quivering torch beam is pulled further upwards, her head turns away though her eyes are fixed. The bully's eyes narrow to slits. Now the beam is on a neck bent sideways, on a face grey like the grey of the banned comic book corpses that jump to life under convent girl blankets when the dormitory sister is nowhere in sight. The hanged woman's eyes are wide open. She's wrapped in a sheet wafting around her like an untidy shroud. She swings creaking from side to side.

'Aah!' the bully gasps.

The hanged woman's head drops forwards. Her pale lips stretch to a smile that causes a frantic scuffle at the door. She unfolds a tongue that flicks at the bully, red and sticky, a lizard's tongue, three feet long. She suddenly drops from where she is hanging, her arms flapping like wings. She lets out a bloodcurdling cackle; lands cackling on the bully who drops like stone.

The girls at the door run screaming in all directions. Beams from their torches race their footsteps up the stairs and out of the library, through the courtyard and the garden back to the dormitories where sleepy boarders sit up in fright. 'Help! Help!' the girls screech. 'A suicide ghost is in the ghosthouse, eating the bully!'

In the basement the bully fights for breath. The bully knocks the hanged woman off with her fists. 'Get off!' the bully snarls.

I push myself off the bully, my feet tangling in the sheet. I am still cackling, choking. I spit the bitter rubber from my mouth. My long red tongue snakes to the ground. The bully and I sit for a minute, panting, our arms draped around each other. I pretend to ferociously eat her neck. We sit for a moment, dissolved in muffled shrieks and cackles, then the bully jumps to her feet. 'Go back!' she orders. I gather my sheet, my crooked wig, my flapping tongue, snatch my scattered bits of laughter from the corners of the basement. In the darkroom I collapse onto the pile of cushions. The bully clicks shut the door.

When the girls come back with the dormitory sister and half the sleepy dormitory they find not the bully's mangled corpse as expected, but the bully walking in circles among the papier mâché horses and chariots with dangling wheels. The bully stares at them with eyes that are glazed. She is covered with bruises, her face and neck with scratches and bite marks that glisten in the light. 'What happened? What happened?' the girls whisper.

The dormitory sister boxes the bully's ears. She herds the girls back to their dormitories where they go sedately in twos, trailing frenetic whispers and hand signals in their wake.

'What nonsense!' the sister pushes the bully to make her go more quickly. 'What do you think you're up to? Waking everyone at night!'

The bully walks along quietly. She squeezes out a penitent tear or two. The next day she is punished severely, given sharp cuts across her buttocks, sent to her chores without breakfast. Made to miss her favourite class. The bully is forbidden to speak or mix with anyone for being a bad influence. She goes about her chores with the air of a martyr, whistling softly under her breath. She gobbles the sweets, rice cakes and titbits I and the other girls bring her, sneaks me her special scrapbook so I can write the suicide ghost story for everyone to one day see. For weeks the bully crouches at the centre of a group of girls, behind this shed or that pillar, or in the furthest outfield where the nuns cannot see. Even the troupe of bandit monkeys invading the library to pelt books and magazines at teachers doesn't interest them. Even the nuns on a monkey hunt with badminton racquets and broomsticks, and the one-armed leader landing with a thump on Matron's shoulders merely makes them yawn. For weeks convent girls want only to huddle together behind this shed or that pillar, in the furthest outfield or the least-used commonroom, open-mouthed and admiring as they listen to the splintered, jagged edges of the bully's storytelling.

Grandmother says: *The world is full of gods, humans and ghosts. Some ghosts are hard to recognise, they are masters of disguise who mingle freely with humans. Others are easily discovered: these are like jungle mist, or their mouths and eyes are extra large, or they are merely a head followed by dragging entrails, or a floating hand. Some ghosts have no bodies, only a weight that presses against you or a voice that bangs inside your head. People with* yin *eyes, eyes of darkness, can easily see ghosts. Other people must watch for signs. A way to spot a* pontianak *ghost is to scrutinise the back of her neck. This is hard to do as* pontianaks *usually have very long hair. Embedded in the neck of a* pontianak *is a nail. As long as the nail remains in place the* pontianak *will appear as a normal woman. This is how they are caught. In these parts men are always on the lookout for* pontianaks *because once caught they turn into beautiful and loving wives. If you see a man in the bushes at midnight, clutching a three inch nail, you'll know why he's there. Men of these parts who cannot attract live women are famous for trying to catch spirit wives. They brave the seas at midnight, hang around jungle edges or at rivers where jungle spirits come to bathe. To catch ghosts or spirits one must turn them. One must change their natures, force on them something human or take something inhuman from them. This traps a ghost in human form, it makes it confused, docile and meek. In these parts men sit in bars and coffeeshops late into the night, arguing the best method. A nail slipped into the neck. A ghostly gown taken from a riverbank, without which the spirit cannot flee. A spirit necklace torn from around its neck, a lock of hair from its head. A spirit knife from its belt. The more ghostly things you take from them, the more human things you give them, the surer the bind. Some ghosts are so good at fooling humans they have led normal human lives and been faithful wives and mothers without anyone but their captors knowing. But ghostcatchers must always be watchful. Captured ghosts are always trying to regain their ghostly part that's missing, to lose their human bit. Careless ghostcatchers have lived to regret their deed. A simple way to recognise a ghost is to spit on it, or smear it with fresh blood. Spitting or smearing will force a ghost to assume its true shape. A way to escape a ghost is to run zigzag, to turn corners, double back at sharp angles on which the ghost will be snagged. Then you will be safe. Ghosts can only run in straight lines.*

Before my mother became a Christian, she believed in the value of walking crooked. She believed in the value of beating, of shoving harder if someone shoved her, and raising her voice louder, and pushing her arms, her elbows, her body to the front of the crowd, the head of the queue. My mother believed in the value of fooling both humans and ghosts. Grandmother trained her to raise her fists and puff out her lungs.

'Do you understand?' Grandmother demanded.

At market, at the height of the food shortages, Grandmother shoved my mother into the paths of fierce housewives and one-leg-kick servants, the most tenacious and ferocious of shoppers, who had only one leg to kick with, their other limbs slaving day and night at their endless work. Every market day my mother went for training.

'No good!' Grandmother scolded when she mumbled apologies, when she cowered in fright and ducked away. Grandmother poked the small of her back. 'Bad, bad, bad! Aiya, stand up! Stand straight! Why are you hiding?' One glare from Grandmother sent the housewives and one-leg-kick servants grumbling away. 'Do you want to be like them?' Grandmother demanded. 'Cooking, cleaning, wiping, shopping, washing. Day in day out, just like a slave. No excitement, no holidays. No fun. Do you want me to send you back?

Ungrateful girl! Do what you're told and you'll become famous! You'll become rich! Now, what must you do?'

My mother wiped her furrowed brow. She filled out her lungs as far as they would go, trying to focus as Grandmother showed her the swirling power of her breath. Her chest swelled out her blouse, her glaring expression, eyebrows drawn in a straight black line, emphasised her ferocity, her don't-mess-about-with-me-ness, her unladylike stance. My mother stood amidst the market bustle looking like a woman warrior, like the legendary Bandit Queen of the jungle, her face unlike her passive mother's face that the bully and I are used to, more like an opera singer's, each feature pronounced. Her expression wild and fierce.

'Good,' Grandmother nodded. 'Remember that face. That will scare anyone, human or ghost.'

My mother tried to remember. It took all her energy and concentration to make that face, when she forgot or became tired, her normal face sagged back. When anyone dared to bump into her or jostle her, or push her out of the way of the best bargains, the choicest vegetables, the least rancid meats, she turned her fierce wild face towards the offender, she unleashed her wild fiery breath. 'Out of my way!' she copied Grandmother's tiger shout. No one was more surprised than she when even the fiercest matriarch, the wiliest one-leg-kick servant backed away, releasing the chunk of meat or vegetable they were both clutching, removing their elbows from her sides.

'Aiya, what a fuss,' came the outraged mutters to mask their fear, the lopsided grumbles to hide their loss of face. 'Why so fighting-cock!'

'Accident!' they cried, hurrying away.

My mother tilted her radiant face towards Grandmother, lurking like a watchful schoolmistress just beyond the bean-curd stall.

'Good!' Grandmother roared, jumping the beancurd seller out of his skin, sending the beancurd watery with fright.

Before my mother began her training, she was always

jumping out of her skin. Though just a girl her skin already bore the first signs of sagging, her bones were watery, her back curled in a stoop that ended with the sad sag of her head. My mother's badluck diluted her courage, her blood. With watery bones and blood, she barely filled her skin. She could hardly stand up. My mother's body was thin and delicate, held gingerly, as though it had no right to be there. As though the very air around her would hurt. She slipped through the days, through her daily work, around people and objects, a streethawker, a roadsweeper, lamp posts and bullock carts, even pots and pans, as though each of these had more substance, more of a place in the world than she. Her hands hesitated in the instant before touching anything, her feet every moment before leaving the ground. Her eyes were always shiny with tears about to be shed.

'*Tauhu*,' Grandmother called her. 'Beancurd. Useless!'

Grandmother's method was to scare the timidity, the fright, right out of my mother. Grandmother set her the hardest tasks, the scariest, the ones to stiffen the blood. She pushed her into telephone booths that were ringing at three in the morning, made her listen to the crackly voices cursing from the other side. If the curses were not so bad, my mother was to ask for a lucky lottery number; if they weren't forthcoming, Grandmother made her curse back. My mother shivered uncontrollably, cursing back. Grandmother made her huddle in midnight graveyards to count the number of creepings over the earth, the number of flittings above her head. She rubbed her eyes with dogs' tears so she could see why they howled, pushed her face to fires to show her a ghostchaser's greatest tool. 'Bad for humans,' Grandmother said as my mother's face swelled red and her eyes sprang cooling tears. 'Even worse for ghosts.'

Grandmother filled my mother with herbs and potions that ran riot inside her and sent her racing to the outhouse, or filled her with energy and euphoria, or swelled her gut to grumbling. Every morning my mother woke before the first stirring cock crow, the first whistle summoning the road coolies to work.

She woke to see the change of soldiers patrolling the street. On special days she rushed around preparing the offerings for the house gods, the earth gods, the gods guarding the door. She learnt the special days and offerings by heart, and the names of the gods and spirits, their origins, the naughty demons and the dangerous ones, and how they could be placated: what they liked to wear and smell and eat. Every evening Grandmother tested her. Grandmother swished her cane to remind her to get her memory right. Every morning they stood side by side in the faint light before sunlight, breathing the difference between day and night. Their movements, flowing one into another, was a dance of heavy shadows. After seven months' intensive training Grandmother finally nodded her head. Grandmother rubbed her palms with satisfaction, clapped my mother on the back. As a reward she let her touch the icy handle of her special, ghostslaying knife. The handle was scarred and partly melted, its blade glimmered in the light. Grandmother got the knife from a captured ghost, she kept it when she thought the ghost was burnt up. She slashed the knife through a chunk of firewood to show my mother its sharpness. My mother touched its handle with the tip of her finger, with great awe, which made Grandmother laugh.

'This knife, cut anything,' Grandmother cried, 'especially ghosts! Now you are my assistant, maybe someday you get to use!'

The story of the ghosthouse is one the bully and I think my mother knows, but no matter how we ask her, she will never tell it. She'll never tell it whole, not without coaxing or trickery, or hugs round the waist to distract her. Without the bully and me begging more than twice. 'Ask Grandmother,' is my mother's usual answer, but the bully and I know her ghosthouse story is different from Grandmother's. We know her story is set in a different time, like a photo taken years later, with a finer camera, or one more dilapidated, anyhow using a different lens. We know it's a story Grandmother won't tell. When we persist, when we wind our arms around her and bob to look silly and pull at her hands, my mother will stop what she's doing and pretend to frown. 'Bad girls!' she'll laugh, sometimes adding, 'All right,' in a voice resigned to keeping us quiet. And she'll settle us at the ironing table, and brush back her hair.

When my mother was a young girl, she will absently begin, turning almost immediately back to her work of lifting, scrubbing, dipping. When she was a young girl, in the days she was Grandmother's ghostchasing assistant, they were called to the ghosthouse in the middle of the night. The midnight ghosthouse looked to my mother like a beast with a ridged backbone, squat and heavy, crouched as if to spring. Moonlight made its roof tiles glisten like scales. My mother, laden with ghostchasing equipment, puffed after Grandmother. Where, even in moonlight, her feet caught themselves in shallow ditches and flowerbeds, and were tricked into stumbling by the rise and fall of the garden paths, Grandmother walked surely, briskly. Grandmother leaned forward, swinging her head from left to right. 'Quiet!' Grandmother hissed.

In all her time as Grandmother's ghostchasing assistant, the ghosthouse was the only house my mother saw Grandmother hesitate to enter. They stood at the entrance with the caretaker and his son, watching the pale lights swinging in lazy arcs from window to window, listening to the tapping of feet in the courtyard, the scrapes and muffled thumps threading their way across the upstairs floor.

'Wah, so many,' my grandmother marvelled.

'There she is!' the caretaker pointed to the shape bustling from window to window, raising puffs of shadow in one corner, a shower of sparks in the next.

'Very busy,' Grandmother admired. 'Wah, she woke everyone up.'

'In life also like that,' chattered the caretaker through his teeth.

'Stay here,' Grandmother told my mother. 'I will look round first.'

'Stay here,' the caretaker said to his son. 'Good boy, keep Missy company, ah.'

My mother and the caretaker's son stood side by side at the ghosthouse window, their eyes just above the windowsill. Sudden loud bangs and screeches made them jump against each other. My mother turned away. She carefully put her ghostchasing equipment down. The caretaker's son turned also, shuddering. They stood face to face, exactly the same size, eyes exactly level. 'Aren't you scared?' the boy asked.

'Why should I be scared?' my mother was scornful. She stared a moment, then asked: 'What's wrong with your face?'

'None of your business!' he snapped.

At the rattle of the caretaker's keys my mother gathered her tools. 'This is the best way in,' Grandmother said. 'Already seen us, no point sneaking.'

Grandmother looked at my mother. 'Useless, remember what you've learnt! Ah Ma's oldest enemy is also in there, very strong!'

The caretaker's fingers shivered so much he couldn't find the keyhole. His son held the lantern that shivered also. Grandmother stamped her feet in their shiny worn shoes. She shot last-minute instructions to my mother, who nodded once, twice, and again. The caretaker's son wandered a little way off. My mother felt the fine hairs on her forearms stiffening. This was her bravery signal. She squared her shoulders, made her liver like lead to weigh her to the ground. She heard Grandmother's low soft laugh. The caretaker swung open the door.

At this point in the story my mother, bending over the steaming laundry tubs, stirring with the paddle till the water turns grey and sludgy, will suddenly stop. 'Bad girls!' she'll cry, her hands on her hips. 'You came to help, or what? How many shirts have you folded, hah? If you're not careful, I'll tell the sisters you're not working, then they won't let you come.'

'We're working!' the bully and I protest, our hands suddenly adept at folding, our pile of ironed shirts suddenly growing. 'Look how fast we work!'

'Anyhow,' my mother sighs, running a damp hand over her forehead, 'you know Grandmother doesn't like that story. That's the one she doesn't like to tell.'

'That's why we ask you,' the bully and I fold faster, the iron hissing between us like our persistence, our hope. We glance at my mother slyly but her back is turned.

'Anyhow,' she continues as if we haven't spoken, 'now it's your turn to tell. What did you learn in your morals class? What did you learn today?'

'Tell us the moral of the ghosthouse!' the bully and I beg, sneaky, but my mother just wags her finger, and shakes her head.

Unlike Grandmother my mother says the crocodile is not an old saying, but one that is relatively new. My mother says she knew the person who made it up: she was present at the time. She whispers that Grandmother's crocodile saying is neither original nor true. Grandmother's saying is an offshoot. The first crocodile saying happened when my mother was a girl, not long after Grandmother sent her to the convent to beg for work. At the convent laundry my mother witnessed the birth of the crocodile saying first hand. The boy who made it up lived in a house next to the jungle—that is why the jungle comes in. This boy's nickname was the Lizard Boy because his skin was cracked and scaly, his body thin and sinewy, his stomach bulging whenever he ate. His eyes were round and lizard-like, hardly ever blinking. Everyone could tell wherever he'd been by the trail of silver skinflakes he left. They watched fascinated and repulsed by the flicking of his tongue. The Lizard Boy stood unmoving for long minutes in the heat of the noonday sun when he should have been working, dragging his basket, sweeping up rubbish and leaves; when he finally moved, when someone shouted or threw a stone, it was in quick silvery darts.

'There goes the Lizard!' convent girls chorused from their classroom windows.

This Lizard Boy, the caretaker's son, was always coming up with sayings. He carried a book scrunched into his back pocket. He was always sorting proof: balancing this tale against that, these stories against those, this article and that, staring for long moments into space as he tried to figure out which was true. During rest periods he sat with his head buried. The Lizard Boy wasn't choosy. One day he'd be reading a history book, the next a five cent novel, then a book of rhymes. Then it would be colourful, bloodthirsty comics filled with ghosts and monsters, and heroes with eyes like ice chips, mosquito-waisted women whose mouths were always rounded, ready to scream. The Lizard Boy accepted bribes to hide these comics when the nuns came on their confiscation rounds; he read and then thrust them under stones and into hedges for convent girls to find. He read anything, everything. Chained up in the laundry for causing a convent riot, he didn't have as much choice; he read books and magazines the caretaker sneaked to him, and soap powder packets, week-old newspapers, even shipping lists. He muttered to himself as he read. 'This one's printed overseas, must be true story. This one local, aiya, can't even spell properly, so many mistakes! Can't be true.' The Lizard Boy tore out the read-over pages, deftly folding and twisting until they became birds, animals, elegant boat shapes which he laid in neat rows. He christened the fleet with sea-conquering names. Then sidled from the corner of the convent laundry where he crouched, to whisper in my mother's ear. The chain attached to his ankle tinkled faintly as he walked.

'Flower of the Orient,' the Lizard Boy whispered, consulting his list, making my mother jump. 'Blazing Sunrise. Queen of the Sea.'

My mother swatted away his whispers the way she swatted the flies that lifted buzzing from her pile of monkey scraps. She made a face fierce enough to scare ten tigerbitten demons, as Grandmother showed her. She turned her shoulder and hurried across the room to where the linen lay ready for sorting. The laundry tubs hissed and spluttered, the steam made a billowing curtain between them. The Lizard Boy lounged against a pile of dirty pillowslips, grinning.

From the time he was a child, my mother says, the Lizard Boy was always being teased. No wonder he was always hiding his face behind paper. He was the only boy in the convent, an experiment, allowed to stay only because of the soft hearts of the nuns; because of the intercession of his godfather, the Old Priest. The Lizard Boy's father, the caretaker, had stood with shoulders drooping and the grey sweat-cloth from around his neck dripping not with sweat but tears on the day the Lizard Boy's mother died. His shoulders slumped with self-pity. His face crumpled at the kindest word. That day the caretaker stood for hours, begging the nuns to let the Lizard Boy stay. No one else would have him, neither friends nor relatives, and if they were both made to leave what would they do? How would the father work and look after the child? No one else would treat him kindly. Surely the good sisters must feel pity, seeing the way the boy stood with his eyes screwed up and one fist rubbing and rubbing at one eye while the other clutched a corner of his father's shirt. The Lizard Boy crushed a tiny handful of the caretaker's shirt in anticipation of the nuns tearing him away. My mother's own eyes cloud with pity when she thinks of this scene. Her hands pause in mid-action, the folds of the half-ironed sheet hang over her elbows like bent wings.

Of course the nuns allowed the caretaker and his son to stay. They looked at the boy's pale flaky face, his ridged skin. When he was just a baby and his mother pushed him away in horror, the nuns cradled him against their starched white breasts. They pushed fingers dipped in sugar water to his questing lips. Such babies were often left at the convent gate: babies born with harelips or disorderly features or missing limbs. The nuns dismissed the old superstitions. They cuddled the babies, planted their cheeks with warm kisses, cooed and chirped to make them smile. The nuns took every child in, even the ones who were dying, whom the Old Priest quickly christened to send their souls to heaven. Badluck children, people called them, pointing, staring when they were glimpsed in the parts of the convent they were allowed to go. Children whose families or ancestors had done something to offend some spirit, or god, or nature.

The Lizard Boy's badluck, my mother says, came back in his nickname to plague him. Unlike my mother's badluck, which before she became a Christian, she had always felt but never seen, the Lizard Boy's luck sat on the surface of his skin. It wafted off in pieces to stick to other people, making convent girls run screeching, mock-dusting their clothes and hair. Worse still, the Lizard Boy's badluck was not even his fault. It happened before he was born: when his pregnant mother accidentally smashed a nest of geckoes, crumpling brittle eggs with one swipe. The tiny crushed bodies stuck to her cloth by their own jelly, their too-large eyes gleamed like jewels. The Lizard Boy's mother threw her cloth away in fright. She ran to scrub her hands. Over the sounds of the splashing water and the radio crackle her husband listened to in the evenings, over the clink and slurp of their bowls and lips at dinner, the Lizard Boy's mother grew pale. Her eyes widened, she raised trembling hands to cover her ears and block out the clicking cries of the geckoes, now quick and furious, now quietly teasing. Always promising—something. The caretaker laughed at his wife's rantings. He gave her money to make offerings, waved away her fears. When the Lizard Boy was born everyone came to look, even the Old Priest and the nuns. The boy's mother fainted at the sight. The Old Priest held out his hand in commiseration and blessing while the caretaker stood scratching his head. Beside his mother's fainted body, the Lizard Boy lay kicking his feet. His eyes blinked round and jewel-like amidst the folds of skin already lifting, flaking. His lips parted to show tiny serrated teeth. The Lizard Boy watched with interest the shadows pressing in a circle around him. He listened to the dips and curves of their whispering. He breathed the moist jungle air; gurgled joyfully.

When I was born my grandmother asked the skywatcher to

chart my future. The chart the watcher gave my grandmother was short—I would not live past seven, he said. The first cycle. That made Grandmother laugh. Grandmother's laugh was loud and raucous in those days, it hung like a beak from her lips.

When I was seven, Grandmother says I became very ill. I burned with a fire that separated the skin from my flesh in layers, like a snake. No one thought I would live but Grandmother sat at the foot of my bed and peered at me relentlessly. A strange woman came into the children's ward. She was the most beautiful woman my grandmother had ever seen. Grandmother recognised the woman even with her extra eye closed. Grandmother's hands and feet grew icy, her face drained to a shadow of her face. She watched as the woman moved slowly from bed to bed, passing doctors and nurses who took no notice. Grandmother admired the woman's smooth walk, her gliding walk like that of dancers and acrobats, boneless. Her shimmering white gown fountained round her feet. Grandmother saw the woman had no feet. She saw her touching the heads of certain children, their heads and lips and hands. Outside the ward the clamour of the hospital, of the city street and the nearby jungle, all sank to silence.

When the woman came to my bed she saw Grandmother looking at her anxiously. She smiled and held out her hand. The woman's smile was dispassionate, her eyes like black stone. Grandmother smelt salt and the open sea, then a cloudy smell of dark places, of jungle mud. The children's ward was filled with a sound like rain on water, like a wind through jungle leaves. Before the woman could touch me Grandmother snatched at her hand. The woman's hand was rough, unexpected, like snatching burnt sticks. The woman's hand was as cold as ice. Grandmother looked up, startled. The woman's face was suddenly shrivelled, the features of her face shifting subtly. Her face shrank to another face, gap-toothed and craggy, her eyes were washed the colour of crinkled leaves. Her face became an old man's face. The old man leaned forwards, his mouth split with laughing. His laughter filled

Grandmother's head. Grandmother rubbed at her eyes. She remembered the old man's face. When she looked again the beautiful woman had returned. Grandmother swallowed. She blurted her wish, her challenge, in one desperate breath. 'One more cycle,' Grandmother wheedled, crafty as an old pedlar, as if she had an ace up her sleeve. Grandmother wept and beat at her breast. She peeped at the woman through her tears. The woman stood at my bed and looked at me tenderly. She looked at me with great thirst. When Grandmother finally stopped, she was gone. The woman smiled and was gone.

'Wait!' Grandmother called.

'Swear by the Sea Spirits that you'll keep your promise, swear first.'

'I swear!'

'Then you shall have your one cycle, you shall have what you seek.'

'What will I give you? What promise?'

'What I've lost.'

'What have you lost?'

'Don't you remember?' came the answer, a cackling answer in a voice hoarse and fire-burned, cracked with the weight of the years. 'Don't you remember what you took? What you burned? You've already promised! You promised your most precious to help me get it back!'

Grandmother shuddered, recognising that voice. The old man's voice. Grandmother jumped in her chair. She thumped her fist against her palm, realising the old man's long ago trick to make her promise. She remembered his long ago voice calling from the jungle with spells and salves to reopen her extra eye. Grandmother thumped her fist like a gambler caught out. She hissed like a curse gone wrong. Passing doctors and nurses stared disapprovingly, raised fingers to their lips, but she took no notice. She knew it was done. Grandmother knew the woman agreed. She left a reminder: Grandmother's breasts shrivelled against her belly, her hands and feet twisted, her hair whitened to the roots. When Grandmother saw the sweat glistening on my hot forehead she started to laugh.

'Is that what you think I've promised?' she murmured. 'Is that what you think you'll get?' Grandmother leaned forward to rest her twisted hand on my cheek. She laughed uproariously.

The next day the children the woman had touched all died, but I lived, and my grandmother's laugh was the sound I woke to hear.

SOMETHING
COLONIAL

When my grandmother was younger she used to specialise in being a Little-People-hitter. This is how Grandmother's reputation first spread. People who were wronged or slighted came to Grandmother seeking revenge. A small hit resulted in a bad headache or a small accident while a big hit caused illness, badluck, serious injury. Small hits cost a dollar, big hits ten. Grandmother sat on a street corner surrounded by other pedlars. Even today the smell of frying chicken wings and worked leather takes her back to this time. Grandmother sat waving her slipper in her hand, but she had no need to coax and call as the others did. In those days the sight of a stern-looking woman seated on the roadside waving a soft black slipper always gathered a crowd. 'What is her name?' Grandmother asked. 'When was she born? What hour?'

Grandmother made customers write the details on a piece of paper. The more accurate the details the surer the hit. She lit joss sticks and offered a bowl of rice to the spirits, then set the paper alight. 'I hit you!' she cried, slapping the burning paper fiercely with her slipper. 'Do you feel the pain? I hit you! Hit you! Hit you! Hit you, you Small Person, you weed, you worm!'

Some people came back every week for their dollar hit. Grandmother assured them it was well worth their money to see their enemies suffer. If nothing happened this week, it meant the spirits were building up their energies for a double dose next week. Grandmother stared through narrowed eyes at people who dared to express doubts about her ability, she fingered her slipper and matchsticks until they reddened and slunk away. Every day people squatted beside her with clenched fists and gleaming eyes while she hit. Although she would never admit it, when Grandmother first set up her stall she was never sure how many hits reached their target. Much later, when her business was booming and she'd branched out from merely hitting, out of curiosity she experimented on her assistant, to see. Grandmother grinned, counting eight hits out of ten. By this time she'd worn out many slippers, both left and right. My mother squirmed as she sat mending the tattered soles, pressing her fingers to her aching forehead, moaning.

Nowadays convent girls seeking revenge wait behind the ancient caretaker's hut while he's busy clipping hedges or sweeping the driveway, or doing his rounds. In between lessons, at lunchtime, during free periods, girls sneak out to wait. They stuff hankies into mouths so no whispers or giggles will give them away. Behind the toolshed the bully pushes their grasping hands aside. The bully makes everyone wait their turn.

'Money first,' the bully says, and I hold out my hand.

Convent girls dig in their purses to drop pocket money into my hand. Ten cents for a peek, twenty cents for five minutes, fifty cents to take it home. For a dollar they get to keep the photo. Every week the bully produces more: photos of the most-feared nuns without their wimples, of overweight nuns stuffing their faces, naughty nuns doing penance push-ups on the floor. Huddled nun-shapes laughing in the bathrooms at night. Girls splutter through their hankies, their shoulders quiver, their fingers snatch at the photographed nuns. The bully shows photos of the nuns' quarters and the boarders' dormitories where the day-girls aren't allowed to go. Convent girls who buy them must cross-their-hearts-and-hope-to-die they will neither show nor tell. If they do may their eyes go blind and their tongues fall out, and the bully will know. The bully will come to get them. Everyone knows the bully always does what she says. For twenty cents extra she lets them use her special candles, stolen from my grandmother's stock. Red candles over which Grandmother's curse-prayers have been said.

'Scorch the eyes, they'll get styes,' the bully says. 'Burn the throat, laryngitis. The mouth, a toothache to swell the face.'

Convent girls cluster over the candles burning blisters into the photos, concentrating hard. Only with the proper concentration will the candles work. The bully shows the more staunch-hearted her special collection, wrapped in a special cloth, tucked in her special scrapbook. She tilts the scrapbook so girls can't see inside. She unwraps the ragged cloth, which she used to mop the Old Priest's forehead before he died. The cloth is heavy with the Old Priest's death, a smell that makes the girls flinch. Vinegar sour, stale. The bully's special collection is not for sale and costs double the ordinary rates to see. These are photos taken in the dead of night, at great danger. Convent girls clutch each other at the sight of the fairy dancers whirling around the library courtyard, suspended several feet in the air. They press their cheeks to see monster shapes lurking behind pillars, blurry shadows of all shapes and sizes in the ghosthouse, standing and sitting and staring right next to girls. Crocodile shadows peer from the edge of the jungle, ghosthouse shadows show their teeth.

My grandmother laughs when she hears what the bully is doing. She pauses between stories, reaches to pat the bully's head. The bully jumps as though Grandmother's fingers burn.

The nuns let the bully out of the convent once every fortnight. They send her home with my mother to sample family life.

The nuns trust my mother to look after the bully because once, after my father disappeared, my mother too had wanted to become a nun. My mother saw a vision of the Virgin Mary while searching for my father in the city streets. She came to sit at the back of the convent chapel, weeping for her disappeared husband, telling the nuns what she saw. The light in her face as she recounted her vision slipped the nuns to their knees. Her tears were a clattering of crystal that melted at their touch. They knelt beside her and held her hands. They stroked the life back into my mother's hands, let her rest her head on their crisp white shoulders, which my mother blotched with tears. They led her to a basin of warm salty water to ease her swollen feet. The nuns let my mother weep the way my grandmother forbade her to at home. My mother clutched at her breast, twisting deep creases into her blouse. This was her spirit weeping. The nuns passed a damp cloth over her face to wipe away her crying. They placed their cool palms on the lines newly etched on her face, propped up her sagging flesh.

'You're not the first girl to be tricked!' they cried. 'Cry hard, now you've learnt your lesson, and offer your tears to God. Offer your thanks to the Holy Virgin!'

Seeing my mother's deep distress, the nuns forgave her absence from the laundry, they gave her half days off work to go for lessons with the Old Priest who read to her from his book of holy writings words that made my mother's head spin. The Old Priest looked at my mother kindly, intently. Her face grew warm at his magic words, on her shoulders she felt the badluck shifting, she felt she was floating on air. My mother began to spend her lunchtimes at the chapel on her knees. The blue-eyed statues with smiling faces stretched out their pale hands to stroke the top of her head. My mother wore the rosary the nuns gave her around her neck where the heavy carved beads made a row of dents and links. Her eyes turned upwards like those of the saints.

'Where is your family?' the nuns asked.

'Only my adopted mother,' my mother sobbed, 'in the city.'

'Can she come and see us?'

'No, Sister, she's sick. She's old. Hit on the head by bandits a few weeks ago, and still can't walk. Can't see properly.'

'Who looks after her, my dear?'

At that my mother's sobs came harder. 'Me, Sister,' she whispered. 'I look after her.'

The nuns patted her hands. 'Then we must advise you not to join just yet, dear child. At least not while Mother's sick. We must wait and see!'

Then the nuns saw my mother's belly growing and had to regretfully turn her away. My mother's calling was not the spiritual but the family life.

The nuns say my mother's family is ideal for the bully to experience family life because in it there are no men. No sons to lead the bully astray. No crocodiles to lure her into dark coffeeshops and butt her with their snouts. The nuns give my mother two dollars to take the bully and the bully follows her, carrying the bundles of clothing and linen my mother takes home to mend for the nuns. For these special outings they make the bully wear a ribbon in her hair. They tell the bully to be on her best behaviour. When she's out the gate they sigh with relief. A whole weekend without having to shout at the bully, without throwing up their hands! The bully tosses her head to loosen the ribbon. She glares at everything, she snarls and grunts under the heavy load as she and my mother weave their way between the cars and motorcycles that honk to make them jump. The bully's hair drips with sweat as they trudge the narrow backlanes to my grandmother's house.

When my grandmother was a girl she spent her days waiting. When she was a girl nobody liked her. The other servants made her sit by herself in the kitchen corner, they made her eat by herself in the courtyard, sleep by herself in the kitchen passage with a pile of gunny sacks over her head so they wouldn't have to hear her breathe. When the rich man was away on his travels the other servants knocked their knuckles on her head, they waved their fists, and shouted: 'Tell who? Who are you going to tell?' Every day of the rich man's travels Grandmother crept to the balcony to scan the roads of the city, the horizon, the darkening sky. Her head turned from side to side, from one end of the horizon to the other, to the city-edged sky. She was never sure which way to look. Which was the right direction. When Grandmother slept she dreamt of walking. She dreamt of sights and wonders she would one day see. Awake, her time was spent in a daze, peering at the world through a mist of uncertainty, hearing whispers when no one whispered, seeing shadows that disappeared when she turned. Wherever Grandmother walked, she stumbled. She ducked and scowled, chin set, glaring, at every moment expecting blame, or objects flying towards her, a housekeeper dragging her off for scolding, a new mistress chasing her out. Her bond-pledge offered to another household, one which knew how to deal with disobedient girls!

When my grandmother was a girl she stuck her chin out at everything. Even nowadays Grandmother has this look. Servants hiding behind doors and cupboards to jump out screeching and cackling gave her a belligerent disposition. She jumped backwards, raising her fists. Sometimes she woke in the mornings with unexplained aches all over her body. Her body was covered with bruises, her ankles with scratches, her feet with cuts that lifted the skin in flaps. The rich man's servants shrieked in mock-terror when she showed them. They pushed her out of the house. 'Kissed by demons!' they cried. 'Kissed by demons!' Strapped to her pallet at night, Grandmother saw the roads of the city stretching before her, shophouses looming, people stooping to stare, and smile. Grandmother woke suddenly. Her bones ached in the mornings as though from a beating all night, as though from trudging and stumbling, from too much walking.

Later, when she returned to the city, when she learnt to focus her extra eye and discovered her life's work, her talent for ghostly advice and chasing, my grandmother no longer woke up tired from walking. When not out chasing ghosts she slept soundly all night. Her face was pink from too much rest. This was my grandmother's easy time, her young woman's time, every day filled not with ducking and scowling but with discovery; charms cleverly cajoled from wisewomen and ghostchasers, the whys and wherefores of ghosts, gods and demons painstakingly learnt by heart. Grandmother hung around the city's shrines and temples watching the monks. She skirted the crowds around marketplace healers and magicians, nudged her way forwards to examine the oils and potions, the strength and virility and cure-all charms. The old men and women selling the future from cards and bowls of coloured water made her laugh. Magicians held her spellbound with tricks of appearing and disappearing, conjurers with the summonings of spirits of stones and bottles, of departed loved ones and distant sea spirits, until she looked with her extra eye. Only if she saw their magic with her extra eye was Grandmother impressed. Only then did she run and carry, and scrape and wheedle, and beg to be taught. Her black-and-white vision sharpened with each passing day. Her own small streetstall became so crowded the soldiers moved her on. The soldiers moved and moved her until she proffered a red packet bulging with hard-earned takings, which they pocketed and left. Those were my grandmother's lucky years, when her fame spread throughout the city. Grandmother's stomach grew round and untroubled, her teeth acquired edgings of gold. In those days she rode to her jobs in a hired taxi, or to the market, or merely down the street. She bought a house large enough to accommodate her stream of clients and her growing repertoire of spells. People came from far and near to ask her advice. Later, when Grandmother was no longer so young, she had to buy herself an assistant to cope with the work. My mother bustled in and out of the kitchen, pounding herbs and mixing powders, serving special teas to soothe despairing clients, special titbits to cool their blood. Grandmother sat just outside the doorway, advising one client after another. The front of the house was her ghostchasing office.

'Turn your bed so the soles of your feet don't point east,' she droned. 'It's the eastern dragon who's offended, who is sending his eastern winds to shake your bed. Take one of your wife's soiled menstrual cloths, burn it until only a pile of ashes is left, bury the ashes outside your doorstep. This way you may rest assured your wife will never run away again. Move your mother's grave sixteen paces to the right, then she will be happy and won't come crying to you at night.'

In those days Grandmother sat in her special chair for hours, hardly stirring, rising only occasionally to make a special charm or send a passport to a ghostly traveller with a fearful whoosh of the incinerator. Grandmother gets angry when she thinks about those days. The memory of those easy days twists her mouth with rage. 'Their fault!' Grandmother shouts, beating at anything, a table, a chair, the earth. Anyone or thing that is passing becomes her target, friends or enemies, cars or bicycles, even bullockcart drivers who yell warnings when they see her come. 'The nuns' fault!' Grandmother cries. 'Aiya, that's how they answer a favour! Their fault, theirs!'

In a more generous mood my grandmother becomes philosophical. 'Everything in good time,' she says with a saintly expression. 'Revenge is sweeter for those who know how to wait. How to plan. Next cycle, it's my turn. Next time, I win!' Grandmother stares at me as she says this, her smile complicit, her eyes narrowing to a secret that excludes the bully and my mother, looking on. 'What do you say, Ah Girl?'

'Yes, Grandmother,' I say. From habit I spread my lips to the thin line yes that my grandmother likes, no matter the question. From training I wink and smile back. The bully and my mother turn their slighted shoulders, frowning, pursing their lips. The bully kicks at the legs of her chair.

From the time I was a small child my grandmother and I have had this secret: the complicity of smile and wink. That is part of Grandmother's plan. My grandmother has pulled me towards her. We have stared into each other's eyes, leaned our faces so close it is easy to imagine we see the same landscape, we draw the same breath. Grandmother points me towards the convent and asks me what I see. Do I see danger, do I see newcomers and people who disregard rules? Do I see fault? 'Yes, Grandmother,' I say. 'Yes!' Her cheek against my cheek feels like crumpled paper. Her eyes are black and muddy orbs.

From the time I was a small child, my grandmother and I have gone walking. Grandmother rested her hand on my head for support, stopping to point at this and that. Nowadays she leans on my arm. Nowadays we only go as far as the gate. When I was a small child my days were spent with Grandmother in front of our house, not the big house of her famous ghostchasing days but our modest house of cement and plywood. Grandmother sat staring at the street. Some days dragged by without even one client. Passing neighbours hailed Grandmother, others stopped to squat by her chair for an evening chat.

'How's business, Auntie?'

'Aiya, you know, like that. So-so only, what to do?'

'Never mind, Auntie. Have patience! Next month is the Hungry Ghosts Feast, customers are sure to come. Wah, like last time, no place to sit!'

'Hah!' Grandmother watched the other neighbours streaming home from their workplaces, some bowing politely, others crossing the street with gazes lowered, quickening their steps. The neighbours opposite, good clients for years, dared not meet my grandmother's eyes. They strung protection crucifixes over their door. Grandmother's mocking cries followed their footsteps long after they disappeared. 'Hah!' she cried.

'Why do they walk so quickly?' I asked. 'Why, Grandmother, why?'

'They are afraid if they look in my eyes, I will see their secrets.'

'Can you do this, Grandmother?'

'I will see their secrets and they will see mine. That is what makes them shudder.'

While Grandmother advised her infrequent customers I

played near the front gate where she could watch. I rattled her collection tin. Already I could tell which coins were right and which were wrong. If a client tried to cheat Grandmother she always knew by the rattle of my tin. One look from her and the client paid up.

'Your girl so big, so pretty,' they stammered, patting my head, shoving extra coins into my tin.

'Come here,' Grandmother called at the end of the day. 'Give Grandmother her tin. We'll see if we can buy a cake today. Aiya, good girl, hug Grandmother! Give Grandmother a kiss.'

As I toddled towards her, Grandmother would snatch the tin, then push me away. We would eye each other. If I held the tin too tightly, Grandmother would smack me. If I let her push me away she smacked me. If I cried out Grandmother would smack me. Looking in her eyes I could sometimes tell where the smacks would land, on the arm, the leg, the head. If I guessed and ducked, she would either hug or smack me. Sometimes I could tell. When her last client left, or it was clear no clients were coming, Grandmother would call me. 'Ah Girl, bring Grandmother's tin.' Then she would smack. Then call again. Then push. Then smack; then call. In between smacks she hugged me. The buttons on her blouse pressed their pattern to my cheek. Her kisses made wet rings on my forehead and neck. 'Come here,' Grandmother called.

Every evening my grandmother and I played this game, until my arms and thighs were bright with smacks. Until the sounds of my rising laughs and howls and grunts crowded the neighbours at the gate. 'Aiya, Auntie, why so rough?' the bravest ventured.

'Your business, or what!' Grandmother snapped, sending them scurrying with her tiger glare.

In those days, when my grandmother was well past her easy middle-age, the gold dug from her teeth, her taxi-riding days over, we often played this game. I knew the game inside out. Grandmother and I played until we were breathless. We shrieked until our shrieks filled the evening and neighbours sheepishly drew their curtains, and my mother came rushing home to drop her laundry bundles and snatch me from my grandmother's arms.

Grandmother was offended at any sign of protest. 'Useless, you forgot what you promised already?' she cried. She beckoned me to her. 'Ah Girl! What! You hurt? You grumbling? Your Grandmother hurt you?'

'No, Grandmother!' I shouted, pushing my too-short legs into the tiger stance she taught me, puffing out my chest with the exercises to harness a tiger breath. I slapped my arms and legs to show that the redness didn't hurt.

From the time I was a small child I have always known to show that the redness doesn't hurt. This is part of Grandmother's plan. Even then she had started my training. Even then she was training me for life. Grandmother peeled a few crumpled notes from the roll of savings tucked into the waistband of her pants. She gave the notes to my mother to buy the foreign picture books and leaded pencils, the notebooks of ugly ruled paper so unlike the pliable brush and clean red squares that Grandmother used. Long before I could read Grandmother asked my mother to collect the discarded foreign newspapers from the convent. My mother lugged home the books and pamphlets once belonging to the Lizard Boy, left in the convent laundry after he ran off to join the bandits. Grandmother pasted newspaper sheets around my cot, on the walls of the corner where I lay. She stacked the musty books around me for later. All day I lay kicking my feet at the foreign words that marked my fingers black when I touched them. The words snaked from left to right like rows of soldier ants, like tiny black bricks. So unlike the winged shapes Grandmother made on her charm papers to show me, shapes now thick, now an eyelash. 'Watch carefully,' she said. 'This is only the beginning.' Every night she peered into my eyes to see the effect of the foreign words. She put her face so close to mine that her eyes became not Grandmother's eyes but two shiny black bowls to cup me. Grandmother's eyes made me dizzy, but still she said I must look. I must practise looking,

I must fight dizziness, for a crocodile's stare would be a thousand times worse. Peering into my eyes Grandmother hmmed and muttered. She made up a charm to counter any change. 'Only the beginning!' she cried.

In the city's records, in the faded inks of its founders and the shiny printed sheets of its successive governors, the hill with the convent and the jungle is called Mat Salleh Hill. It was named for the long ago sailor who was stranded there, who ran maddened from civilisation to live forever on the jungle-covered hill. Nothing was seen of him for years although sometimes his midnight voice came floating down the hill. The sailor's midnight voice made people's hair stand on end. Legend has it that he lives there still, though it was only the grandmothers of old women who swore they saw him, they glimpsed his pale bony body through the jungle edges. Only naughty city children still hear his hoarse voice at night. The mad sailor creeps down the hill to spirit naughty children to the jungle to tear their limbs and crunch their bones. One glimpse of him, so the legend says, brings the worst kinds of luck: the deaths of loved ones, businesses folding, great houses falling to ruin. The proclamation of curfews and new taxes, the scrape and kick of soldiers' boots. The mad sailor lived on the hill for more than a hundred years. A hundred years old and more, still he could run and jump, and leap like a boy. He could outrun naughty children, fell young men with one blow. The mad sailor was possessed by a demon, he'd bargained his soul for knowledge, his afterlife for an immortality as tormented as it was long. City children still shudder at the mention of the sailor, even though nowadays no one ever sees him but the old badluck grandmothers who have long since died, who return every Hungry Ghosts Feast to complain, and tell. In the days before her extra eye closed my grandmother quizzed the flock of hungry badluck grandmothers stopping at the door.

'What is he like?' Grandmother chanted in a trance for the curious. 'How old is he? Is he very strong?'

The hungry grandmothers clamoured and squabbled at the food stations lined along the roadside, stuffing their mouths. 'He's weak!' they screeched between mouthfuls. 'She's strong! He's old! She's older!'

'Venerable Grandmothers,' Grandmother chanted while my mother tended the joss sticks, the hell money and incense, the piles of food. Grandmother's clients crouched in one corner, waiting their turn. 'Is the sailor alive or dead?' Grandmother asked. 'What is he—a he or a she?'

'Aiya, both!' the grandmothers burst out cackling. 'Both!'

'What's the sailor doing? Why is he there?'

'Aiya, don't you know anything?' they shrilled, their mouths dripping flame and ashes, their bony hands snatching at each other as they flapped in a seething cloud to the next mound of food. 'Don't you know? She's waiting!'

'What for, Venerable Grandmothers?' Grandmother chanted, but the hungry grandmothers, out on their once-a-year holiday, can't be bothered answering.

'Useless, who's next?' Grandmother asked, coming out of her trance.

The hill with the jungle and the convent is known to city people not by its official city-records name. Poor cityfolk call the hill King Crocodile Hill. Once, not so very long ago, no more than two turns of a woman's life cycle, a gang of bandits lived there, the most famous of the bandit gangs who made the narrow paths and clearings of the jungle-covered hill their home. Its leader was the most famous bandit the city had ever known. For years he led his gang in a charmed and dauntless life, escaping imminent capture by sheer bravado, by the skin of his pointed teeth. No more than fourteen years ago the hill with the convent and the jungle was a nest of trouble and defiance, of bloody skirmishes and booby-traps, the rat-tat-tat of firearms in the dead of night. There soldiers were stationed in lonely outposts, and jungle trees felled, jungle paths widened to admit the soldiers' trucks. There the bandits planned and staged brilliant guerilla raids and ambushes, capturing supplies of food and weaponry, communications networks, prisoners and trucks. Captured soldiers hobbled back to the city after interrogation with their faces streaked as pale as the foreign masters they served.

Deep in the jungle the gang of bandits continued the old bandit tradition of printing propaganda leaflets and newsletters for distribution in the city by bandits in disguise. *Freedom*! the leaflets proclaimed in the colours of blood and freedom. *Self-determination. Independence. Say no to slavery! Local riches for locals. Act now!* In the dead of night they crept into the villages surrounding the city, collecting village news, letters from relatives, food and clothing the villagers hid in special places for them to find. They left money taken from bandit raids on rich houses, bandit ambushes on prosperous plantations. They noted the villagers' complaints, exacted revenge on soldiers who came to take mothers and fathers, uncles and brothers and sisters away. After a soldier visit whole families disappeared. The bandits assassinated landowners foolish enough to travel without hired soldiers armed with machetes and guns. They cleared the city's oldest landmark, the hill in the shape of the woman turning, of its foreign Pearl, its Boil—they razed its hilltop pavilion so only blackened stumps marked where it once stood. They cut the cables of the rich man's abandoned pleasure railway, overturned the cars. Masked bandits flagged down shiny air-conditioned coaches in the city to snatch gems and handbags from ballgowned women, golden cigarette cases and wallets from the men. They cut jewelled fingers off party-goers, sliced the lips from those who talked back.

The gang of bandits whose headquarters was deep in the jungle-covered hill was notorious throughout the city. Not so long ago, no more than fourteen years, they were known by every city child, woman and man. Their names were spoken by young men and women with reverence, by older folk with a twist to their lips. Like the mad sailor whose hill they had taken over their names were spoken with awe: Old Broken Arm, Old Hairy, Bandit Queen, Handsome, Mat Mat Salleh, King Crocodile. Their physical attributes were discussed intimately, their personalities as though they were personally known. Old Hairy's armpits like the blackest jungle, the Bandit Queen's temper, the red glowing skin of the King Crocodile geared up for a fight. Sayings about bandit doings were woven into songs and stories fast being sung and told alongside those of the Mad Sailor, the Rich Man of the Mansion, the Bandit Ancestors in whose footsteps they trailed.

The bandits were feared throughout the city by those who had cause to fear them. They crept to distribute pamphlets and promises, to whisper sayings and slogans that spread from ear to ear. To propagate their bandit dreams. They fitted their words to poor cityfolk's everyday aches and grumblings; infiltrated the dens of informers and collaborators to drag suspects into dark alleys and slit their throats by moonlight so their collaborator and informer souls would be snatched by passing ghosts. Poor city and village people bowed their heads as the bandits passed, others ran to the telephones, others shook their fists. Poor cityfolk called the hill King Crocodile Hill in admiration; even to this day, almost two turns of a woman's cycle later, some of my grandmother's neighbours insist this is the hill's only name. Grandmother turns on them with her tiger glare. She fingers the lump on her head that once swelled red and throbbing from the hit of a bandit rifle, that even years later still hadn't shrunk smooth. No hairs grow on that part of her head, which swells like a boiled egg, a shiny knob. Grandmother shakes her fist at the old bandit who sent her crumbling with one stroke, who shimmered in the shape of a beautiful woman in the instant before Grandmother fell. My grandmother has no love for bandits. She says the crocodile was merely a thief, and the bravest neighbours may contradict her if they dare. Twisting their fingers into goodluck shapes poor cityfolk continue to whisper the name of the most famous of the famous bandit leaders. Faced with calamity they cry 'King Crocodile!' as if invoking a charm. *King Crocodile for miraculous escapes, for a nose thumbed at death!* In dim and crowded coffeeshops poor cityfolk huddle together whispering the bandit stories. In the bustling din of markets, in dark alleys under tattered awnings, a snatch of bandit song may be heard; a bandit slogan may be shouted in the grey of morning when unfriendly eyes and ears aren't waking, in the dead of night when all but the lovers, the zealous and the lonesome are asleep.

In the dead of night is when the bully suddenly wakes twitching. When the bully lies with ankles crossed and palms pressed flat to the floor. On nights like these she twitches as though with fever. She wakes suddenly, eyes sliding open, just like that. She is suddenly still. These nights there's no difference between the bully's eyes being shut or open. Either way all she sees is the dark. Never a mark like sunlight on a wall, as bright as burning. Never a sight to make her stare and clasp her hands. I turn towards her, flopping over, waking to the pale shine of her eyes. Strands from my tangled braid slide over my face. The bully lies as still as the statues nestling on every spare ledge in every spare corner of my mother's room. Her chest hardly moves, her skin is like pitted stone. I watch her closely. 'Why did you shake?' I whisper. 'What did you see?'

'I didn't shake,' the bully murmurs. 'It was the room shaking.'

On nights like these the bully bears watching. These nights she may go either way. She may fall into her wild fits that make the nuns smack and grumble; she may sit cow-like for hours, eyes filmed with a watery glaze, or suddenly turn smiling, affectionate, greeting everyone with an amicable slap. Everyone knows the bully's moods. I watch her carefully.

'Let's go,' she says, making me jump.

Sometimes, in the dead of night, the bully and I go walking. The bully and I creep from our cushioned mats in the darkroom with our torches, our special candles, our satchels crammed with foodscraps and flower offerings. Grandmother's leaf and root collection bag is tied round my waist. The bully checks her camera. She carefully wipes her lens and tests her flash. She leads us past the dusty props of the basement, out through a loosened downstairs window into the library courtyard where the night-time jungle air is a blast of warmth and dampness that shivers my skin.

'Are you shivering?' demands the bully, who never shivers. 'This is the test of courage,' she says, who although she hates the tests set by the nuns and teachers, will spend hours devising her own. If we can hold our breaths walking past ten lamp posts, when we're held underwater by torturers it will be easy, we'll think of the lamp posts and won't drown. If we can stand as still as the jungle, only swaying slightly, our faces painted the streaky brown of jungle trees, our arms draped with branches, if we can stand unnoticed beside the path, an inch away from convent girls straggling on afternoon treks or soldier patrols swiftly passing, so close we can touch them, then when we're faced with hardship, when we go walking and searching, we will be successful. We will find our jungle treasure. Our photos will hang in hallways along which convent girls stop to ponder our faces in awe. If we can make our bodies into rock when we're chased from the classrooms with everyone laughing, or made to stand for hours in the noonday sun, our palms cut with wooden rulers, or when acid is dripped onto our shoulders like the acid endlessly dripping onto the bully from the mouths of the girls and the nuns, then we will win. The ones who don't shiver will win. 'Keep still!' the bully orders, as I squirm.

Unlike Grandmother, the bully says the crocodile is a creature whose belly is always full. While Grandmother's crocodile stares out from the edges of the jungle, hungering for what is outside, the bully's croc struts through the city, rubbing elbows with city people, hopping into air-conditioned buildings and cars. The bully curls her lip at Grandmother's crocodile, afraid to leave its hide-out in the jungle except for wild skirmishes to poke at lone victims in the dark. When Grandmother isn't with us, the bully sticks out her hip. She raises her forefinger in challenge. Grandmother's crocodile lives on the hollow ache of its belly, on fear. It preys on fear, but is itself always fearful. Otherwise why does it hide? Why does it need a knife to scare? It is a fake crocodile, with rubber teeth. Like a suicide ghost with a rubber tongue.

The bully's croc, however, walks about with its belly distended and eyes glazed from overeating. Its lips are red from constant smacking at the aftertaste of honeyed pork ribs, chilli chicken wings, mashed potatoes and steak, which at the convent the bully never gets to eat. This crocodile picks at its razor sharp teeth which it can stick out or withdraw at will, depending on its mood. When the croc is in a good mood champagne flows like water, gold coins flip through the air, parties are thrown that last all day, all night. When he's in a bad mood people who are smart will flee. No one dares to laugh at this croc or call him names. He is so rich he can buy whole cities. So powerful his enemies clamour to lick his shoes. Everyone knows who he is. His photo hangs in hallways where people come to gape in awe. If anyone angers this croc he bites off their heads with one snap. The bully's croc never wears a school uniform. He has never washed toilets or cleaned blackboards, or perhaps only in some distant past, and has never been slapped on the cheek without giving two slaps back. This crocodile wears movie star sunglasses. Sometimes he wears a suit. Sometimes a soldier's uniform, with a shiny oiled gun. The crocodile is so smart he knows all the spells and stories, he has read a thousand books in his sleep. He has a tremendous memory. When he speaks no one interjects, everyone stops what they are doing to listen. No one laughs and gets angry, and orders him back to his seat. Even if he had only one arm he would be the leader of his country. He would be boss. He would sit at the top of the pile. His crocodile eyes are always tearful, not from crying but from gulping, from swallowing everything whole.

'Like this,' the bully shows us, gulping a handful of groundnuts in one go.

The house on the hill fell into a pattern of the rich man's coming and going. When news of his ship's arrival reached the house, everyone jumped and bustled: dust puffed out of long-neglected corners, windows were polished, every inch of the stairways snaking this way and that were scrubbed. All the servants produced, miraculously, their stashed-away doses of elbow grease. The rich man was famous for his fastidiousness, for spotchecks in the unused parts of the mansion where nobody thought to go. If, on his return, his house was in any way below standard, the culprits would have to be produced. The culprits would be made an example. The rich man's judgments were fair, none could argue otherwise, even the culprits, but his punishments were harsh. No amount of begging would allay the whipping if one was decreed, no tears shorten the long days and nights spent bolted into the punishment room. If no culprit could be found, everyone was made to pay: from the housekeeper to the gardener's boy, all had to work doubly hard, with cut rations and no one allowed even a night off, let alone a half-holiday at festival time. What disturbed the servants most was the coldness that accompanied their master's displeasure. His voice cut like ice at those fallen from favour while the others were lavished with claps on the shoulder and jokes in the corridors, small unexpected gifts. So the rich man's servants were always suspicious of each other. They worked hard only at their own responsibilities, spying on the others for slackness, forming separate groups: gardeners against houseboys against kitchen workers. Everyone carried tales. This method of running the household was a stroke of the rich man's genius. He believed whole cities could be run this way, by division and an iron rule. This way the whole ran smoothly, like clockwork, each part oiled by his favour, and kept separate, gliding against each other in their separate duties, aware yet ignorant of each other, always suspicious; rubbing shoulders but never merging, coveting favour only for their separate parts, never the whole. This way the rich man kept tabs on everyone. Even in his absence he ran a tight ship.

One return, however, everything changed. As usual the house bustled when word came of the rich man's arrival. My grandmother, leaning over the balcony rail, saw the usual train of his luggage and supplies, the trunks of exotic purchases he brought back from other lands. Usually she could see the rich man easily. He strode ahead of the train, his strides quick and eager, carrying him to the house long before his laden-down men. The rich man would raise his hat as he entered the garden, waving to Grandmother, to the row of servants lined up in welcome. This return, however, Grandmother could not see him at first. This time the rich man was at the end of the train, and he neither walked quickly nor looked for my grandmother with red ribbons in her hair, stretching her body, waving both arms. The rich man walked alongside a closed litter draped with scarves of bright cottons and silks. Now and then the draperies shifted to hint at a reclining figure. Now dark strands of hair curled like seaweed through a crack. Beside the litter the rich man walked slowly, solicitously. The servants could hear his sharp voice chiding the carriers when they slipped. This time he strode past the lined-up servants without a second glance. He ordered the litter be carried upstairs to his private quarters. Striding indoors he scraped mud onto the doorstep that only that morning had been polished so bright no one could see it for the glare.

On this return the rich man kept to his private quarters, where only his personal manservant was allowed to go. This manservant, who had followed the rich man from his homecountry, eyed the locals with disdain. He snapped his fingers to send them about their business, his chest swelled and his eyebrows bristled so no one dared to ask. The other servants were agog. They tiptoed to the rich man's door and pressed their eyes to the keyhole, over which a cloth had been draped. This time there were no welcome-home meetings with the household during which the rich man distributed gifts. No tours of the house in which he surveyed and commented on their labours, or enquired about their families, their health. This return there were no lavish parties. Former party guests, curious acquaintances, men and women who had heard so much and waited so long to meet him, all were shown the door. Even his own servants hardly saw him. Even my grandmother was sent away. The servants brought the rich man's carefully selected meals to his quarters, and when he rang, returned to remove the still-warm dishes, some merely pecked at, the rest untouched. The cook was at her wits' end, ordered to prepare a variety of different dishes every day. Every night the servants gorged themselves on the leftovers until they could hardly move. Only my grandmother sniffed at the proffered plates suspiciously, turning to her cold rice congee, averting her face. The sharp smell of seawater heaved her stomach, that rotting smell of rope and ships' timbers that clung to the rich man whenever he came back from the sea. Every mealtime two houseboys carried the laden trays to the rich man's quarters. They rang the bell, handed the trays to his manservant and were promptly waved away.

The story of the ghosthouse is older than the oldest priests and nuns. Therefore it is rubbish; nothing of value in this city can be older than their old. This is what the nuns say. The nuns say convent girls must look forward, progress, forget the backward superstitions of the past. Now this city is growing like a sturdy riceshoot out of the jungle, like the jungle ancestors of old, convent girls must learn to see. They must leave their nakedness behind. This makes convent girls hide their mouths behind their hands, but the nuns only wag their fingers. Convent girls must learn civilisation. They must spread it to their parents and friends and later their children. They must learn to wash their hands after using the toilet, and to not spit, to definitely not blow their noses into the gutters in the street. Manners must be learnt from the civilised books. They must always keep a hankie in their pockets and learn to use a knife and fork, and say with a gentle lilt: 'How do you do?' instead of shouting across rooms and busloads, over heads and under armpits: 'Have you eaten yet? Have you eaten?' They must learn to stop their headlong speech from tangling their tongues like an animal's, from ending their talk in exclamation marks. They must be quiet and dignified.

Civilisation is the convent girl's duty. It is inevitable: something colonial, spreading like fire through the colonial family of the civilised world. Convent girls must read from the holy book what is good and right and learn to stop talking their gibberish, to dismiss their superstitious babblings with one word. To speak the truth they must learn to speak like ladies. This is what the nuns say.

When the nuns took over the house that later became the ghosthouse, everything was a mess. The garden had been claimed by the jungle, undergrowth reached as high as their heads. Great jungle trees had scattered seeds which now pushed up through the tangle: the banyan, the angsana, the meranti, the parasol fern. Monkeys scrambled in and out of the broken upstairs windows, nesting wildbirds rose screeching in feathery clouds. No one but soldiers and bandits had been there for years. The nuns packed the land deeds into a waterproof packet, locked it into a battered travel trunk placed for safety in the middle of their camp. They hired natives to hack a circle around their tents to the places where they planned to eat and cook and worship. From this circle they ordered paths to be hacked in different directions: one to a pit for a toilet, another to a well, others to where the chapel would stand, and the initial classroom and the living quarters for the priest and nuns. The nuns stood and watched while the natives hacked a path to the front door.

Grandmother says: *The ghost of the Christians is a kind ghost, a holy ghost, with relations in high places. This ghost has a split personality and extremely good eyesight. The Christian ghost sees everything. Its eyes will follow you as you walk around its temple. If you steal even a candle the Christian ghost will know, and will make a black mark next to your name. The Christian ghost has a book full of names. This book appears in its hand when you die. It is called the Book of Judgments. Unlike the Chinese heaven where the dead can ask for the most modern houses to be sent, intact, complete with servants and furnishings, the Christian's house in heaven has to be built brick by brick. Each time a Christian does a good deed, she gets a brick. These bricks wait in piles for her to get to heaven. When she gets there she has to start building her house. If you become a Christian you must never bite into the body of the god they feed you with on Sundays. If you're not a Christian, never venture to receive the body of the god. A man who did this once took the god home, removed it from his tongue, took out a carving knife and sliced the god in two. Of course the god bled profusely, blood pumping out of its dismembered body. The blood soaked the man, and filled the room, and flowed out in great, thick globs into the street, and the man screamed and tore at his hair. The man went completely insane.*

My grandmother doesn't like the nuns. She says they are Little People whose words make a shadow too big for their bodies.

SIX

SO YOU
WILL NEVER
LEAVE ME

In the darkroom the bully can be anyone. Anyone at all. Her hair can be oiled and spicy, her skin rugged, her fat not fat, but muscle. Smooth. Her starched skirt like the flap of a dressjacket, the convent badge a carnation on her breast. The bully stands with legs apart like a man.

'Close your eyes,' the bully says. 'Open your mouth. Stick out your tongue.' The bully prepares the papers as she speaks. She puts out the lights. 'I'm going to put mouse shit on your tongue,' she says, 'and you must eat it. You must smile. You must like it.'

The bully pushes me against the wall and I stick out my tongue. I stand there while she develops the photographs, the sound of the solutions like music. My hands resting on my belly brush against a patch of roughened skin, bubbling tough and unexpected through my shirt. Skin in a raised and regular pattern, like plaiting over the bellybutton, like a twist of nail. My hands snatch themselves away. 'Don't move!' the bully orders.

Seeing the pictures arrive is like the opening of Grandmother's eye. Shadows lean against each other, jostling, one on top of another until there are eyes, a nose, a mouth. Tiny beaded teeth. When the bully has finished she shows me the photos. She spreads them in a circle around her oldest photo, puts on her bully's look of concentration to peer first into the old, then the new. Then back to the old. But the new photos don't help the bully. When she takes them she thinks she has recaptured something. She thinks she has made the smoke-burned shadows take shape. The bully is so excited she can't wait to get to the darkroom. But side by side the old and new photos don't match. Still the bully can't make out the shadows in her oldest photo, still she thinks there's more to see. She beckons me from the wall. 'You should be in the movies,' she says. She points to her favourite. In the photo I stand with my side towards the camera. I lean against the balcony rail, my blouse unbuttoned, my hair dishevelled by the wind. In the photo my shadows curve and swish around me like a wave, a tail.

'Are you ready?' the bully says, shaking the things in her hand.

I open wide. It could be anything at all. Mouse shit or wood, bits of glass or candy. I swallow. I smile. The bully laughs and slaps her thighs. I throw my arms around her.

'Not mouse shit,' the bully says, 'but a charm. So you will never leave me.'

My arms around the bully are surprisingly strong, my weight against her she can hardly move. I feel the echo of her heartbeat in my arms, I press my ear to the pounding of her breath for release. I tighten my hold. 'Remember your promise?' I whisper. 'Remember your promise when I won, what you said you'd give?'

'Anything you like,' the bully shrugs. 'What do you like?'

When I only smile for an answer she huffs and puffs till she's red in the face, till we're both laughing, and I have to let go. 'Remember your promise,' I'm panting, but the bully is past remembering. Her breath heaves from her chest in great gusts, earthy, like jungle rocks and leaves.

My grandmother is a teller of stories. She is a keeper of secrets and unnamed things. Grandmother is small, her face wizened, etched deep and leathery by the sun. She perches special sunglasses on the end of her nose out of pity for ordinary people, so they won't suffer the full blast of her tiger glare. The bones of her elbows and knees stick out. Grandmother walks hunched over, she waddles with shoulders stiffened and legs bent like a coolie, like a soldier itching to draw. Her feet are so crooked she walks with great difficulty. 'Slowly!' she cries, beating the backs of my legs with her stick. Grandmother walks fingering her various aches and pains. She is old now so her aches are numerous: headache from car and truck pollution, face ache from neighbours passing without a greeting, swallowed jar ghost ache bloating her belly with wind. The ache of her long ago hospital promise continually nagging at her brain.

'What promise, Grandmother?' I ask 'What promise did you make?'

'Keep quiet,' Grandmother says. 'I'm thinking.'

Grandmother chews and chews on betelnuts while she's thinking, so her teeth are always red.

When Grandmother tells stories she likes everyone to sit quietly. She makes the bully sit at her feet where she can see her every move. My mother brings us hot barley water and things to eat, coconut candy, sugar-coated melon pieces, sunflower seeds. The bully fills her mouth without waiting to be asked. Grandmother slaps the bully's hand.

While Grandmother tells stories, the bully sits transfixed. The bully is pulled backwards and forwards on the thread of Grandmother's telling. She sways this way and that, her mouth half-open to catch every word. Grandmother's words drop from her own mouth like ripe fruit. She stops frequently, chewing, tasting. Everyone else stops too. Our very breath stops. Grandmother moves her words from one cheek to the other. She watches our faces. She sees my mother's hands tremble, one hand curved inside the other, trembling. She watches the bully's back coiling tight as though ready to spring; waiting for Grandmother's next word to spring. For long minutes she keeps us waiting. Sometimes she will stop to write a charm, or flick through her store of hell money. Sometimes she will rise to shamble from the room. At other times she spits her story in a rush we strain to catch. Missing something, it is gone.

'What happened, Grandmother?' we cry. 'What happened?'

But Grandmother won't repeat that part of the story, not for what seems like forever, a month or two or three, if we're lucky. Grandmother will start another story, and another, before she goes back. After she has finished for the day her lips seal tight. I drop my pen, flex my aching fingers. Grandmother bends to peer at her notebook even though she can't make out the words. The bully also turns her disappointed face to the notebook as if the scribbled notes will continue the story halted too suddenly for the bully to bear. The bully fingers her own special scrapbook, in which she wants to fit all the stories so she can look them over by herself, at her own pace. So no one can make her stop. The bully plagues me to write in her scrapbook. Already my different-coloured scribbles thread their way between the pasted jungle leaves and earth once plucked or stepped on by the bully, the small pebbles once lodged in her shoe. The photos prised at random from her old photo album, alongside photos she has taken herself. Her scrapbook cover is made from glued together layers of tough cardboard so it will last forever. It is patterned with star and diamond shapes and strings of pearl so convent girls who see it will think it is filled with treasure; but even if they ask nicely, they will never find out.

'Write here,' the bully whispers after Grandmother has finished. 'Write here too.'

After Grandmother has finished, she takes her notebook from me, slips it back into its special case, to which only she has the key. She digs for her extra special notebook, the one being saved for the book she is going to one day write, using my notes. The extra special notebook is covered with red leather, stretched bright and smooth, soft as an animal, lovingly stroked. Its pages are edged with gold. After Grandmother has finished, her story curls around us on sugary threads. The bully sits licking her lips, fingering her scrapbook. The bully thinks she can taste Grandmother's story on her lips. She swallows greedily.

In my grandmother's house the bully seems to grow smaller. She shrinks to Grandmother's size. The bully's uniform, which the nuns make her wear even on weekends, flaps around her. Her voice loses its rumble, her shoulders no longer stretch taut. Girls at the convent can always tell the bully is coming by her smell, but here she smells only of soap and her crisply starched skirt. Her body sops up its other smells. In my grandmother's house the bully grows pale. She thinks she will fade away. She eats and eats to keep up her strength.

When my mother was a young woman she met another young woman walking in the street. The other young woman was the most beautiful woman my mother had ever seen. This was just before my mother became a Christian, just after her face gave up its struggle, losing the fight between its childhood badluck expression and the fierce black outlines Grandmother tried to train. After her face turned from sad into a tragic face. At first my mother hardly noticed the other young woman. My mother's feet dragged with exhaustion, her shoulders sagged miserably. Only sheer will held her body up. Even her stare into people's faces was a fish stare: fixed. When my mother met the other young woman, she had been walking, staring, for days. This was not unusual. In those days all manner of people walked the city streets outside curfew hours, stumbling, staring. Some walked bare-handed like my mother, others with hurriedly bundled possessions coming undone. Some could be seen stumbling through the city streets with heads wrapped in bloodstained cloths, arms bent at odd angles in slings. Anyone could be seen racing with shirts flapping ragged on their backs. Old men ran with suspected bandits from the scenes of looting and streetfighting, marketwomen dodged stray bullets alongside suspected communists. Rumour mongers snivelled amongst children. In shabby bands of threes and fours, or singly, all manner of cityfolk hurried around unexpected corners, their footsteps echoing the slamming of doors and windows, their faces bumped askew by the butt of a soldier's rifle keeping peace.

Head lowered, hair falling forwards to hide her face, my mother walked in parts of the city she had never before been. She stumbled through the twists and turns of the city's narrow backstreets where the smells of bodies overwhelmed her, of everyday living in cramped quarters, saltfish and prawn crackers laid out to dry. She spied latrines half-open, in which a child sometimes squatted amidst the buzz and swell of flies. The evening sunlight of these alleys, flapping through strung washing, hardly grazed my mother's cheek. She walked with steps trying not to seem too hurried, with shoulders hunched against recognition, against youths whispering in doorways, old men smoking under greasy awnings. Against soldiers in groups of four and five on routine checks from door to door. Shadowy peerings from slatted upstairs windows disappeared in a flurry of movement wherever she looked.

In those days it seemed to my mother she walked an endless twisting and turning, down blind alleys ending in sudden unimaginable openings, through markets where she was almost swallowed in the desperate rush for scanty vegetables, for wild and gamey meats. She brushed past this family heirloom, that family jewel going cheap. She refused slashed prices, ignored curses and pleadings both. My mother hardly noticed the old women and children wailing at roadside altars for their missing dead, the sudden barks of gunfire neither made her run nor duck. In those days she walked until her head began to spin, until the streets blurred one into another and everything and nothing seemed familiar. Surely this narrow bridge had been crossed but not this square of cracked pavings, and this laneway was unfamiliar, but this fringe of washing, this was surely remembered, the wind had reached it down to brush her face as she passed. My mother stopped to press her hands to her cheeks, to still the spinning. She did not know where she was. She had walked too long, stayed out too late. She stumbled forwards, then to her left, then right, then back the way she had come, the street around her spinning, spinning. All the years of Grandmother's training did not help. My mother did not know the way home. She had not noticed that the streets she walked were hurriedly emptying. Doors and windows shut on the curfew hour, side alleys gaped incurious at her frantic stare. The street she walked was empty except for her spinning. At the turn of a sudden corner my mother came upon a huddle of shadows crouched in the darker shadows against a wall. The last of the evening slatted pale bars of light across the alley. My mother stopped on the smell of smoke and metal, on the blacking of polished boots. She stared as the shadows uncoiled into a group of soldiers whose teeth gleamed around their cigarettes. Her hands curved to the shape of Grandmother's sign for demons: *Avert!*

'Out so late,' the soldiers murmured. 'Ah Girl, don't you know about curfew?'

'Come here!' the soldiers called as my mother stumbled away. 'Come and be nice!'

Ever since I was seven my grandmother, my mother and I have spent one day of the year by the sea. Each year we go to the same place, using the same route. At other times Grandmother avoids the sea like a plague, like a scaly-backed beast. When we ask to go there she raises her hand in warning. The sea is filled with spirits of all shapes and sizes, Grandmother says, which can be either harmful or benevolent, depending on their mood. Seeing them more often than one has to is asking for trouble. It's too big a strain.

'Why, Grandmother?' I ask. 'Are they more powerful than land spirits, and jungle spirits, and spirits who live in the wood of trees?'

'No,' Grandmother says. 'But sea spirits are more mysterious, if your own spirit is not from the sea.'

Every year my mother and I can tell when we are going to the sea. Although the time we go changes each year, we can tell by Grandmother's dreams.

'Wait!' Grandmother calls in her sleep, raising her arms in greeting. 'Wait first! What's the hurry?'

'Don't worry,' she calls. 'I'll keep my promise, I'll keep my side. Aiya, still plenty of time! No need to get angry.'

My mother sits beside Grandmother on these nights as she did at the closing of her extra eye. She grips Grandmother's arms that wildly flail.

'Aiya, she's not going anywhere!' Grandmother calls, reaching for my hands, fiercely gripping my wrists. 'Here she is!'

My mother loosens Grandmother's hold, shoos me from the room. Sometimes she sits with Grandmother all through her dream, and is still sitting, hunched over, grasping Grandmother's now quiet arms, when I stumble back in the morning. The light through the curtains dapples them now red, now green. Grandmother's snores ruffle the fine hairs on my mother's neck as she turns with her finger to her lips. In the coloured light they breathe as one. When I go to stand with my chin pressed to Grandmother's chest, she slowly opens her eyes. Her face is shiny, sweat diamonds glistening in the crevices around her nostrils, on her cheeks. Her blouse clings in sticky patches to her shoulders. She shakes my mother's hands away.

'Wah, so tired,' she says.

'Where did you go, Grandmother? Where?'

'To the sea,' she says, and we know it is time.

The place by the sea that we go to can only be reached on certain days, by following a certain path. Only Grandmother knows this path, which winds through the city in sharp twists and ever-narrowing circles, through sidestreets and deserted buildings, down main roads and alleys that no matter how

I try to memorise, look different every time. The place we arrive at is always the same. Here the sea sits flat and tepid, as brown as the melted coconut candy my mother shoves into my mouth to quiet me. The outlying islands make faint blotches through the heat haze southeast. Northeast there's only a faint grey line between sky and sea. The beach curves in a muddy arc on which pippi diggers crouch with their canvas bags and hooked sticks. My mother and I stand watching the oily lick of the waves as Grandmother busily sets up her altar. I kick at the picnic rubbish strewn around the bus stop sign.

'Can we take the bus back, Grandmother?' I bend to knead my aching legs. 'Can we?'

'Shut up,' Grandmother says. 'Come here.'

Following her directions I kneel before the makeshift altar with lighted joss sticks clasped between my palms. Grandmother digs into the heavy bag of offerings my mother has carried. She arranges the plates neatly, makes a pyramid of oranges on a circle of red paper cut with intricate shapes. My mother watches from a distance despite Grandmother's beckoning, one hand clamped over her head, a sudden wind lifting her hair. Grandmother's candles flicker wildly. I bow as she shows me and poke the joss sticks into the sand.

'Great Sea Spirits!' I chant when she signals, following her mouth shapes so I don't make a mistake. 'Your promised daughter has come to see you. She's come to pay you homage, she's brought you offerings so you'll know she hasn't forgotten you. Accept her humble thanks and offerings, O Great Sea Spirits, and send your promised daughter luck!'

Then Grandmother sets fire to wads of hell money and we jump away from the flare, the mad spiral of ash on the wind. All day we kneel at the altar, keeping watch, while my mother strolls along the beach talking to the pippi diggers, playing with other children, making footprints that fill with water and suck at her toes. We sit until my legs go numb, until Grandmother dozes and I try to creep away. Grandmother puts out her walking stick so I trip. 'Don't move!' she orders, her eyes still shut.

At sunset we are the last on the beach. Then Grandmother signals, and my mother begins to pack up the altar while Grandmother and I, starving, smacking our lips to see who can smack louder, devour the offerings. We tear the wings and legs off the fried chicken, squeeze orange juice straight down our throats, swallow my mother's sticky cake whole. 'Eat slowly,' my mother cautions, slapping my back when I choke. Every year she sits beside us, watching us eat. She watches, impassive, even when we dangle the food in front of her and rub our bellies, and breathe onto her face to show her what she has missed. My mother will not share the feast. She stares at Grandmother reproachfully, lips drooping, shoulders hunching under their badluck weight. Grandmother smacks her own lips. Before we go she turns to the sea, hands clasped respectfully.

'O Great Sea Spirits,' she cries, 'retreat to the deep ocean! Your children have paid you homage already. Do not try to follow them! They know your origin, with your great arms like tentacles, and the scales on the backs of your necks!'

Later, on the long walk home with Grandmother leading, hobbling ahead to show us the way, my mother pulls me towards her. She pinches my lips to stop any cry. 'Shh!' my mother whispers, marking my forehead with a cross.

'Hurry up,' Grandmother hisses, scanning the way we have come.

'Why so fast?' I drag my feet. But I too turn to look over my shoulder at the dark, which is full of sounds and shadows that at any moment may leap. I know my grandmother's worry, why she hobbles quickly, why she grits her teeth against the pain licking at her withered feet. Every year she tells me. Why she makes a path through the city so full of sharp twists and turns that even my mother and I, who can go around corners, have trouble keeping up. Grandmother is just being cautious, making sure nothing can follow us home.

But stumbling after her I twitch her sleeve. 'Why do we have to go there, Grandmother? Why?'

'Insurance!' Grandmother snaps.

When Grandmother was a young girl she never needed to run around making trouble. Grandmother never needed to climb up drainpipes waiting to jump on unsuspecting victims or hang from scrawny roadside trees pretending to be a hungry *pontianak* ghost. Grandmother never needed to run around looking for excitement like the bully and I do when the bully is visiting, loitering in backlanes to tease the local madwomen, racing to the sound of any commotion, bursting into the front room where Grandmother is dozing, to dance around her and shout: 'What shall we do next? What shall we do? We're bored, Grandmother! We're bored, bored, bored!'

When Grandmother was a girl she never needed to be entertained. Unlike my mother, the bully and me she never needed to go out strolling in the evenings, stopping for a gossip at every opportunity, marvelling at the neighbours' new possessions, their shiny Morris Minors, their imported hire-purchase furniture, their brand new black-and-white TVs. Grandmother never hung around the house listlessly knocking her feet against the bamboo chairs. She never stretched or yawned to show the back of her tongue, or whined every few minutes: 'Ma, give us some money! We've nothing to play with. We want a top from the breadman. We want an aeroplane that spins!' or 'Grandmother, tell us a story. Grandmother, wake up! Tell us a story, Grandmother, we're bored!' When my grandmother was a young girl she was never bored.

'Why, Grandmother?' I ask. 'Why was that so?'

'I just closed my eyes,' Grandmother says, 'and it happened. I didn't know what boredom meant.'

'What happened, Grandmother?' cry the bully and I, sitting

up from our slumped positions, pushing our bored fringes back from our bored-silly eyes.

'I'll show you,' Grandmother says.

When my grandmother was a girl she didn't have time to be bored. Grandmother wags her finger at the lazy bully and me, she shakes her fist to emphasise her point. My mother, busy ironing or washing or cooking, vigorously nods that it is true. When Grandmother was a girl she worked from morning till night. Did Grandmother get to go to a highclass school and sit around all day only doing occasional chores for payment, did she get her own books and pencils, and a coin for lunchtime, and free periods to do nothing but *contemplate*? Did Grandmother get weekends off? Unlike the lucky lazy bully and me, from the time she was a small child Grandmother woke up early every day. Grandmother rushed here and there when the sun was a mere pale disc, helping, always helping: rolling straws from waxpaper for a few cents a bundle, chopping meat and vegetables for the large family meals, kneading riceflour cakes for market the next morning. Grandmother's list of chores went on and on. Even at the rich man's mansion things weren't easy. Though the rich man liked her there were rules. The senior servants were to be obeyed, small punishments meted out as they liked. For the long periods of the rich man's travels the senior servants were left in charge. In the rich man's mansion Grandmother's sweat dripped in a puddle around her feet. Her back was bent with her labours, her eyebrows lowered from the weight of her frowns.

When my grandmother was a girl there was no neighbour's television to peep at through a hole in the dividing fence, no neighbour's humpbacked car to scrounge a ride in, no cockfights to sneak to at midnight when everyone is asleep. No passersby to be silently stalked and caught in unnatural poses for the bully's collection of candid shots. Neighbours disappear faster than their curses, they run with heads behind newspaper whenever the bully and I appear. When Grandmother was bonded to the rich man's mansion the entertainment was the players that came to his parties: the actors, acrobats and contortionists, the opera singers and dancing troupes. The servants crowded behind hidden partitions to watch. Sometimes Grandmother managed to squash a place for herself amongst them, but more often they pushed her away. 'Go away, Bad Smell!' they hissed. 'Get lost, Tell-Tale Cat! Take your smelly feet away!' So Grandmother went to sit alone in the dark kitchen, furtively sniffing at her feet. She carefully wiped her feet on the Number Two Kitchen Maid's favourite apron. She swung them under her bench in unhappy arcs. Then she closed her eyes.

Unlike the bully, my mother and me, endlessly bickering for a turn at the fence hole in the evenings, jostling for a glimpse of the shadow figures on the neighbours' rectangular screen, my grandmother was never so pathetic. Even as a young girl she wasn't one for jostling. Grandmother just had to sit quietly to hear a myriad whispered voices. She just had to close her eyes to see more than the fire-eaters and acrobats, the dancing girls like shadows leaping in black-and-white: to be taken somewhere else.

Unlike Grandmother my mother says the crocodile saying is nonsense: but she never says this where Grandmother can hear. The crocodile, my mother says, is a fantasy. Its power lies in the fury of its birth. This fury seethed for years beneath the surface, beneath the lidded eyes and tightened lips of the Lizard Boy as he was prodded this way and that, and his skin scraped at, his photo taken, his trousers peeked into to see if he was growing a tail. The fury was a seed at first, dormant, shuddering to life as his mother shuddered when asked to hold him, pushing forward as she pushed him away, growing as he grew, as he glanced up from his books and papers to see convent girls pointing him out to visitors, and nuns shushing, and parents craning to see.

'Better than the circus!' convent girls whispered loud enough for the Lizard Boy to hear. 'Better than the snake woman twined with serpents, and the stripy tigerboy, and the cowfaced girl!'

All this time, over the slow minutes, the months, the long circling years, the crocodile fury simmered. Is it any wonder that one day it finally boiled over, it burst? What a sight it was, my mother says, when the crocodile fury finally burst. That was the day the Lizard Boy ran amok.

Convent girls bolted screeching and screaming in all directions that day. They pelted from classrooms, through the gardens, over flowerbeds that later looked as though a herd of jungle elephants had trampled past. That day the convent hallways echoed with bumped furniture and doors slamming, a cacophany of screams and shouts.

'He's gone mad! He's coming!' convent girls cried, hearing the flatfooted slap of the Lizard Boy's feet in the corridors. 'Hide! Quickly hide!'

'Girls! Be calm, girls!' the teachers ordered, but the girls were already running here and there.

'Three girls stabbed in the middle field!' they wrung their hands in horror. 'The library on fire! Four girls strangled in the toilet block! Who will be next?'

The convent seethed that day. Even in the tucked-away laundry, the furthest corner of the convent where the voices and movements of the girls echoed only faintly, my mother froze midway in her work. Her hands half-lifted from the soapy water, her skin prickled. The convent classrooms were like fishbaskets in which convent girls thrashed and flipped. Their panic glimmered fishtail silver from one end of the convent to the other. Convent girls bumped into each other, they pushed desks and chairs crooked, grasped each other in a frenzy of fear. Their eyes shone feverish, their pink tongues pushed against their parted lips. Their voices quavered, throats trembling like the trembling throats of hungry young birds.

'Call me Lizard!' they heard the Lizard Boy shouting as he rushed from one group of girls to another, as he raced from class to class. The Lizard Boy's body glowed a fiery red. 'Lizard, hah? Look properly. Look at my teeth, glinting brightly! Look at my tail I can swish here and there like a whip! There's no lizard here, see—only—a—Crocodile!'

It took the caretaker, three teachers and two of the biggest, strongest nuns to catch the Lizard Boy. He ran with the speed of rabbits, dodged his pursuers with the agility of a fine young monkey and when finally cornered, turned to attack with the ferocity of a captured tiger. The Lizard Boy kicked and punched at the arms that grabbed him, he pushed furiously at the bodies that sat on him to keep him still. He sank his teeth into any hand, shoulder or thigh unwise enough to dangle within reach. His clenched fists kept up their staccato jabbing long after the thin bamboo rods and angsana branches that he'd ripped from the jungle to swish and beat at the convent girls were prised away. Water was thrown over him to cool his blood. His father, the caretaker, slapped mottled handprints onto both his cheeks, and his wrists and ankles were tied, and a rag wound round his head, so terrifying was his look that day. The Old Priest rushed to sprinkle holy water on his body. Then the Lizard Boy was half-dragged, half-carried to a quiet part of the convent where not many people went. Where convent girls would not see or hear him, and so would recover from the day's shock. Here he would be left until it was decided what to do. Here he was left to drag ragged breaths from the hot, moist air. To lie where a soapy runoff prickled bubbles around him, and think about his many sins, and the many punishments to come, and to rattle the chain that bound his feet to the laundry wall.

'Poor Godson,' the Old Priest stood shaking his head.

'Watch him,' the nuns ordered my mother, who came out of the laundry to look. 'Be careful, don't go near. Run and tell if he does anything wrong.'

'Control yourselves, girls!' they told the girls whose voices remained pitched and fevered for days afterwards, who became even more prone to fainting fits. 'Remember you are young ladies, girls!'

'A charity case,' the nuns soothed the parents who later rushed to the convent to see what went wrong. 'No one was in the *slightest* danger. It was just a highly strung child, who is being closely watched now.'

'Watch carefully,' they told my mother.

Years later, in the days my mother's spirit was weeping for her disappeared husband, the nuns gave her a little plaster saint every week. They gave her a little saint for every spiritual bridge my mother crossed on the long path to salvation, for strength along the way. Saint Christopher for dangerous crossings, Saint Lucy for eye and throat problems, Saint Joseph for a happy death. They listened with breaths held as she told of the vision of the beautiful woman that saved her, they murmured: 'How lucky! How lucky you are, dear child.' The vision of the Virgin Mary came to save both my mother's body and her soul. When the nuns discovered she was meant not for the spiritual but the family life they gave her Saint Gerard to preserve her in the dangers of motherhood and childbirth, to shield the child she bore and bring it safely into God's light. Even destined for the family life, the nuns let my mother continue her lessons with the Old Priest. The nuns gazed at her face, at her pale cheeks and lips drooping, they clasped their hands at the traces of the Virgin, the Queen of Sorrows, to be found there still.

This was the time the Old Priest was dying, although no one yet knew. At that time the Old Priest looked in the best of health, his old eyes radiant, his papery skin transparent from an inner glow. In certain lights his sparse white hair stood up in fiery sparks. My mother sat beside him in the afternoons, tears spilling from her eyes as she turned the pages of his Bible, which were damp from the tears and finger sweat of a thousand turnings. She stole glances at his joyful face. The Old Priest pointed to the faded tear marks. He asked my mother to press her fingertips there.

'These sorrowful tears,' he said, 'have turned to tears of joy.'

'How, Father, how?' my mother asked and asked, but the Old Priest could not say. Every now and then he turned to the small child lounging outside the chapel doorway. He raised one hand in greeting, nodded his head to show he remembered she was there. Every now and then he stared at a point just past my mother's left shoulder, his eyes lit like fire.

'I am coming,' the Old Priest said.

When the small child sidled towards him he cupped her face in his hand. The square-faced child stared suspiciously at my mother, opened her mouth in wide protest when the Old Priest reached for my mother's hand.

'Can you see it?' the Old Priest asked, grasping them both in a fiery grip, burning their faces with his stare.

'See—see what, Father?' my mother stammered.

'Evidence!' the Old Priest cried, but when they turned to look they saw only a bright mark of sunlight on the chapel wall. The mark glowed on the wall with the fierceness of the afternoon's fading, with the clarity of an opened door. The child's eyes narrowed while my mother's widened, my mother's filled with the Old Priest's joy.

'I see, Father,' she whispered, slipping to her knees, hands clasped in supplication. The light on the wall was blinding, like the light on the Virgin Mary's face.

'See what?' the child shouted, rubbing her eyes.

After my mother became a Christian, she no longer believed in shouting. She no longer believed in fighting. All the shouting and fighting of her girlhood, of Grandmother's training, dwindled away. My mother believed in a careful, watchful life. After she became a Christian she emerged clean and wholeskinned. Her voice became soft and gentle, her look a limpid query, never a glare. On the day she became a Christian the badluck howled and whimpered, leaping wildly, making my mother howl and whimper at the sight of the chapel cistern glistening full. My mother scampered on all fours, tried to creep under a pew. Her legs were swollen, her rounded belly squashed against her knees. The Old Priest, frail as he was, held her firmly. The nuns gripped her arms, pushed the hair back from her face. At the first touch of holy water the badluck shrivelled to a hump on her shoulders that she could hardly feel. My mother fell against the arms that held her. After she became a Christian she no longer believed the badluck demon ever crouched on her back. To her its antics became less than dreams. Unlike Grandmother she no longer believed in badluck, in fortune-telling by physical sensations, a tic in the right eye at 2 am meaning someone was thinking of her, a ringing in the left ear at 7 pm meaning money would soon be lost. She no longer joined in Grandmother's early morning exercises to strengthen the breath and promote balance; she no longer believed in the power of human breathing. My mother's faith was set in a more celestial draught.

Eyes raised to the plaster statues of Jesus and the Virgin nesting among the other figures on our family altar, hands clasped till her knuckles shone white, my mother mouthed fervent prayers of hope and reconciliation. She lived each day as if it was a gift of penance, as if saving for a holiday to be taken once dead. The weight on her shoulders was not a badluck demon but a trial from God, glass shattering at her touch, furniture sliding forwards to trip her, all were a test of patience: punishments sent for her sins. My mother's room is filled with religious icons peering from the tops of cupboards, from window ledges and side tables, even from under her bed. Every extra space in the laundry huddles a nest of saints the bully and I spend hours examining when my mother isn't there. The bully and I turn the heavy plaster in our hands, we push our fingers into saintly orifices, eyes and ears and noses, we colour lips pursed in saintly ecstasy with the pots of grease and tinted powders Grandmother lets us use. We streak ghost-frightening faces onto the saints, tiny faces powdered a ghastly white, coloured patterns drawn across pink cheeks. Shoeblack over the lifelike eyebrows, toothpaste above the lips. When my mother discovers our handiwork she flies into one of Grandmother's tempers but being a Christian, she doesn't shout and scream. She quickly returns to calm. She makes us carefully scrub the saints. The bully, my mother and I stand side by side at the laundry basin, singing hymns for penance, scrubbing saints.

Imagine this hill as it must have been all those years ago. They say it is an old hill that started as a lump no larger than my fist, that over the centuries grew. They say it has always been there, it is the root of the world in these parts, it was here that the Big One first moved. They say the hill is evidence of a long ago battle, long before the city became a city, before the time of humans, when the sea and land spirits first fought to grasp what they could of the world for land and sea. The spirits fought for a very long time, longer than human centuries. The land spirits sizzled molten lava at the sea spirits, heaved rocks larger than cities into their waters, the sea spirits ate at the ragged land's edges with typhoons and tidal waves, hurled fountains of water into the heavens to cause storms and floods. The spirits fought longer than human centuries with neither gaining the upper hand. Finally they agreed on truce and less violent competition. The spirit kings each sent forth the most beautiful and canny of their myriad daughters to a battle of wit and beauty instead of arms. Land and sea spirits of every shape and description gathered at their turbulent borders to witness the test. The sea king's daughter rose from the depths in a great wash of seaspray, a mountainside split open to usher the land princess out. Each stood with their handmaidens arrayed around them, each was dazzling to the sight. From the lips of each came the riddle-poems for which the city later became famous. Each promptly answered in kind. Questions and answers flowed from one to the other for longer than human centuries, from lips smiling sweetly, until the smiles were sweetly frozen and the sea king's daughter, eyes narrowing, reached into the depths of the sea, where sea serpents spun their wise and frightful secrets, for a riddle the land princess could not name.

Earthquakes marked the land king's fury, churning sea squalls the sea king's glee. The land princess stamped her foot, cracking the earth farther than human miles around her, which the sea king immediately flooded. In fury the land spirit king and all his minions swept into the split mountainside, the land princess was the last to follow. Halfway into the mountain she turned for a final hateful look. This part of the story, my grandmother says, is a lesson for ungrateful daughters who do not do as they're told, who stare out the window when they should be learning, who go walking in the city for days without saying where. Daughters who don't do what they're trained for, who don't win the fight! Grandmother says this wagging her forefinger at the bully and me, lashing my mother with her sideways look. So great was the land king's fury that the split mountainside closed on his half-entered daughter, it swept its boulders over her feet and sank her halfway into the ground. Earth crept over her above-ground body, bitter vegetation dug in their roots. The half-sunk land king's daughter hardened to green-fringed boulders and veined rock, to a hill the shape of a woman turning, to stand the centuries turning, watching the gloating festivities of the sea spirits through time. The sea spirits gorged themselves on the land king's territory, their kindred river spirits streaked his vast inland with fast-flowing streams and sluggish rivers to shape the world in these parts to the world it is today: a maze of islands southeast of the city, northeast the open sea. An inland crisscrossed with water like the lashes of a whip. For the future city's landmark: a princess-shaped hill. And though a time longer than human centuries has passed neither the sea spirits nor those of land have forgotten their long ago battle, neither the land's resentment nor the mockery of the sea; sea and land in these parts have ever since been enemies who will snatch and claw at each other, and steal from each other what they may. So the children and minions of the land and sea, who later evolved into humans, are age-old enemies. So says the city's oldest and most famous legend, which every city child knows.

Other legends insist the hill is the humped back of an old sleeping reptile pushed up through a crack in the earth, a dragon which will stir and heave if anyone pricks its back in the right spot. The jungle spirits move this spot around to fool humans. Before scratching or digging in the jungle humans must ask their permission, otherwise the place they scratch or dig will be that spot. When the dragon awakens: calamity. The nuns say the jungle-covered hill has always been a hiding place for troublemakers, bandits and other bad elements, although they can remember a lull in the Wars when the soldiers all but wiped out trouble, and the hill became a quiet retreat in which girls could contemplate the glory of God through nature. Simple cityfolk claim the hill is the dwelling place of the numerous war dead who, clamouring for justice in their great numbers, have made the local deities leave for a less crowded place, the gods of thunder and lightning, of fire and fruitfulness, of earthquake and the seven hundred winds. That's why simple cityfolk have fallen on bad times, on food queues and rations and thieves and bandits and ever higher taxes, and soldiers crowding the city streets. My grandmother says the hill is the site of great danger. Grandmother says this to the bully, tilting her head. Grandmother winks broadly, but the bully doesn't see. The hill is the site of a long-buried treasure, Grandmother says, which can only be found by someone who possesses great courage, who knows the jungle paths and is neither afraid to walk with beasts nor sleep in moonlight. Someone who can run with the hairy hill spirits, who can follow where they go. Someone who can gather saliva in times of great danger and change her face to spite the wind.

Grandmother says: *When I was a young girl I was brought to live in a house on a hill. I was bonded to the house as a servant because my family had too many girls. When my mother handed me over my body was slippery with tears. 'Be good, useless girl,' my mother advised. 'If you're bad, your new master will throw you into the jungle, and the wild animals will chew you up. No one will hear you crying. I've told him we don't want you back. If you try to come home, I'll take you to the jungle myself. That will be your fate. Aiya,* stop crying! Try to be good.' My mother tore herself from my clinging arms and rushed away without looking back. She left behind her a faint smell of my family's crowded life in the city, of bodies huddled in a tired sleep, of onions frying and children racing around a cluttered space, giggling for no reason. I breathed so deeply I thought I would be filled forever with my past life, I thought my lungs would burst. The house on the hill was next to the jungle, at night I could hear the sounds of wild animals creeping and crashing. Their cries made me jump and shiver, I slept with my eyes open for fear. I trembled in my sleep. The rich man who owned the house was fond of me. He was always kind. He made sure the other servants gave me enough to eat and sometimes he even let me ride on his shoulders. Sometimes my laughter echoed through the house. The rich man used to be a sailor. He came from far away. Long ago he ran away to sea. He was no longer young, he'd made his fortune years ago, but still he walked the house like a sea captain. His gaze was a restless scan of the horizon, he stood with legs braced apart as though straddling a great sea. Whenever the rich man was in the house I felt the weight of his body in the whole house, through the walls and floorboards, around the pillars behind which I stood. Behind the pillars I watched his every move. I echoed his movements with my own young body, I curved my shoulders to the curve of his shoulders, brushed my hand across my forehead in the arc of his hand. I felt the rich man's weight in my dreams. These dreams started suddenly. Before they started I dreamt only of the things I knew. The city streets of my memory, the jungle edges that were dark and terrible, the passages of the house in which I lived. One night, suddenly, I dreamt the paths of the sea: the circling waves, the winding routes of tall-masted ships. The trails of sea creatures now rising to the surface, now cruising the deep. Sharp sea winds filled my nostrils, churning seastorms quaked my bed. I saw ships tossed on waves like the giant waves I made with the palm of my hand to send my paper boats swirling. The more I dreamed the more violent were the storms. I saw ships break

*into pieces, people blown on the winds like tiny dried sticks.
I saw ships heave and swirl and dip. Strange shapes rising from
the waters, teasing, slipping back. I saw the rich man braced
on the prow: the white of his knuckles on the railing, the curve
of his body leaning over the side. The rich man was peering.
He was smiling, pointing. Men rushed to obey the cries that
were snatched from his lips before I could hear them. They
threw ropes over the side and tied a rope around the rich man's
waist that was thicker than both my wrists. The rich man
clambered over, tossed this way and that. The taste of the
midnight sea made me quiver. The heat of his strokes into
the dark water broke my body into sweat. His hands reached
for a shape caught in a watery spiral downwards, a fish shape,
smooth and fleeting. The rich man caught the shape mid-
spiral, discerned arms and torso, a gown that tangled, a
slippery skin. The sharp glint of a knife. The rich man gripped.
He pulled. The catch of breath in his throat scraped at my
throat. The suck of the sea on his mermaid shape almost pulled
my arms from their sockets. My feet thrashed wildly in bed.
In the rich man's arms the shape bucked and struggled, it
hammered its fists against him to claw at his face. The knife
pinned between them marked a crisscross pattern on his chest.
The sea entering the rich man's body chilled him to the bone.
Saltwater stung his eyes. Storm bubbles whirled around his
head. The shape plunged downwards, struggling to the call
that lures drowned sailors, to the dance of a watery death.
The rich man gripped. His prisoner breath pounded in his chest
for release. In his arms the shape was turning, was a shape
now suddenly long and scaly, now bloating, now ridged with
spikes. Still the rich man gripped. His underwater grimace was
a smile. His fingers on the dragon-shape, the reptile-shape,
the fish-shape eased themselves around a single scale. The rich
man gripped. He wrenched hard. Such were the dreams of the
drowning, of the breath pounding for release. In his arms the
shape was suddenly still. Long sodden hair tickled the rich
man's face, tendrils slipping like arms to encircle his neck. In
sleep my arms tore the tendrils from my neck. The rich man*

kicked upwards. He broke surface, released his gasping breath.
The men in the ship were signalled with a triumphant wave.
As one they heaved. They plucked the rich man and his burden
from the grasp of the sea.

FAINT SOUNDS OF BRUSHING, BREATHING

When the lover emerged from the rich man's quarters, it seemed to everyone who saw her that her eyes were dark pools of red. The lover emerged wearing a gown which covered her from neck to ankles, even her head was covered, and part of her face. All people could see were her eyes. The lover's eyes swelled in their sockets, red-ringed and glinting, darting left and right as she walked. Gold threads on her headshawl glittered when she turned her head. The lover stopped on the threshold of the rich man's quarters to meet the servants lined up in greeting.

'This is the Mistress,' the rich man said shortly. 'From today you'll see to her every comfort. You'll understand that her every wish is mine.'

The lover's eyes darted from one blank face to another. Under the shawl her head moved in sharp jerks. All her movements were jerky, like one whose joints are stiffened.

Like one newly learning to move. The lover walked with swaying steps. At every step it seemed she was almost stumbling, and the rich man reached out to block her fall. He hovered around her, his hand never leaving her elbow, his voice ringing out with orders and directions. The softest pillow for the couch on the balcony, a cool drink against the heat of the evening, a servant to stand wafting a sweet-smelling fan. The rich man's eyeglass to be placed on a table close at hand. Every step the lover took towards the balcony seemed an enormous effort. When a sudden jungle breeze fluttered back her headshawl, it seemed to everyone that her face was too pale for health or beauty. It seemed her eyes were much too big. The lover's eyes were as red as bleeding. Her hair clung in streaks to the sides of her face. Her forehead was beaded with a fine perspiration, her lips too red to be natural, her eyes fever bright. The lover's eyes swelled and dripped with a steady trickling.

When she emerged from the rich man's quarters it seemed to everyone who saw her that her days, her nights were numbered. That her days and nights were spent endlessly sobbing, her lips chewed to a weeping red. The senior servants' practised words of welcome fell like stones from their mouths. The lover passed without a word, without a sign. They watched her slow progress to the balcony without drawing a single breath. When her eyes met theirs, they lowered them shyly, shamefully, as though seeing something forbidden, though who forbade them they couldn't say.

'Shade her,' the rich man snapped. 'Her eyes are infected. Hurry! She cannot stand the light.'

When the lover's eyes healed everyone agreed they were mistaken. To think from those brief sideways glances that the lover's eyes were scary, to suppose she looked like one already dead! Servingwomen chosen to wait on her brought trays laden with rich foods carefully arranged to tempt her poor appetite, they folded back her covers and plumped out her cushions, begged permission to brush her hair. The lover's brushed hair spilled in a shiny mass over the sides of the bed. She looked small and helpless amidst the plumped-out cushions, even her frown was ineffective. Her averted face refused the proffered foods and medicines, her hands pushed at the servants' plumping and fussing, and the rich man's hovering, the rich man's hands that sometimes swooped to pat and stroke.

Even with her eyes completely healed the lover lay for long months on the balcony, some days, some weeks, hardly stirring. A makeshift awning kept out the worst of the heat and light, but·even when the afternoons were at their hottest, when the rich man begged and pleaded, the lover refused to be moved. Some days she was a weight the rich man could hardly move. Even on the hottest of days her skin was cold. Brushing against her by accident sent shivers through the servants' bodies, and they dropped to their knees beside her, they slapped at her hands and feet, grumbling their worry and affection, rubbing vigorously to warm her blood. Long before the lover recovered enough to walk without the rich man's assistance, long before she descended the stairs to his resumed parties with her hair flowing behind her and everyone gaping, she had already won the hearts of the rich man's household. A mistress at last, and one so beautiful, look at those eyes, that hair, who would have guessed it, a new mistress, and one so frail, and fair! The rich man watched as each servant tried to outdo the other, as they took great pains to guess her wishes, and cracked their brains thinking of amusements and comforts, new ways to make her well. To make her say a word. Like the rich man they learnt to read her face in place of a voice, the lift of her eyebrows, the nose wrinkling, the eyes opening wide. The rich man hardly left the lover's side. He sat in an armchair beside her, his own face grown pale and shadowy, an unread book creased open on his lap. The rich man took to sleeping in the armchair, his limbs in sleep sprawled with a careless grace. Awake, his eyes never left her face. When he woke to see her staring he started, he blinked, immediately he leaned forward to smile.

The lover shrank into her pillows. With each passing day she grew stronger. Soon the flaps on her balcony awning could be lifted to allow a glimmer of light. Soon she could hold the heavy eyeglass herself. She scanned the horizon, the infrequent bumps and domes of the city, the fuzz-topped jungle to see what lay beyond. She could not see what lay beyond. The lover shuddered, replaced the glass. She leaned forward, breathing deep. Always her breath held a faint rasp. When the servants finally managed to coax a smile with their jokes and antics, when they saw her pick at her food with a semblance of enjoyment, and stir from her bed of her own accord, one foot to the hesitant floor, then the other, then only did they put away their joss sticks and life talismans, their healing spells. Only then did they unwind their goodluck amulets from her bed and her balcony awning, and scrape away their death-fooling charms. When the lover smiled, when she touched her cold hand to theirs, rich man or servingwoman, regardless of their station, the one who was smiled at, whose hand was touched, was filled with an overwhelming kindliness, an immeasurable delight.

Only my grandmother stood watching from the hidden corners of the rich man's mansion, from the ragged, ringing edges of his laughter that echoed throughout so there was no escape. Only she lay tossing and turning to the unbearable melancholy of the lover's night-time sighs. She stood with her head poked out from behind pillars and around sharp corners, refusing to enter the lover's intoxicating circle even when she beckoned, even when she reached out her hand. My grandmother stood firmly planted at least a room or a pillar or wall away. She could not bear to meet the lover eye to eye, could hardly bear to look at her. Grandmother leapt from the path of the lover's shadow. But still she watched. My grandmother watched everything in the rich man's mansion with her fists clenched and her lips screwed up disdainfully. Her eyes were narrowed to a knife-cut, a glinting slice.

Grandmother says: *The world is full of gods, humans and ghosts. Gods and ghosts alike have different levels of importance and official standing. Like humans they are open to flattery and bribery, and have to be handled carefully. Some ghosts are stuck to the earth, some go to the heavens, others go anywhere they like. The ghosts most humans see are low-level spirits who stick around from confusion, from hunger and desire, who have unfinished business to do. Captured spirits also remain, though some forget they were ever inhuman. Never think you can avoid the spirits of the dead. Life is a continual struggle against the powers of the dead, who will torment the living until their wishes are fulfilled. The most troublesome ghosts are those who have taken their human natures beyond death. These want worship, sacrifice, sometimes even a marriage. Hungry ghosts are earthbound spirits who are abandoned by their families, or those who have died suddenly and violently, or drowned at sea. Food turns into ashes in the mouth of a hungry ghost. A hungry ghost's mouth knows no bottom. Have many children, have filial grandchildren. A hungry ghost with no descendants to feed it roams the streets making trouble while ghosts with reverent families are placid, sleepy from bellies that are always full. Some ghosts retain slivers of their human memory, which gives them disjointed human speech. Others know the secrets of changing shape. Others love to use the telephone. Never answer a phone call at three in the morning. This is the time when* yin *is at its strongest and you can be sure it's a ghost ringing up for a chat.*

In the days before the convent became a convent, my grandmother used to stand on the balcony of the rich man's mansion, leaning her elbows on the cool marble, pushing her knees between the curlicued rails. Grandmother absent-mindedly rubbed her knees against the railings to loosen her scabs. Her knee scabs made swirly patterns on which she would blow and pick. Grandmother shaded her eyes against the afternoon sun. Her eyes were wide and round-shaped in those days, unlike the narrow slits peeping from loose skinfolds that nowadays are her eyes. Grandmother's eyes sparkled. She was in between ages at that time, almost fourteen years at the count of the calendar, no longer a child, not yet a young woman, at that in-between time given to bouts of melancholy and heightened sensibility that would eventually fade away. So the rich man said when the other servants grumbled. 'Leave her alone,' the rich man said. So the other servants grumbled, and let Grandmother be.

Every afternoon Grandmother went to stand on the rich man's balcony. She went only in bright sunlight, when the lover's awning flapped empty in the afternoon breeze. The lover's awning was hung with beaded scarves and cloths intricately woven, it made a tent like the strange tents of my grandmother's imagination, the drawings in the rich man's travel sketchbooks, the handcoloured postcards of the faraway places he showed her in the days she was called to his side. Grandmother skirted the lover's tent. She looked and breathed in its opposite direction. The lover's tent with its glinting scarves and salty tang hurt her eyes and nose. She stood, back turned, on the balcony that was now her special waiting place usurped. Now the rich man never sent for Grandmother. He merely smiled, he flicked her hair carelessly as he passed.

Every afternoon my grandmother stood on the rich man's balcony, pointing her body in the direction of the city, craning to see. It seemed to her the city changed its size and shape almost daily. The city swelled in different places, now on this boundary, now that, ballooning in one direction for weeks at a time. Then the balloon tattered and the city surged in another direction, trailing behind it a wash of multicoloured debris. As Grandmother watched it pushed seashell-coloured blocks against the horizon, it raised shimmering columns. It grew flat patches of lawn and pushed back its jungle edges with rows and rows of colourful shacks. Grandmother leaned against the balcony rail watching the puff of the different-coloured smokes from the different-coloured smokestacks, and the lazy flock of razzle dazzle kites drifting on a breeze. Her bare feet tapped on the marble floor. Her back was turned to both the lover's tent and the jungle, deliberately. Even with her back turned Grandmother felt the surge of the jungle. Even in the afternoons she felt the icy aura of the absent lover, she felt the jungle coldness seeping to claw at her back. She heard the deep-throated menace of the myriad wild beasts. Even standing in strong sunlight with sweat beads dappling her cheek, Grandmother shuddered. Under the lover's awning she knew the air was cold. She turned her shoulder and tapped her feet as if she was walking, walking.

The lover was like a flower in a glass jar. A tear from her was a diamond, a smile like the rarest jade. Her skin was pale like lilies, her hair like the rippling sea. Her teeth charmingly beaded, her movements awkward yet graceful, her body like a body out of its element. Even the smallest movements tired her. The lover was often still. She lay coiled on couches and sofas, silent, limbs serpentine. When people spoke her eyes seemed empty, her gaze moved restlessly from face to face. When people looked at her directly her eyes widened in fright. The lover's eyes were entrancing. When she stared a whole room was moved to silence, to nervous coughs, a fluttering of handkerchiefs. Then the rich man laughed and the spell was broken, he smiled and took the lover's hand. In the photo he ordered taken, their side-by-side portrait, the lover's eyes gaped black. The lover's eyes looked large enough to swallow the night. At night she walked the rich man's house from room to room, listening to the breaths that circled the sleeping air, and the night-time creaks of the building, the windows tap-tapping to the tune of a jungle wind. She listened to the walls breathing.

The lover was like marble, like polished stone. When the rich man wrapped his underwater arms around her he discovered a scaly ridge over her backbone. He slipped his hands upwards, dug his fingers into the ridge on the back of her neck. The knife caught between them scraped skin and flesh from his chest. The sea entering his body chilled him to the bone. In the wide-eyed dream of the drowning the rich man clawed at the back of the lover's neck: tore out a single scale. In his arms she was suddenly still. When the rich man plucked her from the sea he discovered her back laced bloody from the tear. He lost his heart immediately. The lover was as weightless as a shadow draped over his arm. In his cabin she lay like one dead. Her breath was a rattle heaving infrequently past lips turned blue, her chest a bruised mass marking the rich man's frenzy, the rich man's determined pumping and squeezing to make her breathe. The rich man brushed aside the others' sighs of no hope, no hope. He sent everyone away. 'I have you,' he whispered with each thrust of his arms and shoulders. 'You will live. I have you. You won't escape. You will breathe. You will live.'

Saltwater bubbled from the lover's mouth in a reddish gurgle, and then her sobbing breath. Under closed eyelids her eyes flickered reluctantly. The rich man eased the wet gown from her, wrung out her long black hair. The gown clung to the lover, it came away only with tugging, with a sound like skin tearing from skin. The rich man carried her to his bed. The touch of her skin was numbing. He pulled the bedcovers over her, rubbed at her arms and hands, her pale cheeks. His own hands shivered as he poured brandy down her throat, as he wiped the liquid leaking from the corners of her lips. The rich man threw down the glass as the lover's breath gurgled more and more unsteadily. He peeled off his own wet clothes, climbed under the covers to stretch his body against hers. To wind himself around her like a warmer skin. The cold of the lover's body sucked at him hungrily. The crisscross cuts over his heart ached, but did not bleed. The rich man forced his warm breath past the lover's lips, parted sharp teeth with his tongue. His tongue curled involuntarily, parting ice. He dug his fingers into her, sank his teeth just enough to hurt into her soft, cold neck. 'Wake up,' the rich man murmured. 'No more sleeping, no more dreaming the deep.'

The lover was a flower in a glass jar. Even wrapped around her the rich man felt they did not touch. He could not make her warm. For days she lay gurgling her shallow breath. The rich man crawled from the bed, he picked at his salt-crusted clothes, discovered the scale in one pocket, the knife tangled in the cloth of his coat. The scale was no more than hardened skin, a fingernail, half the size of the rich man's thumb; green in lamplight, shimmering like pearl. The knife winked cold and gemlike, its blade not quite the length of his palm. The rich man wrapped both scale and knife in his handkerchief, slipped the bundle into a trunk and turned the key. He dressed in clean clothes, pulled a chair beside the bed to watch. He circled the room, studying the lover from different angles. He turned this way and that; ran his fingers over her curves and sharp edges. One day, days later, he woke to see her looking directly at him. Her eyes were fish eyes, unblinking. The roll of the sea made everything swing slightly, but the lover's eyes were steady. Her eyes dripped with a steady trickling. The rich man's own prickled in response, the breath that was caught in his throat for hours, for the long days waiting, came out in a rush, in a sudden whoop of joy. The lover started at the rich man's voice, her hands groped to cover her face.

'Don't be afraid,' the rich man said.

The rich man named the lover Lily, after the flower that makes people forget their troubles. He stayed beside her day and night, listened to her breathing, wiped at her trickling tears. Every night he listened for the lock of the cabin door from outside. All night his manservant kept watch. At the rich man's call he swung back the heavy bolt. More than once the rich man woke in the morning, or the middle of the night, to find the lover crumpled at the door. The rich man drew her to bed. The lover's eyes darted from left to right, to the door, the porthole, the rich man's face, the bed, the corners of the cabin. She pushed weakly at the rich man's arms. Her eyes were rich with pleading. Her arms coiled around his neck like a candlesmoke coil to the ceiling, like her smell as he stooped to lift her, the cloying saltiness, the memory of the breath pounding for release. The rich man breathed deeply.

'Body and soul,' he murmured, stroking her hair. He pulled the covers to her chin.

When my grandmother was an older girl in the ghosthouse,

when her arms and legs had lengthened and her body thickened, her face narrowed from its childish roundness to her bony Grandmother's face that even in girlhood bore the marks of her coming age and wisdom, everyone in the rich man's house was afraid of making her angry. Grandmother's angry face was a dark and purplish red. Her angry eyes narrowed to slits the other servants saw glinting out of the dark. Her fits of temper shuddered her whole body, they loosened her joints so she looked dislocated, turned her eyes in their sockets so her glare was a chalky shine. Grandmother's glare sent shivers wherever it darted. Her hands reached for any object to be hurled in any direction, her legs shot here and there in a frenzied swirl.

'Take her away,' the rich man ordered, staring at Grandmother. 'The girl's hysterical.'

In those days everyone was nervous of offending Grandmother. Grandmother was now equal size with the other servants. She could look them in the eye. One of her eyes was larger than the other; hers was the three-quarter stare of a bird of prey. The older servants no longer mercilessly teased her, no longer did they set her the most unpleasant tasks, or pick and bitch until her eyes prickled and her mouth set itself in a constant scowl. The other servants merely whispered *Master this, Master that*, and fell silent whenever she came near. In those days the rich man's house became unruly. The senior servants lamented the loss of the old shipshape days, the weekly household meetings, the spotchecks and tiptoeing, the obedient underservants and pride taken in every household task. They longed for the fearful scoldings in the bookroom when anyone dared to break the rich man's rules, the culprits crouching for hours in the dark of the old punishment room, the methodical flick of a bamboo stick. In those days even the basement room, the old punishment room, was changed. The rich man ordered it cleaned and painted, the servants huffed and panted edging into it a large canopied bed.

In those days the rich man grew preoccupied. The running of his household and business held only faint interest; his foreign manservant, a crafty character, arranged everything. To him the rich man pointed when the servants came with their queries and complaints. The rich man left the lover's side only to supervise the construction of the funicular railway to the hilltop pavilion he perched on the green-fringed boulders of the city's oldest landmark, the head of the woman turning that could be seen far out at sea. The railway was built from the finest materials, its cars decorated with mythological creatures, the pavilion carved from the hardest jungle woods. Any obstruction to the seaview was cleared. The rich man and his lover stood staring at the view. The faint fishing boats bobbing on the horizon trembled her in his arms. The rich man held her tightly. Every evening Grandmother listened for the pull of the railway cables, its grinding wheels. She stood with her ear to the door of the rich man's quarters, which the servants were hardly allowed to enter, hardly allowed to clean. The servants stared in horror at the stacked-up dishes crusted with leavings, the stained wineglasses, the books and clothes littering the floor.

Even the rich man's attire became careless, his face was unshaven, his fingernails no longer clipped and polished neat. The lover wore her hair unbound, she wore nothing but her shimmering white gown. They emerged only to lounge under her balcony awning, or to pace the night gardens, or preside over the rich man's increasingly extravagant parties, the laughings and whirlings and clappings that became increasingly unrestrained. Only before the parties did the rich man and the lover submit to tidying, only then did they sit silently facing each other as the servants fussed and grumbled, as they powdered and smoothed, and twitched fine clothes over their shoulders, and dressed their hair. The rich man and the lover leaned their bodies towards each other, their eyes unblinking. Occasionally one or the other smiled, and their smiles made the servants even more gloomy. Their smiles swallowed each other. Occasionally the rich man led the lover, her feet dragging, her hands grasping at wall or banister, down to the basement room. Soon even the famous parties became a rarity.

Now riffraff outnumbered the city's patrons, anyone could enter, anyone at all could trail their curious way through the brightly lit rooms. Soldiers were no longer hired for the evening, poor cityfolk pressed gaping against the window glass. City urchins sneaked sweetmeats into their ragged pockets until the servants caught them and threw them out. By morning the rich man's house was a mess, precious silverplate and statues were stolen, furniture damaged, brawls broken out amongst those reluctant to leave. Soldiers came to inform the rich man that his party licence was revoked.

In those days, when my grandmother was an older girl, the younger servants watched her with awe. Those days Grandmother cared nothing for the rich man's parties. She did not care to dance. The red pyjamas still wafting her long ago fairy dancing no longer fitted her. When Grandmother spun in private it was an awkward, lonely spin. In those days she wandered the rich man's house in a stupor, she dodged shadowy from room to room. No one ever knew exactly where she was, and she was openly defiant, she came only when the rich man called. But the rich man hardly ever called. Grandmother lounged about his bookroom, halfheartedly playing with the dusty toys, the antique clocks in need of winding. The other servants left her to herself. When they saw her coming they lowered their voices. They turned and went another way.

'What is it?' Grandmother asked and asked, but no one would tell. When she saw their unguarded faces she felt a twinge of fear. 'What's the matter?' she cried.

In the kitchen she ran to the Number Two Kitchen Maid, her cruellest tormentor when she was a smaller girl, but the woman only set her mouth and turned her back. Grandmother rushed at that turned-away back. She dug her nails into that broad bent back, scraped furrows in the coarse material of the woman's shirt. The woman's shriek sent Grandmother flying. 'Aiya!' the woman screamed. 'Help! Help me! She's killing me!' Grandmother was thrown into a corner. She was

so angry she did not see the arms rushing to hold her back.
She did not hear the voices calling for patience, or the younger
servants thrusting themselves between her and the other
woman. Grandmother saw only the woman's face reddened,
her lips twisting, her hands snaking forwards in claws.
Grandmother was so angry her mouth leaked bubbles that
scorched her chin. Her hair stood on end, her fingers trembled
as she raised her hand.

'I curse you!' Grandmother cried in a voice hoarse with
anger. 'You hear me, Number Two Kitchen Maid? One day
you'll come crawling, one day it won't be you turning your
back!'

The woman pushed back her dishevelled hair. She grabbed
the nearest object, a frying-pan ladle, and rushed towards
Grandmother. 'You beast!' she swung the ladle with all her
might. 'Dirty beast, take that! Aiya, why do you think we
avoid you? Look behind you! Look over your head!'

'You've killed her!' the kitchen workers cried, but already
Grandmother was rising, already her hand cupped over the
lump on her head felt that there was no blood. Already
Grandmother turned to look. Above her head dark shadows
were swirling. Dark shapes were twisting into each other with
a surge and hiss of air. The air broiled above her, at any
moment sticky streams of darkness would spill onto her head.
Grandmother stared for a moment, then leapt to her feet. The
other servants stumbled as one to the opposite end of the
kitchen, their eyes were rice bowls, their mouths fallen open.
Grandmother beat at the shadows with her hands. She raced
from the kitchen on unsteady feet, staggering against the walls
and kitchen furniture. She ran shrieking like the future
caretaker and his family from the future ghosthouse, like her
future clients when chased by ghosts. The shadows swirled
after her like shots from a cannon, like a flapping of wings.

Ever since I was seven there is one night of the year that my
grandmother sits wakeful, watching my sleep. On this night
the wind howls through cracks in the shuttered windows, the

rain slaps at the doors like someone knocking. My grandmother's hair sticks to her forehead in wispy strands. As we walk back from the sea I am so tired I fall asleep on my feet. First my mother supports me, shaking me, pinching my cheeks. Then she half-drags, half-carries me the rest of the way. At home I slump into my corner like one dead, and my grandmother watches me. When I wake she says I have slept for a night and a day.

'Wah, so tired,' I murmur.

'Where did you go?' Grandmother demands. 'Tell me what you saw.'

'I went into the jungle,' I say. 'I walked on a path that curved like a sickle moon. As I walked the jungle grew close, the trees lowered their branches, the trunks and leaves were the colour of jungle water: dark with secrets. I could not see the sky. My feet dragged on the path, my body on the air which pulled at my skin. The air stopped in my throat, too heavy to breathe. I was pulled this way and that. My face contorted. Strange birds flashed past me, brightly coloured, as smooth as stone. I heard a rustling through the trees and hollow sounds, like the slap of hands on water. I saw dark shapes gliding through the undergrowth. Behind me shadows surged and loomed, disappearing when I turned to look. The shadows breathed now fierce, now gentle on the back of my neck. At the sickle curve the path ended suddenly. It ended at a mound on which a beautiful woman stood. The woman's shimmering gown fountained round her feet. I could not see her feet. Her black hair swept the earth behind her. She was the most beautiful woman I had ever seen. On her head was a crown, a weaving of light. In a half-circle around her were attendants, girls and women threaded in jungle mist, their faces hidden except for here, the flicker of an eyelid, there a sudden glint of teeth. Behind them darker shapes loomed: humpy barnacled shapes. The woman's eyes were soft with weeping. Her skin was as smooth and pale as the statues in the convent chapel, and like them she held out her hand. She smiled. I reached to take her hand.'

Here Grandmother's vice-like grip on my hand stops me. Her twisted fingers feel like wood, her nails bite into my skin.

'You didn't touch her?' she anxiously asks.

'No, Grandmother.'

'You must never touch her,' she raps the side of my head so I won't forget. 'Do you understand? Never.'

Every year I sit rubbing my head, rubbing my palm on my smarting head in small circles. Every year I ask: 'Who is she, Grandmother? Who?'

'She's an evil demon,' Grandmother says, 'inhuman. She feeds on young girls and men. You must never touch her. Aiya, Grandmother has seen the demon with her own eyes! First she will eat you from inside out until nothing is left but your hollow body, growing thinner and thinner. Then she will bare her teeth and eat your flesh. She will cover your body with teethmarks, nothing will be left but your punctured skin.' And Grandmother's lips will draw into a line, and Grandmother won't say any more.

Ever since I was seven I have had the same dream, over which my grandmother sits watching. Every year, although I don't tell her, I have moved further along the path. I am closer to touching the beautiful woman's hand.

Nowadays everyone is afraid to walk out alone, especially young girls, and no young girl would ever think of walking the convent, let alone the jungle or the city, at night. Not even in their dreams. This is what the nuns say. No good young girl from a good family will consider such a thing. Even the night-time convent, a holy place, has come on hard times. Even here convent girls might see things they had better not. A swirling of fairy dancers around the courtyard, mimicking the swirl of nuns' skirts. A man covered with teethmarks whom naughty convent girls up and about at midnight swear they have seen. A beautiful woman clasped to his breast. How much more terrible unholy places are! The jungle and the city are filled with enemies which may be seen even in the light of day. They are filled with dangers that tangle their paths and streets and walkways, making their very air sharp. Pitfalls lurk around every tree and corner, each bush or doorway conceals a possible trap. Raking claws hidden in dense foliage; an old woman spinning coins on the palm of her hand, beckoning girls into rooms where crocodiles come to bid. A crocodile lounging behind a tree or under an archway, mesmerising young girls with his stare. Lifting his knife to rip their skirts. At night good convent boarders lie rigid in their convent beds with arms crossed over their breasts, whispering As-I-lay-me-down-to-sleep with their legs stretched neatly under the convent blankets and their night-gowns arranged so no wrinkle will snag in the folds of their bodies, no skirts ride up to expose young bellies rising and falling in sleep.

At night the bully creaks her bed amidst the snores and snuffles of the other boarders. The bully pushes back her blanket on which jungle flowers tangle like the path the bully tiptoes past the lumps of all shapes and sizes that in the daytime turn into convent girls. The floorboards creak under her feet, and she shivers not from the breeze blowing through the half-open shutters, filling the dormitory now with city smells then jungle smells then city then—the bully shivers with anticipation. Her camera swings on its strap, the special speed film bulging her side.

When I hear the bully reaching the darkroom I am supposed to scratch my nails against the floor like the scratchings of mice. This is our signal. Midnight mouse sounds send any awake nun on the prowl scuttling for the bully, for ratbait, for traps. The nuns hate the darkroom because it is filled with things that scratch. With mice that creep upstairs to gnaw at library books. One of the bully's chores is mouse catching. Every week she brings the nuns furry bloated bodies with paws clenched like fishhooks and heads caved in. The nuns detest these bodies so much they wave the bully away, so she wraps them in newspaper with red string for journey-luck tied to their tails. She takes them to bury in the jungle where she thinks they belong. The bully burns incense to placate the jungle, as Grandmother shows us. She breaks the earth with her knife, digs her fingers deep into the earth. She imagines she is digging up treasure, she has found what Grandmother says we must look for: the old grave in the jungle, at the place where the many tracks meet. The bully loves the smell of the jungle, she comes back out with her face covered in earthy streaks.

When the bully reaches the darkroom she rubs her knuckles on the door three times so I know it is her. The sound of the bully's fingers is like cloth on wood. Like long, slow breaths. I have to listen hard. The darkroom is filled with faint sounds of brushing, breathing. To an undiscerning ear they are like the night ripples of buildings, like a scurry of wind. But Grandmother has taught me to hear. What was the lover thinking of as she hunched in her corner, did her feet tangle in the swing from bedclothes to floor, did she fold her arms to hold her body still? How the close walls must have made her shudder, how the silence startled her, that silence of earth breathing, of a burial deep in the earth. Never a flow or rush of water. Nowadays never a shred of warmth. I shiver on my mat, drape ragged cushions over my legs. I wriggle my feet for warmth, the lover's footprints attached to my feet also wriggling. The lover's footprints slap against the floor. The cold of the darkroom is a bite to the centre of the bone. From where I am crouching I can hear her breathing. I can smell the heaving of her stomach, the fright leaking from eyes and ears and nose. The sweat that has dried to leave trails of whitish crystal on her skin. The lover's frantic scrabbling under the bed, her tugs and scrapes at the locked travel trunk is a scrabble like mice. I listen for the bully over the mouse sounds, over the restless turning of the rich man on the canopied bed. I open the door many times before the bully comes, in case the bully is there. I listen, and listen. The bully doesn't like to be kept waiting.

In the jungle I think the soldiers are the crocodile. Men in green suits and brown faces from which their teeth shine whitely. Convent girls think the bully and I are mad to go into the jungle. They'd never dare, even in broad daylight they shiver and shake at the thought. But the bully and I, she with her knife, I with my amulet, dare go. The bully says the jungle is home. She loves the way the trees knot above her, she loves walking in the shadow of the leaves. The bully strides along the paths stopping only to take photos, to pluck a thick-stemmed leaf on which to chew. The bully chews thought-fully, like chewing cud. Then spits. This way makes a trail. A map to find our way safely out. The bully's gobs steam in the jungle night. Sometimes, at night, this jungle makes me shiver. I jump at the slightest sound. I slip on a mossy patch, fall into a mudhole to make the bully stand tapping her foot. The bully never slips. Never sees the shadows that flash light and dark in the corners of my eyes, never hears the sounds that rustle the undergrowth, stones overturning, the snapping of twigs. The echoing tramp of thick-soled boots. The bully hears nothing: is never afraid. She only believes things face to face.

'Get up!' the bully hisses when I fall.

Walking along the jungle tracks the bully and I move quickly. The bully goes first and I after. I fit my feet into the marks of her feet. In the jungle the bully is always in a hurry. She marches, legs moving like pistons. She peers under rocks, kicks the point of her shoes left and right to send earth clods and mounds of leaves scattering. She barely looks at the rusted tracks of the old funicular railway, now blocked by fallen treetrunks, now more a jungle stream than a track. At the hilltop she stares incuriously at the burned down stumps of the old pavilion that make me shudder and ask to leave. The bully walks searching right and left for treasure, for evidence. Her eyes scan the path for other hidden paths it may suddenly meet.

'What kind of treasure?' the bully asks, but Grandmother only narrows her eyes. Grandmother only repeats that the treasure is buried in an old grave. The site of the grave is a secret which nobody but the hill spirits know, who are hairy and have only one arm. 'We know the hairy hill spirit!' the bully cries. 'We know the spirit with only one arm!'

'What spirit?' my mother later throws up her hands. 'One-armed *monkey*. Aiya, everyone knows. One-armed thief!'

The bully steals a charm for protection against the badluck influences of digging a grave. When Grandmother is dozing she puts her ear to Grandmother's lips. Her ear fills with Grandmother's breath, with the secrets of her breath that the bully struggles to decipher. 'Rubies and diamonds!' she later whispers. 'Bandit money, soldier loot!' The bully can't sit still, she's so excited. When she leaves with my mother Grandmother finally opens one eye. Grandmother's breath becomes a gurgle, then a boom. Grandmother booms out her laugh. She rises from her chair, digs her fingers into my arm so she doesn't fall. Grandmother bends over double.

In the jungle the bully hitches up her skirt. The bully claps my shoulder at the end of our five-minute rests. As we walk I keep a lookout for what Grandmother has told me. I pick the leaf of a plant that curls only at midnight, that cups three dewdrops on its lip. I scrape red-gold moss from rock crevices, break off bark from the roots of ancient trees. I slip small parts of the jungle into Grandmother's leaf and root collection bag, thank the jungle spirits as Grandmother has taught me. The small parts of the jungle scrape against the never-fail matches and ghostburning candles she makes me carry wherever I go. I ask for the jungle spirits' blessing to increase the power of her charms.

As we walk the bully outlines our plans. Treasure to restock the darkroom, evidence to sell more photos. The bully wants to sell a thousand photos. She wants everyone to buy them. She wants to be famous; people to hang her pictures on walls the way the Old Priest's convent photos hang in the vestry. The bully wants evidence so her name will go into the history books the nuns make her learn by heart, so even if they kill her, people will know her name. The nuns laugh when they hear the bully say this, they tweak the bully's nose. They tell her pride will be her fall; she will tumble, this way she'll never

be like the tough little train. She will never make it to the
top of the hill. She will fall off track. The nuns tell the bully
to renounce pride, to have faith, to love everyone. Or the bully
will regret it. Do the tweaks of the bully's nose hurt her? The
bully's regret will hurt a thousand times more. It will burn
welts like acid inside her. But the bully doesn't believe
anything the nuns tell her, at least only against her will. All
her energy is spent trying to prove them wrong. She sits beside
me with her nose flaming red. The bully wants evidence of
everything: even herself, even the devil, even Jesus. Even the
crocodile.

The day my grandmother ran shrieking from the rich man's
kitchen, chased by shadows, was the day she recognised
her future. That day Grandmother saw what her future was.
That was what sent her running, not the flapping shadows
or the black-and-white faces of the other servants like the
faces of their own ancestors, disapproving and grim. Grandmother ran shrieking from the cool breath of the future
tickling the back of her neck. She ran knowing that her life
as she knew it was soon to end. No longer would she stand
staring from the rich man's balcony, waiting, no longer would
she wander his house. Waiting for what would happen: for
the in-between time to be over, the child shed, the young
woman assumed. Although Grandmother had never seen the
dark swirling shadows before, she had known their voices
from birth. Even as a small child in the city, the shadow
voices had come and gone like breaths of wind at night time,
like furniture creaks. At odd, idle moments, Grandmother
saw their fleeting shapes. The shadow voices never harmed
her. When she reported their sayings people ruffled her hair
and chucked her under the chin.

'What imagination!' her own mother cried. 'Aiya, what
next!'

That day my grandmother ran from the kitchen of the rich
man's mansion, shrieking, because now other people heard and
saw the shadows too.

'Did you shriek like this, Grandmother?' the bully and I ask, shrieking our loudest, our *pontianak* ghost shriek, our drowned woman's shriek, seeing who can shriek higher, who can break glass.

'Bad girls!' Grandmother mouths, voice drowned. 'Bad girls, shut up! Sit down!'

The day after the shadows, my grandmother turned fourteen. She woke up feeling strong. She opened her eyes to stare not only at the other servants' waking-up faces but the layers of the other faces they wore: their hopes and fears in feathery shavings, their day-to-day worries gathered in lumps under this ear, on that cheek. Past slights tinged their skins mouldy.

'When it's your turn . . .' Grandmother points at the bully and me so that we are instantly quiet, we clutch each other mock-quaking, shivering our bodies with fear.

The day my grandmother got her grown-up seeing, she woke with an eyelid like butterfly wings. With an eye rapidly blinking. Eyes closed, she rubbed at the lump where the frying-pan ladle had hit. Still there was no pain. Eyes closed, she realised she could see. Her extra eye fluttered and blinked. Grandmother cautiously opened her other eyes to see if sleep had banished the black-and-white shadows. She sighed: rubbed away the last of her childish sleep. The extra eye on her forehead or her left cheek, my grandmother can never be sure, fluttered and blinked. That was the day she woke to a patch the size and colour of a mangosteen in the middle of her bed. Grandmother sniffed at her own blood suspiciously, so unlike her other blood, mottled, dark. Grandmother dared not touch it with her hand. She spat on the mangosteen patch, rubbed with a corner of her pyjamas until it was a pinkish streak. She tied huge rags between her legs and walked like normal.

After that day Grandmother stared at the other servants with such fixity that they paled, they reddened, they shouted and poked out their tongues. They brought out their forbidden amulets, retrieved their hidden-away charms. Under their collars nestled pieces of paper strung with red thread, from their screwed up handkerchiefs a paper circle sometimes slipped, dappled with protection words. Grandmother went about her work as though nothing had changed. She hardly noticed the other servants, too busy bumping into doors and walls, testing her new vision. Most days there was only an ache from squinting. For weeks there would be a blurry black-and-white nothing, then one day, without warning, Grandmother would be able to see. She saw shadows as solid as flesh, some staring at her, startled, others beckoning, others merely passing by. She heard the rich man or the other servants calling, and answered, and knew what they asked, before they asked, or called.

My grandmother watched the rich man and the lover with her extra eye wide open, her lower lip chewed swollen. The lover's sighing grated against her. Her night-time wandering, her footsteps crossing and recrossing the rich man's mansion made Grandmother cover her ears. Grandmother rolled over, wrapping her blanket around her head. She crept to the rich man's quarters when he and the lover weren't there; stood turning a slow circle in the middle of the room. Grandmother examined everything from this circle. All the rich man's possessions were mingled with the lover's. Her gowns and dresses spilled from scented cupboards to tangle his clothes, her perfumes and powders littered his dresser. Her nest of jewelled hairpins stuck into his hairbrush like miniature knives. Grandmother turned and turned. She slipped into her pockets only what no one would notice: a thread, a scraping of fuzz from the furniture, a thin shedding of skin. When the turning made her dizzy she went away.

My grandmother says that sometimes her extra eye hurt her, it was a glowing charcoal lodged in her head. Sometimes she felt it on her chin, other times the tip of her nose. Grandmother twisted my skin to show me. The mark she made was a burn. Her extra eye gave her no peace until she learned to use it right.

'One day I will show you,' Grandmother says.

At first she thought the eye was meant for this-world seeing, so she walked into walls and pillars, into doorways that weren't there. At first the other young servants ran after her, laughing and giggling, snatching breakable objects from her path. Then they too began to scold and grumble, always having to set things straight. They began to lead Grandmother like a blind person into cupboards and pantries, into remote parts of the garden where she spent hours dazzled by leaf shapes and stone patterns before groping her way back. They took her deep into the basement, to the room without windows, the old punishment room, now taken over by the master and mistress, and grandly furnished. There they slammed the door.

'Stay here!' they called through the keyhole. 'See, the master has brought nice furniture, nice hangings on the walls. A nice bed for you to sleep. The master and mistress won't come back from the pavilion so soon. Stay here and rest, ah? We'll bring you food and water. We'll fetch you when they come. Rest until your head gets better, until you can see!'

The young servants left a nest of giggling in the keyhole when they left. They left Grandmother slumped on the soft bed in the room that was filled with shadows. Grandmother jumped when the shadows swirled towards her. She turned her back to the furniture that was also jumping: chairs skittering away from their table, bedclothes slip-sliding, the portrait of the rich man and the lover crashing its silver frame to the floor. Later Grandmother discovered the secrets of concentration and a steely breath. With these she learnt to focus her extra eye. She realised that the bug-eyed shadows crowding around her were bug-eyed from fear, not spite. The flapping shadows curled their terrible lips from their terrible teeth not to eat her, but in imitation of a human grin. The shadows grinned at Grandmother, ingratiating. They rubbed their shadow hands, waiting for orders: this human tormented with icy fingers, that one pinched mercilessly, the other given a plague of sores. The shadows rubbed at their bloated bellies, hungry for food offerings, not Grandmother's flesh. This she discovered later. Before she learnt concentration and a steely breath she walked around crooked. She hung a black cloth over her head to lessen the strain.

Before I could be born naturally my grandmother snatched me from my mother's womb. Grandmother watched and waited with my mother, counting the months, the days. 'Useless, all is forgiven!' she cried, making my mother jump with her sudden laugh. 'Useless, this is how you will pay me back. Your girl will be my assistant, she'll do what you didn't do!'

'If it's a boy . . .' my mother timidly suggested, drowned out by Grandmother's laugh. My mother bit her lip, clasped her hands as if in prayer.

When I was born Grandmother examined me distastefully. She could hardly lift me. 'Wah, so ugly,' she exclaimed. 'So small, but heavy like stone. What were you before? Aiya, hairy, like something leftover! Just like a monkey, like her sign.'

Grandmother wiped my face clean. She pulled open and peered into each of my eyes. Before my mother could stop her she nicked each eyeball with a sharp fingernail in the shape of a crescent moon. My watery cries protested weakly, my hands beat against Grandmother's palm. My mother pleaded and stretched out her arms but Grandmother held me just out of reach. Grandmother knew the marks she made would never go away. In each of my eyes she had scratched a *yin* sign, to help me see.

'You've spoilt her,' my mother complained when Grandmother finally gave me back. 'Now she won't see Jesus.'

My mother rubbed my forehead with the sign of the cross while my grandmother laughed. My grandmother stood with her arms akimbo, laughing, her laugh a roar. Grandmother roared like her sign, the tiger. She threw back her head with a short, sharp twitch.

EIGHT

WHAT MY
MOTHER SAYS

Before I could be born naturally, my grandmother snatched me from my mother's womb. This is what my mother says. The night before she went into labour my mother had a dream. In this dream the people of her childhood village were gambling. Earlier they'd snared a man-eating tiger in a pit and they crouched around its edges to watch. It was a white tiger. Its eyes gleamed red like the edge of the sky. In the distance the boats of the fishing village rocked fretfully. One man strode forward, carrying a monkey, a special monkey. This monkey had been taught to do tricks, to dance and somersault, to box, and use a knife like a man. It was known as a biter, ferocious, baring its teeth to everyone, even its master. Although clever the monkey performed its tricks grudgingly. It had to be watched, it sprang suddenly to bite deep gashes in the arms and legs of anyone who did not watch. The man swung the monkey on the end of a chain. It wore a child's birthday clothes, red shirt and pants. It clutched a gleaming knife in one paw.

The man threw the monkey into the pit. The villagers poked

at it with long sticks when it tried to scramble out. They poked at the tiger to further enrage it. Then people started laying bets. 'Five minutes!' they cried. 'Ten! Two stabs! Five silver pieces if it rides the tiger!' Money flowed from hand to hand, some of it falling into the pit. The monkey's screeches pierced my mother's ears. It flung its wily body this way and that to avoid the tiger's claws. It knifed the frantic air, nicked the white tiger's ears. The night was filled with roars, with screeches and laughter. When the monkey tired, one of the tiger's paws connected with its head. The tiger scraped the monkey's body along the bottom of the pit, the knife rattling in its still-clenched fist like a toy. The tiger hunched over the monkey, blinking up at my mother's villagers, breathing gently. Its breath ruffled the monkey's fur. The tiger opened its jaws.

This dream woke my mother screaming. The twinges of her belly came fast and sharp, like the snapping and clicking of claws. My mother's screams brought Grandmother running and when my mother told her dream, Grandmother rubbed her hands together to fill them with heat. She rubbed her hands with glee. Grandmother squatted my mother on the floor and pulled her legs apart. She pressed her warm hands to my mother's belly. Grandmother leaned over my mother, scolding, breathing gently, passing the strength of her breath to my mother to calm her. She drew from my mother the terror of the dream. My mother grunted. Her face ran with tiny beads of tears and sweat.

This dream she dreamt once, and never again.

Unlike Grandmother my mother says the crocodile is not an evil menacing creature, but one whose luck is very bad. This badluck struck blindly, like lightning, before the crocodile was born. It hangs like a shadow around him, filling his footsteps, eating into his tracks. The crocodile's badluck, my mother says, has hung around him for so long that the poor crocodile himself can't be seen. When he passes people see only his crocodile shadow, distorted and frightful. Like the invisible oily demons which slip out of the night, leaving only oily shadows on walls and stairways to mark their visit, the crocodile too is known only by his shadowy skinmarks, shed here and there, as once he passed. Over the years how the crocodile shadow has grown! As my mother says this, she bends and stretches over the steaming tubs of laundry, seeming to the bully and me to bend and stretch not over the dripping sheets or the boarders' white bloomers, but under the weight of what she has said. Looking over our shoulders, tilting our heads to listen for Grandmother's shambling footsteps before we remember that Grandmother is nowhere near, the bully and I hold our breaths as my mother speaks. As she idly, unexpectedly, answers our tuggings and pullings, our whispered questions now asked more out of habit than hoping for an answer. Sometimes the bully and I strike it lucky. My mother should know, she says. She was there.

The crocodile saying, my mother says, is nonsense: made up in a flash of madness the day the Lizard Boy went amok. The sayings he made later were equally showy, that was his trait. All of his sayings, his doings, got out of hand. The crocodile, my mother says, is not a man but a method. A way of making people do things, the way the nuns mention the crocodile madness so convent girls will stop their teasing and be good. The crocodile is huge, my mother spreads her arms to show us. He is a heavy low sound that hangs in the sky. His laugh stirs terror in the dark places of the heart, where the terrors await stirring. Where the nameless shapes await their naming, and any old name, even the crocodile's, will do. Here my mother beats one hand against her breast the way Grandmother does when she's upset or angry, a thump so sharp it makes the bully and me feel our own chests gingerly. The crocodile doesn't need a knife, my mother says. Although he had one, it did not belong to him, and he did not keep it long. But people like the knife so they keep it. The knife was tagged to offshoot sayings when the crocodile went on to fame. The crocodile offshoots are as dark and tangled as the jungle in which he is said to live. Nowadays even if no one ever sees him for as long as they live, his shadow is enough to scare; to paralyse, the way certain jungle animals are paralysed by light. The way the Lizard Boy was paralysed, crouched behind the laundry for days after the crocodile's birth. But the crocodile is only a shadow, my mother says, whipping her own, swollen and secretive, across the laundry floor. If clever girls shut their eyes and ears they need no longer see or hear him. He will no longer be there.

For days after the crocodile saying's birth, the Lizard Boy sat silent, unmoving, chained to the laundry wall. Neither threats nor pleas nor bribes could move him. Every now and then, as the nuns ordered, my mother leaned out to watch. 'Eat,' she nudged his untouched plate of food. 'Drink.' The enamel cup and plate scraped against the warm cement.

Sometimes the Lizard Boy sat like rock, sweat-covered, glimmering in the light like a delicate carving. His skin seemed to my mother like lace. Sometimes he swivelled away. He crouched with his back towards her, staring at the laundry wall. He scraped patterns with his toenails on the carpeted moss. For days the Lizard Boy crouched, growing shadowy halfmoons under his eyes, which glistened from a steady trickle of tears. The tears splashed off his face onto his knees and down his legs to dribble dark shapes at his feet. The Lizard Boy's feet were laced with fine cobwebs of skin. My mother stared. Where his tears fell the skin was as smooth as her own.

When the caretaker and the Old Priest came for their daily inspection, the Lizard Boy once more became mad. He jumped at them, he rattled his chain and flicked his tongue. He snapped his jaws fiercely, then pulled down his pants to swirl his buttocks in place of a tail. The caretaker and the Old Priest stood watching for some moments, then turned away. The caretaker wrung his hands. He tugged at the Old Priest's sleeve. Even bent as he was the Old Priest stood head and shoulders over the caretaker, whose greying hairs stuck up on his head from worry, whose whiskers poked out like a cat's. The Old Priest patted the caretaker's shoulder, murmuring words of comfort. As they turned the corner the Lizard Boy stopped to listen. His father's voice was cracked from endless pleading.

'Next week he'll be better, Father. You see, Father? Already he's not so bad.'

'Poor Godson!' the Old Priest sighed. 'I'll dedicate a mass . . .'

For days the Lizard Boy crouched sullen, unmoving. Occasionally he sniffed loud enough for my mother to hear. He flicked his tongue at the insects settling in the corners of his mouth. He crouched scratching at the reddened skin around his shackles, eating only when my mother wasn't looking, tossing the plate away when she was. In the evenings he tugged against his chain to sit just inside the laundry entrance. The chain slack curled behind him like a snake. There, rocking on his haunches, he watched my mother. My mother felt his badluck presence pushing against her, creeping slow tentacles around her body, clashing against hers. The Lizard Boy clicked his jaws to annoy her. His hands followed her slow, heavy dance from sink to tub to wringer. Each finger moved with great flourish, neatly, precisely, as though pulling on a string. The Lizard Boy scowled when my mother ignored the pull of his strings. Steam from the tubs wafted in a halo around him, pressing soft and warm against his body, weighing down his flaky skin. The Lizard Boy stilled his lifted arms in amazement. He turned his hands this way and that: spread his face in a long, slow grin. When my mother turned to look his face snapped back, sullen. She came to squat in front of him. She fixed him in the eye the way Grandmother showed her, a fix enough to freeze the blood, to instil terror in the fiercest ghost. She slapped down his favourite books, which the caretaker brought to the laundry, and the Lizard Boy kicked out of reach.

'You're just stubborn,' my mother told him sternly, pointing her finger in accusation. 'You'd rather be mad than say you're sorry. Huh! Coward lizard, how can you say you're a crocodile!'

The Lizard Boy's face screwed up in annoyance. My mother remembers exactly the glint in his swollen eyes. In a flash he darted forward and nipped her finger with his sharp lizard's teeth. My mother swallowed her voice in shock. This swallowed voice, she says, is the reason why, after that day, she has always had trouble speaking. From not being able to bring it up. From having to dig too deep. They stared at her nipped finger, dented on each side with teethmarks, ragged and filling. On each side of my mother's finger was a mirrored smilemark, bloody, like parted lips. The Lizard Boy watched, fascinated. Slowly my mother grunted out her voice. She curled her hands into tiger claws, the way my grandmother showed her, flung herself at the Lizard Boy in rage. This was the only time my mother ever got violently angry, she says, but even though she swears it, the bully and I can't believe it is true. The bully and I can't imagine it. We have never seen my mother lift an angry hand. My mother was so angry she gouged pieces from the Lizard Boy's chest and neck. His skinflakes flew up in puffs. My mother and the boy rolled on the laundry floor, one over the other, pulling against his chain, tangling their feet. They thumped and bit each other, howling. Their badluck bloods smeared and mixed.

Grandmother says: *There are two types of blood, good blood and bad blood. Good blood is fresh, it is bright red and has powerful magical properties. Good blood is the seat of the human soul and any object smeared with it acquires magical powers. Good blood is used to make powerful charms. The blood of a birthing woman is especially strong, its smell is a beacon in the ghostly dark. Pregnant women should plant pineapples in their gardens or under their houses to deter hungry ghosts. Bad blood is almost black. It is smelly and dirty. A woman's menses is bad blood, contact with it brings illness and unhappiness, calamity. When you change your menstrual cloths be sure never to let your fingers touch this blood. Never let a woman who is menstruating go near weddings or important business meetings or gamblers who*

want to win. Her badluck presence will make things go wrong.
Bad blood is good for warding off black magic. Used with
the blood of a black dog, the penis of a white horse and a
large pail of dirty water, it will turn a spell, no matter how
strong, back onto its sender. Bad blood is also good for
catching ghosts. Smearing an unseen ghost with menstrual
blood will make it visible.

Before my mother became a Christian she was convinced that
her luck was bad. My mother's badluck swirled in a leathery
arc around her as she walked. When Grandmother first saw
the badluck she shook her head with pity. She beckoned my
mother over to cup her chin in one hand. 'Does it hurt?'
Grandmother asked, tapping the places on my mother's
shoulders where the badluck hooked.

My mother was so startled she dropped the heavy winejar
she was carrying, she stood motionless in the puddle of first-
quality wine spreading round her feet. The brothel keeper leapt
cursing from her chair to beat at my mother with her opium
pipe, to slap at her head which was already scarred with the
brothel keeper's bracelet cuts, already dented in the shapes of
her rings. Grandmother admired the way my mother planted
her feet. Her hunched shoulders were impressive, the way she
neither ducked nor fended off blows. Grandmother examined
the firm line of my mother's mouth, the dogged tilt of her
head. 'Aiya, old friend, leave her,' she said lazily. 'I'll pay for
the wine.'

In those days, long before my mother became a Christian,
Grandmother, after the brothel keeper, was the second-richest
woman on their street. Grandmother's house was the second-
grandest, her teeth flashed gold, each of her wrists was
weighted with a dragon jade bangle. Her neck was a jangle
of shimmering pendants and chains. At that time Grandmother's ghostchasing business was at its peak, and as she was no
longer young, she could hardly keep up. Her house rang out
with the voices of both the desperate living and the stubborn
dead. 'Go away!' Grandmother hissed when she'd had enough

for the night, banishing both the living and the dead with one wave of her hand. Grandmother was so rich even a dozen smashed winejars was nothing, she was so powerful she could afford pity. She had so much face she could rub some off.

'Stand still!' she ordered, hitting two tender spots on my mother's shoulders. 'How's that? Not so heavy, ah?'

In those days Grandmother and the brothel keeper spent most afternoons in each other's company, sprawled in the brothel keeper's luxurious guest parlour, sipping ricewine and chatting, half-heartedly playing cards. Though similar in most respects, in size and age, temperament and outlook, and the sharpness of their tongues, my grandmother and the brothel keeper were opposites at card playing: Grandmother betting wildly, against all odds and usually winning, and the brothel keeper, usually losing, only betting big when she knew for sure. Each afternoon ended with their cards fluttering around them in exasperation as Grandmother won game after game of small bets and the brothel keeper suddenly won back big. At the end of every afternoon neither had gained or lost a cent. Grandmother and the brothel keeper were the only two women on their street with free time in the afternoons, the only two perfectly comfortable in each other's company, because of their current cycle of existence: their privileged lot. They were thrown together because they were outside women, outside the rules and restrictions binding ordinary women. They were tolerated if not exactly admired, having no husbands to scold them, no children to run after, no household chores. Both Grandmother and the brothel keeper provided essential services for the smooth running of their district, the brothel keeper appeasing the desires of the living while my grandmother tended those of the dead. As the most essential and wealthiest women they could afford to put on airs. They could afford time off. They sat together, congratulating each other on their lucky life cycle, recounting past lives.

'Once I was a bonded servant,' Grandmother said, pointing to my mother. 'Like that girl there, I smelt of woodfire and kitchen grease. I was up before the crack of morning, asleep only past midnight. My arms and legs were lumpy with bruises, my back crisscrossed with scars.'

'That's nothing!' the brothel keeper wagged her head disdainfully. 'I was a drunkard's daughter. When my father wanted money he called strangers to the house to inspect his girls. Whoever paid most got the youngest, me. My thighs grew a calloused pad, my legs learnt to walk far apart. My mother's hair fell out in clumps from seeing her daughters' suffering, her teeth loosened from the strain.'

'Huh, you think that's hard,' Grandmother scoffed. 'In one of my lives I was a great white tiger. Peasants tried to capture me by digging deep pits, but I evaded them. Only princes and holy men could ride on my back, they walked a thousand miles over dry rock and through dense jungles for this honour, but one day the Sea King sent one of his daughters to drag me to the depths of the sea. There he held me prisoner for a thousand years, coming every day to beg for a ride, but I snapped and roared and pulled at my chains. I shook the foundations of the sea, causing cyclones and tidal waves, seastorms that splintered great vessels with one stroke. Finally I shook myself free, and forever afterwards swore vengeance on my enemy, the sea.'

'You had it easy,' the brothel keeper laughed. 'In my past life I was a white snake. To this day, in my deepest sleep, I dream of slithering. An evil magician cursed me to spend eternity with my belly to the ground, but I curled around the base of a peach tree and meditated for a thousand years, in sunshine and rain, neither eating nor sleeping, till the peach leaves laced a blanket above me and the earth below me turned to rock and then back to earth. Till I felt my legs and arms grow back. In this life I still have my concentration, and now you see how my luck has changed!'

As the afternoon shadows lengthened the past lives of Grandmother and the brothel keeper grew more and more impressive and my mother brought in winejar after winejar, and people making their way past the brothel shuddered at the shrieks of wild laughter leaking into the street. But even as the shadows deepened, and slipped Grandmother's and the brothel keeper's grotesquely elongated shapes through the chinks and slats of the doors and windows to stain pitch black puddles across the street, over which people hastily leapt, the brothel keeper and Grandmother remained hunched together in stalemate, each trying their hardest, flipping extra kings and aces into the game. Even when their sleeves were empty, and my mother finally entered to light the parlour lamps in preparation for the night's business, neither Grandmother nor the brothel keeper had gained or lost one cent.

'You win,' they said graciously. 'No, old friend, *you* win.'

'It's just our luck!' they shrieked, flopping drunkenly against each other as they parted at the door. 'Just lucky this time round!'

When my grandmother left my mother rushed to stand bowing at the doorway, defying the brothel keeper's curses commanding her back to work. 'Thank you, Auntie,' my mother said simply, shrugging her shoulders to show Grandmother how her badluck weight had improved. Staggering homewards Grandmother turned to watch my mother through the lighted window. In twos and threes the brothel women sauntered into the parlour to drape their scented bodies over the lounges and divans. They assumed languid poses, chatting amongst each other, stifling yawns at the usual spectacle of the brothel keeper's furious swearing, the brothel keeper's arms and legs lashing out at my mother as she hurriedly gathered the fluttered cards, and cleared the afternoon from the room.

One night, in the middle of making a difficult charm, Grandmother heard my mother's thin voice from the brothel at the other end of the street. She heard my mother through the intervening cluster of shophouses, through the bustle of the nighthawkers, and the clamour of the customers outside her door. 'Auntie!' my mother called once, in a voice expectant with despair. Leaving her charm half-finished, her customers protesting, Grandmother made her way to the brothel, which was even livelier than usual, its doors and windows flung open, its guest parlour bulging with more bodies than it could hold.

In the centre of the parlour, amidst the people surging to separate them, the voices straining to pull them apart, were the brothel keeper and my mother. The brothel keeper beat at my mother's postrate body with her fists. My mother lay with her eyes wide open, her mouth clenched shut.

'Aiya, old friend,' Grandmother called, elbowing her way through the crowd. 'What's the fuss?'

'It's the last straw!' the brothel keeper spat. 'This is what I get in return for kindness. Who does this girl think she is? A customer wants to be friendly and she cuts him with a kitchen knife. Who told her to carry a knife? Aiya, this girl makes me lose so much face! Today she attacks customers, tomorrow who will it be? Get up, girl! I'm going to beat you to death. Shame on your parents' heads!'

Grandmother stared at my mother, lying like one already dead. 'Old friend, remember I said I would take her?'

'Take her!' the brothel keeper shouted. 'She's only brought me badluck. Hah, you're very brave, old friend! You'd better be careful, she'll rub her badluck on you!'

'I'll take her,' Grandmother said.

When Grandmother brought her home my mother threw herself onto her knees, splashing Grandmother's lap with tears. 'Auntie is so kind to hear me, and take me,' she sobbed so hard Grandmother strained to hear her. 'I'm just a servant, but since Auntie has no daughter, may I have the honour of taking the place of Auntie's daughter, and caring for Auntie in Auntie's old age? If Auntie will let me, I promise to look after Auntie like my own mother.'

In those days such a show of gratitude, especially when no fee accompanied it, no sidelong look from the satisfied client to see if gratitude would reduce the fee, both confused and embarrassed my grandmother. She watched in amazement as even the badluck on my mother's shoulders shivered with thanks. Impatiently she wiped away my mother's tears. 'Anything you like,' she said gruffly. 'But don't talk so much. Now get up! We've got work to do.'

My grandmother is a believer in cycles. She says everything has its turn. Only the foolish think they will always be on top, even if it's human nature to keep trying. To stand at the top of the hill with hackles raised and teeth snarling, guarding your territory, your loot. Only powerful wisewomen who know the secrets of bending the cycles have been known to build success upon success. These wisewomen live once in a hundred years. Everyone else must wait their turn. If now you are down, your feet covered with sores, your belly rumbling, your days spent wondering what adversity tomorrow will bring, all you have to do is wait and watch and plot and listen, and soon enough you will have your day. This is what Grandmother says.

When my grandmother was a child, the Number Two Kitchen Maid in the house she was bonded to tormented her relentlessly. This woman made my grandmother's life hell. For years Grandmother wept at the thought of her, at the sound of her voice Grandmother puddled her pants, cowering, ducking the kitchen knives swished to scare her, crunching on sand mixed with her food to break her teeth. Grandmother's baby teeth were all cracked from eating sand. The woman's laugh, Grandmother said, was worse than a cackling ghost's. My grandmother never forgot her. Years later the Number Two Kitchen Maid came crying to Grandmother. Someone had cursed her, her luck was really bad, everything she and her family ventured ended in disaster. Her hair was falling out, her gums creeping away from her teeth. Her hands and feet were always being pricked with sharp needles, and the things she saw in the dark kept her awake all night. Her children refused to come near her, her husband turned her out of the house. Knowing Grandmother only as a famous healer and curse-remover, she came begging for help. She showered Grandmother's lap with her bits and pieces of jewellery, her pawn tickets, her saved-away coins.

'Isn't it funny how life is,' my grandmother told her. 'I have waited and waited, and now you have come.'

The Number Two Kitchen Maid's mouth fell open. She

stared at Grandmother long and hard. At last she recognised her. She dropped to her knees, wailing, moaning, begging Grandmother for mercy. She wept large tears of desperation onto my grandmother's feet, which Grandmother contemptuously shook off.

'Let's forget the past, eh,' the woman wept. 'Let bygones be bygones.'

'I never forget,' my grandmother said.

Grandmother reminds us of this story every time the bully and I do something wrong. Something Grandmother doesn't like: our help offered only half-heartedly, the charm papers we promise to cut for her abandoned halfway through. Grandmother reminds us how unfinished business always finds its path. So humans must always be watchful. They must finish their business, no matter what, or it hangs around waiting to finish them. If they're careless one day it will drop on them like a stone from the sky, like the butt of a bandit rifle. Like a long ago curse gone wrong. Only powerful wisewomen can skip and duck the path of unfinished business, the convoluted path of ghostly favour or revenge. Even powerful wisewomen are sometimes caught out. Then they must twist and turn, they must plot and plan, and sit biting their lips for hours in a special chair by the doorway. Sometimes they must try tricks. They must make promises they will never keep. Only foolish people make enemies of wisewomen, even the ones who haven't yet mastered their art, or those fallen on hard times, forced to ply their trade by the roadside, covered in dirt and sores. Once every city child knew this and paid the proper respect. The foolish Number Two Kitchen Maid finally crept from Grandmother's house to die a terrible death. That is what happens to Grandmother's enemies. When the time is right—poof! Off they go, shouting and screaming in agony. 'Do you understand!' Grandmother shouts, flicking her cane at our legs to make us dance.

'Yes, Grandmother! Yes!' The bully and I run across the room.

The story of the ghosthouse is the only one my grandmother will repeat. .Grandmother repeats and repeats her favourite parts: the thunderous applause after her fairy dancing at the rich man's parties, being allowed to play with his treasures, to slide onto his knee. Grandmother never tells this story from start to finish, it's a story in bite-sized pieces that leave the bully always hungry for more.

'What happened next?' the bully begs, which makes Grandmother's eyes gleam. Grandmother's lips shut tight.

'Next time you come,' she murmurs. 'Aiya, next time.'

When she tells this story no one is allowed to move. To speak. No one is allowed to go to the toilet or reach out their hands for titbits, or cough or sneeze. If they do Grandmother will stop, and no amount of pleading will persuade her to continue. Sometimes, before she begins, she asks the bully, my mother and me which story we would like to hear. Before anyone else can answer the bully asks for this story, which makes Grandmother smile and nod her head. As the bully bounces, as the bully rubs her palms with pleasure, Grandmother will nod and smile. Then begin a different story. The bully will sit scowling at Grandmother's feet. Then will be caught: will be rapt. The bully can never tell when Grandmother is reaching the end of her stories. Grandmother's endings catch her unaware. To the bully the rapture ends too suddenly. Too suddenly is she brought back to her body, to see out of her bully's eyes and smell with her nostrils, and suck at her own bully's teeth. The bully scratches her head.

Sometimes, in a more generous mood, Grandmother will beckon for her tin of old ghostchasing tools. The bully and I scramble through the piles of tins, boxes and plastic bags cluttering Grandmother's room.

'This one, Grandmother?' we call. 'This?'

Her old ghostchasing tools stretch the tin to fantastic mounds and hollows so heavy the bully and I puff and pant dragging it across the floor. Grandmother reverently lifts the cover while my mother sighs and leaves the room. The smell from the tin is enough to chase anyone away, human or ghost, but the bully and I merely open our eyes wider. As we do in the jungle we merely hold our breaths.

'Here,' Grandmother hands us the pots of grease and tinted powders with lids we have to scrape with our fingernails, they are caked so tight. Grandmother mixes the grease and powders into different-coloured lumps which she dots along her arm. 'Who first?' Grandmother asks.

'Me! Me first!' the bully shouts, pushing herself forward, because the bully always has to push and shout, and yet is hardly ever first.

'Close your eyes,' Grandmother says, in a more generous mood.

The bully's face under my grandmother's fingers becomes a pattern of curls and arches as twisted and trembling as Grandmother's hands. Her cheeks become as white as Grandmother's hair, her lips as red as Grandmother's betelnut teeth. When Grandmother has finished the bully is a fearful sight. The bully's brittle teeth look sharp. She prances here and there while Grandmother does me. Grandmother disguises my young girl's face to frighten any enemy, to send any enemy ghost screeching in fright. She powders my forehead an unearthly white, draws coloured patterns on my cheeks. Sweeps shoeblack over my eyebrows like wings. Then, in a more generous mood, she will let the bully and me do her. While we're busy she will sometimes go wandering. The bully and I scoop lumps of colour from her arm while she nods her head this way and that. She absently turns whichever way we turn her, her eyes flit left and right and out the window or up to the ceiling so the bully and I can't tell whether she is really there or somewhere else, she looks a million miles away from our daubing and streaking. Grandmother's lips purse and stretch from scowl to smile to scowl.

'My most precious,' she mutters. 'Is that what you think I've promised? Is that what you think you'll get?'

'What is your most precious, Grandmother?' the bully and I bend close to whisper. 'Who wants it, Grandmother? Who?' But Grandmother only nods her head. She continues to nod and mutter, to point her hands this way and that as if every way she points is a clue, a way out of the maze that is her hospital promise, given all those years ago. But what her promise is and what is her most precious, my grandmother, even wandering, doesn't say. When we shake and pinch her she looks at us fiercely.

'Don't disturb!' Grandmother snaps. 'I'm thinking.'

Grandmother is old now, she has lived many turns of a woman's life cycle, she gets cranky if anyone disturbs her thoughts. She continues to nod and mutter, and point her hands. So the bully and I finish her enemy-frightening face with great flourish. We streak her cheeks red and yellow half an inch thick, undo her hair to make a wild tangle that will scare any human or ghost. We paint her fingernails, drape cut paper over her head; push her hands into the shapes to scare even demons, *Avert!* We twirl her on her trembling feet around the room. The bully and I clap and stamp our feet as Grandmother spins in fairy circles, her twisted feet no longer hitting the earth in uncertain slaps, but flashing in and out and up and down, lighter than a girl's. Grandmother's face runs in sweat-streaks, her skin glints brown through the greasy mask. The bully and I clap and cheer until she breaks into a joyful grin. Until my mother comes to cry out in horror and slap the bully and me away. My mother leads Grandmother back to her chair, she wipes Grandmother's face with her handkerchief and tidies her hair. She rubs at her hands and arms until Grandmother finally comes back. Grandmother blinks. She pushes my mother away.

'What do you think you're doing?' my mother turns her angry face to the bully and me. 'This is your Grandmother. In your Grandmother's house!'

'Ma, we were just joking.' I rub at my slapped shoulder while the bully slumps panting in remorse. 'Grandmother liked it. Aiya, Ma, can't you take a joke?'

The story of the ghosthouse always leaves the bully panting. It leaves the bully slumped beside Grandmother's chair long after Grandmother has left it. When I touch her shoulder she roughly pushes me away. The bully and I have heard this story many times but still we listen, rapt, unmoving. Every time the bully hears it she thinks it is different. She thinks in the spaces between Grandmother's telling the story has changed. Still the bully likes it best. She likes best a story with real people in it, and one about rich men and treasure and the sea. Grandmother tries to describe the sea to the bully. The sea is like the jungle, full of paths that can lead to treasure. The one who can walk the many paths unharmed will possess great magic.

'What magic, Grandmother?' I ask. 'What?'

'Magic so strong it will kill their oldest enemy with one fiery stroke.'

Before the Old Priest died he packed up a crate for the bully. Into this crate he put his precious photo album, his camera, some film, bottles of chemical solutions, a key to the darkroom, some string, some clips, a sheaf of mouldering papers, two leatherbound books. A salt-crusted bandit's knife with a charred handle, and three red bulbs so the bully would never run out. This was the bully's inheritance, in place of the glory box the nuns said she would never need. The Old Priest's one earthly passion was photography. His album was a record of the convent's earliest days.

'Evidence,' he smiled at the bully.

An ancient photo had pride of place in the Old Priest's album, a fire-damaged portrait from an even older time, when the house on the hill first fought back the jungle. The Old Priest cleaned the worst of the damage as best he could, he pasted the crushed photo inside his album cover. Upon opening the bully did not see it at first. Then her eye drew left, and was fixed. The photo was filled with shadows that made her look and look. The Old Priest edged it with a border of intricate gold. Then followed pictures of steamships in a shallow harbour, an unwieldy baggage train winding its way up the hill. Natives rested long knives in the crooks of their arms. There were nuns bustling about the camp in the morning mists, and the jungle being peeled away from the abandoned mansion. Then came pictures of the house from different angles: an eccentric house, all doorways of differing shapes and sizes, corridors twisting this way and that; stairways leading nowhere. The house was like a child's dreamhouse, built in fits and starts. It was passages ending suddenly, columns holding up nothing, windows that looked onto other windows, or walls. Even with the jungle cleared and awkward walls demolished, new ones erected to make classrooms, sickrooms and dormitories, the weird shapes of the place never changed. The sense one was walking a maze.

Years later, when other buildings had been added and the convent became a successful school and orphanage, and the Old Priest retired, resigned to swollen knee joints and white fluff casing his head, his spare time was spent exploring the original building. Knocking on walls to see if anything lay behind. The Old Priest discovered a windowless room in a corner of the basement, behind a boarded-up door. The smell when the room was opened sent him reeling. He stood on the threshold thinking he had entered another time. Rich hangings covered the walls, a silken canopy swathed an elegant bed. The bedcovers looked newly rumpled, the Old Priest glanced nervously over his shoulder to see if the ones who rumpled came back. He felt he was looking at something forbidden, though who forbade him he could not say. The Old Priest blinked. When he looked again the wall hangings were moth eaten, the silken canopy hanging by threads. The bedcovers tattered to mouldy shreds. The smell fluttered his handkerchief to his nose. On the floor were the black remains of a hastily quenched fire from which it came. Fingermarks patterned the caked grease and ashes, running this way and that. The floor was so cold the Old Priest thought he was standing in water, but when he bent to touch it, his fingers came away dry.

The Old Priest wedged the door of the windowless room wide open. It was the perfect room: not a chance of light. He made a foul-smelling bonfire of everything, at the last moment snatched the old photo from the flames. He snatched at the faces staring out of the smoke. The photo was already partially burned. The Old Priest whitewashed the walls and scoured the floor with lye. He coaxed the nuns to let the bully help. Together they strung the ceiling with red fairy lights the bully danced under when they were done. In those days the bully was a square-faced child who followed the Old Priest wherever he went. Whenever he turned, there she would be: his stunted, staring shadow. The bully's eyes were small and bright. The Old Priest took her into the jungle to photograph close-ups of flowers, insects and birds. He slowed his pace so she could keep up, slung her onto his old broad back, heaving and panting, when the going was hard. He showed her what his photographic chemicals did. The bully's eyes bulged watching this magic.

'Not magic,' the Old Priest said, resting his hand on the bully's head, 'but evidence. So everyone can see.'

'What can they see?' the bully asked and asked, but the Old Priest's gaze remained fixed on a point just beyond her left shoulder. His hand absently stroked her head.

The story of the ghosthouse is one the bully and I think my mother knows, but no matter how we ask her she will never tell it.

'Ask Grandmother,' my mother says.

When we persist, when we twist our arms around her and dance to make her laugh, and tug at her blouse, my mother will look over her shoulder into the corner of the kitchen where my grandmother sometimes sits. Seeing no one she will lower her voice. The bully loves my mother's lowered voice which is soft and stroking to the bully, like the licks of fame she says will one day find us, like my mother's hand gently brushing back her hair. Like the soft pinches my mother gives her cheeks when her weekend with my family is over and the bully needs pinches to forget her sulks. When my mother lowers her voice the bully leans closer.

When she was a young girl, my mother says, in the days

she was Grandmother's ghostchasing assistant, they were called to the ghosthouse in the middle of the night. My mother has no idea how long they stayed in the midnight ghosthouse, for who can measure the hours or minutes of the time spent dealing with the devil and the dead? Devilish time, dead time, compared to that of humans, runs either too long or short. When they emerged, dragging their feet in exhaustion, dripping cold sweat from their brows, they emerged to the sound of sirens and the screeching of trucks. To the caretaker quaking between two burly soldiers, insisting they'd been in the ghosthouse for a mere half hour, no more. Yet it seemed to my mother the ghosthouse door had slammed behind them long enough ago for her fingernails to curl into useless talons and her hair to sweep her feet white and luminous, to fall from her skull's head by its own weight. Long ago enough for Grandmother to shrivel to skin and bone, to a puff of dust. It seemed to my mother they'd been in the ghosthouse for a time both forever and black. They stood on the doorstep blinking in the bright trucklights, too tired and bewildered to move. 'You all right?' Grandmother asked her gruffly. 'You're not hurt?' My mother had energy enough only to nod, then shake her head.

'Good,' Grandmother looked around them. 'Aiya, what's the fuss? They've come to thank us, or what? Wah, so tired! So many this time, sure put up a fight, ah?' Grandmother turned to beam at the crowd gathered beyond the door. 'Got most of them,' she announced, wafting the smoke from her ghostburning bucket towards them as proof. 'Tomorrow do the rest. One of them—wah, very strong!'

'Look!' the caretaker's miserable voice drifted towards them. 'Only carrying that badsmell bucket, aiya, I tell you they didn't come to steal. This badluck place, who'd come to steal?' When a flurry of nuns and soldiers crowded around him he stammered: 'I—I don't know! D-don't know why they came. I heard a noise and came to see! That's my job! That's why I'm here! Ask my boy, you heard the noise too, didn't you, Ah Boy?'

The flurry of nuns and soldiers brushed past Grandmother and my mother, other soldiers grasped them firmly by the arms.

'Sirs, what's this?' Grandmother asked politely, assuming not her tiger face but the face she used when talking to soldiers, rent collectors, tax collectors and other officials of city order and law. 'What's wrong, Sirs?' her blank, innocent face darkened as they were frogmarched to the trucks. 'What have we done? Aiya, we were just doing them a favour!'

'Don't you know about curfew?' one soldier snapped.

Grandmother put on her wheedling voice. 'Please Sirs, we can only chase ghosts at night . . .'

The flurry of nuns and soldiers came sweeping back out of the ghosthouse. They clustered together for some moments, the soldiers lifting their palms in calming gestures, the nuns beating at their breasts. The nuns' faces were flushed with anger, their night wimples askew. Other nuns raced here and there, chasing curious convent girls back to bed. The Old Priest wandered about in confusion, blessing everyone. 'Blood everywhere!' the nuns cried. 'A dead chicken, buckets of burning rags. Books strewn all over. The place stinks! What a mess! Where's the madwoman, where is she?'

My mother shrank from the sudden white mass that surrounded them, the sudden white wall of lips pulled back and fingers pointing. The nuns' words flashed hot and fiery towards them. 'How dare you? How do you dare? You dare to come here, where God is, and cavort with the devil in this holy place! You dare to bring the devil into our midst! The fires of hell await you, wretched creatures! You'll be sorry, we'll pray for you, but oh how you'll burn!' The soldiers burst out laughing, listening to the nuns' fury, watching their nuns' bodies twisting into un-nunlike postures, vicious and swift. One daring arm, another, reached out to strike Grandmother and my mother before the soldiers pulled them back. Grandmother's face darkened in the glaring trucklights until it was almost black. My mother's cheeks burnt bright red.

'Is this how you answer a favour?' Grandmother asked in

a voice unnaturally low, with eyes narrowed to slits. Grandmother trembled as she raised her hand.

'Get in!' the soldiers interrupted, pushing her and my
mother into the back of the truck. They fell against the bodies
already huddled there, unsteady arms reaching out to steady
them, curses and grumbles spat in greeting. 'No need to talk
so much now, Grandmother,' the soldiers called. 'Vandalism,
breaking curfew. Wilful destruction of property. Aiya, later
you can talk. You'll have lots of talking to do! You got bandit
friends, or what?' The soldiers flung the used ghostchasing
equipment after them, then crowded in, laughing at their joke.
My mother looked up as the truck roared to life, she saw the
nuns clustered together with their held-up crosses, their
brandished fists.

At this point my mother, bending over the stove, splitting
pieces of wood into kindling, swirling the ricepot to deftly
pick husks from the cloudy water, will suddenly stop. The
bully and I, squatting beside her, dipping our fingers into the
sauces she has made, will look at the thin line of her mouth
and lift our heads to hear Grandmother's breath in the
doorway, Grandmother's hand lifting the doorway curtain
with one sweep. Grandmother will peer at us intently. 'What
are you telling?' she'll demand, and the bully and I will dance
across the kitchen to shout 'Tell us! Tell us!' into both her
ears, and Grandmother will beckon us into the outer room,
and the story of the ghosthouse will continue.

But not my mother's story.

Later, when Grandmother is dozing, when her chin sinks
to flatten its point on her chest or she tires of telling or stops
to tilt her head as if she has heard someone call, the bully
and I will look for my mother. 'What happened *in* the
ghosthouse?' we'll ask. 'What happened next?'

'Ask Grandmother,' my mother says.

Before I was born, and sometimes after, my mother dreamt
another dream. This dream started at the time she walked the
streets of the city every day, looking into every face for a sign.

Every day my mother walked searching for my disappeared father. In the dream she was turning: turning a corner, walking dark alleys, reaching a corner she knew she must turn. In the dream my mother turned endlessly, she walked an endless maze of streets and sidestreets where the only sound rising to meet her was the echo of her feet. The last of the evening slatted pale bars of light over everything. My mother turned a corner, and another, and the next. In the dream she walked until her head began to spin, until the streets blurred one into another and everything and nothing seemed familiar. All the years of Grandmother's training did not help. My mother did not know the way home. In the dream she could put nothing together, not even the way she had come. Around one sudden corner she smelt smoke and metal, the blacking of polished boots. She heard a sharp intake of breath. My mother woke up startled, reached out her arms to grasp the bedrail like an anchor, or my arm, my shoulder, my leg. In my campbed beside her I stirred in grumbling sleep. Only long moments later would my mother let go.

In her dream of turning my mother was still a girl. She was the long ago girl working day in and day out at the convent laundry, long ago leaving the bulk of her ghostchasing work behind her, long arrived on the convent doorstep to impress the nuns. My mother stood with her eyes downcast and her hands neatly folded, as Grandmother told her. The nuns carefully examined her steadfast face and manners, her strong back, her sturdy arms and legs. They listened patiently to her stammered work pleading, any work, without pay if necessary, if she could only join the convent girls at their lessons, if the nuns would only teach her the magic words in the golden-edged books from which they read. 'Not magic, dear girl!' the nuns laughed heartily. They did not recognise my mother as the girl once standing before them with the same look, halfway between terror and pleading. My mother stood unrecognisable in her ironed clothes with her hair parted neatly, neither ash nor ghostburning grease streaking her cheeks, and no Grandmother beside her with a hand raised to curse. To the nuns my mother looked like any city child turned up at the convent doorstep to beg for food or money or a prayer for the dying, awe-stricken and slightly grubby, words tangling as she tried to get them out. 'Now tell us,' they encouraged. 'Why do you want to learn?'

'To—to make—To make myself better!' my mother answered the words Grandmother taught her. 'To see.'

'Not magic,' the nuns warned, 'but a way to God, to Truth. The hardest path, for to walk it the self must be destroyed. A path to eternal Life!'

In the dream my mother was older than the girl who nodded vigorously, as Grandmother taught her, when she heard that her self must be destroyed. 'Agree with everything!' Grandmother said, pinching to make her remember. 'Always say yes.'

In the dream my mother was an older girl, already her girlhood seeped from her body into the footsteps she left behind her as she walked. Even in the dream she walked timidly, her head lowered, her shoulders weighed. She walked, listening for the sharp intake of breath around the corner that always took her by surprise, it could be any corner, and often was not. The sharp intake of breath around the corner made my mother stop. There was no way behind her. The dream swallowed the alleys and passages as soon as my mother passed: she could only turn forwards, never back. The sharp intake of breath made her hunch her shoulders before she turned. Around the dream corner, at the end of a narrow sidestreet, or under a sudden arched window, or in the dim light of a convent corridor hardly warmed by the sun, my mother met a shadow walking the other way: a gaunt shadowshape, solid. My mother and the shadow bumped shoulders, accidentally, for an instant their shoulderbones locked.

My mother's gaze flew from its usual sweep of the ground to the shadow's face: a blurry dream face, pale and shifting. Now the shadow's was the face of a young man with hollow cheeks and skin flaking, now a face dark and brooding, like the demons encountered in Grandmother's ghostchasing,

staring at my mother with the same bulbous eyes, stretching
the same reddened lips. Now the shadow was faceless, no more
than a stretch of skin. My mother saw swirling around it now
the flap of a plastic rainjacket, now a fall of leathery wings.
On its belt she saw the glint of a knife. Her voice froze in
her throat. Her eyes widened with fright. Both she and the
shadow took a half-step backwards. Their eyes were exactly
level, their bumped shoulders and arms curved for balance
curving at the same angle, aching at the same spot. The shadow
and my mother held their heads the same way, slightly
lowered; they held their bodies alike, gingerly. For an instant
my mother and the shadow stood rooted like a mirror image
of each other. Then her gaze reverted to its old angle, her
mouth mumbled excuses, her body slipped around the corner
and the shadow, away.

This, the shadow whispered, *was their first meeting.*

This was not! my mother cried.

My mother woke, crying, widening her eyes from habit to
her old tiger glare.

◄ N I N E ►

THE SMELLS
OF GIRLS

Unlike Grandmother the nuns say there are many different types of crocodiles. During the morals lesson they draw pictures on the blackboard to show us. Thin crocodiles, fat crocodiles, ones with greased hair. Especially beware of the ones who roll up their sleeves and ask girls over to their lair to hear them play guitar. The nuns' pictures wobble across the board. Girls must all sit with their legs together. Crocodiles are attracted by the smells of girls with their legs apart. Girls when walking must always look straight ahead and walk quickly and never dawdle. Crocs scramble after girls who dawdle and butt them with their snouts and nip at their ankles. The bite of a crocodile will never heal. Girls must never let a crocodile, in whatever guise, take their hands and lead them into the jungle, whispering magic crocodile charms. If a girl is charmed by a croc no amount of prayers or penance can save her. She will be spoilt forever and no one will ever want her. Not even her parents. Not even Jesus. If a girl, in all innocence, is captured by a croc using force she must look for guidance to Saint Maria Goretti, aged eleven, who preferred to be stabbed fourteen times rather than lose her virtue to crocodile youths. Like Saint Maria, dying, they must offer each stab wound to God as a gift. It is good for good girls to be afraid of the crocodile. Girls who aren't afraid suffer from a disease called running wild. Girls who gaze out the window when they should be studying, who huddle in corners to shriek over movie posters, who pass banned novels under their desks with pages creased at the juicy bits. These girls are particularly susceptible to the crocodile disease. Crocodiles are born with lumps of sugar on their tongues, they are experts at making promises but they only want one thing.

'What do they want, Sister? What?'

'To plant baby crocodiles inside a girl so she will grow and grow, and the baby crocodiles will snap and slither inside her, and get bigger and bigger, and one day she will burst!'

'How will the crocodile do it, Sister?'

'It's easy, that's why girls must beware. Sometimes just by putting his scaly limbs around her, by putting his hand—'

During the morals lessons the bully and I sit at the back of the class. We sit with our heads together, hankies stuffed into our mouths. Our cheeks are filled with laughter, our faces growing red. The bully flicks through her pile of reject photos. Girls' faces too close up, the backs of nuns' heads, fuzzy arms and necks and legs. As she passes them to me I busily snip. Here a head, there an arm, the bottom half of a body, an unlaced shoe. A smashed red lightbulb on a page of tricks. The bully snatches the pieces before I've finished, making fuzzy-edged tears. She arranges them on the desk under cover of her exercise book. We move the pieces around. We make flying limbs and kung fu stances, arms and legs bent at impossible angles, bodies curling into themselves. We make recognisable monsters: nuns with too-small heads and giant grasping arms; Grandmother's scowling profile with a crooked wimple and her fist raised to scold; girls with soldier legs swelling their skirts. The bully and I make the crocodile. Smiling red lips with a jagged gash of teeth that the bully colours in. All are pasted into the bully's special scrapbook to bulge out its sides. The bully hands me her pen.

'Write,' she whispers. 'Write what you see.'

During the morals lessons the bully and I sit silently choking, fit to burst. We sit with our heads low on the table, our feet almost tapping, almost stamping. The lover's footprints attached to my feet jump and sway on their own, they flap papery from my heels like fever-peeled skin. During the morals lessons the bully and I sit with our fingers busy, paper squares, spirals and triangles flowering from our hands. We sit with our muscles tingling, our legs crocodile-attracting, wafting: wide.

Grandmother says: *Everyone knows that life proceeds in cycles. In waves of good and bad, of ignorance and learning. From the cradle to the grave, a man goes through a number of eight-year cycles, a woman through cycles of seven years. At seven months a baby girl gets her first teeth which she loses when she is seven years old. At 2 x 7 years = 14 the yin path opens, that is, the onset of menstruation. At 7 x 7 years = 49 menopause ensues. Spirits of the dead slowly sever themselves from this world in seven-day periods following death. On each seventh day sacrifices have to be made and ritual ceremonies held. The whole process takes 49 days; by then the spirit has left for the other side. Spirits which are not sent off with the proper prayers and ceremonies become confused and resentful. They cling to the earth and sometimes don't even know they are dead. Never linger about the sites of terrible deaths, for example, places of accidents, murders, suicides or execution. These places are marked forever on the tourist maps of ghosts. They are the spots where malevolent spirits gather to wait and plot, to snare a substitute to take their place. Never stop to help at an accident where you see someone is dying, unless you are a powerful ghostcatcher out to catch a ghost. One may well be hovering, waiting for the completion of death, to slip into the newly dead body and make it sit up straight. The newly dead body will rise and go about the ghost's unfinished business. Ghosts don't like*

*being thwarted. To stop and hinder the dying process would
lead to great ghostly anger, and retaliation.*

My grandmother is a believer in the value of retaliation. She
is a believer in keeping face. Face and retaliation are laws of
conduct more ancient and honourable than the good behaviour
rules of the nuns.

'Why be like a mouse, always afraid to make a noise?'
Grandmother demands. 'If someone insults you, or does you
harm, you must insult or harm them back double, otherwise
you lose face.'

Everyone is born with a certain amount of face which must
be guarded at all costs. Face can be added to, and also stolen,
or lost. The person who ends their life with less face than they
started with is a sorry case. My grandmother believes in the
value of waiting. She believes life is a battle with winners and
losers and the key to success is timing: biding one's time. Great
generals have lost crucial battles through failing to wait for
a propitious time. The one who waits and plots before striking
will win.

'Understand?' Grandmother asks, peering over my shoulder
as I painstakingly loop and thread her words onto paper. I
suck on the end of my pen. Make ink splotches, which
Grandmother carefully blots. Some days her words are too
heavy, they press on my shoulders, on my pen until the nib
curls inwards and snaps. On these days she sits beside me with
a pile of new nibs. She twirls her bamboo cane every now
and then to remind me that the weight of her words is not
so bad. On days like these I crawl after Grandmother, page
by page. I stare out the window when she isn't looking, run
my other hand over the knotted wood of the table, along the
chair arm to scratch at my elbow, to slip under the table and
over the insides of my thighs. Some days, just above an elbow
or knee fold, there's a patch of skin that makes me snatch
my hand away: rough and snagging. Some days there are two.
Skin patches in a raised and regular pattern, scaly, flaking at
the touch of finger, or table, or dress. Other days I fly after

Grandmother, my pen racing her advice and stories. In the pauses when she's thinking, I scribble pictures to go with her words, inky curves and splashes which make Grandmother laugh.

Late in the night, when our kerosene lamp gutters and my mother bends to sweep the shadow curl of ash from under the burnt mosquito coil, my grandmother finally lets me stop. She finally takes the pen from my cramped fingers, signals that it's time to turn back the pages and read our night's work. I stand with one foot forward, the notebook in one hand. I read to Grandmother her words, with actions. Grandmother nods appreciatively, laughing at the right bits. When I finish she claps her hands. I snap the book shut when my mother leans over to look at the quality of the writing, and Grandmother and I put our heads together, the notebook held like a shield between us and my mother, and Grandmother giggles like a schoolgirl, and we whisper and peep over the edge to see if my mother is jealous.

'It's her own fault,' Grandmother whispers, loud enough for my mother to hear. 'She had her chance to help, but she spoilt it. Look at that badluck face! Useless!'

My mother bends to her mending, pretending not to hear. Her mouth is set serenely, her forehead unmarked by the slightest frown; her face unlike the badluck face she turned to Grandmother when she spoilt her chance to help. Then my mother's face was tear-streaked, reddened. Grandmother's fingers swelled her cheeks in stripes, her voice slapped and scraped at her until my mother fell weeping at Grandmother's feet. She neither ducked nor flinched from Grandmother's words and blows. She twisted deep creases into her shirtfront, her mouth also twisting. Grandmother stood over her, breathing harshly, one hand rising to the lump on her head from the bandit's rifle that weeks later still had not healed. The lump on Grandmother's head was a boiled egg, a shiny knob. Grandmother tottered on her feet. She blinked, so angry her extra eye blinked also, open, for an instant the world was once more clear and colourless. For one moment

Grandmother got her black-and-white vision back.

'Useless!' she ranted. 'Your mother's old now. Your mother's sick, can't work now. Look at this lump on your mother's head! Business is not so good, the nuns spoil business, how will we live? Ungrateful beast, I sent you there to learn their magic, why you never do that? What did you do? First you take my knife, you give to that boy, that crocodile! Then you go walking for days. Come home crying. Now this! Soon stomach swelling. You think your mother can't see?'

'Ma,' my mother wept despairingly, her blotched face unlike her calm mother's face that the bully and I are used to. 'Ma, forgive your ungrateful daughter.'

'Useless, stop crying!' Grandmother ordered when she was calmer. Grandmother slumped in the rattan chair she used for advising clients while my mother leaned against her legs. 'Your old mother should be the one to cry. All my time and work, wasted, now must change my plan. Aiya, don't cry! Already done, no need to cry.'

'Ma, your ungrateful daughter will never forget your kindness. Ma's time and work—not wasted! Ma, I promise! I will make it up to you. Your ungrateful daughter will pay you back.'

'Yes,' Grandmother agreed, placing her hand on my mother's belly that hadn't yet begun to swell. 'Yes, you will.'

'Useless!' she calls across the room but my mother pretends not to hear. My mother calmly plies her needle so Grandmother returns to our book. Grandmother flicks her finger over the pile of notebooks kept in the special case to which only she has the key. She pulls one out at random, squints at the pages covered with blurry squiggles that swim from left to right. She puts on her extra strong spectacles but even then can't make out the words. 'Here, Grandmother,' I point. Grandmother mouths the words as I read. Occasionally she traces their shape with her finger, then practises speaking them. The foreign words fight with her tongue, twisting it in ways it doesn't want to go. Grandmother makes sounds that send the bully, my mother and me into peals of laughter in defiance of her scowls.

'Can't you be serious?' she shouts, her hands on her hips. Then she too laughs scornfully at the bulky shape of the words. She collapses in a heap beside her special case, digs deep into it for her extra special notebook. All the scribbled notes from the other notebooks will make a pattern to go into this. Grandmother rests the notebook on her knees to show me the smooth paper on which I will one day write. We breathe its rich papery smell. She fingers the other notebooks which will eventually make up her legacy, her store of seeing that since her extra eye closed has become increasingly dim. The bully and I stare as Grandmother props her eye open with spells and salves learnt from an old man deep in the jungle. The old man called not long after she was hit on the head with the bandit rifle that closed her extra eye. He showed her the love charms, weather charms and charms for profit and prevention that the bandit had rifle-knocked out of her head. But the old man didn't finish telling her everything, so the spells and salves don't last. Her extra eye never stays propped open for long. 'The old bugger tricked me,' Grandmother curses. Only in a more generous mood will she grudgingly admit that the trick that wound its indirect way towards her through the passing of the wet and dry seasons of her living, the habitual twists and turns she made in hope of confusing just such a trick, was cleverly done. 'My oldest enemy, very strong,' she says. 'So strong, and my eye so bad, that at first I didn't recognise her.'

'Who was she?' the bully and I ask and ask. 'Was the old man a she?' But Grandmother never says for sure. Already she thinks she has said too much.

Every day more colour leaks into my grandmother's sight. 'Write faster!' she orders, though I'm writing as fast as I can. Grandmother wants her seeing to be written in shapes and patterns she herself can't read. In the words she sent both my mother and me to the convent to learn, the words of newspapers and city records, not those of talking-story or ghostchasing, or charm. That is a part of Grandmother's plan: to learn the word shapes and patterns of the nuns so her seeing can be printed on golden-edged paper and bound between covers of shiny red leather, and kept in a glass case at night and taken out in the daytime to be read and copied and sung from, and taught to little children by heart. So everyone will know.

'What will they know, Grandmother? What?'

'That theirs isn't the way to answer a favour!' Grandmother says. 'That there's more than their way of seeing, and more to life and the afterlife than dressing in white with a head wrapped in cloth, and making everyone read their book, and always falling on their knees, praying.'

My grandmother is the possessor of a tremendous memory, which she is slowly passing to me. Grandmother says she never forgets. Good deeds or slights, kind words or insults, all are stored in deep dark pools into which she dips and fishes. When Grandmother isn't listening, my mother tells us not to pay attention. As the years pass Grandmother's pools have fewer and fewer fish. That is why she wants them written down.

'Useless!' Grandmother calls from the other room. 'Useless, what are you saying?'

When the bully and I return to sit at her feet with a pot of tea and the sweetcakes she likes to nibble, Grandmother winks at us conspiratorially. There's a big fish that will always stay in her pools, she says. This fish lives on a hill and is filled with other tiny white fish, like maggots. The bite of the little maggot fishes stings like fire, like salt on a wound. Like an endless ride, jumping and jolting, on the floor of a soldiers' truck. Their eyes swing like the swing of a truck lantern. The maggot fishes bit Grandmother when she was younger, when she and my mother went ghostchasing at the ghosthouse one night. They bit my mother too, though now she pretends she can't feel the bites. Grandmother shows us the scars. She sent my mother to catch the big fish, to prise their secrets from the maggot fishes, but my mother spoilt her chance, my mother went swimming instead, and now Grandmother has to wait. Now Grandmother is waiting. Now she is fishing and one day she is going to hook that fish, and we will have it for dinner. The bully and I bend our bodies to the shape of Grandmother's hook, we snap our teeth to show its sharp point. Grandmother leans forward, her words coming so quickly we cannot see her lips, her arms stabbing at us in staccato flourishes the bully and I have to duck. The bully and I fall still, awed by her performance. My mother watches disapprovingly from the door. When Grandmother finishes the bully and I whistle and stamp our feet. The bully and I clap our hands.

'We like fish for dinner, Grandmother!' we shout, smacking our lips. 'We like tasty fried fish!'

My grandmother is a hoarder. Her room is filled with crates and boxes, bundles wrapped in squares of cloth, oddly shaped tins. Grandmother spends hours sifting through her hoard. Beads with inky centres, old ceramic money, cloths worn so threadbare the bully and I can see right through them even in Grandmother's dim light. Grandmother holds each item to her light. She turns it this way and that: peers for long moments the way she peers into her swallowed jar. Eyes narrowed, considering. Grandmother spends hours sucking at her cheeks. Smiling. She is old now, almost fourteen turns of a woman's life cycle, so sometimes she forgets when people are watching. She forgets to be nice to soldiers, she turns on old friends with her tiger glare. In the street Grandmother drags her feet. She sucks at her hollow cheeks, stops to forage in scrubby bushes while the bully and I pretend we don't know her, we are just resting on the roadside, how interesting the opposite roadside is! The bully and I stare just above people's heads. We look at our feet or at the tops of buildings or into the sky until Grandmother shuffles towards us with a triumphal clutch of leaves, an earthy root. Grandmother stumbles, her special sunglasses slipping down her nose. 'Eat!' she orders, shaking the worst of sand and city dust from her find. The bully and I obediently hold out our hands. We toss the leaves or root over our shoulders at skilful angles, move our jaws in exaggerated munch movements so Grandmother thinks we eat.

'Yum,' I say, mock-swallowing.

'Wah, already working!' the bully flexes her arms.

'Come,' Grandmother beckons us to the next roadside clump.

At home she brews foul-smelling medicines of what she has gathered for the bully and me, remedies for the troublesome time we inhabit, our in-between time, now that the bully and I are no longer children but not yet young women, that dangerous time my grandmother knows of only too well.

'But what time *is* it, Grandmother?' the bully and I ask. 'What?'

'Everything shaking,' Grandmother says. 'Everything turning time.'

The herbs, roots and grasses found stubbornly surviving in the odd nooks and crannies of the city are far from satisfactory, so Grandmother grumbles, Grandmother slaps her earthenware pots onto the stove. 'No good,' she mutters. 'No good, no wonder cannot work. Aiya, what to do?' Grandmother glares at the bully and me, about to slip from the kitchen, away from her head-scratching, her pinching and slicing and mixing; her beckoning us over for a taste. 'Next time you go walking,' she tells us, 'don't play the fool so much, don't waste time. Take pictures for what? You want to be famous, do what Grandmother says! Find leaf, find root. You want to find treasure, listen good. Follow the hill spirits, the one-armed hill spirits, then you can find.'

In her room my grandmother digs and scrabbles through her possessions the way she scrabbles and digs for leaves and roots to calm our young girls' restlessness, to stifle our heady in-between girls' smell that will get us into trouble if we don't take care. Our in-between mix of curiosity and skepticism is the target of Grandmother's herbal potions, our annoying habit of asking and wheedling, then doubting what she tells us is true. Our running around looking for other sides to Grandmother's stories. 'Hah!' Grandmother shouts, waving her ladle. 'You think I don't know?' In her room she holds old cloths and papers to the light as though a cure is to be found between the pulped fibres, the woven strands. Sometimes she forgets the bully and I are there. She forgets we are in danger, she slips from danger-watching and warning back to the days when she was just a girl. The bully and I can't imagine my grandmother as a girl. We can't believe she fitted the red pyjamas she carefully spreads onto her knee. Her fingers tremble as she smooths the faded cloth and raises it to her cheek. The bully and I can't imagine Grandmother's skin smoother than the cloth of her red pyjamas, or her hair shinier than its buttons, her cheeks flushed a fresher red. We pull at the tiny sleeves and push our fists up the legs, hover our hands like flies so Grandmother slaps us away. The tattered cloth reeks mothballs and more uncertain smells: sweat and savoury laughter, an air of dancebands and fairy dancing; a hand pressed to Grandmother's forehead heavy with a musk that makes her dizzy, that makes me sniff harder, suspicious of her bowed forehead, her distant smile. In her room my grandmother sits surrounded by half-opened tins and boxes half-spilling their contents, her feet tangled in plastic bags and raffia, her hands clutched like claws to her red pyjamas that even after all these years whiff envious glances and the rich man's laughter, the firm slope of the rich man's knee. A faint and childish certainty of belonging: the assurance of joy.

An older girl in the ghosthouse, an in-between girl, no longer a child, not yet a young woman, my grandmother knew her life as she knew it was coming to an end. The certainties of everyday living crumbled like kitchen ashes in her hand. In those days Grandmother liked to push her hand to the warm ashes of spent fires, to charcoal hearts. The odd red coals to be found in their centres were surprisingly cool. Grandmother watched her calloused fingertips blister, she pushed bead blisters to her teeth to test her skin strength. She spent many hours, many days, on her own. She wandered the rich man's mansion like the shadows that occasionally followed her, passing over everything, leaving nothing but a trail of smudged feet. She went from bookroom to kitchen to balcony to basement room to rich man's quarters, wherever other people were not. Her walk, unlike her dawdling child's walk, was a dodge and skip always to be out of view. Grandmother walked bumping into furniture and doors and walls, squinting her eyes to slices. She walked with arms outstretched as though blind.

Squinting, my grandmother saw not furniture, not doors and walls, but the secrets of wood and mortar, of old arguments pressed into the plaster, old joys seeping from the woodwork, long ago slights. Workers killed laying the foundations pushed their sad faces through the paintwork to stare. In those days the rich man's mansion swirled at my grandmother the secret longings of both the living and the dead. The sight of the secrets spilling to skin and wall surface was terrible, when Grandmother looked at her own body, the sudden shadows sprouting on her arms and legs made her quickly look up. Over her heart the flesh was mottled black. Over painted partitions, around pillars, she watched the secret paths of the rich man's hunger. Through intervening walls she heard his whispers in a voice never used with her. The rich man's whispers sat in her ears like a waxy ache. His gaze after the lover could eat the sea. Only the lover was like glass to Grandmother, reflecting only its image, its one layer. She looked and looked but there was nothing underneath.

In those days my grandmother walked the rich man's mansion from bookroom to kitchen to balcony to basement room to rich man's quarters gathering the bits and pieces of her life as she knew it, that was coming to an end. Pieces of annoyance, confusion pieces, stored up slights. Hate bits eating into the palm of her hand. Grandmother slipped these to her pockets like evidence. She dangled them from fingertips, stuck them like extra hairpins behind her ears. The gathered bits and pieces of her life weighed into her steps. As the weeks passed her back became bowed. Grandmother collected childish laughter now never rich man echoed, she prised long ago fairy dancing from the left over claps and cheers scattered over the ballroom floor; snatched through the bookroom window a slant of sunlight that once brushed the rich man's hair. Grandmother held the rich man's hunger like an injury to the crook of her arm. She walked from bookroom to rich man's quarters to balcony to basement room nursing his thirst like a delicate ache. His sunken cheeks and eyelids were heavy to carry, his musky rich man's smell was tinged with the lover's smell. His hollow body hurt her hands.

Grandmother collected other bits and pieces as she walked. Here started her lifetime of hoarding, the scraping and picking and hiding away as though any moment everything might be lost. Like a mouse she crept her way through those older girl days of the ghosthouse, secreting in this corner red candles and joss sticks stolen from a kitchen drawer, under that ledge matches and stove kindling, scissors, a jar of dirty water, filthy kitchen rags. Amongst the precious statues she slid bottles of kerosene, sparklers left over from a bonfire party, thorny pineapple leaves. Between leatherbound books in the book-room could be found protection charms of all shapes and sizes sneaked from this houseboy, that kitchenmaid. Every day Grandmother shifted her hoard. The weight of her gathered bits and pieces pulled her always lower. The basement room was where everything ended up. Grandmother swayed from side to side, her walk two steps this way, two skips that, to hold everything. Bits and pieces of her life as she knew it spilled from her arms in a trail behind her: hate mixed with joss powder, despair with stray matches, childish laughter snagged to a banister rail. From the balcony awning Grandmother took hairs untangled from the lover's old headscarves, from the rich man's quarters nail parings picked from the wastebasket, a cloth waved in the air to catch the lover's smell. In the basement room, the old punishment room, Grandmother found the side-by-side photo of the rich man and the lover, framed in silver, she found a locked travel trunk under the bed. The trunk's hinges were salt-crusted, its wood cold to the touch. Its smell like water drawn into the nostrils, merciless and sharp. Grandmother felt the coldness of the trunk, of the things inside it, even before she entered the room. The cold seeped into the floor, into each tentative step she took. She chipped at the crusted hinges with her scissors. In the trunk she found a bundled handkerchief. In it, a scale the size of her thumb, a fish scale, green in lamplight. Shimmering like pearl. The knife beside it winked cold and gemlike, its blade the length of Grandmother's hand. Grandmother shuddered. From the scale and the knife the lover's smell came sharp and unrelenting. On them the shadows she could not see when she looked at the lover were layered soft and thick.

In those days my grandmother liked to push her hand to the warm ashes of spent fires. Even nowadays the corner she favours in our kitchen is the one closest to the stove. Grandmother likes the flush of her face next to a stove fire, the waft of ashes onto her feet. In those older girl days in the ghosthouse she first learnt the virtues of flame. The blaze started on the basement room floor could almost still the shuddering of her hands. The greedy crackle as she fed it almost silenced the bug-eyed shadows flapping around her, almost steadied the fearful beat of her heart. Grandmother fed the fire with the gathered bits and pieces of her life as she knew it, that was coming to an end. It took to her past life immediately, shot sparks to the ceiling, lapped at the kerosene trails. The lover's hairs pushed to its centre shrivelled to seaweed shapes, her nails jumped away from the heat. The bundle with its scale and knife hissed like something alive. My grandmother's breath teased the flames to greater fury. The heat singed her eyebrows, lifted the hair from her head in horny spikes. Sweat trickled down her body; her face was wet with tears. The dirty water she sprinkled onto the conflagration hissed and spat with glee.

'I curse you,' Grandmother whispered with all the weight of her gathered life that added up only to the bitter taste of her curse. 'Do you hear me? I send you away. I send you to the wild beasts. I'm burning you up. Go away! I'm sending you to the jungle, where the jungle roots will snag you, and the wild animals chew you up, and the jungle spirits lick your bones. The hill spirits will take what's left of you away. You'll be stuck there forever. Nothing will be left of you but burnt sticks. No one will hear your breathing, your midnight walking. No one will hear you sigh! Can you feel the weight of my curse? I send you away! Go away! Go!'

Grandmother sank to her haunches. The slipping and sliding of the bits and pieces of her life into the fire left her light enough to float. The curse heaving from her body made a hollow cleft in her chest. Grandmother watched the bug-eyed shadows tossing the curse from hand to claw through the flick of a tail into the fire. The shadowy parts they added swelled its shape and size. In the curse's inky centre sat Grandmother's annoyance, her pieces of confusion, her stored-up slights. Her hate bits. Grandmother watched the flames. Smoke curled her breath into a racking cough. She threw the last of the lover into the fire for good measure, to seal the curse: the portrait found by the canopied bed. The flames licked at the silver and glass. Too late, Grandmother saw the figures in the photo, the rich man and the lover, side by side. Too late she remembered to tear the photo in half. Grandmother's cry was drowned in the hiss and crackle of the flames. The hot silver she snatched at singed her fingers, the photo within it already crackling to black. The glass cut her hands. The photo she tore from the frame was already charred. It was filled with smoke shadows, its side-by-side figures merged. Too late Grandmother watched her blood seep into the burned paper, drip into the flames to feed her half-cooked curse. The curse gobbled up Grandmother's blood, it sucked the images of the rich man and the lover from their photo. Grandmother's hands were raw and weeping, like the cries pushing their way up her throat, the shouts and wails pounding at the basement room door. In her lap the half-burned photo of the rich man and the lover, and blood from her half-burned hands, were inextricably mixed.

When my grandmother was a young woman she no longer lived in the house on the hill. Grandmother returned to the city, she and the other servants were sent packing, the house was put up for sale. The other servants left huddled together for comfort, dressed in dull black, in mourning. Soldiers stood in careless knots at the gate to watch them go. Grandmother trailed after them, her cloth bundle dangling from one wrist, her face twisted with crying. Her burned hands were bandaged with rags. Over her shoulder the house with its half-shut windows and front door swinging half-open was a tearful blur. Grandmother ran the back of one hand over her face to set it straight. She looked back once, then turned. The road to the city curved smooth and inviting.

When my grandmother was a young woman, and later, when she was a woman not so young, she used to return to the house on the hill for a visit every now and then. The house remained empty for years, a badluck place, no one wanted it. For months Grandmother forgot that she'd ever lived there, her city work absorbed her, her peddling and amateur charm-making. Then one day she'd wake with her feet twitching, her toes curled into claws. All day she'd sit at her roadside stall, twitching, snapping at customers, carelessly showing doubters her ghostslashing knife. Towards evening Grandmother would find herself walking, she'd find the crowded streets and huddled shophouses falling behind her and the jungle looming ahead. She'd find herself halfway up Mat Salleh Hill: wandering through the overgrown gardens of the rich man's mansion, slipping into the house through a broken window, spying on the bandits who camped there every now and then. Grandmother sidestepped bandit lookouts who stared straight through her. The bandits were a rowdy bunch, unkempt and smelly, breaking what was left of the looted furnishings to build campfires in the middle of the hall. Where couples once swirled they lolled in untidy huddles, arguing, dividing their treasure into piles to be kept, to be given away. They crouched poring over maps and papers, swearing when their wireless gave out only a crackling whine. Off-duty bandits dealt greasy cards with deft flicks of their wrists.

My grandmother walked the house on the hill as if she owned it. The house was her belonging place, the place that had shaped her life and her luck. She walked the walk of the girl she used to be, that in-between girl of the days just before the ghosthouse became a ghosthouse. No one could keep her out. Neither the bandits nor later the soldiers who claimed the house for interrogation headquarters ever stopped her, ever saw her come or go. At the very edge of the rich man's garden Grandmother stopped to peer into the jungle gloom. She stood gathering her breath, steeling her blood. Trying to push one foot forwards, then the other, trying to stop their slide back. Grandmother tried her hardest to enter. Peering sideways she glimpsed the path of her unfinished business snaking its way through the jungle, a path faint and uneven, slippery, scattered with loose stones. Red ants swirled now on this side, now the other; leeches raised their questing bodies at any footfall, spiders as big as her palm dangled from invisible threads. To walk that path Grandmother must push through branches that were like arms to push against her arms, she must snag her skin and hair on plants with curving thorns, and run zigzag alongside the glistening tracks of the rich man's funicular railway, and listen to the terrible screech of its cables, its grinding wheels. She must run the path in terror. Only at the top of the hill could she pause to ease her tattered breath. Only there could she stand bent over with the terror snapping at her feet. Grandmother stood for long minutes on the very edge of the rich man's abandoned garden, trying to swallow her terror of the thing she had cursed into the jungle; of the cursed thing lying in wait. She stood trying to lift her feet. But even the pull and power of unfinished business could not lift her feet. Each return, standing on the very edge of the jungle, my grandmother turned back. That is why I go there: because my grandmother always turned back.

From the time I was a small child I have always known I would walk in the jungle. That too is a part of Grandmother's plan. Grandmother, my mother and I stood on the edge of the jungle peering in. My mother held me in her arms, shifting me from hip to hip. The weight of my body crushed her dress.

'Don't be scared!' Grandmother cried, shivering and shaking so fearfully that I shivered and shook too. Her face drained of its tiger expression drained mine too. 'Grandmother will give you a strong amulet,' she said. 'No need to be afraid!' I stared into the jungle with narrowed eyes.

Although my grandmother can see the twists and turns of her unfinished business through the jungle, she does not know where it goes. She does not know for sure. That is why I go there. The path of the unfinished business is so well-hidden my grandmother only found it by chance. By following the rich man and the lover one night.

Walking along the jungle paths the bully and I keep a lookout for the place where the many tracks meet. This is the place of Grandmother's stories, the place of treasure, where she says we must dig.

'How many paths, Grandmother?' we ask. 'How many?'

Grandmother counts on her fingers. She scratches her elbows, peers into her teacup where the tea leaves swirl.

'How will we know this place, Grandmother?'

'Aiya, hasn't Grandmother said? Follow the hill spirits! When you get there, you'll know.'

Whether at night or in daylight the bully walks the jungle paths with her head turning left and right looking for this place. In the daytime we look for the troupe of monkeys which the bully thinks will lead us there. When the daytime finds us nothing we set hill spirit snares at night. We creep from the darkroom where we've set up our sleeping corner, our mats laid with cushions side by side. We lie in wait for photos. Day and night, since my grandmother first mentioned the treasure, the bully can't wait to walk. She walks with her camera slung bouncing on her back like the bats and balls she carries when convent girls go for sport. She walks with her chin permanently lowered the way some animals do; snuffles in the grasses and under dead branches and rotting treetrunks for what might be an overgrown path. 'Help me look!' the bully scolds, although I am already looking.

In the daytime we creep from the classrooms where we're told to stay while good convent girls go out on excursions. We leave our classroom jobs, our classroom punishments, the blackboard uncleaned, our punishment lines unwritten, and the floor unswept, the desks and chairs unstraightened. Sometimes we leave so quickly our five hundred lines *We will be good obedient girls* flutter after us in confusion. Sometimes we leave when the teacher's back is turned. We slip into the parts of the jungle that push through breaks in the wire fence. We walk with our eyes peeled. Sometimes we leap from the path to stop and stand like trees. We wave our arms like branches, crouch in the heart of a fern where the furry curling tendrils tickle my nose. A look from the bully and I do not sneeze. An inch away from our faces, so close we can touch it comes the slippery pitter patter of convent girls on a biology outing, running from tree to tree; examining leaf and bark patterns, squinting at the size and shape of the various foliage, piercing, pinching, squeezing with their fingers to determine the textures of the different jungle fruits. A sharp whistle and the girls tick their quiz papers and run to the next numbered tree. The girls push and pull at each other, at arm or hemline, to get there first.

'Girls! Girls!' the nuns admonish, their whistles swinging round their necks, their habits flapping white patches through the undergrowth.

In the jungle the bully and I hold our breaths till the jungle leaves are a pattern of dips and slices that merge and break above our heads. We hold our breaths till the sound of our held breaths drowns out the jungle sounds. We make our bodies into rock when we see anyone approaching. We leap behind trees, peer out from under overhanging branches. Ears pressed earthward we gauge the nearing tramp of the soldiers' boots.

Soldiers play at killing soldiers in this jungle reserve, they divide into blue teams and red teams and they lie in ambush, they set elaborate traps. They burst from hiding with cries that send jungle animals scurrying, they shoot dye pellets to mark their kill. The soldiers whoop over the bodies of their fallen enemies, sit them grumbling in dejected groups to wait out the war. They set snares for monkeys in their lunch hour. Shoot slingshots and dye pellets when the monkeys drop to snatch at the laid out food. The bully and I, rock still, watch red and blue patches flower on monkey fur. We hear monkey shrieks at the cut of stone. The soldiers' shouts and cheers, the slaps of their hands on broad backs as they fall about laughing, drown out every other sound. The monkeys crash through the canopy, leaves and jungle vines snapping and tearing, twigs, fruit, anything they can find fall thudding around the soldiers like rain. The bully snaps quick photos, turning her camera this way and that like a professional. Her hands are steady in spite of her giggles whenever a monkey missile hits. Then the bully is lowering her camera, clamping her fist over her mouth.

'Get them! Get them!' she squeezes the words around her fist as the soldiers leap from the stream of monkey piss splattering onto their heads. The one-armed monkey flashes through the trees beyond reach of their stones. 'Got them!' the bully whispers, laughing, tears of admiration streaming from her eyes. The bully and I abandon our rock-frozen postures, we scramble from the startled turns of the soldiers, their shouts beginning, and race after the troupe of monkeys weighing down now this branch ahead of us, now that vine. The bully and I run willy-nilly, bumping into rocks and trees. Bent branches catapult our faces, astonished insects find themselves tangled in our hair. But the bully and I can't keep up. Soon we slow our run to bend over panting, and the last of the monkeys swings out of view. The bully and I turn back. 'We can we will we can we will!' she chants between her ragged breaths.

'We can we will!' I echo to the dragging tempo of our feet.

Before we leave the bully and I turn back to the jungle,

hands clasped respectfully. 'O Great Hill Spirits,' we say, as Grandmother has told us, 'retreat to the deep jungle! Your children have paid you homage already. They have clasped their hands in respect. They know your origin, with your one arm like a broken treetrunk, and your lower lip dangling to your chest!' The bully and I bow as Grandmother has shown us and leave without turning, so nothing will follow us out.

When we emerge from the jungle we are sometimes met by a group of telltale girls and foot-tapping teachers and nuns. The girls cower at the bully's look of revenge but all the same we are hauled by our ears and stood dishevelled in the main hallway, our faces streaked with jungle earth. Punishment signs are strung round our necks: *We are uncontrollable girls*. In the evening the bully is sent to her dormitory with chores doubled and cheeks smarting, while I, my mother and I both well scolded, trudge home to Grandmother in disgrace.

My grandmother laughs when she hears what the bully and I are doing. She pats me on the back. The next time she sees the bully she is all smiles. 'Never mind,' Grandmother tells her. 'Next time, try harder, you will surely find it. Next time, you'll win!' The bully's mouth is a joyful spread. The bully and I sit rock steady, never shivering, even when Grandmother draws the curtains and dims her old-fashioned lamp as our reward. Even when she settles in her chair and looks at us unblinking, and her voice takes on that ungrandmotherly quality that signals the start of her stories, her voice becoming now a rumble, now a needlesharp prickling to our spines. Even then the bully and I sit rock still: when Grandmother's eyes narrow to slits and the lamp shadows leap around her and it seems the night slips damp fingers into the crevices of our bodies, into our ear folds and navels, and the air presses at our backs so we must turn to look, and see nothing, and the air presses harder, and the bully and I lean forward, and the air pushes past us to lick at the red line of Grandmother's mouth where her gapped teeth are glinting. Even then the bully and I are silent, still, our fingers marking dark stripes on each other's arms. Seeing we are rock steady, Grandmother will begin her wandering through the paths where jungle roots stick out to snare her, the caverns where dark waters swirl and secrets may be plucked from the walls. She will spread her arms to show us; crook her finger to a narrow hook. The bully and I struggle to follow. We stumble and call but Grandmother doesn't hear. Grandmother strides forward, turning every now and then to beckon. Her body contracts and expands, now a bit of glass, now a trail of heavy smoke. Her voice is a whisper, then a roar; her hair a white swirl on her head.

'Follow closely,' her voice echoes around us. 'Watch my footsteps. Be wary of hidden turnings. Watch out for the crocodile.'

'Come!' Grandmother calls, striding forward, plunging first upwards to the smoky ceiling then down into the cracks of the floor, pulling the bully and me irresistibly after. Grandmother's calls ululate around us, pulling us ever onward, taking us somewhere we will one day thank her, she says. To her lifetime's hoarding, her treasure more precious than rubies and diamonds and strings of pearl.

That night the rich man and his lover returned to his quarters to find everything in disarray. The bedchamber was strewn with shattered powder pots and trinkets, the rich man's books were torn and scattered, the lover's dresses, scarves and silken underclothes shredded to bits. The curtains torn from their windows, the hangings from the walls. The rich man and the lover stopped on the threshold. The colour drained from the rich man's face. 'Boy!' his one sharp call brought the head houseboy hurrying to stand gape-mouthed at the door. 'Who has dared to do this?' The rich man's voice quivered with fury, his grip on the lover's arm whitened to bone. The other servants who came running flitted here and there in terror, smoothing the rent bedspread, righting toppled ornaments, pricking their fingers on glass. They tidied the curtains and paintings ineffectively, gathered the pieces of the lover's clothing only to drop them in a sudden turn, a swoop to retrieve something else. The rich man's room was filled with a flurry of white-clad servants, a rush like gulls. Their voices skittered with terror so they made no sense.

'Damn you insufferable monkeys,' the rich man said in a low flat voice that silenced them immediately. 'One of you, tell me, or it will go badly for all.' Finally they made him see it was something to do with Grandmother, that disobedient creature, they'd tried to tell him before, that uncontrollable beast, doing whatever she liked, that bad girl! The rich man sent two burly houseboys racing to fetch her. He stood stock-still, waiting, his mouth drawn in a tight line. When the houseboys could not find her, all the servants were sent looking. They raced through the house peering into cupboards and pantries, under beds, behind curtains, anywhere a culprit might be concealed. 'Downstairs, Master,' their voices finally dragged Grandmother between them. 'In Master's downstairs quarters, the basement room. Old punishment room. Aiya, Master, this bad girl make fire, try to burn down house! Open Master's special travel trunk, burn Master's things.'

'Not *Master's* things,' Grandmother scowled. She stared at the rich man anxiously. Her face was ash-streaked and terrible, her hands blistering with burns. Pushed to the centre of the room she half-bobbed in the awkward curtsy that was her special rich man's greeting.

'What have you done?' the rich man asked.

'Master, I tried to stop it,' Grandmother began. 'I tried to make it stop . . .' Then she noticed the wreckage. Her eyes widened to buttons. Her burned hands, her arms and shoulders where the servants gripped her, no longer hurt. Amazement gaped and shut Grandmother's lips in quick succession so no intelligible words emerged; no defence. When the rich man stabbed her with the other servants' accusations, Grandmother's head and shoulders stooped under the weight of every word. Her body bent forwards. She stared in horror at the rich man's words furiously tangled, his body held rigid, his trembling hands. When he shook her she burst into ugly tears. 'It wasn't *me*, Master, I wasn't *here*!'

The rich man released Grandmother in disgust. At his signal the nearest servants bustled her away. The Number Two Kitchen Maid twisted her arm cruelly as they went out. 'Do what now?' she mocked in a fierce whisper. 'So clever at cursing, who's cursed now, beast? Who'll come crawling now?'

At those words my grandmother flew into one of her rages that even nowadays, old as she is, still have the power to make the neighbours hide their faces, and the bully and me run squealing, the bully and me immediately become demure. Grandmother's arms and legs and teeth lashed out wildly, her voice bellowed like a caught animal's, her face scrunched and reddened into what later became known as her tiger face. Her tears burnt their way down her cheeks. 'Not me!' Grandmother cried.

'Master,' the remaining servants continued their tidying at a less frenzied pace now that a culprit had been caught. 'Master, this girl's gone amok. This girl's lost her reason, make servants lose face. Aiya, Master, sell her bond-pledge, that troublemaker. Master, better for everyone, better to send her away!'

The rich man stared until the servants fell silent. 'Take her to the basement room,' he said coldly, 'since she likes it so much.' Then he added, 'Leave that. Everyone get out.' The rich man reached a hand to his forehead, he swayed a little on his feet. His face was beaded with a fine perspiration, his eyes unnaturally bright. Beside him the lover stood as still as stone. Her breathing was harsh, she pressed one hand to her throat. The lover exuded a faint charred smell.

'But Master—'

'I said leave it.'

One by one the servants filed out. The senior servants' averted faces showed their discontent. The lover followed them to the doorway. She stared at Grandmother's kicking and scratching, tilted her head to Grandmother's cries. The lover staggered against the doorpost before the rich man reached her. She stared at Grandmother with eyes grown much too big.

CERTAIN
UNEXPLAINED
ACHES

Exhaustion slipped like a wedge between the Lizard Boy and my mother. It prised them apart like a sizzle of oil in boiling water, threw them hissing and sputtering into different corners of the room. The Lizard Boy and my mother lay panting in their separate corners, their hoarse breaths rising and falling in unlovely unison, their clothes dishevelled, their hair falling over their faces in wildly yanked-at tufts. Steam from the laundry tubs billowed their past frenzy around them. The Lizard Boy lay eyeing my mother. Slowly, imperceptibly, his look turned sheepish. His ears shone red under their whitish flakes. The Lizard Boy pushed himself upright. He crouched fingering his swelled-up bruises, gingerly flexed his jaw. His head was filled with a roaring like a great rush of water, his stomach with seasickness. The Lizard Boy patted his fingertips to the scratches on his cheeks, he licked the blood shadows from around his lips, and turned to my mother with his turned-sheepish look. The Lizard Boy coughed faintly.

My mother lay perfectly still, she lay curled up with only the pale back of her neck visible, and a thin line of skin between shirt and pants where her shirt flapped up. My mother lay secretive in her corner, her face, hands and feet tucked neatly into her like a folded-up toy, a jack-in-the-box before springing. The Lizard Boy stared at the moist curls on the back of her neck. His shoulders slouched dejectedly. Her curved back seemed curved towards him in accusation, the curls on her neck curling in reproach. The Lizard Boy coughed once more. Then, more loudly, but still my mother did not move. He noisily cleared his throat but she did not look up.

'Wah!' he exclaimed suddenly, cheerfully, changing tactics; grinning his lopsided grin. He winced only slightly, slapping his bruised thigh. 'Where you learn to punch like that?'

When my mother made no answer his cheerful face fell. He shuffled his feet to fill the space of her reply. 'Why don't you move?' he asked when the space grew too big for shuffling. 'Are you hurt?'

'All right!' he shouted when her silence grew so big he could feel it suck against the aches of his body. He was awed by its enormity, he thought it would swallow them whole. 'Aiya, don't be like that! Say something! Did I hurt you?'

The Lizard Boy crawled towards my mother, jangling his chain.

'All right, you win,' he said in a voice so low, so grouchy, my mother almost didn't hear him. 'Don't be angry. You win. I'll tell them I'm sorry.'

My mother almost didn't hear him. She lay folded into herself, listening intently to the self inside her, to the one who neither saw nor spoke, who hardly felt her bruises, or her smile-marked finger, or her burning skinscrapes against the damp floor. She lay listening to the soft shifts and gurgles of her inner organs, to her disorderly heartbeat, the jolted coursing of her blood. She listened to the spaces between each breath. Her head was filled with a roaring like a great rush of water, her stomach with seasickness. Her badluck blood with an unfamiliar presence, a scaly quality. A slowing like the last embers in Grandmother's incinerator, like a midday haze of jungle steam. My mother listened to the mixing of her blood. The Lizard Boy's mumblings rudely cut in. Impatiently she held up one hand. 'Quiet!' she ordered. The thickening of her blood filled her with a narrow inside ache. On her shoulders the badluck shifted, heaved once, twice, settled anew. My mother looked up suddenly. Her face through the steam of the laundry was an oval glow, her eyes red-rimmed but sparkling. Her smell was an animal smell, sharp and heady, overpowering the starch and laundry detergent in a way that made her seem both more strange and more familiar, that made the Lizard Boy, breathing deeply, afraid to breathe. Her lips curved in a way that made his curve back.

'Can you hear it?' my mother asked.

The Lizard Boy was awed to silence. Silenced, he heard only the great rush of water, the seasickness. The churning of the badluck bloods inside them: the irrevocable mix. The Lizard Boy stared at my mother in wonder. He flopped beside her the better to hear it. His skin was plastered smooth with steam and sweat, but they hardly noticed the smoothness. They sat flopped against each other, shoulder to shoulder, listening hard.

'Yes,' the Lizard Boy finally said.

Grandmother says: *If you want someone to fall in love with you, go to a wisewoman and ask for a love charm. To make a powerful and long-lasting charm there are things that you must do. You must obtain a part of the loved one: a strand of hair, nail parings, a recent photo, a few drops of blood. Mix the parts of the lover with parts of yourself, take these to the wisewoman and then you will see what she can do. Mixed blood makes the strongest charm. If you want someone to fall sick and die, you can ask a wisewoman to arrange it. The same rule applies; a part of your enemy is the central ingredient of the charm. Make sure no part of yourself is mixed with the enemy, or else you too will be charmed! Even wisewomen, before they have mastered their art, have been known to make mistakes. A miscast charm may loop back on them like a curse gone wrong, like unfinished business chasing them through the years. Like an old enemy stalking the wet and dry seasons of their living, the habitual twists and turns they make in hope of confusing just such an enemy. Charms come in all shapes and sizes. A charm may look deceptively innocent. It may be a piece of paper written with magic words, sewn into a bit of coloured cloth. It may be a bottle of 'water'. Paper charms can be folded into your wallet or hung around your neck, or pasted above your door. Their ashes can be drunk with water. Charms may be used for barring sickness, stopping wild animals and demons from entering houses, preventing birdshit from falling on your clothes. Charms come with varying strengths and durability, depending on the strength of their maker. Once a miser went to a maker with the cheapest rate to get a charm with strength lasting only one hour. In her rush home to use it the miser was run over by a herd of wild bullocks, squashed to a pulp. That's what is known as fate. Only the charms of powerful wisewomen have the power to influence fate. Cheaper charms need concentration to work. If you see a charm lying on the ground, avoid it at all costs. Charms are like landmines. The best way to defuse a loaded charm is by burning. Another is to pee on it. The more people who do so, the greater the assurance that it has been rendered powerless.*

My grandmother is a keeper of secrets. Deep inside her is a heavy small jar in which these secrets mix together, like soup. Grandmother swallowed this jar by mistake, by falling asleep one afternoon with her mouth wide open when a jar ghost passed. Jar ghosts can never resist the sight of an open mouth. Into the mouth they plop, feeling much like an extra-fat raindrop. Grandmother was ill at the time, her extra eye closing, a lump on her head like a boiled egg, a shiny knob.

So Grandmother was careless, her mistake to snap shut her mouth when she felt the ghost. Jar ghosts should be spat out at once, with the help of chants and stomach-squeezing. Vigorous back-thumping. For my grandmother, caught unawares, it was too late. The jar ghost settled in for good. It liked its new home so much it leapt joyfully about inside her, making Grandmother seasick. For weeks my grandmother battled this ghost, she ate sticky cakes to gum it up, she chewed and drank her way through special charm cakes and waters that would shrivel even the toughest ghost. Finally the leaping subsided, as well as the stomach rumbles and smelly burps and farts. The jar ghost shrivelled to a calcified pot-shape that roamed Grandmother's body at will.

Sometimes, when Grandmother is dozing, the bully and I roll back her blouse to look at her stomach, and there the jar will be, nestling like an egg under her diaphragm, or at her side, pushing against a rib. Every time we look the jar has moved. Every time we look it has changed. Sometimes Grandmother's jar is a mangosteen, sometimes a lump no larger than our knuckles. This jar is where she keeps her secrets. In a generous mood she will admit she should thank the jar ghost for giving her a place to hide. A place to keep things no one can find, even if they beat Grandmother and starve her, and shine a light to confuse her eyes. Even if torturers slam their fists onto tables, shouting and scolding, and refuse to take her to the toilet when she asks so she wets her pants. Even if she and my mother are thrown into a cell to count their bruises and languish on cement slabs that mark cement patterns on their cheeks, Grandmother's secret jar will spill nothing. Grandmother will give nothing away, save for sugary pleadings and promises of red packets and no more trouble, no Sirs! Grandmother will spit her curses into her secret jar where they'll sit stewing with her stored-up slights and vows of vengeance: waiting for the right time to come back out. Extra strong. Even under torture Grandmother's jar of secrets remains impregnable. Even then she can't spit it out.

'Where do you keep it, Grandmother?' I ask. 'Where?'

But Grandmother can never be sure. She cups the shape of the jar in her hands to show me. Sometimes she points to her belly, sometimes her left foot. She pats her belly, swings her foot to test the jar's weight. She smiles to feel the secrets swirl. My grandmother likes the swirl of the secrets inside her, she likes their hollow echo, the identifying taste and texture of each. As she does with the soups my mother makes, soup bowl balanced on one knee, nostrils quivering, soup spoon lifted slowly, deliberately, Grandmother rolls the secrets around her mouth, over the tip of her tongue, in a swirl around her tastebuds. She moves them from one cheek to the other, swishes them backwards and forwards over her gap-toothed gums to push against the smile that cracks her lips.

Every dinnertime, long after we have finished, our bowls slurped at, our chopsticks no longer clickclacking, Grandmother sits bobbing her bowl. Picking at the soup pieces, lotus root shavings, the blobs of pig's fat and sliced black mushrooms swollen smooth. Every dinnertime she sits sipping, smiling. The bully and I watch her tongue dart from her mouth like an anteater's as she identifies each taste and ingredient. It's the only game my mother and my grandmother still play, my mother going to greater and greater lengths to find ingredients which Grandmother may not be able to name. Grandmother's cheeks suck inwards just before she spits out the names. Her breath rushes out in triumph at my mother's nods. Most nights my mother concedes defeat. 'Tomorrow I'll try harder,' she promises, picking choice pieces of food for Grandmother's bowl.

When Grandmother can't guess an ingredient she sits all night mulling over her bowl. On these nights the bully and I can expect no stories. We are banished to our corner where we're not allowed to make a sound. We cut and paste photos in the bully's special scrapbook, press our lips to each other's ears to speak. These nights my grandmother sits scowling long after we have left the table. She obstinately swirls her soup, curls her fingers into claws around her bowl. 'I'm not finished,' Grandmother snaps, brushing my mother's hand away. My mother sits beside her, wiping the table, polishing the wiped table in small circles, rubbing at the circles until they shine. They sit together until, minutes or hours later, Grandmother throws down her bowl. 'Useless!' she cries over her shoulder as she hobbles from the room. 'Useless, what's that? Are you trying to poison me?'

The library courtyard is the place. The place to find things.

'There,' I call to the bully. 'Over there.'

'Shh,' she whispers as she stumbles to my side. Her light slides soft and red around her hand. 'Not so loud.'

In the midnight courtyard the bully is always stumbling. The bully's feet, so steady elsewhere, are caught on the smoothest stone. Her heels snag on hairline cracks that turn her ankles, leaves drifting harmless onto her shoulders make her leap. Sometimes the courtyard air at midnight slows her to a shuffle, so thick with finding that it takes great effort for the bully to move. The bully stands with her shaded torchlight the only movement trailing left to right like the bug-eyed shadows once trailing my grandmother through this very courtyard, stampeding feet marks to make the other servants scold. The midnight courtyard is thick with shadows. To an undiscerning skin they are like night insects, felt only in the soft flutter against an eyelid, the pierce of cheek or palm. But Grandmother has taught my skin. Grandmother has watched my skin peel in layers never to grow completely back. She has pinched and slapped at my fever-thinned skin to strengthen it, has taught me to curve like water over a clenched fist. Like a stretch of air: unbreakable. Grandmother has taught me to feel. What was the lover thinking of as she spun in her sluggish circles, did she lean her head back, did she sag to the pull of the rich man's arms? How the courtyard air at midnight must have scraped against her, that parched air like fire to a throat unused to air. From where I am standing I can feel the ache of unnatural breathing, the dryness around lips. I can see the swirling couples, hear the music, the tinkle of glasses as they stop to drink. I can feel the lover's terrible thirst, her thirst of the whole body, untold by my grand-mother, every orifice of her body, every pore, gaped wide. I swallow where I am standing. I swallow hard.

'Over there,' I call to the bully, but the bully swings her torchlight too late. So we stand amidst the shadows that the bully can't see, and since the bully in the midnight courtyard is slow to anger and action, I pull her hands to my shoulder and waist. I pull her to a clumsy imitation of the shadow swirlings so light on their feet. The bully spins half-heartedly, she follows my lead in surprise. She sags against the pull of my arms, treads on the lover's footprints attached to my feet so that we stumble, we fall against each other like dancers who have been dancing too long.

'Stop,' the bully says, but somehow the bully can't stop. The bully can't make me stop. I am like stone against her, she's a feather in my arms. 'What are you doing? Why are you looking like that?' The bully's hand sliding from my shoulder stops on a rough patch just above the elbow. At my waist she prods skin like plaiting through the shirt. Patches in a raised and regular pattern, scaly, smooth when she rubs one way, snagging when she pulls her hand back. 'What's that?' the bully asks.

'Tell you later,' I whisper, spinning her round and round.

'Tell me now.'

'No, later,' and before the bully can get angry I stop and point so she will point her camera. 'There! Take one there. And there!'

In the midnight courtyard the bully is much too slow. She never gets the right shot. Only a spray of shadow in one corner of the photos she later develops, spots like faults in the acid, marks more accidental than secret. Nothing convent girls will pay for, no evidence to show the nuns. In the midnight courtyard the bully takes her photos only half-heartedly. She carelessly swings her camera on its frayed strap.

The nuns scold the bully for her search for evidence. Their smooth brows darken at her evidence craze. They beat at the bully's back in exasperation, set her on her knees for hours to pray for grace. The nuns say it's the devil who has filled the bully with evidence craving, and the bully must resist. The bully must have faith, but no matter how hard she tries she can never find it. 'The Old Father said . . .' the bully mutters, which drives the nuns crazy.

'Bless his soul, that crazy Old Father,' they grind their teeth. 'Filling young girls' heads with senile fancies! Poor child, have you learnt nothing all these years?' The nuns set the bully five hundred Hail Marys and Our Fathers to help turn her stubborn search for evidence to faith. But saying Our Fathers and Hail Marys like a steam engine, shifting her sore knees, peering at the figures of Jesus and the saints poised disapprovingly around her, still the bully can find neither faith nor grace. Peering, she can see only plaster statues. Squinting, she sees nothing but the Old Priest in the days he was dying, his old head lolling, his gaze fixed just beyond her left shoulder. The Old Priest's face was filled with a rapturous light that pierced the bully. She shows me the dull red spot on her chest where she was pierced. In the days the Old Priest was dying she too stared over her shoulder to where he stared ecstatically, nodding and smiling. But stare as she might the bully saw only the chapel wall. She leaned forwards to twitch the Old Priest's sleeve.

'Father, what do you see?'

'Evidence,' the Old Priest's eyes spilled with tears of joy.

When he died the bully lugged the crate he left her to the darkroom where the nuns now ordered her never to go. The bully laid out the Old Priest's things, last touched by his wavering hand. In the darkroom we inspect them. I smell the Old Priest in his mouldering crate, see his fingermarks like trailing insects, now over this, now that, lingering. The bully pokes at the two red lightbulbs smashed in anger when he died. She twitches her special cloth, heavy from wiping his death. I pick up her salt-crusted knife, once owned by a famous bandit, pressed into the Old Priest's hand just before the bandit fled. 'Keep this safe, Father!' the bandit whispered. His body glowed red and fiery, his skin fluttered a cloud of silvery flakes as he plunged into jungle. The soldiers lunged after him. 'King Crocodile for a miraculous escape!' the Old Priest screeched.

The icy handle of the knife fits the palm of my hand. I open my shirt to press the handle to my belly to see if it makes a mark, but the grey of the charred handle stays where it is. My bellyskin stays pale and smooth. The bully slaps my shoulder, laughing, so I lean forward to tweak her ears. 'Remember your promise?' I ask, swinging her knife with idle flicks of my wrist. 'Remember your promise when I won the darkroom game?' When the bully can't remember I remind her, I study the contents of her crate. 'You promised anything I liked,' I remind her, but the bully can't remember. The bully takes back her knife, starts packing up her crate. I look at her sideways. I flick through her books, one the Old Priest's Bible, the other a book of rules. I balance the rulebook's spine on my palm to see which way the pages fall: open at the page marked trick photography.

The story of the ghosthouse is a story the bully and I should heed. The bully and I should take note of this story. Someday the story will make us famous. My grandmother rocks backwards and forwards as she says this, she spits gobs of laughter into the palm of her hand. One eyelid falls in long slow winks when she thinks the bully and my mother aren't looking. Grandmother and I exchange winks until the bully becomes red-faced, until my mother looks up to the ceiling like the statues of Jesus and the saints in the convent chapel, and the bully throws a punch to shudder my arm. 'Aiya, always making like you got secrets,' my mother sighs, while the bully demands, 'What's wrong with your eyes?'

'Be quiet and listen,' orders Grandmother. 'How will you be famous if you don't listen. How will you find treasure? How will you be king?'

In the ghosthouse before it became a ghosthouse, the rich man was king. The rich man's word was law, the rich man's actions were like the actions of the ancient gods and spirits, needing no cause or explanation. Like them the rich man only needed to be humoured, worshipped and obeyed. Worshipped and obeyed correctly, life for the worshippers was easy; otherwise it was hard. Newcomers to the rich man's mansion were informed of this on the day they entered, before they were allowed their first drink of water, their first word. The rich man was his household's reason: their substance. Without him each and every servant might as well go back to their village or city or jungle, to walk barefoot or scrounge for dustbin scraps, or pull on a plough like a beast. The city was filled with men like the rich man, just as the temples and roadside altars were crowded with spirits and gods. Like the gods and spirits, they too had specialties, special names for praising, special favours to be prompted with red packets and prayers. Along with the Kitchen God, the God of War and Gamblers, the Great Sea Spirit King, cityfolk paid homage and asked for blessing from the Rubber Plantation Superintendent, the Assistant District Officer, the Palm Oil King.

'But *why* was the rich man king, Grandmother?' I ask. 'Was it because his blood was blue like the nuns say a king's blood is, or because he had a golden tongue and jade words like the old emperors, and could make dragons and city officials and soldiers come running at his call?'

But Grandmother can never be sure. She sucks at her lip, tugs the long white hairs on her head into wisps my mother tucks neatly back into her bun. *Because*, Grandmother says, which is also the nuns' answer. Because the rich man was. The rich man was king long before my grandmother came to the ghosthouse. He was king because everyone obeyed him. Everyone obeyed him because he was king. Every single word falling from his mouth had the power to become something: a flock of servants cleaning the house from top to bottom, city officials presenting themselves at the appointed hours, new rooms and pleasure gardens springing up where no rooms or pleasure gardens stood. A houseboy stretched on the flagstones after a whipping, his back ripped to shreds. When the rich man scratched his words onto paper their power reached even farther afield. They sailed whims and wants into the harbour: trees from faraway climates, a bird of paradise, prized silks and cottons, a striped horse with five legs. Workers armed with saws, ropes and axes came to clear a path through the jungle to the top of the city's oldest landmark, the hill in the shape of the woman turning. The pavilion called the Pearl or the Boil appeared on her head out of thin air.

The rich man owned everyone and everything in his house. He never raised his voice, had a way of staring until the servants shrank to nothing, to a spot of dirt on the floor. The rich man ruled everyone and everything fairly, but with an iron hand. He was known in the city for eccentricity, for restlessness. The long absences searching—what for no one knew. He was famous for his love of the exotic, his craving for fine articles; his desire to possess what no one else had. The rich man was known for possessing his servants body and soul. For holding their bond-pledges until they paid them off, or died. Those were the rich man's rules: complete obedience until freedom, or death. Everyone and everything in his house had a certain position, bestowed upon arrival, which they strove to keep or improve, like face. Everyone's position was improved by obeying the rules. Only the foolish knew the rules yet failed to obey them; that was like forgetting to lay out offerings—opening the door to let badluck in. Do the bully and I think we have it bad, feeling once in a while the lash of a cane on our thighs, going once in a while without food? Our lashes fade completely after only a few weeks, our stomachs forget their bloated aches after our next meal. Our tears dry up with my mother's gentle scolding, with Grandmother's promise of a new story, or one of her rough, rare hugs. In the rich man's mansion the aches were burnt into everyone's bones. It was burnt into a place just behind their every thought and action.

But exactly what these aches were my grandmother can't say. She can only say she felt them in the looks of the other servants when the rich man lifted her onto his broad shoulders;

in their mutterings and sharp hand gestures when he gave her a special treat. She heard them in their whispers when the rich man took her into his bookroom to play with his treasures, his antique toys and precious knick-knacks no one else was allowed to touch. Playing under the lazy, watchful eye of the rich man Grandmother felt the aches arrowing into the small of her back. Other aches were more subtle, mere prickles when the rich man rested his hand on her head, or set her on his knee. When he rocked her gently, his hand cupping her ugly child's face, his rich man's voice murmuring: 'What are you afraid of, little girl? What makes you shiver? Why are you afraid?'

Grandmother looked into the rich man's eyes, which were the shape and colour of the sea he described to her so often: swallowing everything. The aches welled up inside her. She gripped the rich man's shirtfront in a childish crush, shifted uneasily on his knee. She pressed her body to his, her small tense body.

'You smell nice today,' the rich man smiled. He ran his hand over her back, over the old scars welting through her shirt. 'Have you been bad?' he whispered, his voice slipping like water into her ear. 'What have you broken?'

Grandmother pushed a charm stolen from the senior servants' charm drawer into the rich man's pocket. She rubbed goodluck ointment stolen from the head houseboy behind his ears, strung a come-home talisman around his neck. 'So you'll come back safely,' she said. 'So you won't forget. So you will never leave me.'

'Don't be silly,' the rich man said, wiping his ears, crushing her talismans with one twist of his fingers. The rich man laughed, swinging Grandmother to her feet.

My grandmother's aches were special no-name aches, with no special cures, not like backache, headache, hunger-ache or the aches rich cityfolk felt, and turncoats and collaborators, whenever bandits slipped in the doors. Did the bully and I think that nowadays people still felt them? Grandmother's were aches of an era gone by, of the days when she was a girl, when gods and spirits flitted through the city streets performing miracles openly. In those days the gods and spirits were bold; even city children knew of their powers, their whims and wants. Wisewomen thronged the pavements, magicians and cure-alls were never short of jobs, or face. Those were the days before the local gods and spirits needed extra coaxing and bribing to show their benevolent faces; before the city surged to the very edge of the rich man's hill. Before my grandmother learnt to see.

'We've got aches too, Grandmother!' the bully and I shout when Grandmother pauses her rambling. 'We've got elbow aches and scab aches and aches where the bugs are biting our heads!'

The bully and I scratch at our bug bites in amazement when Grandmother doesn't answer, when Grandmother's eyes remain glassy.

'Grandmother!' we pull at her arms.

But her aches, as they sometimes do, have taken over Grandmother's brain. Grandmother won't even begin a new story. She thumps her fists at her caved-in chest, one shuddering thump, then another, and another, before my mother can intervene. Perhaps only the lover knew the sharp twist of aches like these, Grandmother muses, her hands finally lying quiet in my mother's hands. Perhaps the rich man knew later, when he was no longer king. These were aches that lurked in the chest cavity, that leapt suddenly to tighten the back of the neck: the aches of an overwhelming desire. Of a curse gone wrong.

'Don't pay attention, girls,' my mother tells us when Grandmother has fallen asleep. Grandmother's head lolls against one shoulder, her lips in sleep are generous and slack. Her face is as peaceful as a lucky old age. 'Aiya, girls,' my mother cries. 'Your Grandmother is old now, that's why she has so many aches!'

Before my mother became a Christian she was convinced that

her luck was bad. My mother's badluck stuck to her shoulders like a shadowy appendage, it swirled around inside her, rose to her throat in shiny black lumps to nudge her forwards into disaster, to snatch her back from the jaws of any likely joy. When my mother was a child she thought the badluck would remain unchanged forever, it would be a child-sized badluck, picked up in ignorance, borne like toothache, carried like a limp one manages to forget at odd moments, with which one has learnt to live. All too soon she discovered the badluck could change; unlike her the badluck was moody. As my mother grew it grew with her, like an arm or a leg, increasing in size and weight, but unlike arms and legs, the badluck had a will of its own. Some days it was the luck of a playful spirit, causing only minor calamity, moving brooms and buckets so my mother couldn't find them, switching salt for sugar so the brothel keeper sprayed a soupy mouthful across the room. Some days the badluck seemed to sleep, leaving my mother to her own devices, to tiptoe through the day expecting at any moment, around any corner, a sudden awakening. Other days it weighed into her very footsteps, it flattened the grass, dented the tiles so people could see where she passed. Some days the badluck hung so thick and heavy on my mother's shoulders it made its own shadow in strong sunlight, at night it wrapped her in a deeper shade of night. The badluck made dimples on her shoulders into which each of her fingers exactly fitted.

'Show me,' the Lizard Boy dared, disbelieving.

My mother glared at the Lizard Boy, crouched in his corner, gazing at her in disbelief. But Grandmother's tiger glare had no effect. The Lizard Boy believed nothing my mother told him. He wanted everything backed up by paper, by proof. When she scoffed at the newspaper stories he read her, he circled the relevant sections for her to look at, he tore out the writers' names and photos for her to hold. He crackled the paper between his fingers so she could hear the sounds of proof.

'You think this paper, so big, prints lies?' the Lizard Boy demanded.

'My story also true,' my mother insisted, but the Lizard Boy wanted proof of her heyday as a ghostchaser's assistant, and her sad stories of brothel women, and the account of the terrible night at the ghosthouse when Grandmother lost so much face that her ghostchasing reputation was spoilt. After that night Grandmother couldn't lift her head, everyone laughed and pointed when they heard how the nuns had sent for soldiers to cart her off. 'Who's more scary, soldiers or ghosts?' the bravest cried. 'Who's stronger, ghostchasers or nuns?' When Grandmother turned to glare they pulled a straight face. When she turned her back they burst out laughing.

The Lizard Boy remained sceptical even when faced with stories that happened only yesterday. The pale shimmering shape that floated past the window to make my mother cry out was mere laundry steam. The shouts from the convent library and the accompanying smells of burning that rushed them to the length of the Lizard Boy's chain were only convent girls playing tricks. The Lizard Boy swore he saw only convent girls walking sedately, no sign of flame. He remained doubtful even when he felt the surge of the badluck bloods inside him, dizzy-making, and looked up to see that my mother felt it too. He wanted words on paper before he'd believe anything, he wanted newspaper proof, history book proof, even of happenings just a moment past. Even of stories he'd seen with his own eyes. 'None of your stories here,' he said, flipping the pages.

'But you were there,' my mother said. 'I saw you, the night we came to chase ghosts. You and your father were there. You held the lantern while Uncle unlocked the ghosthouse door. And now you want proof! Aiya, don't you remember?'

'No,' said the Lizard Boy, whose greatest asset was his capacity for forgetting. The Lizard Boy tapped his head. 'No memory, no evidence inside here. No proof. You make your head go blank, then you can't be hurt. Then no more ache. Chained up, no problem. You should try it. Paper proof is easy to handle, not like up here, if you don't control. But sometimes I forget. Like that day, crocodile crazy, go mad. Forget to forget, easy to go mad.'

'Show me,' he asked, gazing innocently, disbelievingly at my mother's shoulders, at her tiger glare. To the Lizard Boy's surprise she tugged at her topmost buttons to slip the shirt from her shoulders. In the hazy light of the laundry he had to peer. My mother's shoulders were ridged with dents like an animal's backbone, five dents on each shoulder linked by a shadow in the vague shape of a hand. One handprint for each shoulder, one heavy, the other light. The Lizard Boy's eyes filled with tears.

Before my mother became a Christian she was convinced the badluck was a winged demon crouching on her back. My mother was convinced the demon came from deep inside her. Touching her finger to the murdered handprint on the path from her house to the river on that long ago childhood morning had merely let it out. The demon was not an unusual demon but one her own mother said every girl child carried inside her, which made her blood dirty, and prompted her to mischief, and let loose a smell so potent it made men dizzy, it attracted madness, dishonour, badluck. This inside demon pressed girl children's faces to the dirt at childbirth, it sold them to strangers for the price of a meal. Good women were girl children who grew up accepting their inside demon, learning to disguise its smell with perfumes and eyes cast downwards, with voices and ways that were soft and malleable. Good women were girl children who learnt to keep their demons still. That day, at the touch of the murdered handprint, my mother's inside demon leapt out. But she snatched her hand away so quickly that instead of tearing off into the world, loose, leaving my mother a mere skin sack on the path to the river, her inside demon only managed to get halfway out. My mother's demon clung to her shoulders, stuck, venting its anger on my mother, bringing her badluck.

'Nonsense!' the Lizard Boy cried, braving my mother's glare.

'My adopted mother can see it,' she said, setting her mouth.

My mother's demon, half-in, half-out, hooked to her shoulders with steely fingers, channelled its frustration into her. It filled her with aches that crawled all over her body: prickled her skin with secret longings, flushed her cheeks hot and cold with cravings she could not name. The badluck demon, stuck, pushed and pulled against her in fury, pressed her further into the earth, almost lifted her into the air. It gave her a dizzy sensation of flying.

'What's wrong?' the Lizard Boy asked, bringing my mother back to the laundry with a jolt.

'Badluck demon,' she insisted, quarrelsome, glaring him in the eye.

When the Lizard Boy touched his finger to one of the dents on her shoulders, the badluck demon sent a scraping like fire through my mother's body. A shivering like ice. The tip of the Lizard Boy's finger was smooth from weeks of laundry steam, his eyes tearful shiny; his touch cool against the badluck scraping, warm against the ice. My mother quickly pulled the shirt back over her shoulders. She collected the pile of sheets, momentarily forgotten, hastily took them to the tubs already filled and waiting. The badluck demon set a hissing in her blood like Grandmother's cornered ghosts in the desperate fight before surrender, a hissing like spite. Like glee. Although she did not turn to look my mother knew the Lizard Boy too shuddered from the hiss. The Lizard Boy too held his body stiffly. Back turned, she heard his shivered breathing. She heard the increasingly familiar mix of their bloods. Back turned, she heard the faint clink of his chain. She bent, slipping sheets and pillowslips into hot water, passing steamy sheets through the wringer, sorting convent girls' clothes for mending, all the time hearing the hiss and shiver of the mixed bloods. The clink of the Lizard Boy's chain. On her slow daily dance around the laundry, from sink to tubs to gas jets to scrubbing boards, my mother heard the swirl of their badluck bloods, the shuffle of the Lizard Boy's footsteps like moth shadows around her, like mothwings fluttered against another moth.

The Lizard Boy followed her with eyes tearful shiny. Crouching in his corner, devouring newspapers, comics, Bible stories, even shipping lists, the Lizard Boy sometimes forgot. He forgot his most ingenious technique, his wall of iron; he forgot to forget. He stopped to curve his hands to my mother's shape, abandoned his lizardly blankness to follow her graceful movements with his hands as he had on the day they bitterly fought. He forgot his cries of 'Nonsense!', turned from his newspaper proofs to listen to the proof of the badluck bloods. The demon crouching on my mother's back nudged her forwards as she bent with his tray of food and water so that their shoulders accidentally touched. It itched the Lizard Boy's feet so he rose from his usual crouch to pace the length of his chain, accidentally brushing my mother as he passed. The demon sat them side by side at the ironing table, scanning newspapers and storybooks, exclaiming at the stories, laughing at silly pictures when my mother should have been folding sheets. It pressed the Lizard Boy's fingers, lightly, to the back of her neck and held them there for a moment so that my mother and the Lizard Boy sat hardly breathing, for a moment, hardly daring to breathe. The demon raced with my mother, shrieking demon laughter, as she raced to shoo monkeys from the shirts they were unpegging, to secure the sheets flapping on a sudden jungle wind.

The story of the ghosthouse is a story not without its other aches, nothing to do with my grandmother. It's a story not without a sudden flapping of jungle wind. This story gives even the bully and me, immune to most aches as we are, she with her knife, I with my amulet, it gives us headache, dizzy-ache, which-part-came-first-ache, which-part-next, as we try to piece the whole. 'Where are we?' the bully asks, lying face downwards on her darkroom cushions, stomach squashed, legs lazily swinging. Scattered around her are her special scrapbook, her old photo album, a pot of glue, scissors, other piles of photos loose. Around me, beside her, are the notebooks Grandmother doesn't know we borrow from her special locked-away case. I stroke the red leather cover of her extra special notebook, peer into the other notebooks for the place the bully and I have arrived at. 'Where are we?' the bully repeats.

'Darkroom,' I answer.

'That's not what they call it!'

'Basement room, then. Punishment room.'

'What's happening?'

'Grandmother is locked in there, she can't get out. Servants laughing through the keyhole, panting after dragging her back. The light through the keyhole swinging, fading away. The smell of burning hurts her nose. Smoke stings her eyes. Her face is wet with tears.'

'Write it down,' the bully waits patiently while I write in her special bully's scrapbook, in a large rounded hand. The bully's scrapbook is filled with red and green passages, with columns black and blue, and arrows linking one to another so the bully can keep tabs. So the bully knows where she is in Grandmother's ghosthouse story, and my mother's, and the one the nuns hint at but will never tell. So that even if we get lost the bully knows she has a map. The bully's notebook is filled with photos of the sites of possible action, of white sheets draped over my shoulders like a shimmering gown; of my hair flapping in a sudden jungle wind. Extra photos flutter from the bully's scrapbook, in the lamplight they look like large silvery flakes. The bully grabs at the fluttering pieces to shove them back in. She wants her book to contain everything. No clue to slip out, no blank spaces left for uncertainty to slide its way in. The bully's book is filled with so much evidence it opens with a great thump of its cardboard cover, its weight dents red her cradling arms. 'What next?' she urges.

'I can't read this,' I complain. 'My eyes hurt. It's too dark, I can't write.'

'Don't stop.'

'It's too dark to see, but Grandmother knows what she's looking for. She saw it earlier, before they dragged her away.

Her hands hurt but she plunges them to the still warm ashes. The sticky grease of the drenched fire coats her hands. She's found it. A curve of metal in the dark, a half-charred handle, cold in spite of the ashes: the lover's knife that she tried to burn. There it is in her hand. The handle fits the palm of her hand. She finds the half-burned photo, the portrait of the rich man and the lover. She crushes it, flings it across the room. She fingers the ashes but finds nothing else. Nothing but her broken curse. She—and then she—Oh, it's too dark! I can't read this. Now she's holding her burned hands, her hands are shivering, fingers folding in and out. Her breath comes hoarsely. Her face is wet with tears. It's too dark to see. She's not doing anything. She's listening. She's looking up. Staring. She's stopping. She's stopped.'

'Go on,' the bully urges.

'It's too dark. I can't see.'

'What do we say?' The bully turns over, fixes me with her unsmiling bully's stare. 'When it's dark, what are we supposed to say? We can we will we can we will,' she chants as I push away the old and new photos, my eyes sore from too much peering, my fingers from scribbling too much. I snap shut Grandmother's notebooks, which the bully patiently reopens, painstakingly tries to make out the words.

'Wah,' she grumbles. 'Your writing's supposed to be good!'

'I didn't write that.'

'It's your handwriting.'

'I didn't.'

'I saw you.'

'Not mine.'

'What are you talking?' the bully asks, her unpleasant look warning, her hands curling to fists. 'What are you saying? You'd better stop.' Suddenly the bully changes her look. She smiles suddenly, reaches out to slap my back. 'We can we will we can we will,' she says. 'Go on, say it. Like the tough train the nuns tell us. We can, we will. Say it.'

'I don't want to. I'm tired.'

'The nuns say that's when to say it.'

'No.'

'We can, we will. Say it!'

'We won't,' my voice is gloomy.

'We will,' the bully is fierce, her fists pounding against each other, her eyes starting with tears. 'Grandmother says so. What's wrong with you? Why are you looking like that?'

In the darkroom I think the bully is the crocodile. I watch her bully's tears that nowadays start at the slightest provocation, at the slightest shape of my mouth that doesn't fit her shape. The slightest turn of my body from hers. The bully's tears have nothing to do with the angry clamp of her mouth, her hands curl themselves into claws. She plants her twice-my-size body beside me, grasps the flesh above my elbows between thumbs and fingers until my skin darkens to a burn. My skin blooms purple. We watch the purple welting for some moments, my eyes unblinking, the bully's first narrow, then widening to surprise. 'Say it,' she orders, and I see that her voice is not the crocodile voice my grandmother describes, low and menacing, but incredulous, almost sobbing, a squeak. Her face is unlike her usual bully's face, twisting now this way, now that, undecided whether to lash out or crumple; an in-between face that makes me smile. I smile at the bully. 'Of course we will,' I agree, 'if Grandmother says so.'

Later the bully sits up suddenly, scraping the sleep from her eyes. The bully claws her hands into my shoulder, my arms, my chest. I stir beside her in grumbling sleep.

'Where are you going?' the bully calls.

I press my lips to her ear. 'Why did you shout? What did you see?'

'Is it time to go?' The bully lies sinking back to sleep.

'No,' I peer at the alarm clock by her head. I brush back her rumpled bully's hair. 'Not yet.'

The ghosthouse story spreads aches of all kinds in all directions, it sends the nuns livid with indignation-ache, exasperation-at-girls'-naughtiness-ache, it curls convent girls' toes and fingers, flutters their bellies with aches for which they have no name. Convent girls go one by one to Matron, nursing their bellies, pressing their hands to their flushed cheeks. They gargle hot water and stick their foreheads under lightbulbs, look faint from pains here and here and here also, 'Ouch! Matron!', and they *are* too dizzy, see, they can hardly stand up. Convent girls crowd the infirmary during measles, influenza and chicken pox scares, which they're sure they've caught. The ones Matron can't weed out for pretenders lie limp and pale during recovery, free from lessons, until Matron turns her back. Until Matron signals lights out.

Then convent girls leap into each other's cots, they huddle three or four to a cot, facing each other, legs tangled, the single blanket pulled to their chins. Convent girls twiddle their toes along each other's shins and press their palms to each other's breasts to feel the thump thump thump of the heart when the body is gripped by fever. They hold their breaths, shut tight their lips to a slow count of sixty, or a hundred and sixty, however many counts it takes, their faces grim, their eyes devouring each other. For convent girls know *that* is the grip of fever: the pounding of the breath for release. Convent girls turn red from the effort, they really turn dizzy. They know the shape of stillness in their arms, taking turns to wind their arms around each other, to lie still in each other's arms. They know the tickle of long wet hair, of black tresses slipping to encircle the neck. Convent girls think they know. In each other's arms they take turns knowing the shadow weight of the lover as the rich man held her, the shadow kisses brushed to her eyelids. The touch of fingertips tracing her earlobe, or the hollow at the base of her neck. Convent girls shudder deliciously. They know the delicious shudder of the lover's terror pushing weakly at the rich man's arms. They lie practising *that* terror, perfectly still, breasts cupped under each other's nightgowns, square fingernails skimming bodily creases, lips pressed to lips perfectly still, until one or the other skims a tender spot, a tickle spot, and they start choking, they start spurting giggles and kicking the blanket askew. Then the lover's terror turns to muffled shrieks of convent girls' laughter, to pillowfights and a belly-holding ache that prickles their eyelids and brings Matron huffing and puffing with sharp slaps and penance prayers, and extra dining-room duty to chase everyone back to their own beds.

◄ E L E V E N ►

THE BULLY
AND THE
BULLIED

After the terrible night at the ghosthouse that spoilt my grandmother's spotless ghostchasing reputation, she decided to send my mother to school. Grandmother sent my mother to the convent where the nuns took her in for free, on condition that half her time was spent working in the convent laundry. The other half dragged its long hours through a room away from convent girls where a nun retired from proper teaching taught my mother to read and write. She peered at my mother over the rims of her glasses and swung a wooden ruler if she was slow, or lazy, or wrong. My mother painstakingly shaped her mouth and pen to the squiggles that seemed no more than ants on the page. Her eyes smarted at the flick of the ruler, her knuckles glowed pink. Steam from the laundry burnt permanent red marks on her cheeks, which the nuns said made her look extra healthy. The nuns set my mother to work alongside the naughty convent girls sent to do penance in the laundry. In the midday heat the place became so hot that naughty convent girls fell over fainting. Other girls carted them out and sprinkled their faces with water. Naughty convent girls called the laundry Hell, but the nuns said hell was a thousand times hotter, filled with demons which would screech, prick, pinch and otherwise torment them. When a naughty convent girl was in hell she would think longingly of the coolness of the laundry. Only my mother's bully worked in the laundry day after day, never once fainting. The bully stood with her arms on her hips, laughing at the fainted girls. She got into fights in which she pulled out handfuls of naughty convent girls' hair. She pinched and tickled and tormented the other girls so much they called her Demon. My mother says the bully didn't care.

In those days, the bully in school was a girl twice my mother's size. She was tall and heavy, with legs like pillars and hair cut jagged, sticking out in tufts. This bully cut her hair the day she got to the convent to spite her parents for sending her there. Her uniform was made from imported cottons smelling nothing like the cottons in the laundry, her shoes were cut from leather so soft they felt like my mother's skin under the slap of the bully's hand. Peering through the steam my mother watched this bully. Whenever the bully didn't like something her jaw would stick out, whenever she didn't want to do something no one could make her. The bully always said no. My mother stared at this bully in shock when she first heard her. The bully dug in her feet and clenched her fists, and when the teachers snaked out their hands, she didn't even look away. Her head hardly moved. My mother followed this bully everywhere, even when the bully hid around corners to jump her, even when she hissed at my mother to go away, and turned suddenly, waving her fist. My mother followed this bully, watching her method: how this bully said no. My mother shaped her lips to the word in her speckled handmirror. Her mouth made an ill-fitting O. When my mother went home to Grandmother she forgot how to make this shape. At home she stood reciting the lessons she had learnt.

'What did they teach you?' Grandmother asked.

'C-A-T, cat,' said my mother. 'D-O-G, dog.'

'Is that all?' Grandmother marvelled.

'T-A-B-L-E, table,' said my mother.

'When will they teach you magic? When will they teach their power? Are you doing everything they ask, are you being nice?'

'Yes,' my mother said.

'Useless, you telling the truth? Aiya, is that all? Is that why everyone likes them, that's how they take the customers? C-A-T cat, D-O-G dog!'

'G-O-D, God,' my mother said.

Standing before Grandmother, my mother's mouth slid to the thin line, yes. Before the nuns, her mouth slipped to this line. 'Yes,' my mother said. 'Yes.' When she followed her bully, she remembered the other shape. For years my mother practised, twisting strange shapes with her mouth, making other girls giggle, and Grandmother smack when she saw her, and the teachers and nuns throw up their hands. Soldiers at the gate stood laughing when she passed. When her bully was expelled from the convent, my mother stood at the gate with her arms outstretched. Only many years later, when the naughty girls she first worked with had grown up and left the convent, and the nuns no longer sent other naughty girls to the laundry for punishment, only then did my mother get it right. That was the time just after her instant passed, just before she became a Christian, when she walked the streets of the city every day, looking into every face for a sign. Weeping for her disappeared husband, my mother's mouth finally hit the right shape. 'No,' she whispered as Grandmother's own mouth opened and closed in fury. 'No, Ma, forgive me. I have to go.'

Years later, when I first brought my bully to visit her, my mother's mouth fell open. She stepped backwards into the laundry.

'What's wrong, Auntie?' the bully, on her best behaviour, asked.

'Aiya, nothing's wrong!' my mother exclaimed. 'Huh, fancy that. I thought you were someone else. So you are my girl's friend. Wah, so long I didn't see you, so big you've grown! Have you eaten yet?'

For years my mother imagined her own childhood bully. My mother described her to us, laughing, showing her size and shape with her hands. I laughed with my mother while the bully scowled. 'Not at all like you,' my mother assured her. For years, even after her own bully's expulsion, it seemed to my mother she watched and followed in her poised and arrogant shadow, her don't-care shadow, always a step before my mother's step. My mother followed even though she thought she would never catch up. This is the way to victory, she says. Suddenly my mother is rapturous. This is the way to calm: following in a Great Path, already laid out, even if it seems impossible to catch up. Calmness depends on learning to shape the mouth when it's necessary, on following and watching, and a prayer or two. No plots or plans. No promises given without trying her best to fulfil them, no years of twisting and turning to get them back. Calmness depends on remembering nothing but the Great Path, on counting each day as a step. On soupmaking and sitting silent, on humouring an old woman, even though it's hard. The one who follows and watches will win, who walks one day at a time. This is what my mother says.

Nowadays convent girls are taught to feel sorry for bullies. Convent girls are taught to love everyone and listen to their elders and always be nice. They are taught that the bully is the friend of the crocodile. When bullies and crocodiles die they hang out in hell together. They call to each other across the flames, they lick their crackling lips and tell each other how sorry they are now that they were bad in life. Their tears sizzle on their cheeks. But in hell it's too late. No amount of sorries or sizzling tears will get them out. Convent girls must always think of the flames. They must remember that now is the time to be good. Now is the time to say their prayers and confess their sins and be kind to each other. Tomorrow may be too late.

The nuns make the bully stand on a chair in front of the classroom to show, us. They kneel her in the corner and stripe her palms with a wooden ruler so we can see how a bully's ways will make her suffer. When the bully makes a disturbance or sings out of tune in the chapel, or a girl runs to tell what she is doing, the nuns stand her in the sun with her arms stretched out for hours. They make her stand, swaying slightly, until they are sure she is sorry. Until the soles of her shoes become soft. Sometimes the bully is so hot I have to snatch my hand away. The top of her head could fry an egg. The nuns say it is better for the bully to suffer now than to burn in hell. Throughout the lesson convent girls look out at the bully standing in the sun with her arms outstretched like Jesus. They nudge each other when they see her head starting to steam. Convent girls call her Frypan Head behind her back.

When the bully is released she goes to her seat on shoes that suck at the cool cement. She walks slowly, arms hanging by her sides. She sits quietly at her desk all day. This makes the nuns say to look at how even the bully can be cured. How the bully can be saved. Only at night, in the darkroom, does the bully finally speak. Only then do her tears fall: one bright tear after another, so hot they burn red trickles down her cheeks. In the darkroom the bully rants and raves. Her teeth gnash together, her hair stands out on end. The bully paces the room, then throws herself onto the cushions. The bully will have revenge. I scoop her bully's tears onto my palm with my fingertips before they drip out to burn her. Some nights I collect a handful of tears.

Imagine this bully as she must have been all those years ago. They say she is an old bully, that is why she deserves her punishment, that's why she should know better than always trying to get her way. Always trying to win. If the nuns knew all those years ago what the bully on the doorstep would be like, why they would have left her there! For wild dogs to take her. For the mad sailor who came to steal bad babies away. All those years ago the baby bully wrapped in her newspaper and scrap of red cloth hollered so loudly the convent doorframe shook. Even then her face was screwed up and livid, her chin jutting, her baby hands bunched into fists. If only the nuns had known. If only their hearts had been hard. Surely the bully, after years of care and comfort, of her own bed to sleep in and never going hungry, even allowed a favourite hobby, the nuns posing patiently for group photos no matter how long she took; after all that, as well as being allowed to attend classes, surely it wasn't too much for the nuns to expect the bully to turn out good. They say she is an old bully, the oldest girl in the convent, by now she should know to count her blessings, she should know to act more grown up. By now she should know to be nice.

But it's hard for the bully to act her age with only faint nicks on a window frame to mark it. Fourteen marks of equal length and thickness, and no new ones added since the old sister who started them died. No one knows exactly how old the bully is, no one cares to count. They say her sign is the bullock because her baby face through the newspaper crackle was as stubborn as a bull's. Other girls get taller and wider, or slimmer and shapelier, but each passing year sees the bully looking the same. The bully grew until she was fourteen, the end of the second cycle, and then she stopped. Perhaps she didn't know which way to grow. She stands at the window, head pressed to the glass, fingering the fading marks. In the darkroom she presses her hand to one corner of the cushions we lie on, a ragged corner patched with her scrap of red cloth. When she wakes suddenly in the dead of night, with her bully's eyes wild and staring, and the room she wakes to shaking, she presses her hand there firmly as though only that scrap of red will hold her still. The nuns say the bully was born bad, the fault of her bad stock. It's the bully's nature to always need a scold, to stay a stone tied around the nuns' necks till the end of her days. But how can the bully act her age when she doesn't know what her age is? How can she know which way to grow? All her time is spent waiting for a yes or no. Before she can turn, before she can sit or stand or go to the toilet, or choose a book to read, a class to attend, she has to raise her hand and wait for a no or yes. The bully has never shaped her mouth to the rounded shape of my mother's bully without having to duck and twist from punishment, to'trick and wheedle and chase the thin line yes. All her energy is spent on her face screwed up and livid, her chin jutting, her hands bunched into fists. Perhaps the nuns are mistaken. For all the time she has cleaned and cried and taken photos for evidence, and disrupted classes, and shown her face in sunlight to be hung with a net of fine lines, perhaps the bully is not so very old.

But how will I know for sure? I only know what I'm told, what I see. I see only what I'm told. This is what my grandmother has taught me: to narrow my eyes and look sideways, and see what she has told. To see what Grandmother sees. Every day I seem to get heavier. My walk to the convent is no longer as light as air, as crooked as a crab baby's; no longer a skip here and there to peek under shop awnings, to crouch at a pedlar's barrow and slip a trinket into my shoe. Nowadays my convent walk is a pull against metal, a straight line, like tugging at the anchor of a ship. My chin is no longer lifted for whistling. My feet press further into the ground with every jungle search the bully and I go on, every page of Grandmother's notebooks or the bully's special scrapbook that I fill. Every glimpse of the lover I see. Each trick the bully and I try on my mother to make her say more hunches my shoulders like her shoulders, every history, morals and storytelling lesson spent listening to the nuns. Each new amulet my grandmother gives me hangs on my wrist like a piece of coloured paper, no more. The purple marks the bully makes on my arms when I disagree stay purple for weeks.

When I complain to Grandmother, when I show her my bully bruises, the screw marks on the insides of my elbows, the accidental scratches at the base of my neck, Grandmother looks at me sideways. Grandmother puts on her tiger glare.

'For what did Grandmother train you?' she shouts. 'Are you following her, are you being nice?' Grandmother sits chewing her lip, her temper crusty, her old bones like iron, immovable. She grumbles as she checks my amulet, slaps her stomach to see if that jangles the jar ghost loose. She doublechecks the amulet whenever I go to the convent, to that crocodile-infested area, she sits shivering and shaking until I come back. But still Grandmother says I must go. I must go with the bully because the bully is part of Grandmother's plan. From the time I was a small child I have always known I would follow her.

'That's her,' Grandmother pointed through the convent gate, past which, since the nuns chased her, she swore she would never again go. Grandmother made my mother lift me so I could see. My mother heaved me from the ground. I wound my arms around her as I turned to stare. The child bully wandered the convent garden with an enormous box camera slung round her neck. She stood with arms akimbo, one foot jutted out. Half-hidden under her shirt came the glint of her bandit's knife, its salt-studded blade catching the light like crystal. I stared at the bully with narrowed eyes. 'That's the one to follow,' Grandmother whispered, her eyes glistening at the sight of the knife. 'That's the one who's got what we want, who'll help us get it! Wah, she's not afraid of anything! Even from here you can see her liver sticking from her belly like stone.'

Before I ever saw the bully I knew the shape of her head going past a lighted window, I knew her leap across a shadowy jungle path. I knew the swing of her arms and her smell at morning and midnight, her bully's smell of jungle earth. I knew the way she raked her fingernails around the convent pillars where my grandmother once hid.

'Didn't you get it?' Grandmother demands when I return from the convent. 'How far did you walk? Did you follow the hill spirits? Aiya, didn't you find it yet? Why not?'

Before my mother became a Christian, she was convinced of the necessity of glaring. She was convinced of having to fight tooth and nail for a decent morsel of meat from the market, of having to chase customers, to nag and wheedle up business ever since Grandmother's ghostchasing reputation was spoiled. Before my mother became a Christian, she was convinced of the necessity of the endless fight to eat, to be clothed, to be housed, to sleep the sleep of the peaceful—in short the fight merely to live, every single day. Day after day she glared at the Lizard Boy as he crouched in his corner of the laundry. She glared at his different life philosophy: his lizardly forgetfulness that floated him above the fight. His blank reptilian stare.

Every morning my mother entered the laundry to see the Lizard Boy crouched in his corner, chain tangled, face grimy with sleep. The Lizard Boy smiled joyfully to see her, seeming to care for nothing, for neither eating nor sleeping nor washing nor being chained with a chain that scraped his ankles raw. Day after day he crouched with his face buried behind paper, careless of the food crusting its plate beside him, or convent girls peeking cat faces through the window to provoke another crocodile fury, making catcalls to see if it drove the Lizard Boy mad. The Lizard Boy crouched oblivious, hearing and seeing nothing save the rustle of the paper proofs before him, feeling nothing, not even his own back grown hunched, his thighs and ankles grown swollen from inactivity. His buttocks flattened from crouching too much. He seemed not even to notice the wet licks of the laundry air around him, or his hands turning the pages without leaving skinscrapes, his body grown sleek from soaking all day in laundry steam. The Lizard Boy went blank for hours every day, forgetting everything around him, neither moving nor speaking, conscious of nothing but the limp pages clasped between his hands.

This was his best defence, my mother says, although it drove her crazy at the time. It made her slap wet sheets against him as she passed. The daily parade of girls, nuns, the caretaker and the Old Priest coming to stand and point and stare, and whisper together, leaking stray exclamations of *Unstable, Poor thing, Too soon* and *Spastic*, made even my mother turn away.

At first the Lizard Boy stood upright as she encouraged him, he cleared his throat and apologised in serious hopeful tones. When the whispers stopped in shock at his apology, only to redouble, his upright stance drooped under their redoubled weight, his limbs resumed their lizardly crouching. His face reddened as it did on the day the crocodile fury burst. Turning his back to the whispers, the Lizard Boy simply turned off.

'Too proud,' my mother scolded when everyone left. 'My adopted mother says, save pride for next time. Add pride to revenge. Too proud, only stay there longer. Stay locked up, stay chained.'

But the Lizard Boy pretended not to hear. For hours each day he practised forgetting. He crouched working his way steadily through the pile of books and magazines the caretaker deposited at the laundry, books secretly salvaged from the stacks of damaged or unsuitable readings donated to the convent library, which the nuns set aside to be burnt. Each week the caretaker trundled his wheelbarrow lined with the offending books and unwanted magazines in a meandering route past cautious pillars around stealthy corners to the laundry where he dug through the camouflage of hedge clippings to heap them at the Lizard Boy's feet.

'How are you, son?' the caretaker asked hopefully, his hopeful face falling at the sight of the Lizard Boy's gape-jawed smile. His head sprouted white worry hairs at the Lizard Boy's crawl.

'Thank you, Uncle,' my mother said, glaring at the Lizard Boy's antics, the lizard's clicking that was his only reply.

When the caretaker left, twisting his sweat-towel between hands shrivelling, fingers steadily wrinkling from the strain of the weekly visits, the Lizard Boy rifled eagerly through the pile. He leafed through the tattered children's Bible stories marked with childish drawings and comments, not good enough for the library shelves. He thumbed the vulgar five-cent novels sent to the convent for a joke, which the nuns skimmed through with exclamations of disgust and consigned to the reject pile. He devoured the spy and detective paperbacks, pored over the latest overseas fashion magazines, puzzled over the poorly printed leaflets which flitted from unexpected pages, covered with tiny writings he could hardly decipher, words and expressions he had never before heard. *Something colonial*, the leaflets said. *Exploitation. Self-determination. United resistance. Necessary covert activity.* The Lizard Boy held the leaflets to the light, frowning. He turned them round and round, read them to my mother, who merely shrugged, and glared. The Lizard Boy scanned the occasional newspapers brought to the laundry, he studied the pamphlets fluttered from mottled aeroplanes, warning against illegal gatherings, against the distribution of food to strangers and known troublemakers, against imminent bandit and communist uprisings, bandit and communist thugs. *Give up*, the pamphlets said. *Amnesty for immediate surrender.*

When the Lizard Boy asked what they meant my mother merely shrugged. 'My adopted mother says, usual soldier business. As long as they don't disturb us, as long as the food comes in, everything all right.'

The Lizard Boy devoured the amateur newsletters stained with jungle earth or kitchen grease, the painstakingly written hand-to-hand messages she absently handed him: furtive leaflets thrust into her basket as she made her way through the city streets to the convent each morning, papers slipped into unsuspecting pockets, used to wrap stealthy market vegetables. Leaflets crammed with urgent calls to action which claimed no owners when she turned to look. In those days before my mother became a Christian, the city was filled with the whispers of opposing bits of paper. Those days before she became a Christian were later known as the Paper Wars. Even the Lizard Boy heard the paper whispers from his corner of the laundry, he grew more and more excited the more he read. The paper whispers made the whispers of the Old Priest, the caretaker, the nuns, the convent girls, even more remote. It seemed to my mother he devoured the separate bits of paper, ate his way through newspapers, storybooks, historical romances, leaflets, even soap powder packets when there was nothing else. Occasionally he dragged his chain to the laundry-door to stare at the edge of the jungle. The mix of novels, pamphlets, Bible stories, fashion magazines from overseas, newsletters and fluttered leaflets made the Lizard Boy so dizzy he could hardly breathe.

'Huh,' my mother grumbled. 'Always hiding your face behind paper. You'd rather be mad than say you're sorry.'

'What!' the Lizard Boy cried. 'I said I'm sorry, but they don't believe. How many times must I say? I say no more crocodile crazy but they say cannot let go. You see the nun come with the key? When I see that, I'll walk, I'll talk, like they walk, they talk. Like my father, hold down my head when the Old Priest scolds. Turn other cheek. Aiya, don't be like that! Don't be angry. I'm just seeing who's got more will power, them or me. They think they got a crocodile, fine! They got one. They think they got a human, they got one. All depends what they think. They got the key. Now I stay here and rest. Read a bit. Help with laundry. Help make company. No problem for you, for me. No problem, ah?'

'You're just stubborn,' my mother said, glaring Grandmother's tiger glare. The Lizard Boy clinked his chain meekly. 'Never say like you mean business. Will power, huh! You think you're having a will power fight. You think you sit chained here, you make them sorry. You think they care! You sit chained here, no one sorry but you.'

Before my mother became a Christian, like Grandmother she believed in scolding the fight into people: in fighting to win. She believed in bunched fists when her back was to the wall, a tiger roar when her roar was all she had left. She believed in wrenching the chain from the mortar if she had to, tearing at the links until her hands bled so as not to lose face. But Grandmother also taught my mother the value of waiting. Life was a battle with winners and losers, but the key to success was not the nuns' key, to be coaxed from the rope around their waists by will power and a show of pride. The key to success was in biding one's time. The ones who waited and watched and plotted and listened would win. Face lost now would be won back double in days to come, and walking like the nuns walked, talking like they talked, not mad but normal, was part of the plan. The Lizard Boy acted the very opposite of the behaviour rules, the rules for living that Grandmother taught. In exasperation my mother slapped wet sheets against him as she passed.

Day after day the Lizard Boy crouched in his corner. Fewer and fewer were the times when even the badluck demon could shake him from his trance. When the caretaker and the Old Priest dragged in a cot for his corner, he crouched under it until they went away. He kicked the pillows and bedding onto the floor, piled the cot with books, papers and leaflets stacked according to proof-value, to truth.

'This one heavier,' the Lizard Boy mused, weighing it on his palm. 'Must be true. This one nicer paper, foreign name on cover, must be true. This one good quality printing—true!' When finished he knocked down the piles, remixed them by tossing, started again. 'This one handwritten, bad hand-writing, carefully copied. So much work—must be true. This one tattered, creased over and over, almost torn. Covered with grease marks, fingermarks, even here, dried blood. Passed from hand to hand, here it says: *Pass to your friends!* So many people reading—must be true!'

When the Lizard Boy finished he started again. He became so absorbed in his piles of paper truth and proof he hardly even noticed my mother, or the seasickness that came over them both at odd intervals, or the persistent hiss of their badluck bloods. The Lizard Boy hardly touched the food or water placed in front of him, he hardly dragged his chain to the toilet, hardly seemed to breathe. It seemed his bodily functions were winding down. His flesh shrank against his bones; his bones, flesh-shrunken, seemed to take on new proportions, limb bones shortening so his arms and legs became stubby, backbone lengthening so that from certain angles he looked as if he was growing a tail. His toe and fingernails grew curved and pointed, his face bones elongated, jutting out over his eyebrows, squeezing his cheeks into hollow pouches that sagged. The Lizard Boy's skin, stretching in places, in others wrinkling, was in some places steam-smoothened, in others ridged leathery and cracked. His eyes acquired the startling fixity of black and radiant jewels.

'You're just stubborn!' my mother cried, but as the days passed the Lizard Boy noticed her less and less.

'If you don't stop, you'll turn,' she glared, tears slipping from the corners of her glare, but the Lizard Boy hardly cared.

'Leave me alone,' he grumbled. 'I'm sorting proof.'

'My adopted mother says this way you'll get to your next life cycle fast,' my mother shouted, hoping to shout the Lizard Boy from his trance. 'She says you're so pathetic you should go faster, not make crocodile fury, not make fuss!'

'Aiya, don't shout. Don't be angry. Can't you see I'm busy?'

Although the caretaker and sometimes the Old Priest still came on their weekly visits, neither of them saw anything amiss. 'Father, see how much better he is!' the caretaker pleaded. The Old Priest, let in on the caretaker's wheelbarrow secret, brought the Lizard Boy new books of his own, which were carelessly tossed onto the piles for proof-sorting. When my mother hung around them, white-faced and anxious, he kindly asked her what was wrong. He stared at my mother with his slightly vacant stare.

'Father, Uncle,' my mother blurted, 'please take away the chain, otherwise too late. Already he's turning!'

The caretaker and the Old Priest stared. 'Turning what?' the Old Priest asked. 'Surely the chain is long enough, the boy has room to turn if he likes.'

'He—he's turning into a—a crocodile!' my mother stammered with a look so fearful the Old Priest immediately felt her forehead for fever. He pronounced her overworked, ordered her home to rest.

'Don't come back till you're better!' the Old Priest cried.

When my mother returned the next day she brought with her my grandmother's special ghostslashing knife. The knife blade gleamed under its usual sprinkle of salt that reappeared no matter how often Grandmother scraped it clean. The charred handle, so often splashed with ghostly blood and muck, burned icy in her hand. My mother stared at the Lizard Boy for a moment, eyes narrowed, hand burned. The Lizard Boy did not notice. While he crouched in his usual position, sorting proof, noticing nothing, my mother sliced through his chain with one swipe. Grandmother's knife cut through the rusted metal like water. Chain cut, the Lizard Boy jumped, startled, scattering his piles of proof. The Lizard Boy stared in alarm at his lengthening limbs, his shortening backbone, his face shrinking to size. His skin smoothened its tough ridges so he appeared no more than a startled boy. The Lizard Boy fell off the cot in surprise.

'What have you done?' he cried. 'I haven't finished yet!'

'My adopted mother,' my mother whispered, 'says you want something, you got to fight. Got to work. Only good sitting back, waiting, if you've got a plan. If you're planning a bigger fight. No plan, no use waiting. Time to go.'

'Go where?' the Lizard Boy demanded.

'Anywhere better than here, you said. Inside paper, better than here.'

'Put them back,' the Lizard Boy begged, holding his ankles out for chaining.

'Too late. Already cut. This knife's special, cut anything. This is a ghost knife, a spirit knife, brought from the other side. Once cut, can't be put back. Here, you take this knife, carry anywhere, no danger. No need to be scared.'

'Go where?' the Lizard Boy cried.

'Aiya, anywhere!' my mother lost patience. 'How would I know? Go sort real life proof, not paper proof. Aiya, you decide! But this chain's cut—can't put back.'

The Lizard Boy stretched his normal-sized limbs in wonder, only half-listening. He ran his hands over his smoothened skin, cautiously rubbed his bottom to see if the pointed tail-lump had really disappeared. He rose from his lizard's crouch to walk like normal, experimentally waggled his chainless feet. Around him the piles of books, newspapers and leaflets lay crushed and tumbled. 'All right,' the Lizard Boy said suddenly. 'I'll go.'

That evening, before closing up time, after the nuns and the Old Priest had settled for the evening and convent girls were crowded into their dormitories; after the laundry fires had been dampened, the laundry tubs scoured of the lint and grease wrung from the sheets of a hundred convent girls' sweatsoaked dreaming, and the gas switches turned off, the lights extinguished, my mother and the Lizard Boy overturned his cot. They shredded his bedding, dug the chain from the mortar with Grandmother's ghostslaying knife. They tossed the tattered sheets and pillows, the chain pieces and the Lizard Boy's books and papers into the air in a tangle of clinks, feathers and rustling. The demon hissing in their badluck bloods raced them around the laundry in imitation of the Lizard Boy's crocodile fury, in tribute to a jungle wind gone mad. The badluck demon coursed its laughter, wild and fierce, through their clasped hands. It howled around their heads, flapping its wings. That night, just after sunset, after my mother returned from diverting the caretaker from his sunset rounds, they stood side by side in the doorway looking at the mess.

'Aiya, have to clean tomorrow,' my mother sighed.

'I'm going,' the Lizard Boy said.

'Yes,' said my mother. 'Go.'

'I will come back different,' he boasted. 'Will you recognise me?'

The corners of my mother's mouth turned down with such determination, such weight she couldn't possibly lift them. 'You won't come back,' she said. 'So much fun, sort proof.'

'I'll have another name,' the Lizard Boy continued, grinning a wobbly grin. 'Will you know it?'

'If you tell me I'll know.'

'Too easy,' the Lizard Boy said. 'You'll have to guess.'

My mother watched solemnly as he slipped over the wire fence, out of the convent, into the jungle, with Grandmother's special ghostslaying knife dangling from his waist. The poorly printed leaflets stuck out from his pockets in crumpled flaps. Instead of skinflakes, feathers from the ripped bedding swirled in a silvery cloud around his head. His legs were long and bony, his face wistful. He waved once, then turned. The next morning my mother flung open the laundry door to shriek out her lungs. She raced to the nuns' quarters to raise the alarm.

Grandmother says: *Some ghosts are hard to recognise. They are masters of disguise who mingle freely with humans. Other ghosts are not so free. They hold on to their human shapes only precariously, they must watch and guard against recognition, against ghostly parts showing, human parts falling off. Humans who go amongst ghosts have the same trouble. Only powerful wisewomen would dare, for ghosts have sharper eyes than humans, sharper noses, sharper teeth. If a captured ghost is your enemy, use every advantage you have extra quick. Captured ghosts are confused, unused to their new surroundings and the human shapes in which they are caught. The way to get rid of a captured ghost is to burn it up. Set fire to its ghostly bits, a knob of flesh torn from its neck, a lock of hair from its head, a spirit knife from its belt; a ghostly gown left on a riverbank. Everything captured with it from the other side. Do not leave any bits unburnt, use never-fail matches and ghostburning candles to be sure. Unburnt bits add up to a half-cooked curse. Before learning their craft even powerful wisewomen have been known to make this mistake, at great cost. Like the men of these parts who like to catch ghosts, some ghosts and spirits also like to capture humans. Once every city child knew the sign Avert! to send kidnapping ghosts on their way. Beautiful women and children are especially at risk. Once a beautiful young girl was careless with her words. On the Sea Spirit King's birthday she stood watching his family procession go by. The girl stared at the image of the Sea King's youngest son. 'Wah!' she cried impulsively. 'So handsome! If I knew a man like that I'd marry him.' That night a handsome stranger appeared by her bed. The girl woke*

*exhausted in the morning from a beautiful dream. Beside her
the bedclothes were dented in the shape of a statue. Every night
the handsome stranger appeared, every morning the girl awoke
more tired than before she went to sleep. Her flesh wore to
the bone. News spread in the city that the Sea Spirit King's
youngest son disappeared from the temple altar every night.
When the girl died the statue finally stayed put. Tucked into
his jacket was a scrap of her dress.*

The rich man crooned at the lover, Lily, Lily, but she was
never kind. She never looked at him kindly. She stared through
him, she turned her face to the wall. On land the lover walked
as though walking the unsteady sway of the sea. She tilted
her head to any watery sound, sand spilling from the workers'
barrows, a wind through jungle leaves. She lay for long hours
listening for the sounds of flowing. She did not stir to dress,
she hardly ate or slept, hardly moved. Her shimmering gown
cleaved to her skin, the tilt of her head was inaccessible. In
despair the rich man cut a path to the highest point of his
hill, he perched his pavilion on this highest point so the lover
could see the sea. He set his workers to a rhythmic frenzy,
patrolled the rough path along the railway tracks to make sure
they did not slack. Nightly the rich man and his lover rode
the funicular railway to this highest point. They listened to
the creak and heave of the cables, the rumble of the tracks.
Nightly they returned. Before dawn slit the sky with light
enough to hurt the lover's eyes, the rich man helped her back
to his quarters. He anticipated every bump and depression,
every stone along the way. He held her tightly so she would
not fall. But still the lover was not kind.

So the rich man took her to the deepest part of his mansion,
to the basement room, the old punishment room, where the
walls were two feet thick. The walls were cut from the hill
on which they stood: impenetrable. Here the lover could hear
nothing but her own breath, and the rich man's voice in her
ear. Here she cringed against him like a child; she was moved
to childish action, to beat against the soundless walls with

her fists. To the lover the dark of the room buried deep in the belly of the rich man's mansion was the dark of a split mountainside, the centre of the earth. In that room her eyes spilled not their watery longing, but a dry and brittle fright. In the glow of the rich man's candle her terror was a thing he could touch. He pressed his fingers to her terror. In that room he felt not her coldness, but her skin. The lover's terror was a thing that creeped and huddled, that could be held. It seeped its way into the floor and wall cracks, the furniture creases, the very air they breathed so that the rich man snorted, the rich man's breath came fast and sharp. In the basement room she fell into his arms. She wound her arms around him, pressed her face to the crisscross scars on his chest. But still she was not kind. When the rich man pressed his lips to one cold cheek after the other she shuddered. She turned her face to the wall. So the rich man pressed; the rich man bent her backwards. He lifted her gown to mark a pattern of nips and bruises on her thigh. On her thighs he patterned his rich man's marks, like hallmarks, layered and repeated, etched deep. 'So you will never leave me,' he whispered.

The rich man bought charms for the lover and she drank them and wore them, and tied them in her hair. He dressed her like a large shapely doll, draped colourful cloths and silks over her shimmering gown. He spun her in his arms in slow circles. In the rich man's arms the lover spun like stone. The lover lay beneath him as he stroked her, as he strained towards her, as he panted and wept and sighed. 'Sit,' the rich man said, and the lover sat. 'Stand,' he said harshly, and she stood. 'Turn,' the rich man hissed. 'Turn over!' And the lover turned. When his fingers bit into her flesh her eyes barely flickered. Sometimes he did not touch her. He sat in his armchair surrounded by books strewn carelessly, now no longer read. He held their framed portrait on the flat of his palm, that other rich man and lover standing side by side The lean of their bodies through the glass was friendly. Their faces were so close together that when he looked carelessly he saw only one face. The rich man slumped in his armchair with his back strangely bent.

'Are you sighing?' his rich man's voice floated towards the lover. 'If you're sighing we'll go downstairs.'

Every morning and night the rich man combed the lover's hair, he put his face to it and thought he was breathing her in. He washed her hair with luxurious oils and potions, clucked around her like an old nursery maid. He held up different dresses for her to wear, which she left tumbled at the foot of the bed. All the while the lover sat, or stood, or knelt, quietly, silently. Sometimes when their eyes met she might return his smile. She might stare right through him. Then she went to stand on the balcony with her back towards him, her back to the jungle and the hill. The lover looked past the city. She faced east, towards the sea.

In the jungle the bully can be anyone. Anyone at all. Her night-time shape I follow on the path before me can be another shape altogether, her voice that mutters in the dark some other than the bully's voice. Her shadows from the lamp she carries can be taller; her footfalls not the bully's clump but a tapping of ballroom shoes. The bully's shoes can be proof of a servant's bent-back rubbing, reflecting the faces of anyone who stooped to look. Her legs can be legs not for the bully's stamping and kicking but for lifting, stepping. For swirling her body around a courtyard floor. Her arms long enough to crook a slender waist, her hands not clenched but curled softly to cup a softer hand. In the moonlit jungle the bully's body can be musky, her smell going straight to the head; her eyes darkened, her lips curved to a smile unlike her smug bully's smile.

'Lie down,' the bully says. 'Lie down and put your head back. Like that. Lower.'

The bully pushes my head to the jungle dirt. I lie across the path she has newly uncovered, a place on the path now swollen with meeting. For weeks the bully and I have dug and wrenched and gathered, we have cleared armfuls of jungle undergrowth, pushed rocks and boulders out of the way. The bully has hacked at jungle trees with her eversharp knife, slashed overhanging branches with one stroke. Over the weeks we have made a crisscross pattern of paths. The bully has widened this part of the path to a clearing around which two girls can swing. Since we have looked and looked and never found it, she says this is the only way: to make a place on the path where the many tracks meet. The bully hopes this will be the place of Grandmother's stories, the place of treasure and fame. She pulls her fingers through my hair, tangling leaves between the strands, and withered flowers, and fruit with seeds that grow not in their bellies but out. The bully traps insects which grumble buzzing behind my ears. She twists small pieces of the jungle into my hair, rubs its earth onto my skin. She makes a nest for jungle things: a snare. I giggle at the touch of her hands, at her serious look.

'Shut up,' the bully says, and I do.

'Bare your throat,' she says, and I do. To show the hairy hill spirits she is serious the bully pulls out her knife. The knife handle gleams grey and misshapen in the faint light of the jungle clearing, its salt-crusted blade is a shimmer like stars. My throat is white in the moonlight like a slash.

'Shh,' the bully says.

The bully squats beside me. Her body crackles the undergrowth, her heart is like the heart of the night-time jungle, filling everything with its sound. The bully's heart is like Grandmother's calling drum. Her breath like the breath of the jungle, cool in places, in others, hot. 'Stick out your tongue,' the bully says. 'I'm going to slice your tongue. I'm going to make ghost bait with your tongue, and you must lie still. You mustn't move. You mustn't make a sound.'

I stick out my tongue. I lie unmoving as the bully begins to chant Grandmother's calling prayer, painstakingly memorised by the bully. The bully shivers and shakes the way Grandmother does when Grandmother is calling, her voice breaks and quavers in Grandmother's voice. The bully spreads out her offerings: fresh meat from the convent kitchen, boiled rice saved from meals, two candles, some hell money from Grandmother's cache. The Old Priest's cloth, a handful of marbles, an incense-burner from the chapel. Anything the bully thinks the hills spirits will like. She holds her knife like a weapon in case the hill spirits get too excited. She digs into the special leaf and root collection bag tied around my waist for Grandmother's never-fail matches and ghostburning candles just in case.

'Are you ready?' the bully says. The bully circles her knife in narrowing arches, brings it down with all her might. At the last moment stops. Merely nicks a thin red line. I open my eyes. The bully wets her lips. 'Not sliced off,' she says. 'Just to make fresh blood.'

And the bully is sweating, chanting, lighting Grandmother's candles, wiping her knife. Kneading the rice into mouthwatering bitefuls between her fingers. The cut on my tongue is a thread of ice. The bully flicks my blood with her finger, smears red streaks on my neck in the shapes copied from Grandmother's calling shapes. The bully and I concentrate hard. Sweat trickles into the creases of her skin. I lean forward slightly. I lap. I sip. The bully tastes both sharp and sweet.

'You should be a pin-up,' she says. 'You look like a feast.'

The bully sets her camera. She sneaks off into the undergrowth to wait.

My grandmother doesn't believe in bullies. When we tell her what the nuns are saying she throws back her head.

'What's that?' Grandmother shouts, cupping one ear.

Grandmother can never hear anything said by the nuns. The things the nuns say go into one ear and out the other without any effect. According to Grandmother ghosts can run and fly and blow a wind to cause havoc, but they cannot speak. They cannot speak human language properly; they cannot function properly in the human world. That's why wisewomen are needed who can talk and act for them. My grandmother has seen the nuns' lips curve and wobble, she has watched the expansions and contractions of their throats, but has never heard a word. Grandmother is like a radio, my mother says, tuned in only to what she wants to hear.

'What's that?' Grandmother shouts.

In the evenings my job is to comb my grandmother's hair. Grandmother sits in front of our house looking at the evening. Some evenings a cloud hangs over the whole city, a soft white cloud, gradually darkening, reflecting the city lights. Grandmother sighs, her shoulders slumping. To her nothing is as heavy as the weight of a cloud. Other evenings she sits tapping her feet, expectant. She holds the soft leather of her extra special notebook to her cheek, presses it to her ear as if she can hear it breathe. She lovingly fingers the creamy pages one day to be filled with her book. Grandmother cheerfully calls out to the neighbours, doesn't even flinch when I pull on a knot. I tug harder. Grandmother's hair is full of knots. Her hair uncurls in a heavy white snake from the nape of her neck when I pull out the fastening pin. It slithers down the back of her chair, twisting in a diamond pattern, bulking with knots. I squat behind her chair, dig in with my comb.

'Slowly!' Grandmother commands, pricking my legs with her pin. 'Start from the ends!'

◄ TWELVE ►

THE
SEA GHOST
TURNING

When my mother was a young woman she met a young man as she was turning a corner. The young man turned with my mother, he watched the hurried trail she wove through the raindrops to the laundry door. He stood watching a moment, then followed the way she went. At the laundry entrance he stumbled, as she had, over the ledge raised to keep out demons. He leaned against the door as she had, breathing as she had, his heart pounding like the drum Old Hairy played to accompany the bandit singing, his throat as hoarse as Mat Mat Salleh's when the ancient bandit elder tried to sing. The young man shook raindrops that fell in silvery arcs from his hair. He shrugged the dripping rainjacket from his shoulders, walked a faltering walk to the centre of the laundry where my mother stood, back turned, waiting. Running her fingers over the creases of her shirt, through the thick black strands of her hair. The strands on the back of my mother's neck,

trimmed short, curled exactly as the young man remembered.
He dropped the rainjacket with his bundle. Of its own accord
his knife with the salt-crusted blade slipped from his belt to
the floor. The young man reached his arms around my mother,
he gathered his body to hers; rested his head on her shoulder.
His breath stirred the curls on her neck. My mother jumped
at the young man's touch. She leaned into his arms in surprise.

'Like I promised,' the young man said, breathing the warm
smell of her hair.

'I thought you were a shadow,' said my mother. 'Face
different, body different. Hard to recognise.'

'Our first meeting,' the young man said.

'What!'

'Everything changed,' he laughed. 'Wah, like new. Like first
meeting, everything new. Name also changed. Do you know
it?'

'Huh! Easy—everyone knows.'

My mother turned in the young man's arms. They stood
face to face for an instant, their foreheads touching, exactly
level. Then she pushed the young man away. Her head was
filled with a roaring like a great rush of water, her stomach
with seasickness. The young man too rocked on his feet. His
face, close up, seemed cased in a net of filigreed silver. His
eyes were fine and dark. On my mother's shoulders the badluck
shifted nimbly, crouching tiptoe, spreading its wings. The air
whistled around them, whirling laundry steam.

'King Crocodile, huh,' my mother pushed feebly at the arms
that held her still. 'Wah, you went away and grew into a big
lizard, that's all. Still doing your crocodile crazy, running here
and there.'

'Still can do my walk,' the young man broke away to show
her, swivelling his buttocks the way he did when chained to
the wall all those years ago, shortening his arms and legs,
flicking an imaginary tail. The sight of the young man, now
tall and sturdy with a face drawn and serious, almost stern,
swivelling his hips to his old lizard's walk brought tears of
laughter to my mother's eyes. It swelled peals of laughter from

her throat, pressed her hands to her lips to muffle the sound. The young man pulled her hands away. Her laugh sprang out. On her shoulders the badluck demon jumped with glee, it pulled at her shoulders, almost lifted her from the floor. 'Last time I saw you laugh like that,' the young man said, 'this place was a mess.'

'Yes, whole day cleaning, still not clean. The nuns very angry!'

The young man pushed back the hair falling over her face the better to see my mother's laugh. He rested his hand lightly on the nape of her neck. The demon straining on her shoulders sent a hissing through their badluck bloods that at first they thought was laundry steam. It pressed a sigh to their breaths, stilled their laughing. It pressed their foreheads, then their cheeks, their shoulders, then the whole length of their bodies together; it wound their arms around each other in sinewy curves. Listening, my mother and the young man slipped to the pull of the badluck bloods, to the warm stones of the laundry floor. Their heads were filled with a roaring like a great rush of water, their ears with shrieks of the demon's laughter, wild and fierce. Their hands with a careful slipping to the natural curves and mounds of their badluck bodies, past clothes tugged carelessly to crevices warm and moist, the folds of thigh and body, of lips and elbows, the shell of an ear. My mother's hands scraped against the young man's skin, crinkled in places, in others smooth. She traced the shape of old bandit wounds. The young man fitted five fingers to the five dents on her shoulder, he kissed her fingertip that was notched with a smilemark scar. The laundry tubs bubbled their brew of sheets and pillowslips beside them, the floor was slicked with a silvery sheen. Around their heads the badluck demon howled, flapping its wings.

Before my mother became a Christian she was convinced that her luck was bad. My mother's badluck flickered its wing-shaped shadow to trip and push, and stumble and poke, and thwart her. To make everything go wrong. 'Ma, it's my fault,' she sobbed in the rumbling dark of the soldiers' truck as they sped from the midnight ghosthouse. 'Ma, my badluck made them come.'

Grandmother and my mother huddled on the floor amongst the soldiers' boots. In the swinging light of the truck lantern Grandmother's face was grim. 'Useless, why so stupid?' she snapped. 'Your badluck's so small compared to that badluck place—wah, you think you're a bigshot, hah!'

At that my mother's crying doubled, her hands tried to stuff the sobs back into her mouth, the tears back into her eyes. Her childish face was streaked with ash and ghostburning grease.

'Aiya, Useless, already happened,' Grandmother said more kindly. 'Can't change, no need to cry.' Grandmother wiped at my mother's tears with her shirtsleeve. Her hands were still trembling, but whether from fear or anger my mother could not tell. The badluck on her shoulders spread its own fearful trembling through her body so she and Grandmother rattled against each other, against the soldiers' legs, the pitch of the truck.

'Sit still!' the soldiers growled, moving their boots sharply.

'Yes, Sirs!' Grandmother called in her wheedling voice. 'Sorry, Honourable Sirs, truck moving, hard to sit still.'

'Quiet, Grandmother!' the soldiers hissed. 'Later you can talk!'

The soldiers laughed and joked, roaring their voices louder than the roar of their truck. Against my mother and Grandmother the other crouched bodies shuddered, hunching their own shoulders. Some miserably wept. Grandmother's arm encircled my mother. 'Useless, don't cry!' she ordered. 'Ah Ma's here, no need to be scared.' My mother squeezed herself into Grandmother's side. She squeezed shut her eyes.

My mother has no idea how long she and Grandmother were in that truck, bumping and jolting over ruts and potholes with the rustle of jungle branches against their passing, and a grumbling whistle of jungle wind: for who can measure the hours or minutes of the time spent dealing with a terror that moves its boots sharply, and crouches, laughing and joking, over one's head? Like devilish time and dead time, the time of terror, compared with everyday human time, runs either too long or short. When they were finally dragged from the truck to stand amidst the ragged group blinking in the floodlights of a galvanised building, it seemed to my mother the jolts and bumps of the truck that only moments earlier had bumped and jolted forever, had in fact, in an instant, passed. My mother stood there, blinking. Everywhere she looked guns and barbed wire blinked back. Grandmother tightly held her hand. In the truck the dark of her squeezed-shut eyelids brought back the dark of the midnight ghosthouse, its shadows and see-through shapes turning with arms akimbo to stare. The smells of ghostburning filled her nostrils, the pitiful screams of captured ghosts her ears, and every eyeblink held Grandmother's face, grim and awful, Grandmother's hands leaping with hairlines of light. The midnight ghost-house behind my mother's eyelids flickered her eyes wide open. Eyes open, the truck lantern swinging over faces no less grim or awful, over cries no less pitiful, hands wrung no less miserably, and the sharp boots and thunderous laughs of the soldiers, made my mother squeeze them shut. It seemed she swung in the truck like the truck lantern, on a hinge: between eyes shut and open. To my mother the night they were ordered into the galvanised building, and the long days after, and the many nights, all passed in the terror of that perpetual swing. In the glare of the floodlights she longed for the pitching shadows of the truck. In their black cell, crammed amongst other crammed bodies, she longed for the flooding light. My mother shivered, feverish. Everything around her swung. Only Grandmother was steady beside her, neither crying nor wringing her hands. 'Useless, Ah Ma's here, don't be scared!' Only Grandmother was like rock. 'Sirs, don't take her,' she begged. 'She's just a child, a useless girl. Aiya, Honourable Sirs, look at her face! Already she's half-mad with fear. What harm to let her stay with her old mother?'

'All right, Grandmother,' the soldiers said kindly. 'You can stay together. Aiya, Grandmother, your girl's half-mad, ah? Your assistant? You training her? Wah, we can see you train her good!' The soldiers pointed at the two madwomen, they fell against each other, laughing at their joke.

In the black cell Grandmother crossed my mother's hands in her lap, she pinched her cheeks and tweaked her ears. 'Useless!' she whispered fiercely. 'Wah, Useless, ghosts don't scare you, but these men do? Useless, come back!' Grandmother's face was a smudge of black in the black cell, Grandmother's eyes two points of light. 'Useless!' she called every now and then in case my mother's spirit was scared into perpetual wandering. She whispered stories in my mother's ears, sang snatches of folksong, hawker's song and bandit song in her cracked Grandmother's voice. She trembled as she pondered elaborate schemes for revenge, for getting back face.

'Ma, so many soldiers, so big place, how to curse them all?'

'Not them, stupid. Aiya, these are just men. You think they're the enemy? Useless, they can't even see! We leave them alone, they leave us alone. Have they taken us before? They only took the red packet before. Look at them! Look here.' Grandmother lifted a corner of her shirt to show the handle of her ghostslashing knife. 'Even this they can't find.'

My mother's eyes widened. 'Ma, they took everything . . .'

'Special hiding,' Grandmother said. 'They can't find.'

Before my mother became a Christian she was convinced of the necessity of hiding. She was convinced of the necessity of lowering her head, of meekly answering 'Yes Sirs, yes,' now, for later raising her head. For later getting back face. 'Useless, don't cry!' Grandmother warned. Grandmother and my mother huddled in the black cell or the lighted one, the one crowded or empty, waiting for a turn of the pattern to send them back out. Awake or asleep Grandmother ground her teeth. Grandmother's hands twisted to fists.

'This is how the nuns answer a favour!' Grandmother cried.

Years later, when my mother became a Christian, she turned from her life of sinful ghostchasing, of dealing with the devil, of spying for Grandmother on the nuns. My mother went for Bible lessons without telling Grandmother. Her days at the convent were cased in a comforting glow. The nuns cradled her sorrow in their soft white hands, and even when they discovered she was meant not for the spiritual but the family life, they neither shouted nor chased her out. So my mother bore Grandmother's rants and ravings in silence, she hunched her shoulders against her blows. The vision of the Virgin Mary that came to save her in her dire need kept my mother strong. In the evenings or the early mornings, if she sat or stood quietly, the vision would sometimes come back. The Virgin Mary appeared with a faint smell of smoke and metal, the blacking of polished boots. She glided from a dark alley, smiling, holding out her hand. My mother reached for that vision like a secret, she cradled it in the curve of her palm. She pressed it to her belly where the other secret grew, her crocodile secret, the one having nothing to do with my grandmother. The one that made Grandmother rave and rant from morning till night, and even nowadays gives her the shivers whenever she sends me to any crocodile-infested area, the convent, the jungle, certain parts of the city. The vision of the Virgin Mary in the city streets filled my mother's face with a light that made Grandmother stare. When Grandmother chased her from the house she sat on the doorstep calmly praying and waiting until it was time to make supper and Grandmother let her back in. Grandmother grumbled loudly at my mother's turned back.

'Useless!' she ranted. 'First you take my knife. You give to that Lizard Boy, that bandit—that crocodile! Then you go walking for days, never say where. Then, stomach swelling. Now you want to be like them! Aiya, is that why I trained you? So you can be like them! Who will help me with my work? Useless, your mother is old. Already business is so bad, we have to chase business. How will we eat?'

'Ma, forgive me,' my mother chopped supper vegetables skilfully, throwing inedible roots and onionskin in a rustling arc into the sink. My mother's belly stretched her shirt, squashed against the sink. She shifted her aching feet, glanced at Grandmother slumped in her corner of the kitchen by the stove.

Grandmother's face was more tired than angry. 'Remember what you promised?' she asked, looking at my mother sideways. 'Remember you said you'd pay Ah Ma back . . .'

My mother hardened her liver for courage. She used the firm voice of the nuns. 'Ma, I promised to look after Ma. I will work so we can eat. Different work, not ghostchasing. Laundry work, full-time, no sneaking around convent. No study. The nuns pay good.'

Grandmother stared at the stretch of shirt over my mother's belly. 'Hah!' she snorted, creaking herself more comfortably into her chair. 'Useless, soon you will pay me back! Aiya, that old brothel keeper was right, huh? You rubbed your badluck on me?'

After my mother became a Christian her slate was rubbed clean. Unlike Grandmother she no longer believed in remembering. My mother subscribed instead to a vague and lizardly forgetfulness, her hope placed not in people, or memory, or being remembered, or bribing the gods and spirits for a peaceful life and afterlife, but in the promised peace of heaven. The empty space of heaven, spent in joyful contemplation, where no shadows lurked. No enemy glittered my mother's past life back at her. No instant lasting an eyeblink or forever waited around a corner for her to turn. My mother no longer believed in the power of charms and tiger glares to make life smooth. Penance and fasting were what she subscribed to, and saintly levitation, and the existence of only one God who was a light like a radiant face in a dark alley. Like a mark of sunlight on a wall. As bright as burning. My mother's faith was firmly planted in the kind faces of the nuns, in their soothing voices and the Bible they taught her to read from every evening, and Jesus, the Holy Virgin and all the Saints. Saint Anthony for finding lost items, Saint Rita for impossible prayers answered, Saint Maria Goretti for womanly guidance and the Blessed Virgin Mary for special intercessions. After my mother became a Christian, her weeping for her disappeared husband stopped. My mother's spirit stopped weeping. She sat dry-eyed beside the Old Priest in the chapel, listening to his fabulous Bible stories and sayings to guide a Christian life. The child bully squatted at their feet. As the weeks passed the Old Priest's stories and sayings became increasingly rambling. More and more he stopped for long moments to stare at the sunlit mark on the wall, just over my mother's left shoulder. He pointed to the chapel ceiling where golden shapes flitted and twirled.

'Then what happened?' the bully coughed politely, nudging the Old Priest's knee. 'What next, Father? What happened next?'

The Old Priest rested his palm on her head. He waved the nuns away when they called for him at mealtimes, ate only nuts and jungle fruit, sipped rainwater from a cracked glass. He asked the bully to help him into the jungle to dig for jungle roots which he patiently chewed. In the jungle the Old Priest flicked thorned switches over his bare back, which left no welts and drew no blood. The bully watched the flick of the jungle branches, she tested their thorns with her fingertips; walked sucking pinpoints of blood. On those last jungle expeditions, just before everyone realised the Old Priest was dying, still they carried his ancient box camera, taking haphazard snapshots wherever and whenever the Old Priest stopped. The Old Priest wheezed, pointing out vistas, trying to catch his breath. Still they descended the narrow stairway to the darkroom where they mixed and swilled the chemical solutions, and watched like hawks, counting on their fingers until the pictures bloomed. The Old Priest carefully packed up a crate with his most precious materials. He smiled at the bully, rapping away her hands. 'This, my dear, is for you,' he said. 'But not yet.'

As the weeks passed the Old Priest shrank to a shadow of himself. Even my mother, her belly jutting out uncomfortably, could lift him with the bully's help. The Old Priest's bones scraped at their hands. They carried him to his favourite pew, opposite the mark on the wall that the bully couldn't see. The joyful glow spread from the Old Priest's face to his whole body. The sunlit mark on the wall grew larger, took on arms and legs, a manly shape.

'Where?' the bully demanded. 'Where?' But though the Old Priest and my mother pointed, the bully could not see.

'It's not yet time,' the Old Priest murmured. 'My child, you'll have to find it yourself.'

'Find what, Father?' Tears of frustration spilled from the bully's eyes. 'What must I find?'

As the weeks passed the nuns became concerned. They sat with the Old Priest, my mother and the bully at their daily sessions, exchanging meaningful glances, throwing up their hands. Week by week the Old Priest's stories became more disjointed, he spoke in phrases turned inside out, began with endings, could keep his words to no linear order. The Old Priest's words came out in blocks of images and characters that made no sense. It seemed to the nuns he spoke a different language entirely, a child's language, a madman's, who juggles the rules of coherence, sparkling and twinkling, in the air. When the Old Priest gazed at the nuns with his burning eyes they nodded their heads, tremulously smiled.

'It's delirium, poor soul,' they whispered to each other. 'His mind is eaten away.'

'Come away,' they called to my mother and the bully. 'It's an old man's ravings—nonsense! Come away.'

But the bully and my mother begged the nuns to set up a cot for the Old Priest in a corner of the chapel so he could attend mass and take communion, and watch the mark on the wall. The bully and my mother sat with the Old Priest every day. The bully ran to the library next door to fetch the books for which he asked. The Old Priest stared at the pages in joyful incomprehension.

'Who are you, Father?' the nuns tested. 'Where are you now?'

'Nothing,' the Old Priest murmured. 'Nowhere.'

The nuns who loved him best, who were old now as the

Old Priest was old, fell sobbing at his feet. They had seen him in his middle age, still strong and supple, striding fearlessly into the jungle to clear a path to the abandoned mansion. Now he was no more than a husk. The old nuns rubbed at their tears with their old gnarled hands which had been tireless then, which hacked at stubborn jungle creepers, flung rubbish onto bonfires higher than their heads. 'Nothing!' the old nuns whispered in their frail voices that once bellowed scores of lazy natives back to work.

'Can you see it?' the Old Priest asked.

When the Old Priest died my mother, the bully and the nuns who loved him best sobbed clutching each other. The bully twisted the cloth she used to wipe his forehead until it was knotted hard. They sniffed at the chapel air, which was filled with a scent of scorched mortar. The mark on the wall faded with the Old Priest's spirit. The altar flowers looked faintly singed.

The story of the ghosthouse is a story everybody knows. Everybody knows a different part of this story. When we listen to all the parts, when we dig them out and hold them to our ears like the glued-together parts of a seashell, the bully and I will know. The bully and I will know the whole story. This is what the bully says. Then we will take a picture of the whole, we will mount it on good-quality cardboard and hang it in the convent hallways for everyone to see. Everyone will come from far and near to stand oohing and ahing. They will rush to shake our hands. Then the bully and I will be famous. The bully and I will no longer be charity students, always kept waiting last. We will be celebrities. We will have roastbeef sandwiches for lunch like the other girls, and the first servings of rice and curry, and be invited to sit with them, and given store-bought uniforms that don't pull at our arms and necks. Not rejects and hand-me-downs. We will be able to pick and choose, we'll be begged to honour every class with our time and the nuns and teachers will stand holding the door. The bully says this lying on her back in the darkroom, one leg crossed over the other, absent-mindedly worrying her camera strap like chewing on a leash. The bully's teeth are yellow, pocked with silver stopped-up cavities that gleam when she laughs her bully's wide-mouthed laugh. The bully laughs as she says this, she beats her legs against the cushions, her stomach ripples with glee.

In the darkroom I count our collection of coins. The coins are grubby from lying in convent girls' pockets, from rubbing against their bits of candy and finger grease, their other coins. I spit and polish until the coins are shiny. I spin them on my palm so they twinkle in the lamplight like new. 'Look!' I show the bully, but the bully is looking elsewhere. The bully is reaching for her book of old photographs, her special scrapbook, her pen. Her fingers are curling around her old bandit's knife with the charred handle and the salt-crusted blade. Nowadays I can hardly lift the bully's special scrapbook, even the bully grunts as she pushes it towards me. The bully's special scrapbook grows continually larger, new pages added as the lines and columns of the ghosthouse fill it, as more photos are pasted in. It grows thicker while the photo album the Old Priest left her grows thin.

'Come here,' the bully says.

The bully wriggles to one side of the pile of cushions and old blankets that makes up our darkroom sitting place, our darkroom bed. She pats the space beside her, opens the disintegrating pages of the old album that slide from their cover with a dustsoft sound. The old album is filled with torn pages and lifted out photos, with spaces where the Old Priest's words and pictures have been cut out.

'I haven't finished,' I complain, reaching for more coins.

The bully uncovers her pen. She beckons with her knife, with her bully's look so I know she isn't joking. I crawl to sit in the still-warm dent made by the bully. She hands me her oldest photo, long scraped from its pride of place on the inside cover with her knife. The bully has tried all kinds of glue to stick it back, but the photo always comes loose. 'What do you see?' she whispers.

I carelessly look. The bully and I have seen the crackled photo a thousand times. The damaged surface never shows us more than what the bully can't see.

'A room. A darkened room.'

The bully hugs herself in anticipation. She twirls her knife with glee. 'Write it down,' she says. 'What else?

'A face. I see a woman's face.'

'Write it down. Another face?'

'Just one.'

'What! What are you saying?'

'A most beautiful face. The forehead sloping, the eyebrows like dark wings. The hair brushing the earth behind her. The smile dispassionate, the held-out hand . . .' My pen moves faster and faster.

'What else?' the bully whispers. The bully can hardly sit still.

'A curl of smoke from under the heavy hair. The shimmering gown now crumpled and earthy. The face now contorted, the skin rough and scaly. The nostrils flaring. The sharp line of—'

'What else?' the bully demands.

I grin at the bully. There's a warm flush on the back of my neck. I flick the photo across the blankets and cushions, inviting her wrath. I lean forward so my face almost touches her face, so we almost draw the same breath. I lick the tip of my finger and lift it slowly. Slowly my fingertip crosses the space between us. The bully watches, fascinated by the glistening tip. The bully watches with her mouth open.

'What?' she draws back slightly.

'Teeeeth!' I hiss, lunging forwards, knocking foreheads, slicking the bully's own blunt teeth with my fingertip.

Imagine this house as it must have been all those years ago. They say it is an old house, a grand house, that is why it must be preserved. That's why it musn't be demolished though the marble floors are uneven and some pillars no longer stand sturdy, and the walls need patching over the old patched-up cracks and crevices, and the roof in the closed-off areas is almost caved in. Look at the fine workings on the marble columns, the delicate carvings on the banisters and window slats. The cobwebbed statues in their enclaves, the faded hangings and paintings, the fine papers seeping through the painted-over upstairs walls. Like the convent that surrounds it, like the overhanging jungle and the city forever surging, the house too is a part of this convent's, this hill's, this jungle's, this city's story. How can such a house be other than a treasure, to be kept neat and handsome for posterity, to be shown like the imported statues of the saints and Jesus, like the chapel windows casting their jewelled light? Like any treasure of old. This is what the Old Priest says. The Old Priest says this in the margins of the bully's inherited photo album, in a faded scribble we turn this way and that, squinting, before we can make out a single word. We read his scribble around the gaps the lifted-out photos make. The Old Priest says there's a lesson to be learnt by looking past the new redbrick walls added willy-nilly to the original building. By blurring the eyesight so one sees not the corrugated iron rooftop but the original tiles. The bully and I walk around trying out the Old Priest's method. We circle the building with half-shut eyes, bumping shoulders, treading our way through flowerbeds newly planted by the gardening class, falling over plaster sculptures put out for airing by art-and-craft.

'Look!' my shout pierces the bully to a standstill. I joyfully point. 'Over there! And there and there, and there!'

But even squinting the bully can't see the figured wooden window frames of the Old Priest's sayings, now replaced with aluminium and slatted glass. She can't see the pattern of sunlight through the carved gables now hanging thick and lumpy with cobwebs, or the courtyard strung with fairy lamps enough to turn night into day. Even squinting the bully can't see the courtyard cobbles worn shiny by a myriad dancing feet. The courtyard stares back only its broken flagstones at the bully, only its dense carpet of nutgrass and moss. The bully and I wander around outside the library, squeezing our eyes half-shut, turning our heads this way and that like the bully turns her camera, searching for the perfect shot. I point there, and there, and there, just like the Old Priest says. I peep at the bully sideways. The bully's look of concentration makes me hold my sides. I lend her my grandmother's special sunglasses to see if that helps. The bully nods vaguely. She squints harder, stumbling after me, scratching her head.

'What are you girls doing there?' the garden nuns shrill over the heads of the squashed roses, the bent-over heads of the gardening girls.

'Come here! Come here this minute!' the art-and-craft nun charges from the artroom, flapping her art-and-craft apron so the bully and I have to open our eyes to see which way to flee.

The Old Priest's sayings are so faded that sometimes we cannot read them. They are so cramped they almost slip off the page, they swell and shrink with blots and watermarks, they are stained with gaps where the ink has run. Looking at what the Old Priest says gives the bully and me double vision, it turns our eyes an aching red.

When my mother was a young woman, the young man she met while turning a corner turned lazily in her arms. 'Like this?' the bully asks, pulling my mother's arms around her, turning like a fish in shallow water, like a drift of medicinal seaweed in Grandmother's soup. The bully's turning makes her dizzy, breaks my mother into a peal of laughter that is joy to the bully's ears. The bully and I skip around my mother, pulling her this way and that, telling her jokes, asking her jokey questions so she won't suddenly stop. So she won't suddenly look up to see her enemy lurking in a corner of the laundry, hard and shiny, glaring at her laughter with Grandmother's tiger glare. The bully and I laugh shrieking, wrapping our arms around each other, turning in each other's arms like a pair of frenzied winds.

'Shh!' my mother laughs. 'Not so loud. You came to help, or play?'

'Of course, help!' the bully and I rush back to our places at the ironing table. 'Of course, of course,' we say solemnly, making her laugh even more. Cautiously the bully asks 'Auntie, then what happened?' but my mother is already biting her lip.

'Work first!' she orders, and the bully and I work, and joke and clown, and fold sheets and pillowslips, and twirl convent girls' singlets and bloomers over our heads. We beg my mother but she won't tell about the young man any more. She'll talk instead of what we will have for dinner, the special soup she is making for Grandmother, and what our chores are for the weekend. She will remind us that Grandmother's medicines are finished, we'll have to stop at the medicine shop on our way home. Though the bully and I ask and ask my mother won't show us how the young man turned. Later we can't remember what she told. How much she said.

'She didn't say that!' the bully shouts.

'She did!' I hiss.

'What are you talking!' snaps the bully. 'I was there! You'd better stop. Why are your eyes like that?' The bully takes a step backwards. 'Your tongue will grow,' she growls. 'And your nose and ears. When you wake up tomorrow your tongue will split in two, you'll be covered in bruises where the saints pinch liars. You'd better stop!'

'Nonsense!' I cry, nipping away from the bully's swipe.

No matter how the bully and I whine and wheedle my mother won't even mention the young man for what seems like forever, a month or two or three, if we're lucky. Even then she will start out slow. She will go for the unpegging, ironing and folding of countless sheets, skirts, shirts and pillowslips telling us only about the crocodile fury: how Grandmother's favourite saying was born. *Beware the land crocodile.* She will describe how years of teasing drove the Lizard Boy crazy, how the Lizard Boy ran amok. How years of meanness seeped into his skin until one day he burst.

'We know, we know,' the bully and I chorus. 'We know the *beginning* of the story . . .'

But still my mother, in the snatches of time she forgets her enemy, will not tell her story of the ghosthouse, her tale of the young man turning. Unlike Grandmother she's in no hurry to dig into tales long past. Like Grandmother she doesn't want to get to the end. After my mother became a Christian the Christian future swallowed the alleys and passages of her life's stories as soon as they were lived. The Christian future gulped down my mother's past. There was no way behind her: she could only turn forwards, never back. If she did, the dark cracks and crevices of the swallowed past snaked out to snag her. The cracks and crevices froze my mother where she stood, drained the colour from her face. They were unforgiving; treacherous with memory-teeth and shiny, like black and radiant jewels. So no matter how cleverly the bully and I ask, how cunningly we phrase our questions, my mother will not tell except in bits and snatches. She won't tell to the end. She will not describe how the young man turned in her arms, or how she and the young man woke, hours or minutes, an instant or forever later, neither could say, and how they stretched against each other, their badluck bodies held both towards and away from each other, suddenly shy.

My mother and the young man silently gathered their clothes, slipped buttons into buttonholes, pulled eyelets to hooks. The young man tucked his knife into his belt. Smoothing the shirt over her shoulders, my mother suddenly stopped; twisted suddenly, snatched back the collar so she and the young man could see. They stared at one shoulder, then the other. The dents crouched on each were dents no longer, were no more than a cluster of fading marks. The young man ran his hands over them, frowning, then shook his head. He reached out to smooth my mother's hair. For the first time in years my mother felt the weight of her hair, she felt the weight of her skin and bones. She felt her face, cheeks no longer sagging, lips drooping no more. She patted her face in wonder. For the first time in years my mother stood wholly upright. She lifted one foot to test the pull of gravity. The sudden joyful jump she took was the jump of her own body, nothing more. 'Wah,' my mother said. 'Didn't know so easy to make it go.'

'Make what go?'

'Badluck demon.'

'What! You still believe that?'

My mother looked at the young man sideways. She smiled, tapping the side of her head. 'Still can do that too, huh? No memory. No evidence inside here, instantly forget. Aiya, you got a good memory to remember that!'

'Some things I never forget,' the young man said with a look that made my mother redden. She wandered to the window to consider the raindrops, to the ironing table to straighten the already straight piles.

'King Crocodile, huh,' she grumbled. 'Aiya, crawl here, crawl there. Start this fight, that fight; write this letter, that letter. Demand this and that. They say your headquarters on this hill, but so close, you never come. King Crocodile, too proud, hah? They say you died, so many times died. Sometimes I wasn't sure. But I think I'd know if you died.'

'You told me to sort proof,' he smiled. 'Too busy, sorting proof!'

'Real life proof? Aiya, no wonder busy. So which pile bigger?'

The young man shook his head. He stared at his hands, which were tinged the colour of his knife. 'Paper proof easier,' he said.

My mother returned to sit where he sat, cross-legged. They were face to face. Shyly she took his hands. 'Wah, so cold,' she murmured.

The young man turned his palms upwards, palms as smooth as Grandmother's ricepaper, mottled a faint and murky grey. My mother examined the smoothness. He held up his left palm, then his right. 'No past,' the young man said, then, 'No future.' My mother made the sign Grandmother taught her: *Avert!* to ward off badluck sayings. The young man laughed at the start of her tiger glare. 'At least, that's what Mat Mat Salleh says.'

'Mat Salleh? Like this hill?'

'No, Mat Mat Salleh. Mat Salleh Number Two. Oldest bandit in jungle, but, wah, he can shoot! He can swing a knife. When he shrieks the soldiers tremble.' The young man smiled at my mother settling herself before him, sheets and pillow-slips forgotten, her tiger glare diverted to the enquiring look she wore when he used to turn the pages, when he read to her the stories from books curling with laundry steam. 'Wah, you should see him!' he said.

Mat Mat Salleh the bandit elder was so old no one knew how old he really was. His face was wrinkled parchment, waxy, burned and washed by decades lived in the open. In certain jungle lights his face seemed baby smooth. The old bandit elder came from far away. He wandered into the bandit camp too long ago for anyone to remember exactly when; placed hands on hips and asked boldly to join. Startled bandits leapt from their meagre campfire, reached for knives tucked into belts, rifles laid carelessly by. Then they saw the old man. 'Who's on watch?' they demanded, jumpy, reluctantly putting their weapons down. The bandits were used to strangers asking to join, but none who managed to sneak into camp unseen and unheard, and none who were so old. 'Aiya, Grandfather,' they told him. 'Go home. Enough that you found us—that's a great feat! We'll fight for you, Grandfather. Go home!'

The old man made a place for himself at the campfire, stared around him with glittering eyes. 'You'd better take me,' he said in a voice hoarse and fire-burned, cracked from the weight of the years. 'I can help. I have jungle knowing. I have luck.' The old man's eyes were pale in the firelight, the colour of crinkling leaves.

'You're not from these parts, are you, Grandfather?' the bandits asked.

'Yes, from here!' he cried, slapping his chest. 'This hill, *my* name!'

'Ya!' the bandits laughed good-naturedly, thumping his old

bent back so he almost tumbled into the fire. 'Tell us some more stories, Grandfather! Ya, you look more than a hundred years old!'

When the young man first came to the bandit camp, the old bandit elder was the one to test him. The young man stood in the middle of the solemn bandit circle waiting for the elder to arrive. Old Mat Mat Salleh, Mat Salleh Number Two as the bandits called him, took his time. The young man stood dry-mouthed, trembling. The knife my mother gave him, hooked to his belt, was cold and heavy. At last the circle parted to let the bandit elder through. The young man rubbed his eyes. On the questioning mound stood not an old bent man, as the bandits told him, but a beautiful woman dressed in white. The woman's shimmering gown fountained round her feet. Her black hair fell to the earth in one sweep. She was the most beautiful woman the young man had ever seen. On her head was a crown of twined leaves, of greenish light. Instead of the ragged bandit circle a cluster of attendants surrounded her, girls and women standing threaded in jungle mist. Their faces were hidden except for here the flicker of an eyelid, there a sudden glint of teeth. Behind them darker shapes loomed: humpy barnacled shapes. The young man's mouth fell open. The woman's eyes were soft and wet, her skin as smooth as statues. She smiled. She held out her hand. The young man reached to take her hand but before their fingers touched her hand shrivelled; the features of her face shifted subtly, her face shrank to another face. Again the young man rubbed his eyes. On the questioning mound stood a skinny old man, bare-chested, scowling. As the young man stared the blurred edges of the old man's face became solid. The bandits standing behind him became bandits once more, wide-faced peasant women, men scrawny from years on the run. Not once did the bandit elder lift his face to the young man's face. His eyes fixed greedily on the young man's knife.

'Where do you come from?' the bandit elder asked.

'From the east,' the young man answered.

'For what do you come here?'

'I come to meet my brothers and sisters.'

'If your brothers and sisters eat rice mixed with sand will you also eat it?'

'I will.'

The bandit elder lifted a broad-bladed sword. Licking his lips, he asked: 'Do you know what this is?'

'A knife.'

'What can it do?'

'With it we can fight our enemies and rivals.'

'Is this knife stronger than your neck?'

'My neck is stronger.'

The bandit elder stepped forward with his sword. A bucket of wine was placed in front of the young man, over which he held his left hand. The elder sliced the tips of the young man's fingers so his blood dripped into the bucket. One by one every bandit pricked his own finger, squeezed a drop of blood into the wine. The wine was passed around the circle, each of the bandits drinking in turn. The young man drank last, gulping until the bucket was empty. Then the bandits crowded round him, slapping his back, shouting welcome, and the solemnity was broken. The bandit elder slipped away.

'He was never friendly,' the young man continued, 'but a good fighter, one of the best. Aiya, there were times I saw bullets plug into him, I was sure he was dead, but later he came back with not one scratch. You should see him! But lately that old Mat Mat Salleh's gone a bit mad, too old maybe, always making trouble, causing fights. So old, Grandfather Bandit, everybody lets him be. One village training campaign last month he beat up small boys for nothing. Make villagers hate him. Last week—' The young man hesitated, looking at my mother sitting solemnly in front of him, face to face, chin rested on the palm of her hand. 'Last week, before I stopped him, he beat up your adopted mother, hit riflebutt on her head. At first I didn't recognise her. Aiya, if he wasn't so old I really make him pay! He ran away into the jungle, no one seen him since. Lately everything's going bad. Soldiers everywhere. Raids—no success! Bandits scattered, ambushed. Everyone lying low. I almost believe you, too much badluck!'

'So it was you,' my mother's eyes widened. 'My adopted mother was very sick, I thought maybe she'd die.'

'She's tough,' the young man admired. 'I tried to help but she knelt there, bowing, bowing. Then the soldiers came, we had to go.'

'She says her oldest enemy beat her—a woman dressed in white.'

'No woman there,' the young man frowned. He rose to his feet, pulling my mother with him. 'Like before,' he said. 'Reading, talking-story, talking.'

'Before you never do this,' my mother pointed to the circle of his arms.

'You neither.'

'Like you said,' she murmured, 'came back different.' Tenderly she rubbed his smooth palms. 'My adopted mother says, people with hands like these born once in a hundred years. Only one man she knew had such hands. People like this, special. Make their own luck. Their own future, their own past.'

'Nonsense!' the young man said, smiling.

Grandmother says: *A sea ghost turning is a frightful sight. Some people are frozen to death when they see it, others unlucky enough to live are chewed to bits. Their bodies are pale and bloated like the drowned. Only powerful wisewomen come away unscathed. Only once have I seen a sea ghost turn. When I was a young woman, newly a young woman, my in-between time over, my girlhood banished and my womanhood begun, the house on the hill in which I lived was a house of sorrowing. The house on the hill became a house of heavy days. Sorrow hung sluggish from the ceiling, it leaked unnoticed through wood and plaster to trail sad patterns on the walls; sprang weedlike from unseen floor cracks to stick to people's feet. In those days everyone moved slowly. Arms and legs brushing this wall or that doorway, bodies resting for a moment against a window ledge, all absorbed the weight of sorrow sinking into flesh. The house on the hill was a house perched tiptoe. It was breath held. Dancebands no longer jingle-jangled their melodies through the great rooms no longer spilling couples into the courtyard to twirl under lanterns brighter than day. Laughter no longer echoed through the halls. No longer claps and cheers. Everything was moisture-laden. Furniture buckled, ornaments and hangings only half-heartedly dusted acquired a coating of mould. Clothes stuck to people's skin. In those days it was hard to tell the difference between statues and people, each moisture slicked to gleaming, each caught in their inertia. All were tinged faintly green. The rich man too was a man of underwater movements, slow and deliberate, requiring concentration, as though at any moment he might rise in a cloud of bubbles from the ground. He no longer left the house on his travels, no longer did he scour the seas for exotic treasures to be admired and catalogued, then locked away. The gardens were allowed to run riot. No longer did the rich man look at people when they spoke. When he was in the house I felt the weight of his body in the whole house, through the walls and floorboards, around the corners from which I peered. I felt his weight in my dreams. These dreams were neverending. Over and over I dreamt the paths of the sea. Crouched in the basement room, I pressed my hands to the spent fire of the half-cooked curse. I shivered and shook at the curse gone wrong, peered at the bug-eyed shadows that flapped around me to see if they knew the fate of such a curse. How to call it back. The shadows stared blankly. They held up bits and pieces of the rich man's wrecked quarters for my approval, the shattered powder pots and trinkets, the lover's scarves and silken underclothes shredded to bits. I stared at the curtains and hangings torn from the walls in the frenzy of my curse. My face was wet with tears. The grease of the quenched fire soothed my burned hands. I searched the mess for what was left, found icy metal, the half-charred handle of the lover's knife. I slipped the knife into my pocket. The half-burned photo I crushed, I flung across the room. There was nothing else: the lover's scale reduced to ash. Crouched* with my hands to the spent fire, I walked the paths of the sea. The circling waves above me, my feet dragging through deep water, my body against currents pulling at my skin. Salt water burned my throat, the burn of unnatural breathing. Strange fish streaked past me, underwater parrots. Seaweed swirled amongst rock and coral like the branches of jungle trees. I heard a rustling like jungle wind. At the sickle curve of the path I saw the rich man and the lover ahead. The path straightened, rising in a straight line. The glistening tracks of the funicular railway stretched their way into the gloom. The lover sagged in the rich man's arms. Her skin was reddened, from the back of her neck came a curl of black smoke. I listened to the pull of the railway cables, the grinding wheels. The lover slumped on the silver-trimmed seats. The open-air cars gleamed their sidings of mermaids and men, their Gorgon and Winged Gods and Sirens as I followed the rich man and the lover up the underwater hill. I struggled against the currents pulling me back. Sea snakes raised their questing bodies at my every footfall, sea urchins larger than my palms dangled their poisonous threads. I pushed through coral like arms pushing against my arms, snagged hair and skin on creatures curved like hooks. I ran the underwater path in terror. I ran forever, as if forever is the time a runner takes to get to the top of a hill. Once there I could go no further. I crouched breathless with the terror snapping at my heels. The rich man and the lover were on the nearby pavilion. The lover stared into the gloom. The currents lifted her hair to show the blackened back of her neck from which smoke seeped like blood. She sank so suddenly the rich man could not hold her. The pavilion dissolved beneath their feet. The rich man reached for the lover, caught in a watery spiral downwards. He caught her mid-spiral; tangled arms and legs in her shimmering gown. The catch of breath in his throat scraped at my throat. The lover's weight almost pulled my arms from their sockets. She bucked and struggled, clawing at the rich man's face. Storm bubbles whirled around them. Still the rich man held her. In his arms she was a shape now long and scaly, now bloating, now ridged with spikes. Her face was terrible to look at, already crackling to black. Her flesh was blistered, her skin in shards like glass. The rich man could not hold her. The dragon-shape twisted to savage him, the reptile-shape slashed its tail, the fish-shape pressed serrated teeth to his flesh. Then all was suddenly still. The rich man's arms slackened, in his arms the lover was shrivelled to burnt sticks. To smoke heaving. To nothing. The sleeves of her empty gown encircled his neck. Crouched with my hands to the spent fire, I reached to tear the lover's gown from my neck. My face was wet with tears.

◄ THIRTEEN ►

IN THE JUNGLE
WHERE WE
WALK AND
PLAY

One night the rich man and his lover disappeared. There was a search but they never found her. Some say the lover was turned by another lover, who came to steal her away. Some say she was murdered by a jealous rival, one of the rich man's old lovers spurned. Others insist she wasted away, everyone could see it, she was so sickly even all the rich man's riches could not save her. Others merely say that the lover went home, across the sea. The rich man went into the jungle on the night she left. He offered his spirit to the jungle, his body to the beasts.

Combing the jungle the soldiers and volunteers found the abandoned camps of notorious bandits, they shone their searchlights through dim jungle clearings, kicked their way around deserted hide-outs where campfires smoked faintly still. The hill was covered with soldier and volunteer foot-prints crisscrossing each other to confuse their hastily carved signals, a broken branch pointing left, a chalked treetrunk arrowed right, marking which way was searched, which way to go. The soldiers and volunteers weaved their calls and shouts, their hackings and scramblings in eerie place of the lack of jungle sounds, the jungle silence hanging over every-thing like an unwieldly skin. A troupe of monkeys appeared and reappeared, scrambling through the branches, strangely silent, now following this group, now another. The soldiers and volunteers pelted stones and jungle fruit at them, but they only swung higher, making no sound. The combed jungle revealed no trace of the lover save for the white gown the rich man's servants confirmed she always wore. The soldiers and volunteers found the rich man instead, sprawled face upwards near the pavilion he'd built on the hilltop, known as the Pearl or the Boil.

Jungle rain puddled the rich man's hair, jungle earth caked his turned-up feet. The soldiers and volunteers surrounded him in an untidy circle. The rich man was stone cold and staring, his arms flung outwards, legs crossed at the ankle, bent at the knee. He was pale and slightly bloated, like the drowned. Over his body was draped the lover's gown. The rich man's face was contorted, eyes starting, lips spread to call; his look so stricken that one of the volunteers bent to press her sobs to his cheek before the others realised what she did. They hastily pulled her back, the silly servant girl, the fool! They wiped her mouth with their shirtsleeves, pressed their palms over the moans escaping her lips to echo through the treetops, to be answered in animal howls and flutters, animal shrieks racing jittered from jungle roots to the topmost leaves.

Grandmother sat with her mouth clamped, her eyes flicking left to right following the crisscross pattern of her cries. Her burned hands, carelessly bandaged, lay weeping in her lap. The jungle terrified her, it bowed her shoulders, it was filled with frightful sounds and shadows. It was filled with unfinished business, a *waiting* Grandmother could hear. The weight of a curse gone wrong. Grandmother forced her head up. A sudden jungle wind creaked the foundations of the rich man's pavilion, pushed jungle trees against each other, sent leaves swirling in a wild flurry to the sky. The soldiers and volunteers stood rooted amidst the cacophony, not a shirt fluttered, not a hair lifted from their heads. They gazed around them. One by one, silently, the monkeys dropped to the lower branches. Then the wind swerved inward, downward, ferocious; jungle leaves and dirt spiralled into eyes and noses, branches snapped, the soldiers and volunteers bent to shade their faces. The lover's gown lifted, flapping on the wind. It tangled in the lower branches amongst the silent troupe of monkeys. Before anyone realised, the gown was untangled by monkey fingers, it was tugged through the branches, away.

'Stop!' the soldiers shouted, rubbing dirt from their eyes. 'That's evidence!'

'Stop them!' the volunteers cried.

One gunshot, another, and the monkey screeches were louder than any other sound. The monkey screeches filled my grandmother's ears. One monkey dropped to the ground, another lifted the bleeding stump of its arm. The lover's gown was passed from branch to branch, from paw to paw, chased by a volley of shots. The troupe of monkeys disappeared, trailing the gown behind them. The one-armed monkey turned to snarl at the soldiers, then it too was gone.

As suddenly as it began, everything stopped: the animal shriekings, the wind snatching at leaves and branches, the dusty whirlwind reeling soldiers and volunteers on their feet. Everything stopped. Grandmother stared after the monkeys, her eyelids gritty, her eyes streaming. She slumped beside the rich man's body to wring her bandaged hands. The knife in her pocket scraped icy against her thigh. The rich man lay with his lips spread for calling, his eyes reflecting the sky. His arms in an open embrace. His tattered clothes had dried stiff and salty. When they lifted him water spilled from his ears. The soldiers and volunteers stared with pity. The rich man was covered with rows of stab marks, teethmarks: the slashings and chewings of beasts.

As in the old days the young man crouched in the corner of the laundry by the door. He crouched, bone tired, staring at the rain. The jungle rain beat against the laundry window for days, some mornings a mere sprinkle, some nights lightning-laced. Thunderous. As in the old days the young man and my mother spent many hours talking and laughing, holding their mouths in case anyone should come to hear. The young man and my mother unfolded his dusty cot from its corner, they sprawled leaning against each other. The young man started at every sound, reached for the knife tucked into his belt. My mother mended mounds of convent girls' ripped skirts and frayed bedding, other laundry work stalled by the rain. 'Don't be scared,' she smiled. 'It's raining, they won't come. Nowadays nobody comes here. Aiya, not like before—nothing to see!'

My mother came to the laundry early every morning, slipped through the doorway with her bundle of food sneaked from Grandmother's kitchen to see the young man curled on his cot. She stood in the doorway, watching. At her lightest step he opened his eyes. He joyfully smiled. As in the old days the young man's eyes were ringed with shadow, his smile tinged with weariness, but unlike those days my mother did not glare her tiger glare. Unlike those days her badluck demon was nowhere in sight. My mother entered and placed the food beside him. The young man ate ravenously. My mother dragged a cautious bench across the doorway, laden with convent girls' watchful skirts and blouses, mock-drying. She hung sheets between the young man and the window, strung pillowslips and washcloths across the laundry at shoulder height: traps for intruders, a spider's web. To get from one end of the room to the other, they had to bump and swerve, laughing, walking a white and flapping maze.

'What news?' the young man asked.

'Soldiers everywhere. Roadblocks. Wah, they're checking

everyone. Even beggars, hawkers, old women and children, anyone not carrying the right pass. Yesterday my adopted mother was stopped again, she spat at the soldiers. But they know her. They say she's mad, a mad old woman. So they let her go.'

My mother watched the young man eating. He ate with a hunger the steaming buns and ricecakes seemed not to satisfy. He ate urgently, methodically, gulping with hardly a chew. The food bundle empty, he slumped back onto the cot; saw my mother watching. As in the old days he smiled his lopsided smile. He rubbed his flat belly. 'Long time eating fern tips, chewing jungle fruit, jungle roots. Wah! These buns sit here—just right!'

'Tomorrow I'll bring more,' my mother promised. She pulled the sheets in a tent around them. The young man sat with his head lowered, his shoulders bent as though the badluck had shifted its heavy crouch to him. The soft flutter of the sheets fluttered the laundry light around them. 'What will you do?' my mother asked.

'Bandits all scattered now—meeting after the storm. In the city, not jungle. Too many soldiers in the jungle, nowadays too hard to hide. When the rain stops we'll meet in the city—somewhere safe.'

'Now—'

'Now I stay here and rest. Help with laundry. Help make company. No problem for you, for me. No problem, ah?'

My mother laughed, remembering the young man's long ago words, his long ago look, both stubborn and hopeful. She slipped into the space he made on the cot, into the curve his body made for hers. The handle of his knife, tucked into his belt, slid through the opening of her shirt. My mother shivered at the handle's cold touch, lifted her shirt to show a faint greyish mark on her belly, like a bruise. The young man pulled the knife from his belt. He laid it to one side, carefully, reverently. He pressed his fingers to my mother's bruise. 'This knife saved my life many times,' he said. 'You were right—special knife, cut anything. Once cut, can't put back. I think your adopted mother want it back.'

'No,' my mother said quickly. 'You keep it! My adopted mother's got other magic. Strong hands, strong eye. Doesn't need the knife like you need. She was very angry when I took it, but not any more. Now she says the knife wasn't hers—a badluck knife. Aiya, for badluck people like you and me. You keep it.'

'Lately it's growing heavy on my belt. Growing colder in my hands. Cut anything, but hard to carry. Your adopted mother's right—a badluck knife. If the soldiers take it . . .'

'You keep it safe,' my mother said.

As in days not so very old the young man and my mother lay whispering in the soft whisper of their makeshift tent. Asked slyly, suddenly, about this time, my mother will look up for an instant. For an instant she will look at us directly, she will look through us so the bully and I shift uncomfortably on our feet. 'The smell of clean sheets,' she will murmur with a smile to shock the bully and me, a look we aren't used to seeing. 'Dipped in clean water and drying. Dipped and drying, day in, day out. And the sound of jungle rain.' The bully, unnerved by my mother's fixed stare, will turn to look over her shoulder for a mark on the wall. She will scan the laundry wall from floor to ceiling, and see nothing. The bully will turn back, relieved. 'Auntie!' she'll whisper to bring my mother back.

As in the old days the words of the young man and my mother passed from one to the other, they were weighed and handled, nibbled for tastiness, chewed for sustenance, then passed back to the other to be weighed and nibbled and chewed. Their mouths were filled with their own richness. Unlike the old days, rosy wordshapes spilled from my mother's lips, no black badluck globules. The flutter around her was a flutter of clothes and sheets, of heartbeats, not leathery wings. My mother shrugged her shoulders lightly. The words between them were both a comfort and anxiety, circling and circling, turning and returning from the jungle to the storm, from the bandits to the soldiers, to the city, to the jungle, the storm. To the city, the safe place the young man said he would go. Their words circled and circled, lifting and swooping, until they lay back, sated, dizzy. Until one edge of the window was streaked with a faint band of light. My mother went to the window to stare at the fat droplets of rain. 'Storm over soon,' she said.

The young man swung his feet to the floor. He cocked his head to one side.

My mother also listened to the sound under the sound of the rain. 'Trucks,' she whispered.

Before she could turn the young man's meagre belongings were already thrust into a bundle, his knife tucked into his belt. My mother stood bewildered, the sheets fluttering around her. The young man, for days bone weary, indolent, seemed to uncoil before her eyes. His arms became arms not for curving around shoulders but for swinging a knife. His legs, feet shoved into jungle boots, became legs for running, for forcing paths through the jungle, for kicking down doors. His eyes shone hard and bright. The young man turned to my mother, pulled her towards him. They pulled towards each other in a close, fierce grip. My mother's head was filled with a roaring like a great rush of water, her stomach with seasickness. She listened to the thump of the young man's breath, to other lesser sounds, the wavering patter of rain, footsteps in the passageway, the creak of the laundry door. My mother and the young man sprang apart.

The caretaker and the Old Priest at the door could hardly believe their eyes. The young man's fists unclenched, his knife slipped back to its sheath. He grinned his lopsided grin. 'Father,' he murmured. 'Pa.'

'Godson!' the Old Priest stumbled backwards. 'At first I didn't recognise you. Why are you here? The soldiers are searching the convent!'

'Father, look at him,' the caretaker cried, bumping into the Old Priest, eyes shiny with pride. 'Didn't I say he would get better?'

'Father, Pa,' the young man pushed past the zigzag fall of

sheets and pillowslips to the window. 'Father, Pa, your son must go.'

'Hurry,' the Old Priest peered out the laundry door. 'We were showing soldiers the way, unlocking doors . . .'

The young man brushed past my mother to slide the window open. 'Don't be scared,' he whispered.

Before my mother knew it he had rested his hand on the back of her neck, he had slipped out the window with hardly a scrape of the wood, hardly a backward glance. For an instant the young man's shape filled the window, framed by rain and thunderclouds, then he was gone. My mother stood frozen, pale. She did not see the soldiers burst into the laundry, pushing the Old Priest and the caretaker aside. She jumped at the sudden outside burst of gunfire. Behind her the caretaker fell fainting, the soldiers cursed at the tangling maze of sheets. My mother stood at the window, pale. She saw the Old Priest stumble into view, saw the spit of gunfire around the young man's feet; shuddered at the cry 'Take him alive!' as soldiers rushed to grasp him. The Old Priest dashed forwards. For an instant the young man and the Old Priest stood pressed together as though embracing. The Old Priest's arms bent oddly, the young man slipped something into his hand. My mother glimpsed the charred handle of the young man's knife before the Old Priest thrust it into the folds of his cassock. Then soldiers pulled the young man away. My mother stood frozen, her head filled only with the sound of water, her stomach with the sickness heaving. The badluck demon fell like a stone from the sky to fix her shoulders with its old familiar weight. The badluck laughter hissed with the water in her ears. My mother saw the nuns gather in a flutter around the Old Priest, making a wall of their bodies, a fluttering white wall of hands wrung and palms raised beseechingly. The soldiers paused in confusion, riflebutts raised.

'Don't mind Father!' the nuns begged. 'Don't shoot! Don't mind the Old Father, can't you see his mind's wandering? Can't you see the Old Father doesn't mean it, he's just an old man, he doesn't know what he does?'

The Old Priest trembled with passion, his collar crooked, his wispy hair plastered to his forehead in rainy streaks. One hand was buried deep in his skirts. He shivered as though bone cold. His face was filled with light. 'God bless you, Son!' he shouted to the young man struggling on the edges of the jungle, twisting this way and that. The young man's body glowed a wild and fiery red. The soldiers threw up their arms to shield their eyes. 'King Crocodile for a miraculous escape!' the Old Priest screeched as the young man broke and fled into the jungle in a splatter of gunfire. The soldiers plunged after him.

When my mother was a young woman the other young woman she met in the street had a face which was filled with light. The other young woman was the most beautiful woman my mother had ever seen. This was in the days when my mother walked the streets of the city every day, looking into every face for a sign. My mother walked searching for a kindly face. How hard it was to sift through the features of a person's face; which features were they that distinguished the enemy from the friend? The one who would tell her where to look: where somewhere safe was. My mother stared and stared. In those days she could put nothing together, not even words. Her voice, swallowed in shock on the day the Lizard Boy bit her, rose in her throat like jagged badluck globules never making sense. This was the time when my mother's instant passed. When her face changed from a young woman's to her mother's face that the bully and I are used to, calm and weathered, etched with weeping lines that never fade. A face that won't take a joke.

In those days my mother walked amongst all manner of cityfolk searching for her disappeared husband. My mother had not seen her husband since the soldiers chased him away. She tried to describe him but her words came out so broken people stared their incomprehension. They gave up and turned away. In those days my mother walked an endless twisting and turning through parts of the city she had never before been. She walked until the last of the evening slatted bars of light across dim alleys, until the only sound rising to meet her was the echo of her feet. When asked how she met the other young woman my mother recalls the smell of smoke and metal, the blacking of polished boots. At first she thought the other young woman was just another woman. My mother stares at the bully and me to make sure we understand. At first the vision of the Virgin Mary looked to my mother like the most beautiful woman she had ever seen, no more. My mother did not know it was the Blessed Virgin Mary until the nuns told her. She hopes someday the bully and I will get to see her too. When we go walking she makes us carefully look at everyone we meet. If the bully and I aren't careful we may miss her. We may not see the sign when it comes to save both our bodies and our souls.

When my mother first saw the other young woman she stared at her, seeing, unseeing. Surrounded by soldiers, my mother stood tiptoe, she arched her neck to stare. She craned her head past the leering caps and helmets, the arms reaching for her, the heads thrown back. The smell of smoke and metal filled her nostrils, the blacking of polished boots. The soldiers stood in a close circle around her. Their laughter was a swooping like birds. My mother stared at the woman. She hardly noticed the hands that shoved and jostled her, spinning her round and round, or the tugs to her wrists and elbows, her clothes. Surrounded by soldiers, my mother admired the smooth walk of the woman through the dark alley towards her, a walk like that of dancers or acrobats, boneless; having nothing to do with the earth. Spinning round and round, stumbling, still she wondered at the woman's shimmering gown, so bright in that dark alley, and her face like a beacon of light. Her hair sweeping the ground at her feet. My mother saw the woman had no feet. The soldiers broke their circle to look. Their arms hung slackened, their mouths drooped open. The woman stopped to smile at my mother. Her smile was blinding, her eyes pinpoints of light. She held out her hand. My mother pushed past the soldiers to take her hand. No one stopped her. The woman's hand was as cool and smooth as the chapel statues my mother later knelt under, the plaster saints she drenched with tears for her husband who disappeared.

When the woman released her my mother was filled with the urge to run, she was filled with energy and euphoria, like the aftermath of certain herbs Grandmother made her eat. My mother stumbled from the circle of stupefied soldiers without a backward glance. No one stopped her. No one called her back. She ran stumbling and panting. She raced through the twists and turns of the streets and sidestreets, past the makeshift dwellings and eyes peering from furtive windows, the smells of rancid food and unwashed bodies, back to the city she knew. Not once did her steps falter. Her long strides were like an animal's, muscular and smooth. Her head tossed from side to side. Even the badluck on her shoulders did not weigh her down.

When her breath was cut to pieces, my mother slowed to a dogged walk. No one followed. In those days no one walked the city at night except for soldiers. Even the band of soldiers who patrolled my mother's area did not scare her. She looked at them disdainfully when they ordered her to stop. These soldiers recognised the wild-haired ghostchaser's assistant, they pushed her about, then let her go. 'Long time no see!' the soldiers laughed. 'Aiya, you know your mother's red packet is late? Tell her to pay up, or we'll come and see her!' My mother stumbled from them. Already the touch of the beautiful woman was wearing off. The energy and euphoria that made her run and run drained from her body. As she stumbled home she began to twist deep creases into her shirtfront, her mouth also twisting. She staggered but did not stop. She blindly brushed away her tears.

Grandmother says: *Always watch where you are walking. The paths humans must travel are filled with dirt and danger, not only jungle paths but the tarred roads of the city that are swept morning and night. Ghosts also adapt with the times. Always wash your feet or leave your shoes outside your house before*

*entering as a ghost may have attached itself to your feet.
Ghosts can never enter a house unless invited or carried in.
Never step on cracks. Cracks lead to holes in the earth in which
a ghost may be lurking. Never lean against a wall during a
thunderstorm or you will get stuck there. Never make faces
at the wind, which is vengeful, and will freeze your features
out of spite. A woman who once did this was doomed to spend
the rest of her life searching for that particular wind, to beg
it to change her back. Always ask permission before walking
deep in the jungle, or picking jungle fruit or flowers, or
relieving yourself under a tree. Jungle spirits are easily offended
and will follow you home to seek revenge. If you mess up
their house, they'll want to mess up yours. Never step on
chickenshit with bare feet as this will rot the private parts.
Never be cruel to animals. Animal memories extend beyond
death. Each animal has its spirit, the characteristics of which
may be carried into its next life: a nose like a pig, or hairy
arms, or skin patterned light and dark like diamonds. The
ability to crow loudly, or swing and scuttle, to dangle upside
down from trees.*

My grandmother is a maker of charms. She hates the Jesus
people so she never comes near the school. She will never go
past the gate unless it's to claim victory, until the nuns bow
and scrape, and bend over with apologies as they beg her in.
That is part of Grandmother's plan. That is why I go there.
'What did they teach you today?' Grandmother asks. 'Tell
me what you learnt.' Grandmother wants to know their
secrets, to rival the golden-edged books they chant from. She
wants to know what they are. 'Did you find their origin?'
she asks. 'Did you learn their rules?'

'I learnt that life is going up a hill,' I tell her. 'You must
struggle and struggle. Demons will tempt you to stop but you
must carry on. There is only one path. You must be like a
tough little train. If you read the sacred book and keep your
eyes to the path, then only will you be saved. You will be
eternally happy. When you reach the top of the hill, that is

when the happiness begins. That is when you die. Everything becomes easy then.'

This makes Grandmother laugh. The more notebooks I fill, the heavier the special case in which she locks them, the louder Grandmother laughs. 'Is that all!' she cries, slapping the arms of her special chair, pressing her hands to her sides.

After she was hit on the head by the bandit rifle my grandmother heard a voice calling from the jungle. Grandmother lay in bed, tossing from side to side, soaked in sweat and spittle and piss. My mother turned her gently and wiped her. Grandmother rose to follow this voice. My mother's frantic calls, her arms pinning Grandmother to the bed could not stop her. For days Grandmother followed the voice, for weeks. For years she stumbled after it, until her lips were cracked with age and thirst and her fingernails curled crookedly, and her hair grew wispy on her head. Grandmother watched the flesh hang from her bones like hung waterbags and her legs shrivel to sticks. When she could walk no longer she fell to the dark jungle earth. All her years of walking had not prepared her for this. The earth twined itself around her. It flowed on dark currents, pushing her this way and that, pushing into her nostrils, her mouth, under her eyelids, into her ears. Grandmother felt herself sinking. The earth was filled with the hands and mouths of jungle spirits which pinched and sucked. Grandmother curled herself into a ball, a knob of flesh, a leaf folded over in which a worm huddled, ravenous and trembling; hollow with a hunger that was Grandmother's need. Slowly, painfully, she opened her eyes. The jungle earth slapped against her. Grandmother saw gnarled feet planted in the earth. She curled at the feet of an old bent man who leaned forward with a baleful look. The old man wore a tattered and filthy gown which shimmered faintly, his hair was matted with jungle leavings, twigs and small branches. Insects crawled their intricate patterns halfway down his back. The old man's eyes were the colour of jungle leaves.

'What are you seeking?' he asked.

'What I've lost,' Grandmother said.

'What have you lost?'

'My seeing.'

'How will you find it?'

'If you show me, I'll find.' Grandmother looked at the old man sideways, crafty as an old pedlar, as if she had an ace up her sleeve. She knew the old man was a powerful magician.

'How will you keep your seeing?' he asked.

'If you tell me, I'll know.'

The old man's face cracked into a smile as he nodded. 'What will you give me?'

Grandmother threw back her head, reckless. She counted her meagre belongings on one hand, weighed what she had against what she lost. 'Anything you like!' she cried.

This made the old man laugh. Grandmother laughed too, spurting gobs of earth from her mouth, cracking the fine crusty layer that stuck to her cheeks. Grandmother laughed joyfully. She knew the old man would show her potent jungle charms to bring back her seeing, to reopen her extra eye. Love charms and weather charms and charms for profit and prevention. Revenge charms to make every enemy quake. For hours, for days, Grandmother squatted beside the old man, watching. For months, for years, she breathed the warm jungle earth, she watched the old man pound and mix, and sniff and point, and squeeze a plant between two fingers to make a bright dewdrop, a jewel. Grandmother memorised everything the old man showed her. At the end of each lesson she felt a faint flicker of her closed extra eye. She filled her hands with charms, used her charmed fingers to prop it open. But the eye never stayed propped open for long. Soon her seeing faded away. The old man's grin split his face from ear to ear. When Grandmother opened her mouth to protest the earth spilled into her throat. The old man beckoned her closer. She leaned towards him, straining forwards, starting to run, but he pulled further and further back. His voice became fainter and fainter.

'Wait!' Grandmother called. 'You haven't finished, you haven't told how to keep—'

'Tell you later,' the old man promised.

'When?'

'When you see me again.'

'When will I see you?'

'Then you will remember your promise,' the old man said. 'You will give me what I want, and if you're careful and lucky, you'll get to keep your seeing. If you're clever, you'll get what you seek!'

'What will I give you?' Grandmother asked. 'What promise?'

'Your most precious,' the old man said. The old man leaned forward, his old split face suddenly looming up against Grandmother's. Grandmother squeezed her eyes shut. Her head was filled with the old man's laughter, hoarse and fire-burned, cracked with the weight of the years. Grandmother laughed and laughed. The most precious thing she owned was a bagful of charms, useless since her extra eye closed. When she opened her eyes she was slumped in front of her mirror. My mother's warm fingers massaged her back. Grandmother jumped at the dusty image leering out of the mirror. She leaned away from the old man's face.

'Did you see him again, Grandmother?' I ask. 'Did you?'

'Many years later,' she says. 'He was different, but I knew her. I remembered my promise, and took her hand, which was as cold as ice.'

The bully and I scratch our heads. 'Grandmother!' we cry. 'What are you saying? Was he a he or a she?'

'Aiya, haven't you been listening?' Grandmother scolds. Grandmother stares at our puzzled faces, begins to cackle like the hungry old badluck grandmothers flapping at her doorway during the Hungry Ghosts Feast. 'Aiya, both!' she cackles. 'He was *both*!'

Since my grandmother's extra eye closed she has kept her seeing in a secret jar the size of a rounded thumbnail, wrapped in an oilcloth under her breast. This jar came from deep inside her. Only recently did Grandmother manage to get it out. Once it knocked about her insides, giving her a swollen knee joint, a knotty lump pressed to the base of her neck. It bent her sharply forwards, groaning, flung her arms in odd directions to point at this or that ache. My grandmother spent fourteen years, two turns of a woman's life cycle, trying to bring it out. She spent half that time pondering what the old man said. By then she knew what he meant. The old man came back to tell her. Only then did Grandmother see who he really was. In the hospital ward the old man showed my grandmother his true face, he swept his long black hair over the hospital floor, stood dressed in white at my fever-soaked bed. His shimmering gown fountained round his feet. His shrunken features shifted subtly, his face swelled to another face, smooth-skinned and lovely. A beautiful woman's face. My grandmother jumped with recognition and fright. The old man stood looking at me tenderly. He looked at me with great thirst. Passing doctors and nurses took no notice.

My grandmother thumped her fist against her palm when she realised the old man's long ago trick to make her promise. She ground her teeth at the sudden sharp memory of his bandit riflebutt dropping like a stone from the sky, like a frying-pan ladle, to make a boiled egg on her head, a shiny knob. To close her extra eye. His calling from the jungle not long later with offers of spells and seals to reopen it made Grandmother twist her fingers to bruises. Grandmother thumped her fist like a gambler caught out. Only in a more generous mood will she admit that the trick was cleverly done, the trap of the unfinished business neatly set. Even powerful wisewomen have been caught by such a trick. Even powerful wisewomen have had to twist and turn, and plot and plan a way to get themselves out. Sometimes they've even had to try their own tricks. They have had to make promises they will never keep.

'What promise, Grandmother?' I ask and ask. 'What is Grandmother's most precious? Is it Grandmother's house we live in or Grandmother's customers, or Grandmother's spells and seals? Is it your notebooks, Grandmother, is it your memory pools?' But Grandmother will never say for sure. She sits in her special chair, staring out the doorway, twisting her already twisted hands. She sits cursing after the neighbours who don't bow respectfully as once they used to, who defiantly lift their chins at her tiger glare. Already Grandmother thinks she has said too much.

When I tell her what I've learnt at the convent she makes me write it down. She makes me write in her notebooks that now fill two special cases to which only she has the keys. Grandmother's notebooks spill her spells and stories, her ghostly advice and admonitions, the ghostchasing methods and tricks I will use when I take over her business one day. When I finish what she has trained me for, what she has sent me to the convent to do. That too is part of her plan. The spells and stories, the advice and admonitions, the tricks and methods spread from notebook to notebook, from page to page. They spill into the corners of the cases to mix with the dust and dead insects, to stick in the locks so Grandmother thumps and jiggles the keys. Grandmother pauses over her opened cases like a child led to a tray of candies and told to pick only one treat. Her fingers hover to and fro. The notebook she finally extracts is held reverently, the way my mother holds her saint statues, as if their contents, their saintliness, can seep right into her hands. Grandmother never tires of hearing her own words read back. I stand with one foot forward, the notebook in one hand. She stares at the pages covered with blurry squiggles, presses her extra strong spectacles further up her nose, but even then can't see.

'Here, Grandmother,' I point. 'I'm here.'

As I read I watch her mouthing the words, her face twisting to a clown's face, an imp's. Grandmother grows pale from the strain. I read until my mother has trimmed the last of the lampwick, until my eyes ache with squinting and I cough and stretch my shoulders. I slow the words to a yawn, but still Grandmother won't let me stop. Grandmother pokes me in the ribs. 'So soon, already tired. Like that how to chase ghosts? How to finish Grandmother's business? No stamina, how to burn ghosts up!'

So I read faster. I read with exaggerated actions, my face

a copy of Grandmother's tiger face, unlike my usual girl's face, more like an opera singer's, the way Grandmother likes it. Each feature pronounced. I plant my feet firmly, throw out my hands. The pages flutter as I swing the notebook in wide arcs, as I read with an A for expression, a gold star pasted next to my name. I read without looking. The words race away from the page. I hold the notebook upside down, flip three pages at a time. By now I know Grandmother's words by heart. I leap over the gaps in her words, the times she stops her stories with her lips clamped tight. Into those spaces I slide my mother's words, and the bully's, and the Old Priest's from the margins of his depleted album, and the nuns' which trip and tumble into the fray. I creak my own tentative words into the leftover spaces, look at Grandmother sideways to see if she'll notice. If she'll fly into one of her tempers. But Grandmother is old now, almost fourteen turns of a woman's life cycle, so sometimes she doesn't see. Sometimes she sits in her special chair by the doorway with her twisted feet tapping, her eyes flitting left and right and out the window or up to the ceiling, and neither my mother nor I can tell whether she's really there or somewhere else. So I ease her extra special notebook from the tumble of other notebooks out of its case. The red leather stains my fingers the faintest pink. I hold my pen firmly for a moment, then put it down. The creamy pages are filled with a terror that thumps my heart so loudly I am sure Grandmother can hear it. But her lips merely purse and stretch from scowl to smile to scowl as they do when she's trying to guess soup ingredients, when she's in the middle of making a difficult charm. Grandmother doesn't even look my way. 'What do you think I've promised?' she growls. 'What do you think you'll get?' She stares at my mother and me as though for a moment she can't imagine who we are, as though we no longer swim in her memory pools. She doesn't even protest when my mother gently leads her to bed.

'You have learnt well,' Grandmother tells me just before my fourteenth birthday. Grandmother gives me her jar of secrets to eat. The jar is rusty red, shrivelled from soaking all these years in her thick, salty blood. Its walls are ridged and leathery. 'My strongest amulet,' Grandmother says.

'Wah, so heavy,' I hold out my wrist so she can snip the thread of my old amulet. The jar dimples my palm.

'Eat it,' Grandmother advises. 'It will make you strong. Protect inside you, make you like rock so you won't turn seasick, you won't turn reeling or dizzy, or become like jelly, like your mother, turning at the first sign of danger, the first sniff of the crocodile. So you'll know your way home. So you won't turn.'

I keep the jar under my tongue. I know it is a powerful charm.

Waiting for the hill spirits to take the bully's bait is like the instant before the closing of my grandmother's eye. It's like the long slow fall to the ground, the moment between recognition and when the ground hit. In that instant Grandmother saw everything: the storm-laden sky, the jungle trees reaching over the road like chapel arches, her scattered porkscraps and talismans, her broken bowl of coins. The bandit circle loomed like cut paper around her. The lover's ghostly message fell with the butt of the bandit rifle onto her head. For an instant the lover stood before Grandmother in her shimmering gown. Robbed of her body by Grandmother's curse, her human shape burnt to nothing, the lover showed herself only for an instant. She used anything for an instant's showing: a decrepit madman from deep in the jungle, a shadow at the top of the library stairs, watermarks like footprints next to a balcony rail. Anything to get the ghostly message across. The lover smiled when she saw her message hit. In that instant Grandmother realised everything. Grandmother saw that the passing of the wet and dry seasons of her living, the habitual twists and turns she made in hope of confusing just such a message, were only steps on a path begun the day the lover was carried into the rich man's house. The day the lover's salty tang made Grandmother suspiciously sniff. All the intervening years of her ghostchasing fame and fortune led only to this moment of perfect clarity. Grandmother watched the dips and rises of her life's pattern with great admiration, all the steps she had taken, the goodluck curves, the treacherous folds. The beauty of the pattern surprised her so that she felt no pain. The pleasure before falling was very great. In that instant time and space stretched endlessly, then suddenly, rudely, was cut short. By the time she hit the ground she'd forgotten the pleasure, the clarity. By then Grandmother could no longer see.

Waiting for the hill spirits to take the bully's bait is like looking at crystal, tantalising; like watching lamplight on a salt-crusted blade. It seems I have been waiting forever. The moon has almost travelled the length of the jungle-laced sky. I press my body into the earth, eyes closed, ferns rustling around me. The jungle earth seems buoyant, barely holding me up. If I tip sideways I will sink into the ground. I lie very still, watching crystal. Insects may nip at my earlobes, night animals tread over my belly and still I will not move. Behind my eyelids the jungle dark grows to enormous proportions, in my ears jungle sounds make a pounding like drums. The minutes swell and stretch until I lose sense of everything except their stretch and swell, and I become alternately large then small; infinite, then nothing. Time and space stretch endlessly. I try to imagine that instant before the closing of my grandmother's eye: my life's pattern dipping and rising before me as hers did, seen with perfect clarity. My life's pattern curving and folding according to her plan. Unlike her I watch the pattern not with admiration but a shivering and shaking that's barely noticeable at first. At first even I don't notice. Like Grandmother I can see exactly where the pattern started, and where it goes. How it has led to my lying as ghost bait on this part of the path in this jungle. Unlike her the intricate hooks and sweeps of the pattern only make me shiver and shake. Only the press of the jungle earth against me, the leaves tickling my ears, hold me steady; hold me still. Unlike the jungle of my grandmother's stories, the one that presses against me is neither a jungle of jumps and shudders nor one to slide my sleeping eyes open for fear. The jungle earth is warm and silent. The jungle beasts are mere jungle beasts, no more, which scurry at my footfall. The cursed thing lying in wait is not a thing of terror but a huddled thing, thirsty, fitting a parched space at the back of my throat. One swallow and the thirst will be gone. My tongue tingles where the bully has cut it. Grandmother's strongest amulet sits under my tongue like a stone. The blood symbols the bully painted on my neck have dried in stiff streaks.

When the hill spirit arrives I am almost caught unaware. The screeches echoing through the jungle almost pass me by. The bully's low hiss from where she is hiding brings me back. I rise from the jungle earth as if from water, slowly at first, then in a jolt that sits me bolt upright and reaches my hands for any steadying root or treetrunk. I open my eyes to see the troupe of monkeys swinging through the lower branches. I hear the crash through the undergrowth, branches bending, shrubs uprooted, the quickened tramp of soldiers' boots. I know the soldiers are playing their games. In the branches overhead one of the monkeys is jerked from its perch to the ground. The monkey dangles on the glint of wire, it gnaws at the wire, leaps back into the branches only to fall swinging once more. The one-armed monkey's screeches fill the jungle night. Its desperate tugging against the snare shivers the nearby trees. The bully hisses her annoyance that it's not our snare which has caught the hill spirit, I hear the angry thump of her fists. 'Move!' comes her urgent whisper. 'Quick, out of the way!'

I roll from the path to crouch beside her. The soldiers pass so close we can reach out to touch them, but we lie as still as rocks and trees. The laughs and shouts of the soldiers drown out even the monkey's screeches, the crunch of their boots is louder than any other sound. The soldiers gather in a circle around the snared monkey. They slap at their elbows and thighs.

'Wah, at last we've got you!' the soldiers shout and hoot.

'Aiya, do your monkey dance!' they poke their riflebutts and sticks.

'Break it! Break it!' they cry, and they do.

In the circle the one-armed monkey with the mangy coat and the broken arm does its monkey dance. Its turns are faster than my grandmother's long ago fairy dancing, its spins just as wild. Its eyes bulge, flicking from side to side. The soldiers' claps and cheers rise louder and louder, their voices jab like the rhythmic jabs of the monkey's arm and legs. Their bodies are held rigid, their movements coming in bursts that make the bully wince. The monkey stretches its jaws wide open, its fangs curve yellow and sharp. The one-armed monkey swings from the wire, scrambles from boot to boot.

I begin to tremble as I watch the bully's hill spirit wildly scrambling. The trembles start at my feet, they creep their way up my body to shudder the grasses and leaves. All my life's walking and listening and waiting bubbles up my throat, all my years of treading the path of Grandmother's plan. The trembles turn into giggles and small shards of laughter which tingle my tongue and push against my teeth. I press further into the undergrowth, holding my mouth so the soldiers do not hear. Furry leaf tendrils tickle my nose, my shoulders quiver as my laugh leaks out. Beside me the bully is hissing. The bully is choking back her tears. Her breath is pitifully sharp as she turns to snarl at me. She twists my arm until my eyes too are spurting, until my body twists also, to keep up.

When Grandmother is asleep the bully and I lie her arms across her breast. We pat her hands into place, pull her fingers to the sign: *Avert!* Toothpaste over her eyebrows, shoe polish in careful blobs on her cheeks. We press our lips to her cheeks to make kissmarks she will laugh at when she wakes. We paint a smile onto her sagging lips, tiptoe from the room with the pots of paint and polish slip-sliding in our hands, our hands pressed to our mouths to hold our giggles in. Grandmother snuggles into her chair.

◄ F O U R T E E N ►

A Train on
a Track

That's the place to finish. The hill with the convent and the
jungle is called Mat Salleh Hill. Rival schools call it Mad
Sailor Hill. In defiance convent girls dress up as sailors on
special carnival days, they sew elaborate flounces onto their
shirtfronts, lace their cuffs and collars, wrap black plastic
around their calves to make knee-high boots. They wear curly
cardboard hats with the cross-and-bones and painted mous-
taches fierce enough to make everyone immediately hand over
their loot. Instead of a hand some brandish a silver hook. On
special carnival days the convent is hung with rainbow-
coloured streamers, its rooftop festooned and garlanded,
balloons of all shapes and sizes flit and pop at their moorings,
and sag as the day wears through. Hand-painted flags proclaim
the festival: speech day, saints day, sports day, prize day,
foundation day. A marquee in the largest playing field doles
out paper cups of chocolate for extra energy to teachers,
parents and girls. The convent's ancient loudspeakers crackle
modern music, there's an air of suppressed excitement trailing
the groups of sailor-garbed girls, of sedate walking suddenly

breaking into a higgledy-piggledy run. 'Girls!' come the nuns' voices at regular intervals. 'Remember you're young ladies, girls!' Special carnival days see convent girls butterfly flitting with groups of visitors on guided tours of the convent, city officials linking arms with leading patrons, the parents of prospective boarders nudging their sulky-mouthed girls. Here are the classrooms, plenty of air and light, there the dormitories, the narrow beds train young girls to sleep sweetly, they encourage young bones to grow straight. There are the quaint old chapel and infirmary, and there the library, newly renovated, where—of course not!—nothing unsightly has *ever* been seen. The leading patrons and city officials admire the sense of colonial history the buildings inspire in young girls, that legacy of pathfinders and founders, they examine the fine marble statues and pillars, the imported tiles.

After the speeches and luncheon, the judging of the art-and-craft and best-flowerbed competitions, and the egg-and-spoon and Mad Sailor races with Matron lifting her skirts to win; after the shirtfront flounces hang drooping and the sailor hats have been sat on, and nuns and parents merely stand around talking, convent girls trail off in bands of four and five to really show the new girls around. They take them to the convent chapel where the late afternoon sunlight catches a figure in black wafting around the saint statues, smiling and waving, disappearing in a burst of radiance through a mark on the wall. New girls are invited to examine the courtyard flagstones, crossed and recrossed with the silver scuffmarks of a thousand unearthly feet. They are sneaked past the nuns on guard duty at certain parts of the convent library, the upper stairway and balcony, they're crouched in the deepest shadows, but though they wait and wait, and whistle the ghostly callings convent girls teach them, and jump squawking at the cold fingers trailed down their spines, the new girls can't see her. They can't see the lover paused at the balcony doorway, to them her shimmering gown is merely the last of the sunlight, her hair a black shadow that disappears as soon as the convent lamps are lit. The new girls crouch blinking. They neither smell her salty tang nor hear her sigh. The lover sighs as if she has been sighing forever, but the new girls can't hear. They scramble to their feet at the sudden clang of the convent bell calling the carnival day to its end.

That's the place to finish. The convent on the hill next to the jungle is the oldest and best in the whole city. It is the site of sayings and stories going back to a time long before I was born. Its stories and sayings are known throughout the city: its Mad Sailor, its Rich Man of the Mansion, its Ancestor Bandits planning breathtaking raids and ambushes in the days of old. Even if no one tells them, convent girls can feel the scrape of the stories against their shirtsleeves as they wander the ancient hallways, their feet have to be lifted with extra effort at the stick of the sayings to their shoes. In the ancient hallways convent girls sometimes feel a press and slide of water. Late in the evenings or the early mornings certain rooms and corridors waft a salty tang. The walk up certain stairways is a walk pushed and cresting, it is feet almost lifted, buoyant, it's a trill of bubbles going past convent girls' ears. Insubstantial shapes swirl around them, mermaid shapes smiling with the heads of beautiful women and the tails of seadragons, ruffling convent girls' hair as they pass. Colourful fish shapes nibble at toes and fingers, the air moves in moist ribbons. At the top of the stairs convent girls stop in confusion, their hearts pounding, their breaths heaving like the too-fast rise from a pool. Convent girls are filled with a wild urge to run, their mouths are stretched with laughing. They walk with the memory of the cool green depths all the hot day, that silken slide of a weightless body. Theirs is exhilarated walking. They check to see if their skins are wet.

The memory of the cool green depths is what keeps the lover sighing. It is what keeps her staring and staring though from where she's standing there's not even a glimpse of the sea. The lover presses against the balcony rail. The memory of the cool green depths is a salve to her skin, it's a bead of moisture in a parched throat. The convent air grates against her, suffocating, the air is dissolution. It is arms wrapped around her, a rich man's arms gripping and pulling, stumbling her round and round. The air is fiery, it is the crackle of a curse-fire, a shrivelling to burnt sticks. The air is a sound turned inward, swallowing her, it's the sound of speared creatures, of creatures plucked from the depths. Only gradually does the lover realise that the sound of the speared creatures belongs to her. Only then does she see that it's not the air that is burning, but her. The lover is smoke heaving. She is nothing. No more than a breath of wind to flutter small twigs and leaves. The jungle leaves are cool to rest on for a moment, the jungle dark doesn't hurt her eyes. The lover has no eyes. She is smoke heaving. She is a slipping through the treetops, a sliding over the slow minutes, the months, the long circling years. She is a waiting even the jungle beasts can hear, they stiffen when she passes, and scuttle from her path. Save for thirst these could be underwater rocks and stones that she glides over, those branches could be coral, this, a seaweed green. These jungle paths could be the paths of the sea. But the air is fiery. The singsong chatter of an old man sprawled under some bushes draws her, that clatter of a breath so aged it's soon grinding to a stop. The old man sags in his skin and bones. Only scraps of sailcloth patching his pants indicate his origin, only the tattoos on his arm: an anchor, a rose, another rose. His face is wrinkled parchment, waxy, his eyes the colour of crinkling leaves. A faint swish through the treetops draws his head upwards. The shape hovering over him squeezes his last breath to a screech. When the lover enters him, it's like a bad case of overeating, the *whump!* of an unexpected fall. The old man's mouth stretches and stretches, swallowing gallons of seawater so he chokes and retches, but his bones grow sturdy, his flesh puffs up smooth. The mad sailor sits up suddenly. He opens his eyes wide.

Before I could be born naturally, my grandmother snatched me from my mother's womb. That was part of Grandmother's plan. In my mother's womb she nudged and prodded me, she watched the seashell bow of my body curl to arms and legs;

listened for heart murmurs or limbs growing crooked, for frailty in the gurgle of my blood. My head was bent to a nod of Grandmother's liking, my lips forming to the thin line yes. The boiled herbs she made my mother drink strengthened my marrow and liver and bone. Side by side they sat in the evenings, Grandmother in her chair by the doorway, my mother beside her, watching the coming and going of the evening. My mother was hardly allowed to move. She eased her weight into her chair. Passing neighbours stopped for a chat, joked at my mother's belly to make her hang her head. Grandmother prodded my mother's chin up. She turned on the neighbours with her tiger glare, boomed out her silencing laugh. She fetched and carried for my mother, fussed around her like an old nursery maid. When I was born I fell into my grandmother's hands like a long-awaited gift. Like the heavy brass key needed to set the rich man's clockwork toys in motion, to start his miniature railway rattling on its track spread over half a room. The rich man dangled the key over Grandmother's head while she jumped and strained; sometimes he let it drop. Grandmother cupped her fingers to make sure of the catch. She cradled me carefully. The first breath I took was heavy with her smell, that smell of her overwhelming desire scraping my breath to burning, swelling out my lungs. The first sound I made was an echo of her laugh, the first thing I knew was her looming face. Grandmother brushed away my mother's outstretched arms to press me to her own breast. She guided my lips to her wrinkled teat; poked and pinched at my skin. She scratched my eyes so I could see.

All that was part of Grandmother's plan.

From the time I was a small child I have always known of my grandmother's plan. I have repeated it after her like city sayings shouted at children after this or that wrongdoing, like convent sayings learnt by rote. Every morning my whispers rise singsong to the beat of Grandmother's hand. My mouth shapes itself to the shape of her mouth, listing the things to be remembered, the steps to be taken before the end of my second life cycle, the secrets I must never tell. The complicity of smile and wink that we have shared for as long as I can remember is only one of the bonds pulling us close. I have always known of my grandmother's secrets, even the ones she doesn't like to tell. The ones no one else knows. My grandmother's secrets layer her face when she's sleeping. Her hopes gather in lumps under this ear, on that cheek. Past slights tinge her skin mouldy. I know her fears of telling too much. No one can bully Grandmother into telling before it's time. Ever since I was a small child I have been waiting with my grandmother for the right time. Grandmother says all things must be endured. Though the waiting is hard and the walking cakes my feet with blisters, the writing grows a knob on my middle finger like an extra bone, Grandmother says I must keep on waiting and walking and writing. I musn't give up. The ones who endure will win. Grandmother showed me the steps to be used in the pursuit of endurance and victory, the roots of life. She showed me the steps of her plan. One step after another, each like walking a path. *First: going to the convent. Second: following the bully. Third: getting back Grandmother's ghostslashing knife. Fourth: searching the jungle for her other unfinished business. Fifth: burning it up. Sixth. Seventh. Eighth.* Grandmother made me write these down. Whenever she thought of a new step she pushed her book towards me. The steps that fill her notebooks are almost as many as her years. Grandmother is old now, so sometimes she mixes them up. She can't remember which steps I've taken, or which she has told me are no longer necessary, which are to come.

'Which next, Grandmother?' I ask and ask, running my finger down the list, some items ticked and underlined, some written over, others smudged out. But Grandmother can never be sure. She makes me read with long pauses so she can think. She makes me change the order, rewrite whole pages at a time. As the years pass my grandmother's plan branches out in all directions, its steps slip and slide against each other, cut zigzag across the pages so my pen skitters after and I can hardly keep up. Even through narrowed eyes the plan seems secretive.

Upside down it looks like a great jungle tree. *Thirty-fifth: showing contempt when the nuns finally beg and crawl for another favour. Twenty-eighth: cursing the neighbour's daughter for answering back. Fourteenth: destroying Grand-mother's oldest enemy with one fiery stroke.*

'Which, Grandmother? Which do you want next?' I cry, as yet again she changes the order of her plan. I turn dizzy at the twists and turns of the pages, snag myself on every fork.

Grandmother slaps my wrists to bring me back. She tugs on my tightly braided hair. 'Haven't you been listening? Haven't you heard what Grandmother said? Aiya, hasn't Grandmother taught you to see?'

Before I could be born naturally my grandmother had already taught me to see. The eye-strengthening soups poured down my mother's throat in spite of face-pulling and a quick turn of the head bred sharpness where ordinary eyes are curved. Looking sideways, holding my slapped wrists gingerly, I see that the body of Grandmother's plan doesn't change. Her plan is a treetrunk split down the middle, its numerous forks and branches are mere diversions, sidetrips to be taken when there's more time. Grandmother's two most hated enemies come first. I stand with my back plank-straight, my tugged hair smarting, my arms unwieldy branches clutching at Grandmother's notebooks. My toes dig questing into the floor for cracks and crevices to hold me up. But my back aches in spite of all the years of training. There's a catch in my voice. My feet make indentations wherever I walk, so I'm not allowed in certain parts of the convent, on lawns and walkways and polished floorboards; at home Grandmother trips into my footsteps, and my mother patiently cements the floor smooth. I'm not allowed to walk where other girls walk. In spite of all the years of scribbling my grandmother's steps and stories, her advice and admonitions, of exercising my fingers for flexibility and strength, sometimes the pen flies out of my hand. The pen lies rocking between my grandmother and me.

By the time I turn fourteen I will know all the ins and outs of her plan. Already I know the fabulous growth of its branches, their twisting to a pattern my grandmother likes. Sometimes the bend of the branches is a snapping like bone. Grandmother listens with relish; bone-breaking is necessary when moulding a satisfactory shape. A foot arched like an earlobe, the relationship of skin and flesh rearranged. Grandmother knots her plan the way she rubs her knots into my hair, each one carefully considered, painstakingly twirled between forefinger and thumb. Her shrivelled hands deftly plait the long black strands into place. I kneel squirming from one leg to the other while she scrapes at my skull. She watches unblinking as I lace her words onto paper. She pulls the corners of my eyes upwards, stretches any possible frown smooth. 'Grandmother, it hurts!' only makes her tighten her knots. It makes her list more and more steps. When Grandmother has finished, the pages of her notebooks are as bulky as my braid. Their special cases are bursting at the seams. I can hardly lift them. My braid is so tight I can hardly move my head, it pokes out this way and that with knots so intricately woven that my mother whistles through her teeth trying to undo them. Grandmother's pattern of knots tips my head sideways.

From the time I was a small child I have always known the pattern already laid out long before I was born. I have always known that sideways tip of the head. My life pattern was laid out by my grandmother, my mother, my disappeared father, the rich man, the lover, the nuns, the mad sailor, all the twistings and turnings of their stories, the walking and slightings and yearnings and sighings and hatings and weepings that they did and did not do. All the stories they told, and did not tell. I have always known how far there is to walk, and how there's precious little time. This is what my grandmother taught me. Already I know what her most precious is. I know for sure. Grandmother's most precious is a treasure that shrinks or grows according to whoever she shows it, and how well they listen, and whether they have learnt to see. It's a treasure stretching to whole caverns of rubies and diamonds and strings of pearl, it's the size of her notebooks, the grain of her voice rising and falling, plunging the bully, my mother and me first upwards to the smoky ceiling then down into the cracks of the floor. Grandmother's treasure is an instrument of revenge, a way to get back face. She nurses it like a special hate. It is voluminous, filling whole days and nights, seeping from her chair by the doorway into the street. It's no larger than an in-between girl. By the time I turn fourteen the sideways tip of my head will be an acute angle, I will be so heavy I'll hardly be able to lift my feet. I will be filled with everything my grandmother has tried to teach me, all the years of training and telling will stiffen my blood to sap. My arms will be lifted in whatever direction Grandmother likes, my fingers pointing, my head tilting that way too. My feet planted firmly in Grandmother's earth. Already her stories swell my chest and head, they crust my skin with swirling knobs. I will breathe slowly, carefully, into the spaces that are left. I will make these spaces my own. A jungle wind will rock me. A sudden jungle wind will stir the earth at my feet. The pleasure of falling will be very great.

Grandmother says: *People who strike bargains with ghosts or demons sometimes lose out in the end. People who give their promises recklessly have been known to regret it. Ghosts know things that people don't. The favour a ghost grants always has strings attached and often turns out to be a nightmare benefit for the one favoured. Never think you can outsmart or outbargain a ghost, unless you happen to be a powerful wisewoman, well-versed in the arts of magic. Unless your hair is firm at the roots and your eyesight as sharp as piercing. Sometimes even powerful wisewomen get caught out. Never whistle to yourself to pass the time when walking alone at night. The whistle is a call which can wake a sleeping ghost. Let sleeping ghosts lie. Never dismiss ghosts as figments of the imagination or shades left over from nightmares. Ghosts are as real as you or me, and as susceptible to insult.*

When my grandmother was an older girl in the ghosthouse, she knew her life as she knew it was coming to an end. In those days Grandmother spent many hours, many days, on her own. She walked the rich man's house like a shadow seen only in the corner of the eye. In those days her favourite place was the rich man's bookroom. There Grandmother went when everywhere else seemed unfriendly. There she first imagined her pools of memory, her memory rising and dipping in slippery arcs like a silky sea creature, like ornamental fish. There Grandmother remembered better days.

The rich man's bookroom was larger than the childhood house of my grandmother's memory, the place in the city where she and her family had lived. Grandmother imagined her brothers and sisters running around the bookroom, weaving their way around and into its corners and enclaves, confused at so much space. She imagined her mother stretched out on the polished floor, arms and legs stretching to their fullest without touching a thing. That was her mother's daydream as she rolled the endless ricecakes for market, as she hunched over basins of water reflecting her face in oily streaks: to stretch the length of her body on a clean floor without touching piled-up storage boxes, kitchen utensils, bundles of children's dirty washing. Without baskets of dry goods and vegetables creaking suspended over her head.

Grandmother stretched herself on the rich man's bookroom floor, dipping into her memory pools. The shelves of leatherbound volumes reached up to the ceiling from which no baskets hung suspended, safe from the gnawing of rats. The bookroom floor stretched in all directions, no boxes or piles of smelly clothes to bump into as Grandmother wriggled about on her back, only a couch by the window, a table on which the rich man's reading glasses lay like a pair of flinty eyes. Grandmother walked along the shelves, bumping her finger over the spines of the books. She carefully inspected one volume after another. The combined smells of leather and fine-quality papers went straight to her head. First she sniffed at the book covers daintily, then she opened them with one swift movement to fill her lungs. The room was filled with the sound of Grandmother's breathing. Grandmother's delight. Every book smelt different: of where it came from, and the hands that made it; of the faraway shelves on which it once lay. The rich man's favourite books wafted his musky smell.

When Grandmother was a smaller girl she'd carried the books to where the rich man sat at his desk, the pen in his hand flowing over paper. Grandmother admired the sweeping motions of the rich man's hand, the hooks and shifts that left a trail of ink now fine now heavy in its wake. She admired the magical power of that trail of words she couldn't decipher, how it left his hand in its thick envelope and returned in the form of supplies from the city that took a whole day to be delivered, or new uniforms for every servant, or soldiers coming to patrol the jungle borders of the rich man's property, to keep the city riffraff from his gates.

'No, it's not magic,' the rich man said absently when Grandmother asked. 'It's words. Now run along.'

Grandmother stood by the rich man's desk, watching his smooth looping words, so unlike the swift cuts and dashes of the language of her childhood memory, scratched onto scraps of paper by the roadside letter-writer for her to carry to the pawn shop, the medicine shop, the benevolent society store. Grandmother stood for long minutes holding her pile of books, saying nothing. If he was in an agreeable mood the rich man would finally smile. He would lay down his pen. He'd take the books from Grandmother and sit her on his lap. 'One day when I've time I'll teach you to read and write,' he promised, sweeping his arm around the bookroom. 'Then you'll see for yourself. You'll know everything there is to know. Will you like that? And what will you give me in return?'

When the rich man opened the books, he and Grandmother inhaled their precious smells. The rich man and Grandmother laughed. As he read she studied his face, his deep-set eyes and hair curling fine and golden around his ears. Grandmother's own hair stuck to her head in a shiny black cap. She copied the unfamiliar shapes of his mouth. When he explained the words and pictures, she stared hard. When he continued reading, she breathed in deep. She saw the words vibrating with their own strange power. Grandmother breathed deeply. She thought she could breathe the power of the words, their shapes and meanings, right off the page.

When my mother was a young woman there was an instant between the time she was a girl and the time it seemed to everyone she became a middle-aged woman, worn, the features of her face caved in. In that instant my mother was a young woman, no more, no less. Her eyes widened slightly. Her gaze abandoned its usual scuttle to linger on shapes and colours unseen before, on smoke shadows in the stovefire, insects dangling in the light. Her cheek rested for long moments on any convenient windowsill, a strand of hair was twirled between forefinger and thumb. In that instant, which seemed to my mother to last both an eyeblink and forever, she stood poised on a hinge: turning a corner. My mother stood there, perfectly balanced. She could swing either way, but she stood there, an eyeblink or forever, perfectly still. Then my mother discovered that stillness doesn't stop the swing. An eyeblink or forever later her instant passed.

When she was no longer so young, when her face was lined with work and old weeping, and her hands calloused, her legs threaded with vein roots like an intricate map, some evenings saw my mother's instant come back. Some evenings the bully and I have to stop and stare. The bully and I drop whatever we are doing to sit at my mother's feet. Her face on these evenings is luminescent, tilted slightly, her needle poised between convent girls' mending and the stretch of the thread. My mother stares just beyond our left shoulders, she stares like the still surface of water, endlessly receding. Soon she is so far away we have to reach out our hands to call her back. The bully and I rest our heads against my mother's legs, and she smiles, she touches our heads with her hands.

My grandmother is a gambler. For someone who is the enemy

of havoc she is not very neat. She lives life like loose strokes of an ink-heavy brush, like the bully's blackboard cleaning. Grandmother's life spills from the countless boxes piled to head height in her room: a cascade of scarves in this corner, early ghostchasing costumes sliding from their paper, cardboard cases containing nothing but their long ago smells. Grandmother breathes deeply. When my mother tries to tidy the room she chases her out. My grandmother likes loose ends. She likes winning against the odds, that infinite moment just before winning, when silence fills the room. The imminent round of shouts and incredulous applause, the enemy bowing and scraping in defeat. Grandmother never wants anything finished, she never wants to get to the end. She is always afraid of telling too much; of giving away the story before the end. She hobbles around with her ears filled with the sound of imminent applause. To her the *expectation* is as great as the actual sound. Like her long ago fairy dancing, her jumping and spinning to tear her breath to pieces, once the applause comes and the dance is over, the gamble paid off, the cards laid face upwards on the table, all the jumping and spinning, the waiting and plotting and worrying till her hair falls wispy to the floor, will be forgotten in an instant. In an instant the years of twisting and turning, of sitting in the doorway with her hands beating and beating at her breast, all will have passed.

In Grandmother's early ghostchasing days she was known as a show-off. Grandmother's stall was the largest, the most colourful, it was hung with mirrors and peacock feathers, with paper cutouts and pieces of beaten metal tinkling to the tune of any passing wind. Grandmother's was the most flamboyant routine. Her calling drum the loudest, her songs and chants the most impressive; her cures so miraculous that even disbelievers came from far and near. The slave spirits she summoned were so frightful they could only be seen through finger cracks, even Grandmother had to wear her special sunglasses, seeing them was such a strain. Customers flocked to see my grandmother's style. They jostled with shoulders rubbing, sweat gathering in the spoon-shaped parts of their bodies as they stretched tiptoe for a better view. Smoke from her makeshift incinerator reddened Grandmother's tiger glare, her costume swirled and fluttered with every move. The bug-eyed .shadows flapped around her like flame, they tossed coloured lights into the air to send the crowd oohing and ahing, hurled fireballs to make them duck and shriek. The clearing in which Grandmother performed was stamped uneven by a myriad shadowy feet. Her box for donations was crammed so full she had to bring a spare. For a treat she stood with one leg arched, arms spread like wings. She beat on her drum for silence, spun and twirled so the crowd could hardly see her feet. Her held up hand signalled she was ready to speak.

In earlier days, when she was newly a young woman, my grandmother met a ghost as she was walking one night. This was in the days she was an apprentice ghostchaser. The ghost suddenly appeared at Grandmother's side. 'Who are you?' Grandmother asked.

'I'm a ghost. And you?'

'I'm a ghost too.'

'Where are you going?'

'To the city.'

'In that case, let us travel part of the way together.'

Grandmother and the ghost walked side by side. 'Aiya, how slow walking is!' the ghost exclaimed. 'We'll go faster if we take turns carrying each other.' The ghost offered to carry Grandmother first. After a few miles it grumbled: 'Wah, you're so heavy. Are you really a ghost?'

'Of course I am!' Grandmother cried. 'I'm a new ghost, that's why I'm heavy.' When Grandmother carried the ghost she could hardly feel it. 'As I'm a new ghost,' she said conversationally, 'I don't really know what we ghosts are most afraid of.'

'Why, human spit is what we hate.'

Grandmother walked until she came to a swampy area. She invited the ghost to cross first. The ghost skimmed over the water, hopping neatly over mangrove roots, while Grandmother followed stumbling and splashing. 'How come you're so clumsy?' the ghost asked. 'How come you make so much noise?'

'Please excuse me,' Grandmother apologised. 'It's because I'm a new ghost, I'm not used to passing through water.'

'Not at all,' the ghost replied.

When they reached the outskirts of the city, Grandmother flung the ghost over her shoulder. She dug her fingernails into its legs. 'What are you doing?' the ghost cried, begging to be put down, but Grandmother took no notice. Grandmother hurried into town. At the marketplace she flung the ghost, which in its fright had turned into a pig, at the porkseller's feet. She spat on it so it couldn't turn back.

'What a fine pig!' the porkseller cried, not having seen such a pig since the food shortages began, and promptly gave Grandmother a handful of coins. Grandmother jangled the coins in her pocket as she walked. She stopped spinning and twirling to stare at the crowd gathered around her stall. Lamplight glittered the mirror shards sewn onto her dress. The last beat of her drum signalled the end of the story. The crowd broke into claps and cheers and her donation box was passed from hand to hand. People harassed by ghosts clamoured to tell her their woes, to buy anti-ghost potions and make an appointment with the only ghostchaser in town who could turn a pesky ghost into a pig. The smell of roast pork tickled their nostrils. 'One by one!' Grandmother ordered, taking up her brush with great flourish, painstakingly noting their names.

My grandmother reminds us of this story whenever the bully and I come flopping into the front room to throw ourselves onto the floor. The bully and I tear off our sweatsoaked shoes to sprawl pressing our legs to the cool cement. We kick at the bundles of convent laundry we have helped my mother carry home. 'Did you find it?' Grandmother demands, nudging us with her cane, and the bully and I look at each other. The bully and I sheepishly shake our heads. We burst out laughing, shaking our heads until our hair flips wildly and our eyebrows stand up straight. Grandmother reminds us of this story to keep us on track. One musn't get distracted when searching for treasure, she says. One must be brazen when dealing with ghosts. No matter how fearful the walking, how tiring, how sharp the ghostly teeth glint in the moonlight, one must keep pace. Shivers must be banished from the voice, the urge to run steadied to a sauntering walk. One must think of the roast pork.

'Tell us the story of the ghosthouse, Grandmother!' the bully and I butt in to stop her scolding. 'Grandmother, tell us the end!'

But Grandmother only looks at us vaguely. 'Where did Grandmother stop?' she murmurs, and even when we tell her she hmms and hahs, and goes off in different directions, grumbling about aches and bandits, and the mad sailor on top of the hill. Grandmother begins to tell us again about the rich man's parties, which the bully and I have heard so often we can describe them ourselves. She reminds us of the darkroom before it became a darkroom, about the servants in the servants' quarters, and the view of the city from the balcony, has Grandmother told us about this view? Grandmother's story goes here and there, trailing off at every turn until she ends up silent. Until she sits with her mouth clamped shut and her knob-boned fingers twiddling themselves into shapes that make the bully and me stare.

'What?' we scratch our heads, our heads and shoulders swivelling like Grandmother's fingers as we try to follow the train of her thoughts, the convoluted story-threads she tosses for us to snatch at and hoard, and weave and swallow, and twirl and photograph, and do what we will. Only my mother sits calmly sorting the laundry, her head and body held still. 'What happened next, Grandmother?' the bully and I urge. 'What next?' Grandmother's face as she stares past us is haloed in the lamplight, the hairs escaping from her bun frame her head like a fiery cloud. She is old now, so her tremendous memory sometimes fails her. She dredges her memory pools but doesn't come up with anything new. 'Have I told you the part about . . . ?' she asks, and once again the bully and I look at each other. 'Yes, Grandmother,' we chorus, 'you already told us, yes.'

'No harm hearing again . . .' she mutters, pointing towards her special cases so I dig and scrabble until I find the notebooks to go with whatever story she is telling and can prompt her when she falters. I flick through the pages in which I no longer write. Grandmother's extra special notebook is crammed to one side of the jumbled pile. From habit the bully tears at her hair. Only from habit does she grind her teeth when Grandmother suddenly stops telling. The bully sits grinding her teeth, then begins to fiddle with her camera. She is always polishing and wiping, twisting this or that knob, blowing imagined dust from the lens. She's always counting her saved-up coins for the time when the Old Priest's camera finally wears out. Already the camera strap is frayed, its body marked with dents and scratches, its winding mechanism full of groans. The bully examines the portfolio of photos she is beginning: her landscapes of the convent and portraits of convent girls, teachers and nuns in introspective poses, her nature shots of the jungle and jungle animals caught unawares. The bully reshuffles them in order of good, better, best. She spends long minutes staring into each. Little curls of steam puff out her ears.

Nowadays the gaps between my grandmother's tellings get longer and longer. Every story she tells can be found in her pile of notebooks, noted more than once. Every retelling is different, coloured by a different emphasis, a smell, a mood, the flutter of a garment glimpsed in the corner of my grandmother's eye. I have to listen and look carefully to find the notes that match. But nowadays her stories aren't often told. Nowadays she sits for whole evenings in her chair by the doorway with her eyes filmed over, her eyebrows an unfurrowed ridge. Her hands resting limpid in her lap. Through the long silent evenings the bully and I no longer sit straining, rapt, waiting for her to continue. Grandmother's half-told stories curl around us on sugary threads we lick at only occasionally.

Nowadays the bully's special scrapbook is laid to one side, bulging its cardboard covers, shedding photos and scraps of scribbled-on paper, dried leaves and earth and the odd desiccated insect too. Nowadays the bully is careless of the bits that fall out. She neither grabs at every fluttered piece nor puzzles over the whole, trying to make a single picture that will add up from beginning to end. A map to find every nook and cranny of the stories my grandmother tells, every site of treasure the bully hopes to one day find. The bully has given up on treasure. No longer does she try to make sense of stories the way the nuns tell her; no longer does she search for a moral to tag to the end. The bully is resigned to gulping stories section by section, she is learning to listen like shooting photos, seeing life frozen a moment at a time. The pattern made by shuffling the stories together is interesting. The blank spaces in her newest album are as valuable as the photos they frame. Nowadays, unlike the nuns, the bully thinks stories are full of inconsiderations, and it's only real life that tries to make them fit. These days her tough little train travels more than one track, it travels sideways and sometimes stops halfway up the hill for a rest. These days she hardly ever takes revenge photos of the nuns. Her oldest photo lies crumpled with the others in the last pages of her scrapbook, and now that she looks at it sideways and fleetingly, sometimes she glimpses through the photo's smoke-damaged surface its two faces chiselled in black-and-white: the rich man and the lover standing side by side. The rich man stands slightly behind the lover, one hand cups her frail shoulder, the other the crook of her arm. His hair is pale and shiny, hers a midnight fall. Her shadows curve and swish around her like a wave, a tail. The rich man's head is turned towards her while she stares straight ahead. She stares past any careless watcher, her eyes fathomless, her face a lure for drowned sailors; a memory of the unbearable breath pounding for release.

In the gaps between my grandmother's telling I rub at the

photo of the rich man and the lover until the paper slides with the movement of my hand. Until I rub away more than the smoke. The old crackled paper lifts and frays. The bully doesn't notice but I am rubbing her photo of the rich man and the lover away. I ease my grandmother's extra special notebook from her pile. The other notebooks slip and slither out of the way; there's a faint sucking sound as I pull it loose. Its red leather cover is creased and dusty, dented with the shapes of the other notebooks, scratched from careless packing, but the pages are clean. I breathe their rich papery smell, run my fingers over their fine edges. I pick up my pen. I make my first mark, hesitant, then another, more firmly. Then another. The pen fits neatly between my thumb and forefinger. The ink runs black and smooth.

Unlike Grandmother, who has only heard the crocodile's deep-throated whisper snaking out of the dark and seen only the shadowy thrash of his tail, I have seen the crocodile in daylight. I have looked the crocodile in his gleaming eye and run my hands over the firm ridges of his backbone, the sharp seesaw of his teeth. The crocodile and I have wrapped our arms around each other, his short arms hardly reaching around me. We have pressed our lean bellies together in a madcap dance and run skipping through meagre jungle sunlight like friends of old. We have slashed through jungle cobwebs with his sharp crocodile's knife, pierced jungle fruit to assuage our hunger and thirst. Our strange mix of laughter, human and crocodile, has risen to shake the birds and small animals from their perches, the leaves from their jungle trees. Ever since I was a small child I have watched and waited for the crocodile, shivering and shaking whenever he was mentioned, ready to run. His crocodile doings have stuffed my ears, his teeth scraped with every scary shadow over my skin. Until now I've never seen him face to face. The face-to-face croc is surprising, his expression more kindly than the one I've been expecting all these years. To me he's more timid than menacing, his smile is lopsided not from an innate crookedness but to lessen the shock of his teeth. Seen from a distance his hunched shape is what stands out, and the glint of his teeth, the formidable reach of his tail. Close up his eyes are limpid, they are a mirror to the watcher, they are black and radiant pools. The croc I know is not the evil creature my grandmother tells me, the stealer of daughters and faithful assistants, that stalker of street corners and jungle paths. As my mother says, he's merely a creature whose luck is rather bad. My poor croc can no more help the shape of his face than I can mine, but he knows to make the most of his life and his luck. My crocodile is not one for cursing. His is a fury that starts out slow, that boils and bubbles, and hitches its back against the weight of all the jokes and jibes, the petty slights and discriminations accumulated over the years; all the back-bitings, jealousies and injustices involved in the scramble for favour, the aches of being owned body and soul. The gatherings at the barb-wired gates to sniff at foreign cakes and sweetmeats while the city markets sweat only their rancid smells. The croc's broad back creaks under the weight of the elongated shadows attached to him, all the fears and fevers stitched to his feet: fear of dark alleys, of enemies lurking in every shadow, sniffing and snouting for any trace of convent girls' legs accidentally eased apart. Heave onto him the fever of a pounding breath, of nightly tossings and turnings, and the croc will carry them too, he'll stretch wide his Y-shaped mouth and arch his neck so nothing slips off. He'll shrug his shoulders against the shadowy weight of all the hinted-at secrets and half-told stories that pattern the years; against the patterned fixity of the years. That's why the crocodile's back is bowed. Sometimes he carries this weight for generations; at first he thinks it's the weight of his own body, then one day he stands up straight. The sound of the crocodile fury is more than a breaking of bone. It's more than the gathering of the bits and pieces of his past life as he knew it, that standing straight is bringing to an end. More than a hate-fire in a windowless room. The croc doesn't burn up the past, he sifts through it like treasure. His fury always comes as a shock, even when one has been watching and waiting for years. It hits like a sudden jungle wind, shaking the trunks of giant trees, churning the earth at their roots. Sometimes it bubbles to the skin surface, it's a terror like sudden hairs sprouting, sudden roundings and softenings of flesh. It roughens the skin on unexpected parts of the body, on thighs and elbow creases, it makes patches of a raised and regular pattern, scary, smooth when rubbed one way, snagging at the pull of the hand back. Face to face the croc and I run our hands over each other, our face-to-face skins hold no terrors, each hump and crack is touched tenderly, is shivery with the acknowledgment of hump and crack; with discovery, not fear. When the crocodile fury hits there's a wild urge to run. The in-between time is over, the child shed, the young woman assumed. Everything, the view out the window, the ground, the air, the world, is irrevocably changed. The patterns are rearranged.

Grandmother says: *If you know the charms and can see the many shadows on the paths, you can be sure they know and see you.*

When the soldiers have finished the one-armed monkey is a huddled lump of monkey fur in the clearing the bully has made, where the many tracks meet. The one-armed monkey lies bloody and still. I turn to the bully's snuffling and snivelling beside me. I look at her sideways. I have never seen her weep as now she weeps. The bully runs the back of her hand over her face to set it straight, she crawls from her crouch to stab at the earth with her knife. She stabs at the soldiers' footprints, digs at them and pulls them up in clumps. The bully is furious, her tears burning red furrows down her cheeks. The soldiers are gone now and she is digging a hole. The bully digs and digs. When the hole is done she picks up the monkey's carcass and tosses it in. She runs her hands over its broken body, begins to push the earth back in. 'Don't just sit there!' the bully snarls.

I crawl towards her. I creep like an animal from the

undergrowth to sprinkle jungle earth and leaves. I drop clods onto the dead monkey, dig my fingers into the ground to help shovel its body from the bully's sight. I dig deep. The tips of my fingers touch something soft and silky, cool in the warm jungle earth: something that slips against my fingertips like an underground current. I dig deeper. I grip. I pull. As Grandmother says, isn't it funny how life is. The bully and I have walked and walked and now we have found it. The lover's gown slips out of the earth as streaked as a precious metal, stained and tattered but shimmering still. I heave it out with one sharp tug. The bully and I have found it, as Grandmother told us, but the bully doesn't know. The bully sits stabbing at the earth with her knife. She is so disappointed she can't lift her head. She kneels at the graveside and weeps. I kick off my shoes, twist to look at my heels. There's a crack of light on the slope of this jungle, we have stayed out that long. I lift one foot, then the other. The lover's footprints attached to my feet are dangling loose.

And then the bully is in one of my grandmother's tempers. The bully is so disappointed she has had enough. She tugs at her frayed strap so hard it snaps and her camera smashes to the ground. She doesn't even try to catch it. She slaps her fists together and stamps her feet.

'We have lost our spirit,' the bully says. 'How will we find treasure? What will we follow? It is dead.' As the bully says this she swings her arms. She shuffles more earth onto the one-armed monkey's carcass which sags stiff and crooked, and stretches its broken arm towards her like an accusation. A plea. I feel a stirring inside me as I stare into the half-filled grave. 'No use staying,' the bully points her fist to show she is serious. 'Let's go. Let's ask Grandmother what to do.'

But the stirring inside me won't stop, the bubbling up my throat that makes me laugh. I am laughing. I am holding my sides with laughter, brushing the tears that spout from my eyes. In my hands the lover's gown is caught water, it slips and spills between my fingers so I have to keep snatching it back. I press my face to its shimmering folds, breathe the lover's salty smell. I clasp her gown to my breast like rubies and diamonds and strings of pearl. One deft turn and my arms are into its armholes, my shoulders shrugging to a perfect fit. The gown fountains round my feet, my hands are lifted to stroke its fine pleatings, my chin to smile at the juxtaposition of branch and leaf patterns just over the bully's left shoulder, the sudden wreath of jungle mist curling to the shape of a woman turned. The woman turns to face me. She is young and beautiful, her face only partly singed. Her skin is white china, the pearly underbelly of a fish. Her hair is a slice of a long past night. The dawn edging its way up the jungle-covered hill crowns her head with a greenish light. The lover and I smile at each other. We look at each other with great thirst. The bully twists to stare over her shoulder, but sees nothing. 'What are you doing?' she snaps. 'Why are you looking like that? Take that dirty thing off!'

'Something to tell you,' I say, but the bully doesn't like my look.

'Tell me later,' she bends to retrieve her camera. 'Let's go.'

'Something to show you,' I laugh.

'Show me later!'

But the bully can't stop me showing, the bully can't shut her ears.

'Remember your promise,' I say. 'You gave me your promise when I won the darkroom game. You promised anything I liked, and I want it now. Not photo, not rulebook. Not borrowing camera!'

'I'm warning you—later!'

'No, now.' I'm still laughing as I tug at the ribbons fastening my too-tight braid. I ease Grandmother's leaf and root collection bag from around my waist, dig into its folds for the never-fail matches and ghostburning candles she makes me carry wherever I go. I have another plan for Grandmother's unfinished business, other than burning it up. I have another plan for finishing. I crumple the matches and candles, slip their pieces into the grave. I slide Grandmother's strongest amulet out from under my tongue, toss it into the grave where perhaps a lily will grow. I lift my skirt to piss on it for good measure. This spot: the end of my second life cycle. The beginning of the next cycle, where the lover's footprints have left my feet and are pointing.

'Something to do,' I say, my hair lifting on the sudden wind. My hair uncoils from Grandmother's braid, it slithers untangled and free. The bully can't help staring. Suddenly I am the most beautiful woman she has ever seen. My gown glimmers so bright she can hardly bear to look. She stands with her mouth drooped open as I hold out my hand. 'Give it to me,' I say, and the bully doesn't want to, but she knows what I mean. The bully doesn't want to but obediently her hands drop her knife onto my palm, her salt-crusted knife, once owned by a famous bandit, once known as a famous ghostslashing knife. The charred handle fits my palm like a homecoming, the blade sheaths into its special pouch in my gown. All the years of the knife's passing from hand to hand presses against my belly. Like the lover's ghostly message her knife too has travelled a convoluted route: from the rich man to my grandmother to my mother to the Lizard Boy to the Old Priest to the bully to me. The knife and the gown cleave together with a faint sound of waves slapping, a memory of the toss and pull of the sea.

'Wait here,' I tell the bully, but I know the bully won't wait. I know when I come back she will be different. My bully will be gone. Her in-between face, that fourteen-year-old face she has worn far more than fourteen years, will crease to its natural lines and pouches. When I come back the bully and I will no longer be the same. The bully will be older. But for now that isn't what troubles her. Now her bully's eyes are widening. For the first time she is looking at me with fear. I hold out my hand, and it's not the bully who takes it. The lover smiles like a girl, her hand is girl-shaped, her flesh like a cooling breeze.

'Where are you going?' the bully shouts as we turn. The bully stands with her fists clenched, twitching from head to toe. Her eyes are as startled as a sudden waking. She stands bolt upright, lunges forward to throw her arms around me. Her liver against my belly is as hard as stone. The bully grips. She pulls. In her arms I am a shape turning, I am a shape now suddenly long and scaly, now bloating, now ridged with spikes. Still the bully grips. When I turn to face her my teeth are long and pointed. I show her the hole in my neck where the rich man woke me. I show her the smouldering space of my plucked scale, which my grandmother burnt. The way my jaws click in and out, and then I swish my tail and widen my mouth to hiss my thirst, and the bully's face is pale. The bully's lips are slackened. Now she is face to face, and her mouth stretches to a scream. The bully knows if she doesn't let go there will be teethmarks on her skin.

So I laugh, and run. The lover matches me step for step. There's a wild whistling above our heads, a rush of wind. I turn for a last look at the bully slumped on her knees, shaking her fist. I run to the foot of the hill, the edge of the jungle, my long hair flowing, the lover's gown waterfalling in my wake. The lover's gown shimmers like water in sunlight and wind. I run to start the next cycle. The lover clings to my hand like a promise, her hand fits the palm of my hand. Her joy is something I can touch. Our laughter shakes the birds and small animals from their perches, the jungle leaves from their trees. Our thirst is a scraping that makes us run and run.

East, towards the sea.

My grandmother wakes in fright
when she sees her face.
We laugh uproariously.

The Women's Press is Britain's leading women's publishing house. Established in 1978, we publish high-quality fiction and non-fiction from outstanding women writers worldwide. Our exciting and diverse list includes literary fiction, detective novels, biography and autobiography, health, women's studies, handbooks, literary criticism, psychology and self help, the arts, our popular Livewire Books series for young women and the bestselling annual *Women Artists Diary* featuring beautiful colour and black-and-white illustrations from the best in contemporary women's art.

If you would like more information about our books or about our mail order book club, please send an A5 sae for our latest catalogue and complete list to:

The Sales Department
The Women's Press Ltd
34 Great Sutton Street
London EC1V 0DX
Tel: 0171 251 3007
Fax: 0171 608 1938

Also of interest:

Sheri Reynolds
Bitterroot Landing

Jael is a survivor. A scrawny wild-child, she will survive her
Mammie's illicit liquor shack and the drunken men who visit. As
a ward of the courts, she will survive River Bill, her surrogate
father who makes her his secret surrogate wife. And she will
survive the fleeting kindness of the strangers who rescue her.

But once rescued, Jael is unprepared for the wider world she
must enter. Only the voices of women, both real and imagined,
make her stronger every day. Until, one day, she is so strong she
can survive without them . . .

For all those who loved the vitality of A Thousand Acres and
the spirit of The Color Purple comes Sheri Reynold's magical,
inspirational and compelling new novel of redemption, salvation
and hope.

**'Wonderfully compelling, powerful, moving and
complex.'** Booklist

'An original, lyrically written tale . . . Beautifully realised.'
Publishers Weekly

Fiction £6.99
ISBN 0 7043 4462 9

Kathleen Tyau
A Little Too Much is Enough

Surrounded by countless aunties, uncles and cousins, Mahealani
Suzanne Wong grows up amongst the rich traditions of her
Hawaiian-Chinese family where a little too much is never enough.
But encouraged by her mother, Mahi knows that one day she
must leave to forge her own life. As this time approaches, she
digs deep into the memories of childhood, finding in
remembrance the strength and knowledge needed to carry her
heritage always in her heart . . .

In the tradition of Maxine Hong Kingston and Amy Tan, Kathleen
Tyau weaves the resonant, vivid and often hilarious story of one
young woman's struggle to discover herself amongst her large,
loving and complicated family.

'Candy-coloured and fragrant . . . Tyau is a beautiful
writer, strong and funny and with a wonderful delicacy of
touch.' *Village Voice*

'A feast of a novel. When you are finished, you will push
yourself back from the table, rub your belly and wish
there was more.' Sherman Alexie

'Heaven in small bites.' *The Washington Post*

Fiction £6.99
ISBN 0 7043 4459 9

Githa Hariharan
The Thousand Faces of Night

Winner of the Commonwealth Writers Prize

Returning home to India after two years abroad, Devi finds herself drifting into an acceptable marriage and a future as a full-time wife and mother. But how much can she give of herself to fulfil the expectations of family and society?

Troubled by the gods and goddesses of her childhood, whose fabled lives she has been given as a blueprint for her own, Devi turns her gaze to the women around her. From Mayamma, her husband's family retainer, she learns of women's capacity to endure. From her mother, the secrets of self-sacrifice. And from her runaway mother-in-law, the avenues of escape. Yet, in the end, only Devi herself can lay to rest the thousand faces of night . . .

'Compassionate yet ruthless . . . Beautifully written . . . Githa Hariharan is an outstanding new writer.'
J M Coetzee

'A startlingly effective narrative.' *Sunday Observer*

'Githa Hariharan's fiction is wonderful – full of subtleties and humour and tenderness.' Michael Ondaatje

Fiction £6.99
ISBN 0 7043 4465 3

Stevie Davies
Four Dreamers and Emily

Eileen Nussey James. Single, over sixty and a self-professed expert on the Brontës and passion. Marianne Pendlebury, an overworked wife, mother and academic, whose career could be in jeopardy. Timothy Whitty, the ailing widower, sustained by nocturnal visits from the ghost of Emily Brontë and his cherished correspondence with Marianne. And Sharon Mitchell, a young waitress, resigned to life as an outsider until she is embraced as a 'real reader'. Four dreamers, each pursuing a solitary path until a routine conference brings them together with profound and hilarious results . . .

From one of the world's leading writers on Emily Brontë's life and work and one of Britain's most acclaimed literary novelists, comes a contemporary, sharply observed, tender and lyrical comedy of manners.

'Powerful writing, fine character drawing and splendid storytelling.' *The Times*

'Stevie Davies holds you in a narrative spell.' *Guardian*

'Powerfully moving and uplifting.' *Time Out*

'Impassioned and brilliant.'
Times Higher Education Supplement

Fiction £6.99
ISBN 0 7043 4468 8

Patricia Grace
The Sky People

The Sky People. Born of Earth and Sky. Rebelling against the guardianship of their parents. Wayward, precocious, troublesome and dispossessed. But there is a compelling force to which sky people everywhere aspire. A yearning to love and in turn be loved; to create and to belong; even perhaps to fly.

Award-winning author Patricia Grace draws on ancient Maori legend to weave her extraordinary contemporary narrative of today's sky people. Capricious, ephemeral beings who walk the earth and live seemingly ordinary lives . . .

'A beautiful collection of ancient Maori legends woven by Patricia Grace into a modern context using oral history to reveal the plight of her people . . . Patricia Grace's storytelling skills are illuminating . . . a very special book told with wisdom and insight.' *Detour*

'Patricia Grace can really write . . . [She] not only tells a remarkable narrative but does it so beautifully with such remarkable style.' *Times Educational Supplement*

Fiction £5.99
ISBN 0 7043 4415 7

Octavia E Butler
Parable of the Sower

Lauren Olamina lives in a community under siege. One of the lucky few to have a home, she is protected from the desperate violence and lawlessness that threatens from outside. But despite her community's armed vigilance, Lauren Olamina knows her neighbourhood cannot survive. Convinced there must be other ways of living, Lauren sets off on foot along California's coastal highways. And, as her dangerous journey unfolds, she sows the seeds of a whole new philosophy of life . . .

'Gripping stuff.' *The Sunday Times*

'Beautifully written and utterly compelling.' *Company*

'Brilliantly handled . . . A cracking visionary tale, both worrying and fascinating, and Butler's prose has an immediacy and vitality which is hard to ignore.' *Time Out*

Fiction £6.99
ISBN 0 7043 4421 1

Kindred

Also in print, her universally acclaimed novel of the realities of slavery, both past and present.

'Compulsively readable.' *Daily Post*

'Butler's spare, vivid prose invites comparison with Kate Wilhelm and Ursula K Le Guin.' *Kirkus Reviews*

Fiction £6.99
ISBN 0 7043 4162 X

May Sarton
A Shower of Summer Days

Violet Dene Gordon has returned to her beloved childhood
home after an absence of thirty years. But over Dene's Court
looms the long shadow of her unhappy sister, Barbara. Now
Barbara's child, Sally, is coming to visit – ostensibly to overcome
her infatuation with an American actor. Much is to be resolved
that summer – a marriage, a love affair, a career, and the meaning
of three lives – as Sally's visit reawakens memories and
remembered passions stretching far back into the past . . .

'**May Sarton ranks with the very best of distinguished
novelists.** *A Shower of Summer Days* **establishes once and
for all her unmistakeable authority.**' *New York Times*

'**A poet-novelist with an unfailing eye for all that is
eloquent.**' **Elizabeth Bowen**

'**Unusually delicate. I shall look forward to anything else
she does.**' **J B Priestley**

Fiction £6.99
ISBN 0 7043 4455 6

May Sarton
The Single Hound

When a young English poet struggling to make a name for himself
finds his life and art destroyed by his love for an older, married
woman, he turns for help to the poetry which first inspired him
to write. The beauty of these poems takes him on a search for
their mysterious author. But instead of discovering the great man
behind the art, Mark Taylor finds himself on the doorstep of an
extraordinary household. The home of three remarkable women:
Clare, the short-story writer and beauty; Anne, the teacher and
nurturer; and Doro, the intense, elusive poet . . .

Based on her firsthand experience as a young aspiring writer and
member of the Bloomsbury Group, *The Single Hound* is May
Sarton's celebrated and acclaimed début novel.

**'Only a poet and, perhaps, only a young poet could have
written this beautiful and distinguished first novel.'**
New York Times

**'The characterisation, the account of the love affair, the
beautiful skill of Sarton's writing throughout are
warranted to rivet the attention.'**
Saturday Review of Literature

Fiction £6.99
ISBN 0 7043 4449 1

Dacia Maraini
Isolina

Verona, January 1900. A bundle is washed up on the banks of the
River Adige and inside are the remains of a pregnant woman. The
identity of the body is never in doubt: it is Isolina Canuti, a young
working-class woman. The discovery sparks off a fierce media
battle in which Isolina's lover is challenged to prove his
innocence. But Trivulzio is a highly respected army officer from a
noble family and a cover-up of astonishing proportions ensues . . .

In this stunning historical investigation, bestselling author Dacia
Maraini brings to powerful new light a long-submerged story of
corruption, injustice and oppression.

**'Isolina's life haunts this book . . . All these years later,
she is listened to again, heard again . . . A work of
unforgettable impact.' Michèle Roberts**

**'A riveting tale . . . It's good to feel that murder will out,
and the truth be known, though it takes 100 years.'
Fay Weldon, *Mail on Sunday***

Biography £6.99
ISBN 0 7043 4426 2